Peter Sasgen ca...
sounds of sub...

Be sure to read his riveting novel
War Plan Red

"A knuckle-biting voyage. Gripping and razor-sharp!"
—Joe Buff, best-selling author of
Seas of Crisis and *Straits of Power*

"[A] realistic background of international diplomacy, reactor sirens, and sub-versus-sub combat, with all the dark uncertainties and deathly risks."
—Michael DiMercurio

And don't miss his nonfiction account of a legendary wartime submarine and its relentless sailors

Red Scorpion
The War Patrols of the USS Rasher

"A fine adventure story and well told. Sasgen has added another worthy chapter to the history of a too-long 'silent service.'"
—*Submarine Review*

"Detailed . . . thoroughly researched. . . . Sasgen has cut to the quick."
—Associated Press

Red Shark is also available as an eBook

Also by Peter Sasgen

War Plan Red

Nonfiction by Peter Sasgen

Red Scorpion: The War Patrols of the USS Rasher

RED SHARK

PETER SASGEN

POCKET BOOKS
New York   Toronto   London   Sydney

The sale of this book without its cover is unauthorized. If you purchased this book without a cover, you should be aware that it was reported to the publisher as "unsold and destroyed."   Neither the author nor the publisher has received payment for the sale of this "stripped book."

An *Original* Publication of POCKET BOOKS

 POCKET BOOKS, a division of Simon & Schuster, Inc.
1230 Avenue of the Americas, New York, NY 10020

This book is a work of fiction. Names, characters, places, and incidents are products of the author's imagination or are used fictitiously. Any resemblance to actual events or locales or persons, living or dead, is entirely coincidental.

Copyright © 2006 by Peter Sasgen

All rights reserved, including the right to reproduce this book or portions thereof in any form whatsoever. For information address Pocket Books, 1230 Avenue of the Americas, New York, NY 10020

ISBN-13: 978-0-7434-8360-5
ISBN-10:   0-7434-8360-X

This Pocket Books paperback edition August 2006

10 9 8 7 6 5 4 3 2 1

POCKET and colophon are registered trademarks of Simon & Schuster, Inc.

Cover design by David Rheinhardt;
Front cover photograph by Kulik Photography

Manufactured in the United States of America

For information regarding special discounts for bulk purchases, please contact Simon & Schuster Special Sales at 1-800-456-6798 or business@simonandschuster.com.

To Pete and Chuck

The U.S. imperialists are trying to provoke a war against the DPRK. Since the U.S. has made this clear by its reckless saber-rattling, the North is compelled to increase its military deterrent to defend against a U.S. preemptive nuclear attack and armed invasion against it.

—Korea News from Korean Central News Agency of DPRK (Democratic People's Republic of Korea) http://www.kcna.co.jp

Notwithstanding the current peace agreement, the question is not *if* North Korea will self-destruct, but *how* it will self-destruct, by implosion or explosion, and when.

—Statement by a former Defense Department official testifying before the United States Senate

I do not believe that the current U.S. president, his predecessor, or any future president, would or will launch a preemptive war against any country, even one wishing to do us harm.

—A former U.S. official writing in the mid-1950s, about the possibility that the Soviet Union would launch a sneak atomic attack on the U.S. mainland

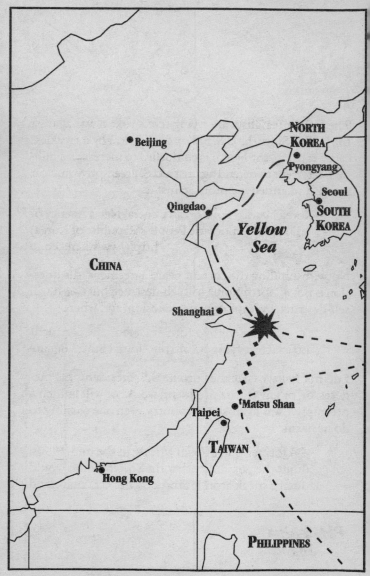

Map by Karen Sasgen, 2006

RUSSIA

Vladivostok

Sea
of
Japan

Tokyo ●

JAPAN

Pacific
Ocean

TRACK CHART

Red Shark __ __

USS *Reno* _ _ _ _ _

Kilo 636 ◆ ◆ ◆ ◆ ◆ ◆

*Philippine
Sea*

PROLOGUE

New York City

South Korean special envoy Nak-chung Paik emerged from the Permanent Mission of the Republic of Korea to the United Nations on East 45th Street and entered an armored Mercedes-Benz. The doors thunked shut and the car drove off with its NYPD escort. At Second Avenue the motorcade turned onto East 44th Street. Up ahead Paik saw the United Nations building, the edge of its eastern facade turned gold by sunrise.

Paik wiped damp palms on the leather seat cushions. The reunification of a divided people and the ending of the threat of nuclear war on the peninsula turned on the meeting about to take place under the aegis of the secretary-general of the UN. Paik knew that his North Korean counterpart, envoy Kil-won Sim, was a tough negotiator and had prepared accordingly. Still, he feared making a fatal mistake that would scuttle the talks and doom the agreed-to exchange of representatives to Seoul and Pyongyang. Though Paik felt the weight of years of faltering negotiations bearing on his shoulders, he took comfort in the fact that the meeting was simply an opportunity to explore possibilities.

The motorcade slowed. In the middle of the block, a red, white, and blue FedEx truck had sideswiped a cab. Both drivers were out of their vehicles, arguing, while the police tried to open a narrow lane past the accident blocking the street. Sidewalks were filled with determined-looking pedestrians heading to work. Those who had stopped to gawk at the crumpled sheet metal now gawked at the approaching motorcade with its flashing red and white lights.

Two blocks away on East 42nd Street, North Korean envoy Kil-won Sim sat stuck in traffic near his hotel. His Mercedes-Benz and NYPD escorts had run afoul of a yellow Hertz truck that had stalled backing into a parking space and was now snarling traffic. The truck's engine cover was propped open, and the driver, perched on a tire, was bent double, apparently troubleshooting the balky diesel engine.

Sim looked back and saw that his car was hemmed in by one of the police escorts, a fleet of honking cabs, and more delivery vans. Pedestrians jaywalking around the stalled truck added to the chaos. A police officer got out of the escort vehicle heading up the motorcade and waved to Sim's driver.

New York frightened Sim. It was too big, unruly, and dangerous. It was not at all like Pyongyang, with its rigid system of controls. New Yorkers were too carefree and too self-absorbed. Like America. He hated America's arrogance and power, its unfettered freedoms, but most of all he hated America for its military might and for meddling in North Korea's affairs. He would speak at length about this, to impress upon the UN delegates that, regardless of what agreements were signed, North Korea would remain forever independent from South Korea.

Sim's Mercedes, guided by the police officer, inched forward around the Hertz truck onto the sidewalk, while another officer, bawling into a handheld radio, called for a tow truck.

Sim recalled how shocked he'd been to learn that Kim Jong-il, North Korea's Dear Leader, had crumpled to U.S. demands to halt production of nuclear weapons. Kim's decision had not only roiled the leadership of the People's Armed Forces but was also said to have caused a violent confrontation between Kim and Marshal Kim Gwan Jin, first deputy minister of the People's Armed Forces. Jin had for years opposed any accommodation with the United States or South Korea. Now the unthinkable was the new reality in Pyongyang. Rumors had circulated too that after the confrontation, two senior military officers had been executed—shot dead by the Dear Leader himself—as a warning to Jin and any other officers who might oppose Kim's policies. Who knew what was true and what was not, thought Sim. All he knew for sure was that he faced a difficult meeting at the UN. It was said that his counterpart from South Korea, Nak-chung Paik, was a tough negotiator.

The Mercedes slowly crawled onto the sidewalk to get around the stalled yellow Hertz truck. As the car inched by, Sim looked up at the driver working on the truck's engine and was astonished to discover that he was a young Korean. For a moment their gazes met and held; just long enough for Sim to feel the full icy measure of the man's contempt; until a thousand pounds of Semtex packed inside the Hertz truck exploded, ending Sim's last living thought.

Over on East 44th Street, South Korean envoy Nakchung Paik heard and felt a tremendous thunderclap rock Midtown Manhattan. Air pressure rose sharply inside the armored Mercedes, and Paik felt it hard against his eardrums. The stuttering boom made pedestrians bolt for cover, while others froze in their tracks. A policeman went into a crouch, hand on his holstered pistol. Another officer standing beside the FedEx truck was waving wildly at Paik's driver and shouting, "Move it! Move it!"

Paik suddenly felt a strange sensation. He looked down and saw that his body had been cut in half by a piece of jagged armored steel that a split second earlier had been part of the Mercedes' rear door. Paik, horrified, yet fascinated, watched his dissected body disgorge its vile contents over the leather seat cushions at the same time that he felt a wave of scorching heat from exploding Semtex, which tore apart the red, white, and blue FedEx truck, the Mercedes-Benz, the terrified pedestrians, and the waving, shouting policeman.

Pyongyang

One hundred and forty miles north of the DMZ, in the fortress-like edifice that served as the nerve center of Communist North Korea's hermetic and paranoid government, Kim Jong-il smoked a cigarette while he waited for the arrival of the two men he'd summoned.

Kim, The Dear Leader and supreme dictator of the Democratic People's Republic of Korea, blew threw his teeth as he paced his gargantuan office. Kim's volcanic temper was on the verge of erupting when he heard a pair of booted footsteps echoing like gunshots off the marble corridor outside his office.

Marshal Kim Gwan Jin and General Chung Hyun Yi, his deputy, passed through three separate scanning devices designed to detect hidden weapons, then submitted to a careful examination by security guards equipped with electronic wands. Only after a full body pat-down and thorough inspection of their possessions—cigarette packages and lighters, fountain pens, eyeglasses, tie clips, even the medals pinned to their brown wool uniform tunics—were the two officers admitted to the anteroom outside Kim's office.

Security bolts slammed open. The door to the Dear Leader's office shivered open to reveal a blue-uniformed, white-gloved bodyguard. He gestured stiffly that the two officers should follow him inside.

"Greetings, Dear Leader," Jin said as he approached Kim, who was standing behind a glass-topped desk fifteen feet long and six wide.

The only objects in view on the desk were an ashtray, a package of cigarettes, and a white telephone. Harsh overhead fluorescent lighting turned Kim's chubby face a sickly green.

Jin said, "I am as appalled as you are by the—"

"You two have betrayed the State!"

Jin and Yi stopped dead in their tracks. Jin tried to speak, but Kim cut him off.

"You both are traitors and I have ordered your arrest! Your people set off the bombs that killed the two representatives in New York! *Don't deny it!*"

Jin, a wiry man in his late sixties, and with a bald head blemished by ridges and fissures of bone under taut skin, didn't react to Kim's outburst. Instead the general stood stolidly at attention while Kim came out from behind the desk under a full head of steam, waving his arms wildly and jabbing the air with a finger.

"The warmongering Americans claim that we betrayed them," Kim bellowed, raining spittle on Jin, "that we lulled them into trusting us. Now they are threatening a preemptive attack with nuclear weapons. Because of your criminal acts we are facing an all-out war on the peninsula and an invasion of the DPRK by the fascist pigs!" He sucked in his ample belly and tugged the skirt of his tailored khaki tunic.

"Dear Leader," Jin said calmly, "we did not betray the State, nor have we betrayed you."

"Silence!" Kim took a breath and wiped his mouth on the back of a hand. He gestured that his bodyguard should get out and close the door. The guard did as ordered, and Kim waited until he heard the security bolts slam shut before continuing.

"Everything I have worked for has been destroyed because *you*, Marshal Jin, refused to support me. Instead you insisted we keep our nuclear weapons, that we cheat on inspections, that we attack South Korea. Now we have disaster. More than three hundred Americans are dead, and the fascists are accusing me of murdering them. But it is you two who are the murderers. I should have had both of you shot months ago."

Kim wiped his mouth again. He stood, silent, collecting himself, diamonds of nervous sweat glistening on his high forehead, which was topped by tufts of fuzzy hair. Fluorescent light reflecting off thick-lensed glasses hid his eyes. "Tell me how you did it," he said. "Tell me how you betrayed the State."

"But Dear Leader," Jin said evenly, "it is *you* who have betrayed the State."

Kim lurched forward as if to grab a fistful of Jin's tunic. Instead he checked himself and pointed a trembling finger at Jin. "How dare you say that to me—"

"It is true, Dear Leader, *you* are the traitor. It is *you* who capitulated to the Americans. *You* who agreed to surrender our nuclear arsenal that we need to defend our nation from Western imperialism. *You* who agreed to sign a peace treaty to end the Korean War, to allow UN inspections in return for international loan agreements. And it is *you* who agreed to open talks with the criminal regime in the South and exchange representatives."

Jin held Kim's astonished gaze. "Given time we could have solved our problems through *Juche*—self-reliance—and in the bargain made the American pigs and their flunkies, the Japanese and Chinese, cave in to our demands. We could have kept our weapons, our missiles, and our power. Now we have nothing. And it is *you*, Dear Leader, who threw it all away because you were intimidated by American power. It is *you* who should be arrested and executed for committing treasonous acts against the State."

It was the first time Jin had ever seen Kim at a loss for words. But he also knew that a silent Kim was unpredictable and that time was running out. Jin looked at Yi, who subtly raised an eyebrow.

"You two are scum," Kim sneered. "Scum of the worst kind. Arrogant, deceitful, hateful."

He fished a cigarette from the package on his desk and with trembling hands put it in his mouth.

"You are describing yourself, Dear Leader, are you not?" Jin said as he produced his own package of cigarettes. He held out to Kim a handsome engraved silver cigarette lighter inlaid with jade and ivory. "And now we must decide what to do about it."

Kim inclined his head toward Jin's lighter, which was rock steady, and said, "There is nothing to decide. You will both be executed for treason." When the expected flame failed to materialize, Kim looked up, into Jin's eyes, which flared like lasers.

A spurt of colorless, odorless gas shot from the lighter and struck Kim Jong-il in the face. Instantly Jin and Yi produced specially treated handkerchiefs, which they pressed to their mouths and noses to block the powerful Z-10 knockout gas. Kim's eyes rolled up into his head as his knees buckled. Before the two officers could catch him, the Dear Leader toppled to the carpeted floor on his face, crushing his glasses under his flattened nose.

After the gas had dispersed, General Yi pressed a button under Kim's desk to summon the bodyguard. The security bolts released and the guard entered the office. He took one look at the unconscious Kim, a mound of khaki lying on the floor at Jin's feet, then removed his peaked cap and wiped sweat from his forehead with a shaking hand. He put his cap back on, came to attention, and smartly saluted Marshal Jin and General Yi.

"Handcuff him," Jin commanded the bodyguard. "Then take him away."

The bodyguard snapped, "At once, *Dear Leader.*"

Part One

WARSHOT

1

Virginia Beach, Virginia

Jake Scott lay in the dark, his mind racing, refusing to shut off, remembering, until a pale dawn crept into the room and brought him back to the present.

Why torture himself? His breakup with Tracy hadn't been one of his finer moments. It was over and there was nothing he could do about it, but God, he wanted to see her again. He pictured her standing in the bedroom of their apartment with her head thrown back, striking a vampish pose. She had on a black thong, black high-heeled slides, jewelry, and nothing else. Her black hair, cut short, hugged her head like a shiny helmet.

Scott's eyes had gone to the ugly greenish-yellow bruises on her wrists, which she had tried to hide under a riot of jangling bracelets. But she couldn't hide the angry red bite mark on her left breast below the nipple.

Who gave you that? he had asked. Rick? No, you did, she'd snapped. Bullshit. It was Rick, wasn't it? He's a toy, that's all, she had said. He understands me, knows what I like. Yeah and getting knocked around isn't it. What did he do, tie you to the bed? Is that why your wrists are bruised? She'd cursed him and slammed the bedroom door in his face. Driven by the agony of sexual jealousy, Scott succumbed to the darkest fringes of his imagination and saw the toy plunging between Tracy's slim, white thighs.

He saw himself with Tracy. Her body arched against his as he'd sucked her swollen left nipple. He remembered that she had grabbed a fistful of his hair and yanked his mouth from her breast. "I said, stop! It can't take any more. Look what you've done to it."

"Sorry."

She had bared her teeth. "No, you're not."

A moment later he'd been in her, deep, then convulsing, breath exploding into her scented hair, whispering in her ear the things she'd liked to hear him say when he'd come.

It was a scene that had been repeated countless times. After their violent lovemaking, she'd hurled accusations at him. Then taunts. It was Tracy who'd broken the fragile bond between them on the eve of his departure. With it broken, she could do whatever she pleased while he was away and not feel guilty.

He swung out of bed and went to the window. A motorcycle ripping at speed up Shore Drive made the glazing rattle. He shivered. Too many days at sea had forced him and Tracy apart. Too many days spent driving submarines into dangerous waters where one mistake could spell disaster for him and his crew: In the Yellow Sea the North Koreans and a botched SEAL insertion; in the Baltic a battle with Chechen terrorists who had stolen a Russian sub and planned to blow up its nuclear reactor in St. Petersburg.

The phone rang. He saw the time—not yet 6:00 a.m.—and hesitated. Then he snatched the phone off the nightstand. "Scott."

It was a familiar voice, that of the chief of staff to Vice Admiral Carter Ellsworth, who was the U.S. Navy's Atlantic Fleet submarine boss—ComSubLant—in Norfolk, Virginia. "Commander Scott, hold for Admiral Ellsworth."

Scott braced for trouble.

Ellsworth came on the line. "Got your TV on, Scott?"

"No, Admiral, I don't usually have it on while I'm sleeping."

"Well, turn it on to CNN, then get back to me."

"What's going on? . . ."

"You ready to travel, Scott?"

"Travel, sir? Where to?"

"I think General Radford will want to see you."

Scott groaned inwardly. "I'm on leave, Admiral; the *Tampa*'s on stand-down."

"CNN. Get back to me." Ellsworth rang off.

Scott looked at the dead receiver in his hand as if it smelled bad.

Major General Karl Radford, USAF (ret.), head of the Strategic Reconnaissance Office—the SRO. Scott knew that a summons from Radford always spelled trouble.

He aimed a wand at the Sony, and a CNN anchorman in Atlanta appeared over a crawler at the bottom of the screen announcing a special report.

The anchorman said, "To repeat, the North Korean Central News Agency, in response to yesterday morning's bombings in Midtown Manhattan, which killed at least three hundred and twenty-seven people, including the North and South Korean special envoys, has issued a statement.

"A spokesman for the DPRK reported that the North Korean leader, Kim Jong-il, has been arrested for treason and for having ordered the bombings in New York City. Marshal Kim Gwan Jin, head of the DPRK's armed forces, has taken control of the country. Jin has issued a pointed warning to the United States and its allies in East Asia that any attempt to interfere in North Korean affairs, or to take any military action against the Jin government, will be, quote '... countered by the full force of the North Korean People's Army and its arsenal of conventional and unconventional weapons,' unquote.

"In Washington, the White House issued a statement. . . ."

Scott turned off the TV and started packing.

From eighty stories aloft, evening rush-hour traffic flowing down the Ginza looked like a river of light. Iseda Tokugawa, dressed in a silk sea-green kimono, watched the river flow across Tokyo from his office at Meji Holdings. As he watched, he heard the female news reader on NHK TV say, "To restate our main news story, the North Korean Central News Agency, in its first response to yesterday morning's bombings in Midtown Manhattan . . ."

So, the first phase had started. Exactly as described. And precisely on time.

Tokugawa entered the *tokonoma*—an alcove kept hidden behind a folding floral screen—and admired the scrolls and seasonal flower arrangements on display. He fussed with a favorite bonsai, snipping and pruning here and there. Satisfied with his handiwork, he turned his attention to the *kamidana*—the god-shelf that hung on one wall of the alcove.

A miniature Shinto shrine made of cypress sat on the shelf. Ostensibly the shrine housed the spirits of Tokugawa's ancestors. He removed a small ceramic bottle of saki from a cupboard, filled a cup to the brim, then placed the cup on the shelf in front of the shrine as an offering. He stepped back, bowed his head, and clapped his hands twice. Tokugawa did this every day, morning and evening. Old habits were hard to shake.

Earlier that day he had concluded a two-hundred-billion-yen deal to supply computerized electrical switching equipment manufactured by one of Meji's companies for use in Iran's nuclear electric power grid. Now he communed with spirits. How to reconcile two such contradictory worlds, one ruled by hard-nosed pragmatism and a fat bottom line, the other by folk spirits and mythological beings represented by a simple wooden box on a shelf. Tokugawa had no satisfactory explanation for this dichotomy.

Shortly he would exchange his kimono for a Savile Row suit, then play host to the Iranian officials and their lawyers at a sex club in Kabukicho, Tokyo's so-called pink entertainment zone. But a vague feeling of disconrent flooded over him, and his jubilant mood gave way to unease: Once embarked upon the path to which he was committed, there would be no turning back. The consequences of what he was soon to set in motion would be like nothing the world had ever experienced. Yet he had lived too long and traveled too far to doubt that his actions were justified. After all, his family's loss of face had been too great. And he believed with all his being that in the pursuit of vengeance ends always justified means.

Tokugawa's unease suddenly lifted, and he felt a surge of delightful anticipation. The girls being provided for the pleasure of his Iranian clients were young and exceptionally beautiful. Perhaps he'd partake of one himself.

Tokugawa nodded *"Domo arigato,"* to the god-shelf.

Scott stood at the foot of King Street in Alexandria, Virginia, by the Waterfront Marina shopping mall, his back to a raw wind whipping off the Potomac River. Old Town was busy. Expensive cars clogged the streets while a dating crowd of well-heeled professionals waited for tables at chic restaurants. Dressed in jeans, turtleneck, and a worn leather bomber jacket, Scott felt conspicuous and out of place.

He had felt the heat as soon as he'd gotten off his plane from Norfolk. A political firestorm had broken over the capital. Congress, reacting to the bombings in New York City, had threatened to declare war on North Korea. Members of both houses had demanded that the president fire the heads of Homeland Security, the CIA, and the FBI. Karl Radford had escaped their fury only because he'd kept a low profile and had powerful friends on The Hill and in the White House. Even the declaration by North Korea's Marshal Jin, that Kim Jong-il was insane and under arrest, facing trial and possible execution for his crime committed in New York, had not placated Congress or the American press. The president was still fighting to get control of the situation before it spun completely out of his grasp. How hot it would get, Scott had no idea. All he knew was that the heat was rising fast and the clock was ticking.

He noticed a gray Buick Regal circle the block twice. Each time, its occupants, a man and woman, glanced at him. After a third circuit the Buick jockeyed into a tight parking space up the block. Scott watched the couple get out and stroll toward a restaurant. Was he being watched? By them? Or someone else? He was a sub skipper, not a spy. Yet the two occupations were so often synonymous that there was little difference between them. He'd worked for Radford before and could only guess what was in store this time. For sure, something to do with the North Koreans. His experience with them had been limited solely to torpedoing an NK frigate, playing hide-and-seek with one of their subs, and snatching a SEAL team out from under their noses. There were plenty of other ways to put pressure on the NKs that didn't require a sub recon—which could turn into a suicide mission—if that's what Radford was contemplating.

"Commander Scott?"

The man was tilting against the wind, tan trench coat plastered to his legs. Though Scott had a commanding view of the area around him, he hadn't seen the man approach. Now he was standing there and Scott felt like an idiot.

"I'm Scott."

"The general's waiting. Would you please come with me?"

Scott looked the man over. "Who are you?"

"Tom Kennedy. I work for the general." He didn't offer to shake hands or show ID.

Scott fell in behind Kennedy, loping north on Union Street, until they approached an idling black Mercury Marquis. Kennedy opened the rear passenger door for Scott, then slid into the front passenger's seat.

Scott smelled aftershave. The general, his grizzled mien raked by light from sodium vapor lamps, sat deep in the far corner of the rear seat, a black cashmere topcoat open over a dark double-breasted suit. Scott felt not only underdressed but also out of place.

"Good to see you, Scott," said Radford.

They shook hands across a bolstered armrest, then Radford rapped the glass partition between the driver's and passenger's compartment. The Marquis pulled away from the curb, turned left, and hurtled toward Washington Street.

Scott started to speak, but Radford held up a silencing hand. His Air Force Academy ring glittered like a diamond in shadow. "All your questions will be answered. Suffice to say we have a new crisis on the Korean peninsula. Marshal Jin says he wants peace, but the president doesn't believe him. We think Jin and his cronies, not Kim, are behind the bombings, that they blamed them on Kim as a pretext to seize power. Hell, Jin opposed the disarmament agreement from the start. That NK defector we have, Jao, warned us that this might happen. Too bad we didn't listen."

Radford peered out at heavy traffic and said, "No one would shed a tear if Kim was stood up before a firing squad, but that's not the point. We had an agreement with him, and it took years of hard negotiating to get it. We averted a bloodbath on the peninsula only because Kim had no other choice but to buckle to U.S., Japanese, and Chinese demands for disarmament. The damn South Koreans were ready to appease him and refused to believe that the whole goddamn regime was rotten, a house of cards waiting to collapse. And now we're back where we started. Jin and his generals are hard-liners and liars to boot. He's also a dedicated Communist. What's worse, he's out of touch with reality. Maybe even a little nuts. They all are. So it's no surprise that Jin may be hatching a new plan to engage in nuclear blackmail."

"What kind of plan?" Scott asked.

"Ah." Radford turned his gaze full on Scott. "That's what the president wants to know." He lit a cigarette and replaced the lighter in the bolster's socket before continuing. "Does this bother you?" He cracked the side window. "We've picked up, among other things, some signals intercepts that seem to indicate the NKs are up to something and that Jin is directly involved. We don't know with what, but we'll go into that when we arrive."

"Where?"

"Not far, just down the road a ways."

2

Mt. Vernon, Virginia

The car turned south onto the George Washington Memorial Parkway, away from Radford's Crystal City headquarters. Whatever Radford had cooked up, Scott knew that there was no way he could avoid being shanghaied into service.

Radford was saying, "By the bye, there may be a citation in the works for you."

Scott said nothing.

"Did you hear what I said?"

"Yes, sir, a citation."

"From the president."

One minute they wanted to cashier you, Scott thought, the next, hand out a citation. Anything to get you on board.

"For the Baltic operation," Radford said. "We are not unaware of the risks you ran to kill that Chechen bunch before they could blow that Akula sky-high."

"Yes, sir, thank you. All in a day's work," Scott said, not caring how trite that sounded. What had Alex Thorne called him, the Navy's garbage man? Always cleaning up their messes. How apt, Scott thought. He had bragged about, had worn as a badge of honor, his status as likely the oldest commander in the Navy. He'd been passed over for promotion to captain once, though temporarily frocked as a captain for his mission to Russia to head off the Chechen terrorists. Once again a commander, his career would be finished if he was passed over for captain again. Though they always seemed to find a way to use him, the Navy couldn't see fit to promote him to captain.

"You should try taking that chip off your shoulder," Radford said, sounding riled. "You might find it does wonders for your career. What's past is past. Try thinking about the future for a change."

"I'm sorry, General, but that's a little hard to do, especially when I have no control over it. Fact is, sir, it seems that you and Admiral Ellsworth have a lot of influence over any future I might have. Or whether I even have one."

"Ellsworth holds you in very high regard."

Scott said nothing.

"It's true. When the chips are down he comes to you for help. That says it all. He even got your old command back, put you aboard the *Tampa,* I hear."

"He did. But I'm not aboard her now. Instead, I'm here with you."

Radford mused for a long moment, then said, "Well, the chips are down again. We need your help."

Scott waited for Radford to say more, but the general merely looked out the car window at the moon rising over Maryland across the Potomac.

They turned off the GW Parkway into a Mt. Vernon town-house development and drove down streets lined with quadplexes, Japanese SUVs and sedans, then into a cul-de-sac and the driveway of a lighted end unit. Scott and Kennedy followed Radford into a modern suburban home furnished in the spare, generic style favored by the SRO for their safe houses.

"Hello, Scott." Carter Ellsworth stood in the middle of the living room, one hand wrapped around a coffee mug, the other outstretched in greeting. He was short and had pale blue eyes, which were magnified by the thick steel-rimmed glasses he wore. Scott had never seen Ellsworth in civilian clothes and almost didn't recognize him.

"Admiral," said Scott, looking past Ellsworth at a handsome black man. The man was clean shaven and wore a well-tailored blazer and slacks, which flattered his good build.

"Jefferson," he said. "McCoy Jefferson. Lieutenant Colonel, U.S. Air Force."

"McCoy's my deputy for special-ops," said Radford.

As they shook hands, Scott sensed that Jefferson was sizing him up. "Combat Control Team?" Scott asked.

"That's right, CCT."

Air Force combat controllers were trained to support special-operations forces such as Navy SEALs and often deployed with them to assist their insertion and extraction.

Radford turned and acknowledged an elegant Japanese woman who had entered the room.

"How do you do, Commander Scott?" she said in perfect English. "I'm Fumiko Kida." She offered Scott her hand, which was smooth and warm.

He held her hand a tad longer than courtesy dictated while his eyes roamed her striking features: silky black hair that grazed her shoulders and framed her face; a pair of full, encompassing lips that were moist and very red.

"I've heard a lot about you, Commander." She saw a man in his early forties, well built and with dark hair flecked with gray. He had rough-edged good looks and a bearing that indicated he knew how to handle himself in tough situations.

"Please call me Jake." He released her hand. "I don't know what you've heard about me, but most of it's not true."

"Come off it, Scott," Ellsworth snorted. "You're among friends. Ms. Kida knows about the Baltic op."

"What brings you to Virginia?" Scott asked her.

"Marshal Kim Gwan Jin brings her to Virginia," said Radford, making himself comfortable in a wing chair. "Ms. Kida works for the Japan Defense Intelligence Headquarters. She was sent here by Director General Kabe to share information about Marshal Jin."

"Information we believe is tied to the recent coup in North Korea," she added.

A woman, whom Scott recognized from the gray Buick Regal in Alexandria, entered the room with a tray of sandwiches, which she placed on the coffee table. The man Scott had seen driving the Buick carried in a tray of soft drinks and condiments.

After the couple departed, Radford said, "McCoy, why don't you and Ms. Kida brief Scott."

Jefferson popped open a soda, took a quick pull, then put the can aside. "As you know, Jin has abrogated the agreement Kim Jong-il negotiated with us to dismantle his nuclear arsenal. Apparently he believes we'll launch a preemptive strike against North Korea as payback for the bombings in New York, and is threatening to start a nuclear war in the Far East or to launch missiles at the U.S. The problem we face is compounded by the fact that the DPRK is on the verge of collapse. Should that happen, we'll have to find and secure the warheads so they won't fall into the hands of terrorists. Either way, it's a huge problem."

"Do we know where the warheads are?" Scott asked.

"Not all of them," Jefferson admitted. "At any rate, five days before the terrorist bombings in Manhattan, the JDIH picked up intercepts which indicated that Jin is planning to attend a meeting with an unidentified individual near Taiwan. Right now it isn't clear what this meeting is about or what his intentions are. We know from JDIH intercepts that the meeting was scheduled in advance of the attacks in New York. We think the meeting may have something to do with Jin's seizing power but can't be sure."

"Do you have any idea who this person is that Jin is meeting?"

"Not yet," Fumiko said, "but we think he is a Japanese."

"What kind of comms intercepts are you picking up?" Scott asked. "Maybe that'll tell you something."

"It has. We're seeing line discriminators and jumped wave band with blocks and filters. Very sophisticated stuff, probably a Geng auto-crypt system, definitely not European or Scandinavian."

"Any guesses what this meeting is about?"

"Jin is one of the most reclusive individuals in North Korea," said Jefferson. "As far as we know, he's never traveled out of the country. For him to do it now means that the meeting is damned important."

Scott turned to Fumiko. "How many Japanese can there be who would have a legitimate reason to meet with Jin at a time when things are so unsettled? And for what reason? A business deal maybe?"

Fumiko said, "Until recently Japan has had very bad

relations with North Korea. But then our new prime minister agreed to open the door a crack to allow trade and cultural exchanges with Pyongyang."

"So maybe someone in Japan is meeting with Jin to discuss a deal for, say, food, fuel, and other goods that they desperately need."

"I don't think so," Fumiko said. "The North has trade ministers who negotiate such things with the Japanese government. Given the new reality in Pyongyang, Jin wouldn't leave the country unless the meeting was vital to the DPRK's survival."

"You mean the survival of their *nuclear arsenal,* don't you?" Scott said.

They all looked at him; their silence conveyed comprehension.

Scott began to see the outline of the plan being hatched by Radford and Ellsworth, and he didn't like it. "You said this meeting is being held near Taiwan. Where?"

Fumiko said, "On an island called Matsu Shan. We identified it from our intercepts."

"So what's on this Matsu Shan?" Scott asked.

"A villa owned by a Taiwanese druglord."

3

Safe house, Virginia suburbs

"General, do I understand," Scott said, "that you want to insert a SEAL team into Matsu Shan to find out what Jin is up to?"

"We absolutely must know what the meeting is about," Radford said. "And the only way to find out is by putting SEALs ashore."

"We need your expertise on this one," Ellsworth chimed in.

Scott felt his gut tighten. He saw it again, the North Korean frigate charging, the race to get the SEAL team back onboard the *Chicago;* her torpedoes slamming into the frigate; its bow and stern folding into a V. . . . "With respect, Admiral, I seem to recall you once had doubts about my abilities to carry out a similar mission."

Ellsworth pointed a finger. "We're not here to rehash the past, Scott. Your actions in the Baltic squared the account." His temper held in check by the presence of Radford, Jefferson, and Fumiko, Ellsworth said evenly, "You inserted SOF teams into Dubrovnik and North Korea, so this job at Matsu Shan should be a piece of cake."

"Sir, they're never a piece of cake."

Jefferson, his face an unreadable mask, said nothing. Fumiko, perhaps unaccustomed to verbal fencing between superiors and subordinates, looked uncomfortable. Radford, smoking a cigarette, seemed content to let Scott and Ellsworth slug it out.

"What I'm saying, Scott, is that you'd be operating in friendly waters, Taiwanese territorial waters, not in the damned Yellow Sea off Korea."

"Admiral, the Chinese Navy patrols those waters. So do the Taiwanese. Getting in and out undetected, much less making an insertion, can be nasty business. Have the Taiwanese been told about this op?"

"They won't be brought into it," Radford said, lurching out of his chair. "This is strictly our show. All we want is a recon job, not an assault. McCoy will head the team. We need first-rate intelligence on this. So we need someone who knows what to listen for and what to look for. That means you'll go in with them."

Scott felt as if he'd just been kicked in the gut.

Fumiko set up a presentation for viewing on a wall-sized flat-screen monitor mounted behind drapes in the living room. Radford, Ellsworth, and Jefferson ate sandwiches and drank sodas while waiting for the show to begin.

Fumiko's long, tapered fingers flew over the keys of her laptop. As she bent close to Scott to retrieve a CD from her kit, he caught a whiff of her scent. She knew he was looking at her and seemed to realize the effect she was having on him.

"Are you based in Washington?" Scott asked.

"No, Tokyo. In fact I'm flying back tonight."

"Thirteen hours. That's a long flight."

"I'm used to it. I'm away from home a lot."

"Must be rough on your family."

"I have no family. The JDIH is my family."

Scott knew that Fumiko represented the new breed of liberated Japanese woman. Freed from the traditional roles of homemaker and dutiful wife of a salaryman, Japanese women were now free to pursue careers that had formerly been considered appropriate only for Japanese men. And she'd obviously made the most of it.

"How long have you been with them?"

"Ten years."

"You must be good."

She turned her lovely almond-shaped eyes on him, the intensity of her gaze penetrating to his core. She smiled and said, "Yes, I'm very good."

He'd seen the same intensity in other women he'd known—and loved. Tracy. If only she could have channeled her intensity, like Fumiko had, into something that wasn't destructive. How different could two women be, he wondered? Suddenly he remembered: Tracy was in Tokyo with her toy, Rick Sterling, the navy attaché. . . . He pulled back from the edge just when Fumiko announced, "Ready when you are."

An aerial photo of the northeastern portion of Taiwan came up on the screen.

"As you can see, we have excellent satellite coverage of Matsu Shan." Fumiko spoke as she uploaded images from the laptop to the video screen.

The still photo went into motion, and they were propelled, as if in free fall, onto a small kidney-shaped island off the northeast tip of Taiwan. Scott saw rifts of narrow inlets sawtoothed into sheer rocky bluffs, and coastal waters peppered with outcroppings of volcanic rock capable of ripping open the hulls of ships and, he thought, submarines.

"Matsu Shan is about seventy-five square acres," Fumiko said after halting the free fall.

She moved a white arrowhead pointer across the island, which was covered with dense jungle and stands of palm. A sumptuous villa squatted at the summit of a high bluff overlooking the sea.

"On the Taiwan side of the island," Fumiko continued, "is a narrow channel from the Pacific Ocean. It terminates at a beach below the villa." She pointed with the arrow to docking facilities and a thirty-foot motor launch.

She moved on, saying, "As you'll see, the villa is well guarded and virtually impregnable from assault by sea and air."

"Who did you say owns this island?" Scott asked.

"Wu Chow Fat," said Jefferson. "He's a druglord, pirate, and hired killer. He runs North Korean–produced drugs for the Chinese Triads in Mainland China and Taiwan. And for the *yakuza* in Japan. Fat is the main conduit for North Korean heroin and methamphetamine—ice—into Taiwan. The Mainland Chinese know the NKs need hard currency and that drugs are their biggest cash crop. They produce more than half the illegal drugs the world consumes."

"How much territory does Fat control?" Scott asked.

"All of the southern East China Sea between Ningpo and Hong Kong."

"The Chinese crack down hard on drug smuggling into Mainland China," Fumiko said, "but when it comes to Taiwan, they let it go through on the principle that drug use by the Taiwanese will eventually undermine their resistance to unification with China."

"So Fat has an understanding with Beijing," said Scott.

"Yes. Fat is Cantonese. At one time he did business simultaneously with Chiang Kai-shek in Taiwan and with the Reds in Beijing, worked both sides of the street. China's General Administration of Customs—GAC—officials are in his pocket. They see to it that small amounts of heroin and ice get through to the Mainland, while the rest gets funneled into Taiwan."

"And everybody makes money, tons of it," Scott observed.

"Billions and billions," said Jefferson.

"Just like the Colombian cartels," Ellsworth said. "Our subs have monitored and helped interdict drug shipments from Peru and Colombia. Still, some of it always gets through. We've never monitored Asian drug trafficking because we naively trusted the Chinese to police themselves. Now we know better."

"But now," Radford added, "smugglers like Fat are joining forces with the Russian Mafiya. They're both flush with cash and are buying weapons to sell to Middle Eastern terrorists. Hell, Fat tried to get his hands on a Russian diesel sub and helicopter gunship, as well as shoulder-fired surface-to-air missiles. That's why we're concerned about this meeting on Matsu Shan."

"Got anything stronger to drink than Coke?" Scott asked.

"In the sideboard," Radford said. "Make mine a Scotch. Anyone else?"

There were no takers. Ellsworth, a teetotaler, said, "Now you see why we need your expertise, Scott."

"And Fat is no cowboy," Jefferson added. "He's smart and well protected."

Scott handed Radford an iced Scotch and had one himself. His gaze fell on Jefferson, who didn't look away. Scott felt certain Jefferson was measuring his resolve, probing for any weaknesses.

"What kind of hydrographic data do you have on Matsu Shan?" Scott asked.

"Tides, soundings, approaches, the usual," Fumiko said.

"How recent?"

"Ninety-eight."

"Christ."

"Don't worry, I've seen what they have," Ellsworth said. "It's good. Very detailed."

"Sir, as I recall," Scott said, "the Ryukyu Trench kisses Taiwan. We'd have six or seven thousand feet of water east of Taiwan, but mostly shallow water inshore."

"True, but it's nothing you can't handle," Radford said.

Scott considered: A sub designed to deliver SEALs needed water deep enough to cover her approach inshore. He didn't like having to hug the bottom to make an insertion with hardly any water to cover his ass.

He pointed to the monitor. "Let's see this villa."

Fumiko zoomed in on an L-shaped structure photographed at a 45-degree angle from an orbiting KH-12 satellite. Crisp moving images crept diagonally across manicured grounds and stepped terraces. Details stood out with amazing clarity.

The villa, with its arched galleries, ceramic tile roof, and spacious veranda, sat on a bluff, surrounded by a low masonry wall. All around were hardwoods, palm, and camphor. At the foot of the bluff was the beach, where the narrow channel from the sea ended.

"Whoa, what's this?" Scott said.

A swimming pool and cabana with diving boards

and striped awnings inched across the screen. An Asian woman in dark glasses was sunbathing naked beside the pool on an inflatable mattress, surrounded by beach chairs and colorful umbrellas.

"Looks better than Club Med," Jefferson said.

Ellsworth coughed into a fist.

The KH-12's cameras picked out more details—a paved parking area with SUVs and trucks, which could also double as a helicopter landing pad. A dark-skinned man in jungle fatigues and stripped to the waist changed a tire on a green Toyota Land Cruiser.

Scott also saw that aside from a long, steep set of stairs hewn from living rock that faced the beach, the only other way to gain access to the villa was up a twisting service road cut into the back side of the bluff.

Fumiko said, "As you'll see, the villa is heavily guarded."

Scott saw armed men moving about the grounds on foot and in vehicles. "What kind of weapons are they carrying?"

"Russian PK machine guns," said Jefferson. "Also H&K 13s."

"Is that a guard tower?"

"Yes," Fumiko said. "There are three of them. Here's a better view of one." She manipulated the sequence; the view widened.

The tower, constructed of open steelwork, had a red tile roof that matched the villa's roof. PK machine guns pointed into the surrounding jungle from the tower's four sides.

"What else do they have?" Scott asked.

"Figure on grenades and mortars," said Jefferson. "RPGs, too. We're betting they have enough hardware to fight a midsized army."

"Not good."

"Look, we're not going in there to start a war, we're going in to get intelligence."

"How?"

"With Micro Air Vehicles," Radford announced. He put his drink down and rose from his chair. "MAVs."

"You're serious, General?" Scott said.

MAVs, some only six inches long, had been under development by the SRO for years. Intended to keep soldiers out of danger on the battlefield during recon missions, they had failed to materialize as a deployable weapon. Until now.

"Of course I'm serious. The SRO has put two billion into their development, and now we've got one that works and is perfect for this mission. Ms. Kida."

She switched channels. On the screen was a machine that resembled a dragonfly, complete with multiple wings made of shiny, paper-thin Mylar. Lying next to the bug, a newly minted twenty-five-cent coin provided a sense of scale. Radford was indeed serious: The MAV was barely three inches long.

"This bug can stay aloft for a half hour," Radford said. "It uses an RCM—Reciprocating Chemical Muscle—a noncombustible engine, attached to the wings to make them flap at high speed. The body of the robot contains a camera, guidance system, and either an olfactory sensor or a listening device."

"We could have used one of these in Yongbyon," said Scott, "instead of those Krypton 85 sensors that looked like plants we stuck in the ground to detect radiation from the NK's fuel rod reprocessing plant. Let's hope it works."

"Oh, it works," Jefferson said. "I've seen what this spy fly can do. Trust me."

"How much range and speed does it have?" Scott asked.

"About two miles and under ideal conditions, thirty-five miles an hour."

"That might work," Scott said.

"It *will* work," Radford said, making himself a fresh drink. "The way we see it, you won't even make contact with Fat and his men. They'll make themselves scarce for the meeting. All you have to do is get ashore, turn those flies loose, get what we need, and get the hell out."

"What do you mean by 'make himself scarce'?"

Fumiko said, "Fat's job will be to provide security. He and his men won't be expecting any visitors, so it should make the insertion less dicey."

Scott said nothing. His gaze fell on Jefferson, who said, "What's bothering you, Scott?"

"The usual. Like, how many bad guys will we be up against? How the hell do we get that damned bug into the villa and get it out? And how can we avoid contact with Fat and his men?"

"We've run a computer model on the op a half-a-dozen times. Ashore, we can insert the bugs from a stand-off position on the beach and record what they see."

Scott frowned. "Computer model, eh?" It always sounded so easy, so clean. But it never was. Computers didn't fight back and kill people for real. "You say Fat's not going to be expecting visitors . . . how can you be sure?"

"Would you be?" Jefferson said. "Hell, it's his private island. He and Jin think no one knows what's going down. It'll be over before they know anything happened."

"Fat's a drug runner and knows better than to let his guard down. And if you think we can run this on a fast clock, that's a prescription for disaster."

Jefferson gave him a hard look and was about to speak when Ellsworth said, "There he is."

The monitor flickered. A grossly obese Wu Chow Fat appeared on a white sandy beach. Points of light reflecting off water glimmered like miniature donuts, proof that the digital photo had been taken with a mirror telephoto lens from long range, possibly a sub.

Fat's tiny head, perched atop a mound of blubber, bobbled. He was assisted by a lithe young woman as he moved with heavy plodding steps through the sand. Fat hanging from his body in thick folds all but hid a pair of gargantuan yellow swim trunks. His arms and legs, their girth enormous, looked like overinflated balloons that might burst at any moment. He continued down the beach, supported by his companion, until out of camera range.

"Well, they got his name right," Scott said.

"Don't be misled by what you see," Fumiko said. "Fat is smart. He's also a cold-blooded killer."

Scott munched a sandwich while Fumiko squared away her computer gear and tidied up cables.

Radford, smoking, said huskily, "According to the information Ms. Kida has from JDIH intercepts, this meeting on Matsu Shan is scheduled to take place in fifteen days. That doesn't give us much time, so Admiral Ellsworth has worked up a schedule that has absolutely no room for slippage but will get the job done."

"Right." Ellsworth looked up from a document he was reading and said, "We have a SEAL team on standby at

Pearl Harbor. Colonel Jefferson will fly on ahead tonight and join them. You, Scott, will follow him out ASAP, go over the plan, then do a workup with the team for an over-the-beach op. You'll get all of this in your op-orders from ComSubPac. For now, consider yourself detached from the *Tampa* and reassigned to the *Reno* in Pearl. She's been fitted out with an ASDS and everything else you'll need for the job."

The ASDS was the Navy's Advanced Seal Delivery System, a 65-foot mini-sub designed to covertly insert SEALs ashore from a nuclear attack submarine.

"The *Reno*? Sir, she's one of the oldest *Los Angeles*–class boats we have. What kind of shape is she in?"

"The *Reno*'s had a refit and she's like new. Quieter than a *Seawolf*. And she's got a new BSY-2 sonar suite and BQG-5D wide aperture array. She's been through the pre-overseas movement and is surge-ready."

"Weapons load-out?"

"Mark 48 ADCAPs."

"Tomahawks?"

"Can't give you everything."

"Crew?"

"Sam Deacon's troops."

"Who's exec?"

"Rus Kramer."

"I hear Kramer's good."

"Tops. Now, you're senior to Deacon and in charge of the mission, but you know Navy regs—he owns the ship. He'll work with you, just don't put his nose out of joint. Any questions?"

"No, sir."

Scott knew it would be a close-run op with no margin for error. Success would turn on the application of a new weapon, the MAV. He also knew that little time had been allocated for training with Jefferson and the SEALs, to form a bond with them, to check out on weapons he'd not handled in a long time, and to prepare himself for the rigors of insertion from an ASDS. He hoped that his prior Basic Underwater Demolition/SEAL training, or BUD/S, undertaken at the Naval Special Warfare Center in Coronado, California, would see him through any crisis. Like riding a bicycle or driving a stick shift, it was ingrained, a thing you never forgot how to do.

The others went on ahead. Jefferson lugged Fumiko's gear, which was packed in black aluminum cases, to one of the cars. She stopped Scott in the town house's foyer and said, "I know you have doubts about the mission."

Scott, pleased by her show of concern, said, "I always have doubts about a mission like this one."

"Because of what happened in Russia?"

Scott gave her a look.

"I heard about the Baltic mission. They said it was Chechen terrorists with a Russian sub."

He laughed. "Hell, Chechnya doesn't have a navy."

Fumiko didn't laugh.

"Look, it was nothing, just a routine recon."

"They said there was a woman involved . . . an American woman . . ."

"Don't believe everything you hear."

". . . and that you and she almost didn't make it back." She put a hand on his arm.

Scott considered, then said, "You're right, it was touch and go. A group of Chechen terrorists led by Alikhan Zakayev commandeered a Russian sub based up on the Kola Peninsula. They had a plan to drive the sub into the harbor at St. Petersburg during the recent summit meeting between the U.S. and Russian presidents and blow the reactor, to contaminate the city and every living thing in it. I took command of a Russian Akula, tracked Zakayev down in the Baltic Sea, and prevented it from happening."

"You mean you torpedoed Zakayev's sub."

"Couldn't have done it without help from Alex Thorne. She's a scientist attached to the U.S. Embassy in Moscow. Very bright. She figured out what Zakayev was going to do and, well, more or less saw us through a reactor casualty of our own. We lost coolant to the Akula's reactor and almost had a core meltdown. If it hadn't been for a Russian officer who patched it up, I wouldn't be here now. And most of the Baltic region would have been radioactive and uninhabitable for who knows how long."

Scott heard loping footsteps, someone returning to the house. Fumiko took her hand away.

"Commander Scott, we're waiting," Kennedy said from the driveway.

"Sorry you won't be there in Pearl to see us off," Scott told her.

"Me, too," she said.

4

Chungwa, North Korea

The new Dear Leader, Marshal Jin, arrived at the special detention center, twenty-five kilometers south of Pyongyang. The high-security facility, a squat, ugly concrete blockhouse, its walls punched through on four sides with rows of narrow, vertical windows, sat at the end of a paved road, one of the few in the Chungwa region.

The stamp of the guards' booted feet and their presentation of arms greeted Jin inside the main entrance. Jin and an aide swept past their ranks and fell in with the prison commandant, who was dressed in full military regalia, including jodhpurs, aiguillette, and Sam Browne belt.

The commandant ushered Jin into a spartan office furnished only with a coal-burning stove and metal table and chair. One end of the table had been set with cups of rice wine and bowls of *kimbap*—sushi—and *kimch'i*—fiery cabbage.

Jin, his full attention on the closed-circuit color video monitor at the other end of the table, ignored the food. The chair, held by the commandant, materialized under Jin, who sat, gripped by an image on the monitor of Kim Jong-il, transmitted via hidden camera inside his cell deep within the detention center.

Jin almost didn't recognize the former Dear Leader. Shoeless, dressed in a filthy powder blue jumpsuit, and without his trademark black-framed glasses, Kim looked exhausted. He'd lost weight, which had caused his pudgy face to collapse. The jumpsuit hung from his body like a sack. His bare feet were purple from the cold and disfigured by bunions. Kim sat, not moving a muscle, on the edge of his bunk, which was suspended from chains bolted to the cell's stone wall.

"He refuses food, Dear Leader," said the commandant, inclining his head slightly toward Jin.

Jin couldn't care less if Kim starved himself. It would save the time and trouble of executing Kim slowly in a vat of boiling salt water laced with lye. Or throwing him alive into a furnace. A bullet in his brain was too quick.

Jin studied Kim's ashen face. Kim the traitor; Kim the drunk; Kim the womanizer. The Swedish prostitutes he favored should see and smell him now. They might think twice about allowing all that unwashed flesh to crush them, two and three at a time, against satin sheets, or they might balk at the idea of licking French wine off his body while he writhed with pleasure and called for another bottle to be uncorked.

Jin stood. "I'll see him."

The cell door shivered and swung open. Kim blinked; a flash of recognition ignited his dull eyes.

"I have nothing to say," Kim croaked, his throat blocked with phlegm, his doughy lips barely moving. He warmed his hands under his armpits.

The cell was filthier than Jin had thought. Kim, in addition to refusing food, had refused to use the bucket provided and instead had defecated and urinated on the floor of the cell. Jin almost gagged on the smell, which cut his nostrils like a knife. The commandant lifted, then dropped, his shoulders, as if to say there was nothing he could do about Kim's bad habit, which was his only means of revenge for such a grave loss of face. *Let Kim breathe his own shit*, Jin thought.

Jin motioned that he wanted privacy; the commandant stepped into the passageway but left the cell door slightly ajar.

Hands linked behind his back, Jin looked down at the hunched figure of the man who had ruled North Korea for almost twenty-five years and who, during that period, had unleashed a wave of brutality that at times had sickened even Jin, a master himself at using terror and pain to control his enemies.

"Go away." Kim hawked and spat between the polished toe caps of Jin's boots. "I have nothing to say."

"And there is nothing you can say that I want to hear," Jin said. "Instead, you will listen to me. An indictment has been handed down by the People's Council of Ministers. You have been charged and found guilty of treason and have been sentenced to death."

Kim, gaze planted on the gob of gray phlegm between Jin's boot toes, said nothing.

"The People's Council of Justice has given me the task of carrying out your sentence. I am free to choose the time of your execution and, most importantly, the method."

"Then kill me now."

"There is more." Jin waited until he had Kim's full attention. "Your uncle, your sister and her husband, and both your sons have been arrested. They, too, will pay for your crime. I will rid the State of all traitors who have disgraced your father, the divine leader, Kim il Sung."

Kim looked up. "Are you trying to frighten me?"

"Frighten you? No. Those are the facts."

"As I said, kill me now."

Jin bent at the waist to make sure Kim heard his words clearly. "No, not now, but very soon. After you watch your relatives die one at a time."

"Is that what you came to tell me?"

"No. I came to tell you that your Japanese friend has agreed to meet me."

Kim reacted like a muscle poked by an electric current. His gaze bored into Jin.

The marshal straightened his back. "He and I have a commonality of interests. He also has the technology I need and the means to turn our raw materials into usable tools."

Jin did an about-face to make his exit. Kim said, "Wait. Stop talking in riddles. What are you saying?"

Jin halted, a hand on the cell door. "This: Very soon the United States will no longer be a threat to our existence or to the rest of the world. With your friend's help we will have the means to cripple the U.S."

"He won't go through with it. He's lying to you."

"If you think that, you don't know him at all. Believe me, he'll do it, because he wants revenge as much as we do."

"Then you're both insane. You'll turn the entire world against us."

The cell door slammed shut; Jin's polished boots hammered the stone passageway. Their echo faded, and Kim clamped both hands over his ears to block a dying prisoner's desperate cry for help from deep in the bowels of the labyrinthine detention center.

5

Crystal City, Virginia

"Evening, Karl, Admiral Ellsworth, I trust you have good news."

The president of the United States appeared on the Secure Video Tele-Conference monitor in Radford's office at SRO headquarters. It was late, and the president, a handsome black man who spoke with the measured tones of a Harvard-trained lawyer, which he was, looked very tired.

"Evening, Mr. President," both men answered.

The president was in the White House's private residence, where the SVTC had been set up for the broadcast beamed across the Potomac River. NSC staff had conferred with Radford and Ellsworth earlier in the day to discuss broad objectives, and now the two men were ready to brief the president on the details.

"Are we launched?" the president asked.

Radford sensed the president's deep concern leeching through his veneer of cordiality. The pressure put on Radford from the White House to launch the recon mission to Matsu Shan had been unrelenting, and he knew it would only increase in the days to follow.

"Yes, sir. Admiral Ellsworth is here to brief you on it."

"Please go ahead, Admiral, but hold the jargon and give it to me in plain English."

Ellsworth cleared his throat. "Mr. President, Commander Scott has orders to Pearl Harbor. He'll link up with Colonel Jefferson and the special-ops group being ferried to Matsu Shan aboard one of our ASDS-boats, I mean, a sub equipped to insert, er, put SEALs ashore and retrieve them."

Ellsworth reviewed for the president the meeting held at the safe house, then described the technical details of the mission and difficulties Scott faced.

When he finished, the president said to Radford, "Scott did a hell of a job for us in the Baltic. He's an asset we sorely need now, but is it necessary that he risk his neck ashore in this Matsu Shan operation?"

"I believe it is. Colonel Jefferson knows his way around special-ops, and he's been part of the planning team we put together the day the North Koreans hit New York City. Jefferson knows how to conduct the tactical side of the mission and he's sensitive to the political side as well, but he can't be expected to also handle the intel side. Scott's versed in intelligence collection, and I felt we would benefit from his experience. He's got a keen analytical mind and won't miss a thing."

"Do you concur, Admiral?" asked the president.

"Yes, sir, I do. Scott's one of our best officers, both as sub driver and in intel ops."

"And now we're putting him ashore in Matsu Shan. He's carried out this type of mission before?"

"Yes, sir, a few years back, in Dubrovnik. A special-ops team launched from one of our subs and took out a Croatian Serb rebel headquarters. Scott went ashore with them to sweep up intelligence and to liase . . . um,

I mean, stay in contact with our headquarters in Brindisi. He also had orders to find and capture the terrorist known as Karst. Scott almost had him, but the bastard got away. Scott knows how to handle himself, so a couple days of work with Jefferson and his men and a weapons refresher is all he'll need."

"What about Commander Scott's penchant for taking matters into his own hands?"

"Sir, we've imposed severe limits on the interpretation of his orders. Mr. President, the purpose of this mission is strictly a sneak 'n' peek, I mean, to find out what Jin is up to, not to engage him and his men. Scott understands that."

"Very well, Admiral," the president said. "I've put through your request for a citation for Scott. Seems to me he deserves it, if any officer does."

Radford said, "Mr. President, I'd like to add that we've had help from the Japan Defense Intelligence Headquarters. One of their agents, Ms. Fumiko Kida, has provided us with everything they have on Marshal Jin. I've been impressed with the state of Japanese intelligence gathering and the high level of interpretation and cooperation they brought to it. Nevertheless . . ."

The president waited.

"I sense the JDIH has some problems with the identity of this Japanese who has had contact with Jin."

"What kind of problems?"

"They're trying to save face. They're embarrassed that he's a Japanese citizen."

The president considered this. "Are they protecting someone?"

"I don't think so. I know Director General Kabe, and he's not likely to do that. Still . . ."

The president wiped an eye; he looked very tired. He

recovered and held Radford's gaze on the monitor as he spoke in a sharp tone. "If a Japanese national is involved with Jin and they know who it is and don't tell us, then the Japanese are as guilty as the North Koreans for the murder of three hundred Americans in New York City."

"Sir, if we can identify who it is, they'll have to give us their full cooperation."

"You mean, arrest him? Question him?"

"Yes, sir."

The president blinked rapidly several times, then said, "Would they?"

"If we had irrefutable proof."

"What's your opinion, Admiral? No bullshit, please. Can Scott get in there and get what we need?"

"Yes, sir. It'll be tight. Their TOT—time on target—is minimal, virtually timed to the minute. There's no room for slippage, and exfiltration should be clean. He can do it."

The president stood, walked out of camera range. His voice came as if from offstage, still earnest but sounding very tired. "Understand, gentlemen, if Scott can't help us diffuse the situation, we could be at war with North Korea in a matter of days. Nuclear war."

The president departed and the monitor's screen went blank.

6

Tokyo, Japan

A chauffeured Maybach 57 carrying Iseda Tokugawa swept across a rain-wet Shuto Expressway No. 7. The big car flashed over the Sumida River and exited at Kabukicho, Tokyo's Pink District, where last night Tokugawa had entertained his Iranian clients. Now the driver inched through a fine drizzle into the heart of the district, which glittered under a greasy pall of smog.

Tokugawa gazed from behind the car's tinted windows at sex emporiums, sushi bars, Burger Kings, and discos; at clubs with names like In and Out, Climax, and Boys and Girls. He saw fortune-tellers' stalls, disco joints pulsing with heavy metal and rock, and knots of long-haired young men loitering in the streets. On every corner touts shouted enticement to wide-eyed *sararimen*—salarymen—and European tourists parading past theaters displaying naked women on their marquees. A tout waving a flyer lunged at the Maybach; Tokugawa turned away. At the Koma Theater, he ordered his driver to pull to the curb.

A wiry Japanese known as Ojima stepped from under the theater's flashing marquee and got into the car. Ojima gave Tokugawa a head bob but said nothing. He settled back and stuffed his hands awkwardly into the pockets of his rain-spotted, jade-green suit.

"Drive us," Tokugawa commanded through the car's intercom. The big sedan hissed away from the curb and blended into traffic. At Yasukuni-dori, the driver turned left and rocketed onto the Shuto Expressway loop toward the Imperial Palace grounds. He exited at Hibiya-dori, cruised past the Babasaki Moat that surrounded the palace's Outer Garden, then around the perimeter of the Imperial Palace grounds.

Tokugawa silently watched the passing scene with the air of a jaded tourist. Now and again he studied his reflection in the door glass, smoothed his thick, silver-white hair, and adjusted his black silk necktie. Ojima remained silent.

They sped past Tokyo's Marunochi District, where blocs of banks, investment houses, and trading companies that made up "Japan Incorporated," the heart of the nation's financial empire, stood shoulder-to-shoulder like stones in a fortress wall. Tokugawa noted the gleaming marble headquarters of the Commerce Bank of Japan, Nippon Heavy Industries, Sumitomo International, and Chikara Electronics.

Tokugawa was on a first-name basis with the executives who ran these businesses. His connections and influence had helped many of them build their empires. In return, their enormous financial resources were always at his disposal. Yet there were times when Tokugawa needed more than financial muscle. Sometimes he needed the kind of muscle only a man like Ojima, Kabukicho's most powerful *yakuza* chieftain, could deliver.

Tokugawa looked at Ojima and said, "Business is good, yes?"

The wiry man shrugged. He had a hard face that remained immobile, like a Kabuki mask. Tokugawa knew he was a good judge of refined heroin and had an unquenchable lust for money. "Yes, Iseda-*san*. But the foreigners, the Taiwanese Mafia, AIDS," he shrugged again, "they all take a bite. I miss the simpler times."

Tokugawa said, "Yes, we are both vulnerable to the vagaries of economics and social turmoil." A long pause. "And our friend Naito, he poses a different kind of problem, no?"

At one time Masayuki Naito had been Ojima's protégé and partner. Now he wanted to oust Ojima as Kabukicho's supreme *yakuza* and take control of Tokyo's pink industry. Worse, he was muscling in on the lucrative drug trade Ojima controlled.

Ojima said, "Yes, he is a problem. I have enough trouble from the metropolitan government without worrying about him. And now the foreigners are making inroads, trying to buy up the clubs. Even women are becoming club owners."

Two wealthy Indonesian women had recently opened The Crystal Palace, a lavish sex club that catered exclusively to high-level salarymen who paid to unwind in private rooms with classy prostitutes. The women's success angered Ojima. "Naito backs them," he said, his face stony.

Gaze fixed straight ahead, Tokugawa said, "And now he is going around you, trying to do business directly with Wu Chow Fat. Yes?"

Ojima nodded.

"Then it is time to put an end to his entrepreneurial spirit. I don't want Wu Chow Fat caught in the middle, between you and Naito."

Ojima barked a laugh. "Caught in the middle, Iseda-

san? But that's what Wu Chow Fat is, a middleman. He works the road between us, the North Koreans, the Mainland Chinese, and the Taiwanese. And now Naito."

"Then there is even more reason to cut Naito out of the chain."

"It is not easy to do. He pays for protection from the head of the prefecture police."

The Maybach had reentered the Shuto Expressway and was speeding back to Kabukicho.

Tokugawa, his white shirt so stiff with starch that it crackled when he reached into his inside jacket pocket, removed an envelope and laid it on the seat cushion next to Ojima. "Please."

Ojima opened the envelope and looked at a document.

Tokugawa said, "That confirms a final payment of two million dollars has been transferred from Daiwa Bank to Chase in New York. The funds are already in your designated account. A similar amount is in the Swiss account owned by the head of the prefecture police."

"Ah . . ."

"Sometimes things require certain measures."

Ojima gave Tokugawa a small head bow. "With respect, Tokugawa-*san*, for a stupid man, Naito has been extremely lucky—"

Tokugawa's eyes bulged ominously. "He is clever!" he snapped, "not *lucky*. Above all, he is not stupid. *You*, Ojima, are the stupid one. You allowed Naito to make a fool of you." Tokugawa's eyes were about to pop from their sockets. "You should have tended to this business when it was clear he had plans to challenge your control of Kabukicho."

Again, Ojima bobbed his head. "I apologize for my shortcomings."

The car exited the expressway and dove into Kabuki-cho's narrow streets.

Tokugawa said, "You have two days to conclude your business with Naito. Before I depart for southern waters."

"I understand."

Tokugawa's driver pulled up in front of the Shinjuki Ward Office. The Maybach, its twin-supercharged V-12 engine idling imperceptibly, sat at the curb while rain, cold and steady, beat against the passenger cabin's darkened windows. Tokugawa watched pedestrians, salarymen, and secretaries scurry through wet streets. Those without umbrellas held folded newspapers over their heads. Ojima, Tokugawa noted, had no umbrella and no newspaper.

Tokugawa said gravely, "It would not please me to see Naito doing business with Wu Chow Fat. Naito is a hothead and too involved with those Colombian powder merchants and Russian arms dealers. And frankly he's not as easy to do business with as you are. I like our arrangement better." He looked at Ojima and actuated the automatic door lock. "Two days."

Tokugawa watched the downpour turn the *yakuza*'s jade-green suit black as he ran for cover.

The Maybach departed Kabukicho and sped east through the crowded Ginza to the Ichigaya section of Tokyo.

Tokugawa didn't blame Wu Chow Fat for entertaining offers from Naito; Fat was a businessman, after all. Instead, he cursed Ojima and seethed at the loss of face he'd suffered. Ojima had forgotten how business was conducted in Japan. And also how to show proper respect to the person who saw to it that doing such business in Japan was possible in the first place. Lately Tokugawa had detected a subtle shift in his relationship with Ojima, who, lately, had seemed more like a lover whose ardor had grown cold. Tokugawa blamed it on the young and ambitious Naito. Ojima had two days to make amends. He knew what would happen to him if he failed.

Tokugawa arrived at the headquarters of the Japan Pacific War Veterans Association's office north of the Imperial Palace grounds, which overlooked the abandoned but still imposing World War II Imperial Army Headquarters building.

Tokugawa stepped from the elevator and was greeted by a row of six smiling, bowing executives wearing dark, shiny suits, white shirts, and, like Tokugawa, black silk neckties.

The association's president, Ichiro Hatoyama, chairman of Nippon Technologies, Ltd., a short, stubby man in his late fifties, greeted Tokugawa. He bowed deeply, hands held flat against his thighs. "It is such a great pleasure to see you, Iseda-*san*. Welcome!"

Tokugawa greeted the others and was escorted into a conference room, which doubled as a museum. Preserved artifacts from the Pacific War—swords, bayonets, grenades, Arisaka bolt-action rifles, Nambu pistols, and sunburst flags—were displayed in glass cases. A battle scene painted in oils covered one whole wall. The work glorified determined Japanese troops and civilians turning back an American amphibious assault, one that never materialized, on the beaches of the Tokyo Plain in 1946. It was titled *Defeat of America*.

The other members took seats and sat stiffly and silently around a huge, black conference table while a servant set at each man's place hot tea and sweet, sticky rice cakes. Tokugawa stood at the glass curtain wall, looking out at the ugly granite edifice that had once been the headquarters of Japan's Imperial Army. Like his colleagues, Tokugawa believed that the spirit of the Imperial Army and that of its leader, General Hideki Tojo, still dwelled there. To most Japanese, the building personified the malignancy of Japan's wartime savagery and was therefore hated.

Tokugawa rolled back the calendar, changing the scene outside to early summer 1945: Instead of sleek Toyotas and Hondas clogging Tokyo's streets, he saw jinrickshaws and, overhead, not fat 747s but formations of silver B-29s raining devastation on a mammoth scale. His memory of the carnage at Hiroshima and Nagasaki that was then yet to come made Tokugawa shudder.

He surveyed Tokyo's smoggy, disordered skyline and saw a nation long risen from the ashes of war, poised now on the cusp of world domination. How easy to forget that the war had ended his father's life and the lives of thousands of men like him. Sadly, for the generations of Japanese born after the surrender, the Pacific War was as unimportant in the scheme of things as the arrival of Commodore Matthew Perry and his Black Ships in 1853.

But for Tokugawa, the war and Japan's defeat burned in his mind as brightly and as fiercely as if it had happened yesterday.

Hatoyama spoke to Tokugawa's back. "The members have asked me to speak on their behalf."

Tokugawa turned and faced the six of them.

Hoshino, almost ninety, a millionaire investor and survivor of the New Guinea campaign. He'd served under the command of a general who, after the war, had been executed for atrocities his troops had committed against Australian and American POWs.

Satsuma, late seventies, chairman of Daiwa Properties, Ltd., a holding company. He was that rarest of breeds, a shamed kamikaze pilot who had lived only because the war had ended before he'd been able to sacrifice himself for Hirohito.

Yukawa, sixty-year-old playboy multimillionaire owner of Nippon Image, Inc., publisher of lurid tabloids. He was the son of a war criminal executed for the mass murder of Filipino women and children in Manila. Many of the victims, the court said, had been burned alive.

Fukuda, fifty-year-old investment banker, grandson of an army officer convicted of killing American POWs forced to build a railroad through the impenetrable jungles of Burma.

Ishigari, sixty-five-year-old magnate, owner of IKE and J-Global shipbuilding. He was a nephew of the notorious General Homma, "Tiger of Malaya," hanged for committing atrocities against civilian and military prisoners.

Hatoyama, grandson of an army officer hanged for ordering the ritual beheading of three captured Doolittle fliers shot down over Japanese-occupied territory in Kiangsi Province, China.

Hatoyama tugged his cuff links and said, "As you know, Iseda-*san*, the situation in North Korea presents both potential problems and potential opportunities for Japan. I refer, of course, to the trade and defense agreements under consideration by the United States and Japan."

The agreement had sprung from a bruising trade embargo and heightened tensions between Washington and Tokyo over the enormous trade deficit the U.S. had rung up. The defense agreement negotiated to solve the problem, if approved, would permit the deployment of an American-designed theater-missile defense system on Japanese soil. The system was supposed to blunt any threat posed by Chinese and North Korean ballistic missiles.

Critics argued that the agreement was too one-sided and favored Japan, that it was a give-away of American technology. They claimed that Japan, instead of being a democratic, free-market trader, was engaging in predatory trade policies. They charged that an elite group of right-wing Japanese politicians and businessmen were working behind the scenes to push the agreements through in an effort to have access to technologies too expensive to develop from scratch in Japan. More than one critic had denounced Japan, saying its tactics were like those it had used in World War II.

Hatoyama said, "Our enemies in America say that we are once again out to conquer the world, this time with our economic prowess. Some interpret our actions as a modern version of 1930s expansionism."

Tokugawa said nothing.

"These are lies, but now, at the very moment Japan may be threatened by the new regime in North Korea, the Americans are threatening to launch a preemptive attack on North Korea. Which leaves the defense agreement in limbo."

Hatoyama paused before continuing. "It will be a disaster if the Americans and North Koreans go to war. We will be caught in the middle."

Tokugawa surveyed the others, then said, "And what is it that you expect of me?"

"May I speak frankly?" asked Hatoyama.

Tokugawa nodded.

"You have great influence with the prime minister. He owes his office to you—please, Iseda-*san*, hear me out—therefore, you must make him see that he has to give in to American demands and resolve the trade issue in their favor. That is the only way we can prove to the Americans that we are allied with them against North Korea."

Tokugawa glared at Hatoyama. "*Give in to the Americans—*"

"Yes, Iseda-*san*, we need their help."

Tokugawa drew himself up. "We don't need help from the Americans. Not after they have denounced us as predators and refuse to accept us as their equal. The Americans are arrogant and belligerent. They pursue a goal of global and economic hegemony. They created the North Korean situation, not us. We owe them nothing. Have you forgotten what we stand for?"

Hatoyama and the others had heard it all before. Tokugawa's loathing of the U.S. for having defeated Japan. For dropping atomic bombs on Hiroshima and Nagasaki. For the deaths of his mother, brothers, and sisters in Nagasaki. For his father having committed *seppuku*—ritual suicide—at war's end after his indictment by General Douglas MacArthur as a Class A War Criminal.

Tokugawa's goal, when he'd founded the Japan Pacific War Veterans Association, had been to rehabilitate the images of former Japanese war criminals, like his father, into heroes of Japan. But Japan had changed, and the names Tojo, Homma, Araki, Kido, and Tokugawa had all but faded from collective memory.

Hatoyama said, "I have forgotten nothing. Certainly not the generation that fought so gloriously in the Pacific conflict. Nor that America and Japan have sharply divergent views about that war. And we will never bend to those in the West who say the Pacific War was an act of brutal aggression by Japan. We glorify our war dead for the blood they shed fighting an enemy bent on our annihilation. We must never capitulate to the dictates of revisionism no matter how fashionable it may be."

Old Hoshino, the veteran of New Guinea, suddenly croaked, "We went to war because America wanted to destroy us. We created the Greater East Asia Co-Prosperity Sphere to liberate Asian peoples from European colonialists. We brought them independence." His voice faltered, but he managed, "I am very proud of that."

"And your father was a brave man, Tokugawa-*san*," said Satsuma, chairman of Daiwa Properties.

"He was a simple army lieutenant caught up in circumstances beyond his control," Tokugawa told his colleagues. "He did his duty."

"But let us also be practical," said Yukawa, the playboy publisher. "While we honor the past, we must protect our future. No one here needs to be reminded of the heroic deeds of our forebears. But now we face a serious challenge to our economic well-being, and if the North Koreans—"

"The North Koreans are not our enemy," Tokugawa said with an edge in his voice. "The United States is our enemy. U.S. multinational corporations are our enemy. Emboldened by America's unilateral employment of military force around the world, they will eventually penetrate every market we control. But General Jin and I will blunt America's influence, not only in Southeast Asia, but in the world."

The association members reacted to Tokugawa's pronouncement with silence.

"What I have said is true." He looked at the members, daring them to say otherwise.

Hatoyama bowed deeply. "Iseda-*san*, I apologize for our shameful manners. None of us have ever doubted you. Instead of exchanging harsh language, we must reach a meeting of the minds and seek the path of tranquillity through stormy seas. After all, each of us has a stake in seeing to it that this problem is resolved to our mutual benefit. The hundreds of billions of yen we have invested in our businesses are at risk. "

"You have nothing to fear from Marshal Jin. America will be defeated." Tokugawa turned his gaze on the ugly granite headquarters of wartime Japan's Imperial Army. "I promise you."

Two men decked out in glossy double-breasted suits eased down a second-floor hallway above a sex club in Kabukicho. The mawkish aroma of cheap incense hung in the air; pulsing techno from 10,000-watt amplifiers vibrated the floor under their feet.

At the end of the hallway slivers of yellow light spilled from around a sliding door that opened onto a small, private room. The two men approached, listened, and heard throaty, urgent grunting, and, in sync with the techno beat coming from downstairs, the rhythmic slap of naked flesh on naked flesh.

With caution, one of the men slid the door open a crack and peeked in. He saw flickering lantern light and leaping shadows, and in the center of the room on a tatami mat, the intertwined bodies of a wiry Japanese man and two Thai girls. The man was fucking one of the girls doggie-style, while the other one, on her back at the bottom of the pile, urged them on with her mouth and hands.

A *yakuza* body tattoo covered the man's sweaty back and buttocks. Intricate and colorful, it depicted the mythical Japanese boy warrior Kintaro astride a bear, fighting a pair of coiled, evil-looking serpents. Only one man in all Japan had that tattoo: Naito. As if alive, the tattooed serpents' thick coils swelled and flexed as Naito rammed his cock into the girl.

The two men burst into the room brandishing unsilenced Glock 17s. The girl down on all fours screamed. In the split second she had left to live, one of the killers recognized her as the *shofu*—prostitute—he had fucked the night before. He remembered that her name was Peach Blossom. Under contract to Ojima, Naito's boss, she had just arrived from Bangkok. Young—not yet sixteen—and petite, very pretty, she was already Naito's favorite.

Before Naito could pull out of her, the two men opened fire. Nine-millimeter Parabellum slugs shredded soft young flesh, gristle and bone, tore into wiry muscle and ripped apart the boy warrior Kintaro and his serpents.

The killers took a moment to survey their work: A fine red mist hung in the room, clotted on walls and floor; fragments of straw matting floated in the air; smoking cartridge cases lay scattered across the floor and on the bodies. Satisfied, they snuffed the lantern and departed, sliding the door closed behind them.

Downstairs, the techno hadn't skipped a beat.

7

The Pacific Ocean, east of Taiwan

Jake Scott entered the USS *Reno*'s torpedo room, reconfigured to the needs of the SEAL team. Nine men, their equipment and weapons, had been crammed into an already tight compartment fitted with Mark-48 ADCAP torpedoes strapped to their cradles, and where sailors hot-bunked due to lack of space. Scott relished the familiar smells of ozone, sweat, and lubricating oil.

McCoy Jefferson stood in the central aisle between the waist-high torpedo storage tables, stripped to his skivvies. He had been working out, and his muscular upper body glistened with sweat, as did his shaved head.

One look at him and Scott felt the torment his own body had been through during a highly compressed training session at Pearl that had had the SEAL team wondering who the hell this guy Scott was and what did he think he was trying to prove.

Scott *did* have to prove himself, through physical workouts, SCUBA training, and refresher courses on tactics and with weapons in the SEAL armory. He had to refine his shooting skills, marksmanship, and magazine manipulation. He also had to relearn how to safely handle C4 explosive and get reacquainted with casualty care. The sessions had left Scott exhausted but exhilarated by the knowledge that he still had the physical and mental stamina to handle the mission they were training for.

A full day had been spent test-flying MAVs. Ominously, two micro bugs had crashed during the last flight, which had left Jefferson surveying their wreckage and frowning. He had cautioned them that with only a primary bug and one backup—due to their enormous cost—any crashes on Matsu Shan, like the ones at Pearl, and they'd be shit out of luck.

To wrap up training, a full day had been devoted to maneuver at sea to test the ASDS, a 65-foot-long, battery-powered miniature submarine designed to deliver SEALs to their objective from specially configured full-sized submarines. The eight-foot-diameter, titanium-hulled mini-sub had a range of 125 nautical miles and a top speed of eight knots. The sub could accommodate ten men: two pilots and eight SEALs and their gear. The pilot and copilot handled navigation through an advanced sonar and electro-optical surveillance system.

With its extended range, speed, and payload, the ASDS was capable of operating on its own, and without Deacon having to run the *Reno* virtually onto the beach—Scott's nightmare—to launch the mini-sub. Instead, the *Reno* could lay in deep water, where she wasn't likely to be detected. Even so, Deacon had agreed to take the *Reno* in as far as he could to make the swim-in as short as possible and to minimize the problems they might have with currents, tides, and also with bioluminescence, which could reveal to an enemy ashore the presence of an ASDS and its swimmers. Scott knew Deacon was a damn good sub driver, and, like himself, was willing to risk his balls for a mission.

But during the maneuvers, Scott had found scant opportunity to mesh with Deacon. Scott was nominally his boss and in charge of the mission; Deacon was ultimately responsible for the safety of his ship and crew. Still, Scott and Deacon had worked well together, and the *Reno*'s crew had been eager to prove just how good they were.

Hours after a final mission briefing from Radford via SVTC from Washington, and with the SEAL team embarked, Deacon had had the *Reno* at sea. Scott had watched Hawaii's Diamond Head disappear off the horizon behind the *Reno*'s boiling wake. Minutes later, with the sub's wave-wrapped bow pointed due west, Deacon had ordered, "Dive! Dive! Diving officer, make your depth six hundred feet."

Reactor spun to full power, the *Reno* had flanked it west under the Pacific, destination Taiwan.

In the torpedo room Scott stepped around disassembled weapons laid out on a rubber mat: 5.56mm short-barreled M4A1 carbines, some with M-203 grenade launchers; suppressed 9mm Sig Saur pistols; and Remington 870 12-gauge choked shotguns.

SEAL Petty Officer First Class Zipolski sat cross-legged, cleaning and checking the weapons and filling M4 20-round magazines with sub-sonic, hollow-point man-stopping ammo. Nearby were night observation devices, PRC-148 inter-squad radios, and a miniature SAT-COM—satellite communications—receiver, and cell phones with embedded crypto-systems. Each piece of equipment had received a thorough going-over by Zipolski. The rest of their weapons—20-pound demolition charges, breaching charges, and grenades of various types, including white phosphorus and fragmentation—had been stowed in the ASDS secured to the *Reno*'s afterdeck over an escape trunk, which provided access.

"Morning, sir," said Zipolski, not looking up from his work. An M4A1 bolt slammed shut in its receiver.

Senior Chief Petty Officer Tom Brodie grunted a hello as he watched Zipolski work. Built like a brick, Brodie was the mission coordinator. The other members of the team assembled in the torpedo room also greeted Scott: Petty Officers Caserta, Leclerc, and Ramos, and SEAL corpsman and shooter Van Kirk. Also present were Lieutenants (jg) Allen and Deitrich, the ASDS's pilot and copilot.

Scott stood with his back to the central torpedo local-control panel and the four tubes canted outboard from centerline of the amidships torpedo room. He addressed the SEALs: "We have another mission briefing update in fifteen minutes. If you have any last-minute questions or comments about the mission, I'll tell General Radford. It'll be your last chance for a face-to-face with him."

Van Kirk said, "Yeah, we don't want no last-minute cluster-fucks, right, Colonel?"

Jefferson, as he toweled off, said, "Especially from you, Zipolski." They all laughed.

Such studied insouciance masked the fact that their line of work was sometimes deadly, something they took in stride because they were ready, eager, and good at it. Scott had seen it in their eyes: confidence and a hunger for action. And a need to prove that they could handle the worst anyone could throw at them. It was a fraternity Scott was not part of and likely could never be part of because, good as he was, the SEALs considered him a liability and knew that to guarantee his safety one of them might have to die while babysitting him.

"No one's expendable, not even you, Zipolski," Jefferson added, eyeing Scott.

Zipolski slammed a loaded magazine into a Sig Saur with the heel of his hand. Then he joined the other SEALs headed for the wardroom.

"You okay on this, Scott?" Jefferson said as Scott crabbed through the cramped aisle.

Scott halted inches from Jefferson. He smelled the man's sweat, felt his heat. He met Jefferson's steady gaze. Scott knew what Jefferson meant. During training at Pearl, Jefferson had constantly measured Scott's performance, probing for any weakness. He had observed how hard Scott had been breathing, how much trouble he'd had keeping up with the others in rough surf and during the slog across wet sandy beaches at night loaded down with gear and weapons. And above all, how good a marksman he was with the M4 and Sig Saur. Very good, as it had turned out. Scott knew that despite his performance, Jefferson didn't want him on the team, had said more than once that Scott belonged in the control room of a sub, not risking his neck on a mission with SEALs armed to the teeth.

"We can handle it," Jefferson had flat out told him at Pearl. "The intel, I mean. Nothing we haven't handled before. Maybe you should sit this one out. Radford would understand. Hell, I don't know a damn thing about driving a sub, no reason you should know about—"

"Stow it," Scott had said, while nursing a badly bruised thigh after a workout. "I'm along, like it or not." He knew Jefferson resented the crossover into his territory. And why not? He wouldn't want Jefferson driving his sub.

Now Jefferson finished seesawing the towel behind his neck and gave Scott a look. The tension that had been slowly building between them during the voyage was threatening to break into the open.

"Briefing in ten minutes," Scott said.

Scott entered the *Reno*'s control room. The size of a small bedroom in a typical American split-level, the compartment was crammed with equipment and watchstanders.

On the port side forward was the ship-control station, with its seats, control yokes, and instrument consoles looking very much like those found in a jet airliner. Here, two men seated side by side controlled the *Reno*'s course, speed, and depth. The man on the left controlled the stern diving planes, the man on the right, the bow planes and rudder. The diving officer, a chief petty officer seated behind them, supervised their actions. To their left, the chief of the watch sat at a wraparound console equipped with monitors that displayed the status of the ship's various systems.

A glance at the console and Scott noted the *Reno*'s depth—still 600 feet—and speed of advance—almost 40 knots. On the ship's status board, Deacon had posted orders to maintain flank speed until they reached longitude 135 east. Only then, or for an emergency, would they slow down and come to PD for a look-see.

Scott moved aft to the two periscopes mounted athwartships—to the left a Type 18; to the right a Type 2. Aft of the scopes were the twin plotting tables on which the *Reno*'s track under the Pacific Ocean was being recorded automatically, and also by hand by the navigator and the quartermaster of the watch.

Portside of the control room, behind the plotting tables, stood the ship's inertial guidance system, gyro, and navigation equipment, all surmounted by racked radio equipment, video monitors, digital chronometers, and depth indicators.

Deacon and his exec, Rus Kramer, stood at one of the tables, the captain stepping off ranges on a chart with a pair of dividers. As Scott approached, Deacon said, "We're making good time. Might break the record for transit, the rate we're going."

Scott gave Deacon a thumbs-up and said, "Ready for RDT whenever you are, Skipper."

"Aye, sir," Deacon said.

The *Reno*'s Rapid Data Transmission system worked in conjunction with GPS satellites to capture super-high-frequency transmissions at moderate depths while moving at high speed. Thus equipped, the *Reno* didn't have to slow down or poke up a mast to communicate with ComSubPac at Pearl Harbor, or with the SRO in Virginia.

"Hold present course and speed," Deacon commanded. "Make your depth five hundred feet."

The planesman at the ship's control station responded smartly: The *Reno*, her deck and hull vibrating from the changed angle of attack through the water, tilted up and sped toward the surface.

8

The *Reno,* mid-Pacific

Scott, braced against the submarine's up angle, entered the wardroom located one deck below the control room. It was outfitted with comfortable seating and a long table that accommodated the *Reno*'s officers for meals, watching movies, or conducting councils of war. At the moment the wardroom's flat-screen video monitor displayed a wobbling dark blue background with the message RESTRICTED MEDIA.

Senior Chief Brodie, Zipolski, and the other SEALs, drinking coffee, waited for the show to start.

"Where's Jefferson?"

"Showering, sir," said Brodie. "Said he'd be right along."

Scott chose not to ascribe sinister motives to Jefferson's absence. To prepare for the broadcast, he made sure the video camera was rigged so that Radford would see all the SEALs seated around the table.

Ready, Scott checked his wristwatch. Underfoot, the deck leveled out as the *Reno* came shallow. The digital repeater indicated a steady 500 at the same moment the sound-powered phone squawked. Scott uncradled it and identified himself.

Deacon's voice leaked past the handset. "Sir, we're at five hundred feet. Course two-seven-zero, SOA forty knots. RDT is powered up and on standby."

Scott hung up the handset and turned to Brodie. "Anything we need to discuss with Radford?"

"One thing, sir." Brodie's thick fingers, better suited to crushing an opponent's windpipe than secretarial work, skipped through the pages of a small notebook. "Those Chinese pirates."

"Drug-runners," corrected Scott.

"Yes, sir, whatever. We sure as hell don't know much about them. I mean, how many of them are on Matsu Shan? We don't have anything definite in the way of numbers."

"Agreed," Scott said. "The SRO says that from their satellite coverage, there's not more than twenty."

"Beggin' your pardon, sir, but that's bullshit."

"What's bullshit?" asked Jefferson as he entered the wardroom, washed and polished, wearing fresh black cammies and matching T-shirt.

Scott looked Jefferson up and down, not masking irritation at his tardiness.

"Satellite head-counts," Brodie said. "They're almost always wrong."

Jefferson said, "It's the best we can do. We're lucky to have anything."

"Chief, I'd trust Ms. Kida's numbers," Scott said. "JDIH says there's closer to thirty men on Matsu Shan, not twenty."

"And if I were you, Scott," said Jefferson, helping himself to coffee, "I'd trust the SRO's numbers. Their data is damn good."

Brodie said, "Colonel, you know as well as I do that those nose-pickers always count heads twice and miss the other ones. Shit, there could be forty, fifty China-men on that rock for all we know."

Zipolski said, "Hey, Chief, what's it matter, we ain't pokin' no stick in a hornet's nest, just doin' a sneak 'n' peek."

"One that could turn into a hornet's nest," Scott said. "Assume it will."

The other SEALs kept silent as they followed the discussion. They knew that a mission's success or failure hinged on good intelligence; bad intelligence was for losers.

Jefferson pulled a face on Scott. "How many spec-ops did you say you've been on?"

"Enough to know we can't underestimate what we might encounter on Matsu Shan."

"Hell, we don't need a lecture on the basics," Jefferson retorted. "We all know how this works. I mean, it's good that Brodie posed the question, but I'm inclined to trust the SRO's estimates. Trust me, this won't be like Croatia."

Scott ignored Jefferson's snide reference to the bungled Balkans op and turned to Brodie. "I'll bring it up and see what General Radford has to say. Maybe they have fresh data they can share with us."

"Right, sir. Thanks."

Jefferson said something but was cut off by the tone signal indicating an SVTC transmission was about to start. The blue screen rolled to the SRO seal, then a fuzzy picture of Karl Radford. His image was distorted by transmission through space and 500 feet of seawater, into the RDT antenna aboard the speeding *Reno*.

Radford adjusted his necktie and cleared his throat. "We on?" The image faltered but returned, clearer this time. "Commander Scott, Colonel Jefferson, men, good to see you."

"Good to see you, sir," Scott said.

The SEALs greeted Radford with nods and casual waves.

"We'll be joined by Ms. Kida from JDIH headquarters in Tokyo, that is, if the patch can be made. . . ." Radford looked off camera. "It is? Outstanding. Ah, there she is."

The screen had split in half. Fumiko appeared on the left side, her image beamed to the *Reno* from a broadcast studio inside JDIH.

Scott saw that she had on a dark man-cut suit over a white top and that her long silky hair was pinned back in a bun behind her head. Though she looked austere and businesslike, Scott noted with pleasure that her eyes sparkled brightly and that her lips had been painted glossy red. He thought she looked as lovely as she had when they'd met for the first time at the safe house in Virginia.

After they exchanged greetings, Scott said, "How was your trip back to Japan?"

"The trip, oh, well, it was long," Fumiko said coolly, adjusting her posture.

"You should have stopped off in Hawaii, spent a day at Waikiki."

Fumiko looked down at papers in her hands.

Radford cleared his throat and said, "Gentlemen, we seem to have a gap in our coverage of the movement of Marshal Jin and his entourage from North Korea. Fact is, we've lost him."

"*Lost him* . . . ," Scott said.

"We were keeping tabs on him right up through yesterday. Take a look."

The screen went to green, then to an aerial view of a

sun-spanked harbor at a low angle—less than twenty degrees off horizontal—taken from an over-the-horizon-looking KH-12 satellite. One of the satellite's cameras zoomed in on a rusty cargo ship.

With the image in motion, a Mercedes-Benz limousine rolled up to the ship's gangplank. Men in uniform poured into the picture and came to attention. A man in civilian clothes got out of the limousine and boarded the ship. Scott easily recognized Marshal Jin from briefing photos of him he'd seen earlier. Jin took a salute from the ship's captain and disappeared from view.

"The harbor is Nam'po; the ship is the *Sugun*, a 1900-ton North Korean rust bucket. Note the chopper on her fantail," Radford said. "An SA 365N Dauphin 2, in gray and olive drab, no markings. Ms. Kida, why don't you take over."

"Thank you, General." The image changed to an oblique view of the *Sugun*, wallowing like a hog in moderate seas. "She sailed three days ago. Here, you can see that we tracked her by satellite into the Yellow Sea, where we lost her just north of Shanghai."

"Lost her, how?" Scott asked.

Fumiko met his gaze on the video monitor. "Coastal traffic in and out of Shanghai is very heavy. Many ships look alike; it's easy to confuse them."

"Why wasn't one of our SSNs put on her ass?"

Fumiko trapped her lower lip under white front teeth. "I—"

"We're short of assets," Radford grumped. "Go on, Miss Kida."

"We thought we'd picked her up again the next day, near Wen-chou. The NKs trade with Mainland China, and the *Sugun* has called at that port in the past."

"But not this time."

"No. The ship we thought was the *Sugun* turned out to be another one that looked like her, and without a helo."

"So where is she now?" Jefferson asked.

"We don't know," Fumiko said. "We're searching for her," she added as if that would make things right.

"Holy shit," Chief Brodie rumbled under his breath.

The other SEALs looked at each other and silently rolled eyes.

"Have you any fresh comms intercepts that might tell us something?" Scott said. "Like maybe where Jin disappeared to."

Fumiko said, "No, no comms. Even so, there's no reason to believe anything has changed."

An infrared picture on the screen showed the incredible volume of coastal traffic plying waters between Mainland China and Japan. Hundreds, if not thousands, of green deltas representing vessels of all types, infrared heat signatures from their machinery and cargoes glowing bright red and orange, swarmed off the coast of China at Shanghai and other ports.

"Scott."

"Yes, General?"

"Take a look at this." The picture shifted to macro view. Radford jockeyed a pointer up against a bright red delta outlined in white, north of Taiwan. "We think this one may be a Chinese diesel submarine. Don't have a positive on it yet, but its heat bloom comports with a Chinese Kilo 636."

"Think she's on routine patrol?"

"Don't know that either. We've counted heads up at Tingchow, their Northern Fleet sub base. Couple of their boats are missing, and this guy might be one of them."

"Okay, we'll definitely keep him in mind. Thanks for the heads-up, General."

Jefferson shifted in his chair. "General, if you have no reason to think Jin has aborted—"

"None."

"—then we still have a go, right?"

"Right. And as soon as we find the *Sugun*, we'll let you know if it appears anything has changed."

Scott knew how quickly a situation could change, how it could scuttle plans and endanger lives. Their lives. For all its vaunted technology, the SRO was too often left in the dark; unlike the JDIH, Radford had pushed for and received heavy funding for electronic intelligence-gathering—Elint—via satellites and the like rather than human intelligence—Humint—on the ground in hostile territory. Satellites were useful for finding submarines like the Chinese Kilo, and large, unmovable facilities like air bases and weapons dumps, but not people.

"Fumiko, do you have anything new that might help to identify Jin's guest?"

"Nothing," Fumiko said. "We're still monitoring comms, but they've gone down. I know that's an ominous sign. But we've also been monitoring commercial and private flights from Japan to Taiwan, looking for someone who might fit our profile. And not just those from Narita and Osaka, but also the smaller airports that serve Taiwan. We're also monitoring seaports south of Nagoya. But so far nothing. We've had a report that Wu Chow Fat was seen somewhere between Taiwan and China, but that's all."

"How was he seen?" Scott asked.

"Aboard his junk, the *White Dragon*. She puts to sea at least twice a week."

"To pick up drugs from North Korean ships and deliver them to his customers?"

"We think so."

Radford interrupted. "I'm meeting with the president. I've scheduled another briefing twelve hours before you commit. Perhaps by then we'll know more. Any questions?"

Brodie waved a paw at Scott, who said, "General, we need an update on how many of Fat's men are on that island. How about rechecking that for us."

Radford's image began to break up. "I stand by our numbers—there are not more than twenty men on Matsu Shan."

Rolling diagonal black bars replaced Radford's and Fumiko's faces on the monitor as the RDT satellite connection faded. Scott heard Radford say, faintly, "What's that, I can't hear you . . ."

The monitor went to blue.

9

Taipei, Taiwan

Engines spooling down, the yellow and white Tori-Air Boeing 737 rolled to a stop in front of a ghostly cargo-sorting facility on the fringes of Taipei's Chiang Kai-shek International Airport. Only a few service lights burned in empty hangars and around a solitary UPS 330 Air Bus waiting to be loaded.

Tokugawa disembarked into a muggy night spiced with the tang of burned jet fuel and the roar of passenger jets taking off and landing. A black Toyota Land Cruiser pulled up alongside the 737's companionway. The driver got out, welcomed Tokugawa to Taiwan, then bowed him into the backseat. Tokugawa settled back in comfort as the big SUV swung out of the airport onto the motorway and sped toward Chi-lung.

Many things had to be accomplished, Tokugawa mused. Wu Chow Fat's vulgar attempt to wrest control of heroin distribution from Ojima had to be addressed and tamped down. Likely Fat already knew Naito had been eliminated. Dozens of eyes and ears reported everything that happened in Tokyo, especially Kabuki-cho. It was said that one couldn't step on a cat's tail without Fat knowing about it. If so, it would demonstrate how seriously Tokugawa took such matters. Because the Chinese were unfailingly polite, Fat might feign ignorance and simply express shock over Naito's misfortune. But Fat knew better than anyone that operators who freelanced in the billion-dollar Tokyo sex and drug business usually ended up dead.

Naito, Fat, and Ojima were insignificant compared to what the North Koreans had proposed. The deal Marshal Jin was eager to consummate was of another magnitude altogether. It was a deal, Tokugawa thought with pleasure, that would bring untold riches, and with it, his long-sought revenge on America.

He remembered what had happened as clearly as if it had occurred yesterday: A solitary silver B-29 seen through a break in the cloud cover over Nagasaki. The flash of light brighter than a million suns. The hard, angry shadow his body had cast on the ground. The unimaginable heat and the mushroom cloud turning everything black, ending his world.

The Toyota, its knobby tires thumping the length of a wooden pier lined on one side with godowns, drew up beside a waiting motor launch. The driver doused the lights, after which Tokugawa got out and, orienting himself, heard the incoming tide chuckling under the pier. He couldn't see her, but he knew that the *White Dragon*, Wu's Hainan-style four-masted junk, lay anchored in the roadstead.

Two Chinese in black BDUs and armed with Beretta submachine guns stepped from blocky shadows and approached. One of the men aimed a blue-lensed flashlight beam at Tokugawa. Satisfied, he bowed deeply.

The men escorted Tokugawa aboard the launch,

where the captain, a leathery looking Chinese, made him comfortable in the cabin below decks. They cast off, and fifteen minutes later Tokugawa was welcomed aboard the *White Dragon* by Wu Chow Fat.

Fiber mat lugsails reefed, the *White Dragon*'s powerful twin diesels drove her into the Pacific, away from the twinkling lights of Chi-lung. Seated in heavy brocade armchairs brought topside for their meeting, Tokugawa and Fat faced each other.

"I hope you do not mind, Iseda-*san*, that we take the night air," Fat said in excellent Japanese.

A warm offshore breeze lifted the lapels of Tokugawa's suit jacket and ruffled his hair. He breathed deeply and savored the hiss and splash of water tumbling past the junk's hull. Due west, he saw the fading glow of Chi-lung; due east, strings of milky colored lights at Pitouchiao. He didn't need a compass to know that the *White Dragon* was on a northeasterly course toward Matsu Shan, a two-hour voyage.

The turbocharged diesels cleared their throats, and their throb deepened. The deck vibrated as the twin screws dug in hard and the *White Dragon* speeded up. A steward set out bottles of rice wine, pots of steaming green tea, and Taiwanese delicacies. Tokugawa and his host toasted with wine drunk from translucent cups dating from the Tsin Dynasty.

"Business has been good?" Tokugawa said, his gaze on Fat, whose face was illuminated by gently swaying lanterns hung from rigging.

"*Very* good, Iseda-*san*, *very* good," Fat said.

When Fat spoke or moved, his flesh quivered like freshly kneaded bread dough. His enormous girth, spilling over the chair, threatened the seams of his hand-sewn black-and-red silk pajamas. It was said that

Fat kept a pistol hidden in his rolls of flesh, and Tokugawa wondered if that was true.

"I owe my success and great, good fortune to you,
Iseda-*san*." He smoked a Marlboro to its filter, lit another from its ember. "I am pleased to offer you my
humble services. I am always at your call."

Tokugawa was not taken in by Fat's obsequious
manner and insipid mutterings. He knew that no Chinese ever conceded the upper hand to a foreigner, much
less a Japanese. "I appreciate your kindness, Wu-*san*.
Now, please allow me to speak frankly."

"Yes, please, speak as you wish. We have no secrets
from each other."

Tokugawa knew better. "I have sad news. Ojima's
protégé, Naito, is dead. Murdered. So unfortunate."

Fat said nothing as he puffed on his Marlboro, the
smoke carried away by a sharp wind that made the hal-
yards whistle.

"Apparently Naito wanted to do business on his
own. I don't know the details but was told he offended
one of his customers and was . . . removed. Perhaps
Naito failed to see that his link to the present was a
bridge to the future. Failed to understand that trust, respect, fealty, openness never go out of style. Perhaps if
he'd not forgotten that, he'd still be alive."

Fat toyed with his Marlboro. With the rippling red-
and-black silk pajamas plastered to his body by the
wind, he mulled this over. "An unfortunate turn of
events, Iseda-*san*. I didn't know Naito personally but of
course have heard his name. I believe he had connections to individuals wanting to invest in Kabukicho.
Perhaps he offended one of them."

"Perhaps." Tokugawa shrugged.

"I don't think this affair need have any effect on our

relationship, do you? Naito, as you say, was an irritant and now a forgotten artifact. We have a fine arrangement, and nothing will change that. After all, we are businessmen and must look out for each others' interests, and, if possible, advance them, is that not so?"

Tokugawa looked away, into a dark and sinister sea.

"Mistakes are made and mistakes are corrected," Fat said, not unwilling to grovel to make things right. "Things will continue as they have."

Tokugawa turned his gaze on Fat. "Excellent."

They toasted, after which Tokugawa said, "Marshal Jin. How do you read him?"

"Confident. He is quite eager to meet with you. Whatever your arrangements with him are, I wish you great success. If it is a new business venture, I would like to say that my own arrangement with the North Koreans has always been cordial."

"And mutually profitable."

"They have products and we have lines of distribution and, of course, influence. Very profitable. But also dangerous. As you know, Beijing wants to exert control over the East and South China Seas. The Americans are trying to prevent this. Some day China and America will go to war to decide who controls what. Such a war would bring an end to my arrangements with North Korea, and thus with the Mainland Chinese and Taiwan."

"There will be no war between China and the United States."

Fat regarded Tokugawa with naked skepticism. "If you believe that, Iseda-san, then you must have the ear of powerful individuals. Marshal Jin, for one. And so I say with great humility that if I can assist your future dealings with the North Koreans in any way, I hope you will ask me."

"I would not impose upon you further, Wu-*san*, nor on our friendship. You have provided both privacy and security, and that is sufficient to prevent others from intruding."

"I understand. After all, I, too, loath the Americans. And despite past differences between our two countries, I commend the work of the Japan Pacific War Veterans Association. This new generation, ah, they look only to the future, to the next day, to the next hour. They have no connection to the past. No respect for history. None." Fat waited for a response.

Tokugawa finished his wine. The wind had turned cold, cutting him like a knife, and he shuddered. Recovered, he recited, " 'In all things foreign, I come across a man who Does not forget our Empire.' It was written by Akemi Tachibana. Let history record that the Americans forgot our empire, and that forgetting, failed to see the end of their own empire. Now I would like to rest. Perhaps there is a cabin I may use."

Three hundred yards off the *White Dragon*'s port beam, a steel pole painted mottled gray-and-black camouflage, with a sea serpent's eye at its tip, popped out of the water. Sixty feet below the surface, Commander Deng Zemin screwed his eye into the rubber buffer surrounding the periscope's ocular and toggled to infrared. The *White Dragon* changed from a chunky black silhouette into a speeding bluish-green dragon with a glowing red heart—the heat bloom from her roaring diesel engines.

Zemin's submarine, a Russian-built Kilo 636 diesel-electric attack boat, one of a dozen in commission with the People's Liberation Army Navy, or PLAN, steamed a course parallel to the *White Dragon* while Zemin looked her over. The Kilo's MGK-400 EM digital sonar had picked up the *White Dragon*'s snarking, sputtering diesels the moment she'd upped anchor in the roadstead off Chilung. Zemin had orders from North Sea Fleet Headquarters to monitor drug trafficking across the Formosa Strait, especially by Wu Chow Fat. He knew Beijing suspected that Fat was siphoning North Korean heroin to the Russian Mafiya, but that they had no proof.

While Zemin observed Fat's activities, Zemin's first officer watched the periscope's video repeater and made notes with a stylus on a data pad, from which he could prompt the Kilo's combat and command system's computer for automatic fire control if needed.

Zemin's inspection of Fat's vessel revealed not only a pair of super-heated diesels but also an M-168 Lockheed Martin 20mm six-barreled Vulcan chain-gun, its snout poking from under a tarpaulin, and a pair of Browning .50-caliber heavy machine guns midships.

"Fat departed Chi-lung for Matsu Shan at high speed," Zemin said. "I wonder what waits on his island that is so important."

The first officer smiled. "Indeed, Comrade Captain, he has both throttles wide open."

Zemin folded the periscope's handles and stepped back. A sailor yanked a hydraulic lever in the overhead; the periscope hummed into its well. Zemin folded his arms and frowned while he considered options. He was a handsome man with delicate Mandarin features of the type favored by the younger members of the Central Committee, whose job it was to hand out choice commands within the PLAN. Zemin's officers, handpicked by him, had been encouraged to think for themselves, a rarity in the PLAN.

"Perhaps, Comrade Captain," said the first officer, "we should sprint ahead to Matsu Shan."

"I agree. The ministers in Beijing might be interested in what we report. You may give the orders."

The first officer swung into action. The stubby, teardrop-shaped sub sheared away from the plodding *White Dragon* and sprinted north.

"We will see what this powder merchant, Fat, is up to," said Zemin.

10

Northwest of Sakishima Gunto

Scott finished a workout, then showered. Dressed in fresh cammies, he sat at the small folding desk in his stateroom and pondered the mission. Jefferson was trouble. The man wanted to run the operation himself and didn't want someone looking over his shoulder, perhaps believing that Radford lacked confidence in him by assigning Scott to the mission. Bad enough he had to deal with Jefferson's bruised ego, Scott feared there was little time left to figure out what the NKs were up to. Were Marshal Jin and his henchman bent on launching nuclear weapons? If they did, U.S. Trident SSBNs would launch nuclear-tipped missiles against North Korea. *It's what we all train for*, Scott thought, *but you can't train for the possibility that a maniacal general in North Korea will overthrow an equally maniacal dictator.*

He thought about Tracy in Tokyo. What if she knew? Would she leave her toy, Rick, and come home? If she did, could they patch things up? Why did he care if he didn't need her anymore?

The sound-powered phone chirped.

"Scott."

Sam Deacon said, "We're just about at point X-ray. Thought you'd want to know."

"I'll be right up."

Scott found Deacon, Kramer, Jefferson, and the quartermaster of the watch huddled over one of the plotting tables in the control room.

Jefferson made room, then pointed to two marks penciled on the chart east of Taiwan. "Captain says we're here and that X-ray is there." X-ray was a prearranged holding box twenty miles northeast of Matsu Shan.

Deacon said, "We'll have you in position to kick out at twenty-two hundred."

Eight hours to go, Scott calculated. So far it was running like clockwork. "How's the traffic upstairs?"

"Sir, like Times Square," answered the quartermaster. "We're tracking close to twenty targets."

Ships of all sizes entering and departing Taiwanese ports posed a potential hazard to the *Reno*. To prevent detection and to avoid a possible collision as she crept silently toward X-ray, Deacon had ordered a depth of 500 feet.

Deacon said, "You should be launched by twenty-two-thirty latest."

Scott turned to Jefferson. "Did you pre-flight the mini-sub?"

"Checked out and ready to go. We'll run a final pre-flight, say, an hour before we kick out." He came upright from the chart table and stretched. "How about that brief from the old man. About time, isn't it?"

Radford was due on the RDT net in fifteen minutes. Scott hoped that Fumiko would join in so he'd have a chance to see her one more time before shoving off.

"Skipper, can we pipe the conference into the control

room?" Scott asked. He pointed to an auxiliary video monitor rigged over the starboard plotting table. "I'd like you to sit in so you know what's what in case we need backup later."

Jefferson reacted. "No way. . . . Sorry Captain, no offense." He jerked a thumb at the officers and men on watch in the control room. "These people aren't cleared for this conference."

Scott said, "Let me worry about that. I want Captain Deacon in the loop. He and his crew got us here and they've got to get us home."

"I said they're not cleared—"

Scott gave Jefferson a flinty look. "I heard what you said."

Jefferson and Scott looked at each other. After a long moment, Jefferson nodded and said no more.

Deacon tugged his nose while Kramer said, "Sir, we can patch the conference through to this monitor."

"Do it," said Scott.

Radford's normally rocky mien looked haggard. Fumiko appeared on the other half of the split-screen looking alert and polished.

"General, I've asked Captain Deacon to be present for this update," said Scott.

Jefferson's jaw tightened, but Radford was past it, saying, "As far as we can tell from satellite IR and laser imagery, nothing's changed on Matsu Shan. However, we spotted that chopper from the *Sugun*—it's parked on Matsu Shan. We also found the *Sugun*. She's on a racetrack about a hundred miles off the China coast at Fuzhou, killing time, we presume, waiting for Jin to fly back from the meeting. We'll keep you updated on her movements."

"Anything new on the other dude, like how he got to Matsu Shan?" Jefferson asked.

Fumiko said, "We think he was met by Wu Chow Fat in Taiwan and ferried to the island aboard the *White Dragon*. But our surveillance is inconclusive. There're just too many vessels and too much traffic in and around Fuzhou to pick out Fat's junk from all the clutter."

"How did he get to Taiwan?" Scott asked.

Fumiko said, "We just don't know. JDIH has monitored flights into Taipei, but I was told by my director that no one suspicious was seen arriving via a scheduled flight. And there's been no private charters. Well, I take that back, there's a Taiwanese movie star who has her own jet. She arrived yesterday."

"Were there any unscheduled flights to Taiwan?"

"Only one in the last forty-eight hours, from Tokyo to CKS. A ToriAir 737 filed a last-minute flight plan to deliver a cargo of electronic switching gear for transhipment to Iran."

"What's ToriAir?" Scott asked.

"A Japanese air cargo service. They're trying to compete with UPS and FedEx in the Far East, but it's a loser."

"And there were no passengers aboard that 737?"

"I was told just the regular flight crew."

"What about a ship from Japan?" Jefferson asked.

"It wouldn't be practical, Colonel. It would take too long, plus there's no regular passenger service from Japanese ports to Taiwan, so we've ruled it out."

"So how did this guy, whoever he is, get to Taiwan from Japan and then to Matsu Shan?" Scott said.

"Hell, what's it matter?" Jefferson said. "We've got our orders, let's go."

"I agree with McCoy," Radford said. "How he got there

is purely academic. What's important is that we find out *why* he's there. Later we can retrace our steps and see what we missed. In the meantime, I've asked Director General Kabe to redouble efforts to identify him. Ms. Kida is still working with them on that."

"Sir, any update on how many people are on that island?" Scott said.

"Um, we're working on that, too. Recounting heads. Fair enough?"

"Yes, sir. We'll have that open channel ashore from the sat com. I'd appreciate an update as soon as you get it."

"Anything else?"

"That PLAN Kilo. Where is she now?"

"Yes, the Kilo." Radford consulted a document. "We think she's north of the Formosa Strait."

Deacon spoke up. "Sir, do you have any information that we can use to plot her track?"

"Yes, we do, Captain. It's not terribly accurate, but I'll see that it's uploaded to the *Reno* immediately."

"Anything you have will do, sir."

"McCoy?"

"No, questions, General. The clock's running."

"Scott?"

"McCoy's right. It's time to go."

"Very well. I spoke with the president. He's confident the mission will succeed. And so am I. Please convey that to your men."

"Yes, sir, we will. Thank you."

Radford signed off. Jefferson and Deacon, lost in their own thoughts, peeled away from the video monitor.

"Jake." Fumiko looked at him across space, her beautiful, almond-shaped jade green eyes sparkling. "Take care of yourself and your men."

"Don't worry, I'll call when I get back."

* * *

Deng Zemin peered through the Kilo's raised night-vision periscope and saw a curtain of rain slanting over Matsu Shan. The scene was rendered an acid green by the NV optics. Still, he could identify the high, rocky bluff topped by the Sino-baroque villa and below it, in the mouth of the channel, the anchored *White Dragon*.

"Forward and aft up ten degrees," Zemin ordered the planesmen.

The deck tilted up; the Kilo rose slightly. Zemin twisted the focusing handle's detent into high magnification and was catapulted past the *White Dragon* to a motor launch tied up at a pier illuminated by a string of dim lights. Zemin counted five men standing on the pier and two more in the launch's stern sheets. Next he examined the villa, with its gaily lighted interior and silhouetted figures behind curtained windows. Perhaps Fat was entertaining his visitor, Zemin thought. Someone important. Someone *very* important.

11

Key Largo, Florida

The president toweled off after doing fifty laps in his pool. The first lady, clad in a skintight white maillot, lay in a lounge chair with a gin and tonic in hand.

Diamond-hard Florida sunlight slashing through palm fronds and crepe myrtle almost blinded Paul Friedman, the president's national security advisor, as he approached the pool after having concluded a video conference inside. A sheer curtain billowing out the sliding glass door to the pool snagged on Friedman and wrapped him up like a mummy until a Secret Service agent set him free.

The first lady, a former actress, gazed listlessly over lowered pink-framed sunglasses and saw Friedman approaching. He was dressed in baggy shorts and a colorful Hawaiian shirt on which a bevy of scantily clad girls played beach ball. A head of thick, unruly hair exploded over his ears and collar.

"Darling," said the first lady, sotto voce to her husband, "it's Paul. Hello, Paul."

"Hello, Mim," said Friedman, using the first lady's nickname, which she preferred to Cole, her real name, which she hated even though she'd used it on the screen.

The president, looking grim, absently seesawed the towel around his neck. "Drink, Paul?"

"Coke, please, sir."

The president, shod in zoris, flapped to the bar, popped a can, and poured it over crackling ice cubes.

"Karl tell you the latest out of Pyongyang?" asked the president.

As was her habit, the first lady departed when discussions turned serious and were necessarily classified. As she strode toward the open glass doors, Friedman remembered to tear his gaze from her long legs and snaking buttocks, made all the more luscious, he thought, by the white maillot clinging to silky, satin-black skin.

"Yes, sir, we discussed the latest threats coming from the NK Central News Agency. It's nothing but bullshit, an NK temper tantrum. We've heard it all before."

"And the satellite photos of Tongchong?"

"Right, the NK nuclear storage facility. Karl thinks they want us to see activity there to give us something to worry about."

"I know what Karl thinks; I know what Defense thinks; I know what the joint chiefs think; I even know what my wife thinks. Now I want to know what you think."

Friedman, heavyset, his wiry hair more unruly than normal from the Florida Keys' towering humidity, flicked moisture from his chin. "Well, they did everything but wave at our KH-12s and at the UN's surveillance cameras surrounding the area. The KH-12s recorded the thermal signatures the weapons give off when they're on alert status. This was after the NKs broke the UNSCOM inspectors' seals and entered the storage facility. That's forbidden under the treaty Kim signed, which is now worthless. We know they have twenty nuclear warheads in that mountain cave complex of theirs, and I don't think they're doing an inventory. Like I said, Jin's trying to scare us by making us think he's willing to go to the brink of nuclear war. But I don't believe he's got the balls for it."

"No? I saw the IR pictures of that truck driving away from the facility at night. Kim tore up the sole rail line into the Kangnam Mountains, so there's no other way to get in or out of Tongchong except by road. So what are they up to? What does our contact in Pyongyang say?"

Friedman shook his head and sweated. "Nothing. He's gone silent on us. I'm not surprised. What with the coup, he's walking a tightrope. Maybe when things settle down, when it's safe for him to pay a visit to the Danish ambassador—"

The president said, "In the meantime, Jin is moving nuclear warheads around like a shell game and we haven't a clue to their whereabouts or his intentions. I can't operate on the premise that he's bluffing. What if he's not?"

The president toweled prisms of water clinging to his close-cropped hair. He turned away from Friedman to the fleet of sailboats that gathered daily in Florida Bay off the president's Key Largo estate, hoping to catch a glimpse of him and his glamorous wife. A Coast Guard vessel with a whooping siren chased a sailboat that had violated the one-thousand-yard-offshore security zone designed to protect the Florida White House from suicide bombers.

He rounded on Friedman. "Paul, let's assume they *are* moving warheads. Where to? The SRO lost track of that damn truck we think was transporting them. When it didn't show up at their test rig in Pyongyang or their missile launch complex at Hamhung, our people on the ground started looking for it, couldn't find it, and panicked. So where the hell are they? Clearly the warheads are tied to Jin's meeting with this . . . this, whoever he is . . . on Matsu Shan. But *how* are they tied to it?" The president spoke in a voice so pinched with distress that, Friedman flinched as if in pain when he heard it.

An aide with a document in her hand entered the pool area and approached the two men. In panty hose, heels, and a suit, she looked oddly out of place. Friedman, glad for the intrusion, said, "Hello, Karen."

She said, "Sorry to interrupt, Mr. President, but there's a message for Mr. Friedman from ComSubPac. Priority."

He skimmed the message and announced, "The *Reno* has departed X-ray. Scott's going in."

Part Two

BLACK OPS

12

Matsu Shan

Jin and Tokugawa strolled from the dining room onto the terrace. A warm breeze scented with orange blossoms made the candlelight dance. Tokugawa saw a shadow move silently among the dripping orange trees and knew it was one of Fat's armed men patrolling the grounds. He and the other guards on patrol had orders to remain out of sight while the two men conducted their business. Earlier, Jin's aide had swept for hidden bugs and announced that none were present.

Jin took a seat on the veranda and lit a cigarette. Tokugawa, silent, contemplative, sipped brandy and listened to the ocean's relentless assault on the sheer bluffs a hundred feet below where he stood. At length Tokugawa turned to Jin, who, during supper, had been remarkably composed, considering what had been discussed. Tokugawa had listened to the marshal and had felt the earth shift under his feet: Together, he and Jin would change the course of history.

The difference between Jin and Kim Jong-il could not have been greater, Tokugawa had marveled. Jin, long suppressed by a Dear Leader who, with good reason, had feared his latent power, had proved to be not only bolder in action but also far more treacherous than Kim had ever been. Tokugawa had been pleased to learn that Jin was a man just like himself.

"My dear friend," Jin said in perfect Japanese, "I want to emphasize that, for all intents and purposes, Kim Jong-il has ceased to exist. The Korean People's Court has convicted him of treason and ordered his execution. Even if Kim had not buckled to pressure from the Americans to disarm, I would have deposed him. He and his father, Kim il Sung—and everything they represented—have passed from the scene. We live in a new era." As if to confirm this, he lifted a hand and, with a gesture of dismissal, chopped the air.

"After the operation has been completed, the United States will need all the help it can get from its allies to recover. The European nations will be able to provide only a small fraction of what they will need. Naturally, Japan will provide the largest share of both financial aid and personnel expert in civil and medical affairs. As for America's economy, it will be left a shell. In fact, it may never recover. I see the United States breaking up into smaller self-governing units, all of them fighting for scarce resources. Should that happen, Japan would be in a position to dictate its own terms with each entity, rather than with a weakened central government in Washington. Either way, Japan will dominate the world. As a result, Europe's importance will wane, as will the Canadian and South American economies that have harnessed their future to America's. And with the collapse of South Korea, another of America's client states, the DPRK will take control of the peninsula—with Japan's help, of course."

Tokugawa's face betrayed no emotion as he said, "To accomplish this goal we must brush aside the animosities that have existed between our two countries for centuries. How do you propose to do that?"

"Under my leadership the DPRK will open its doors to Japan. The West believes that we will never modernize. They think we are a feudal society, closed and self-absorbed. They believe we lack modern science, technology, and medicine. But we will prove them wrong. If the United States had not attacked us in 1950 and forced us to defend all of Korea against their aggression, we could have powered one of the greatest societal transformations in the history of East Asia."

"But that is history," said Tokugawa, "and now we face the future."

"I assure you, dear friend, that the DPRK harbors no ill will toward the Japanese people for past misunderstandings. When the Americans are neutralized, and with Pyongyang's doors open to Japan, the North will prosper and both of our countries will benefit. Equally important, you will have avenged your family."

Tokugawa remembered the sorrowful eyes of his grandfather and grandmother, who had survived the war and with whom, at age twelve, Tokugawa had been sent to live. He remembered how day after day they'd drummed into him like a mantra: "You are Japanese. Be brave. Be proud!" He remembered that his father had joined them upon his return from wartime duty at Unit 731 in Manchuria. He'd been thin, haggard, and still in shock over the deaths of his wife and two older children in Nagasaki, and over Japan's defeat and his personal failure to prevent it.

And Tokugawa remembered the tall American MPs in their white helmets and leggings, and two army officers who had pulled up in front of the grandparents' house to arrest his father.

There had been talk that the Allies intended to prosecute Japanese army officers accused of committing war crimes. General MacArthur had published a list of those slated for arrest and trial, and Shigeru Tokugawa's name had appeared on the list of Class A criminals. One day the boy had heard his father say, "I won't be judged before a conquerors' court." His grandfather had used a word Iseda had not been familiar with: *koshukei.* He'd looked it up in a dictionary and learned that it meant "to be hanged to death."

The Americans had waited while Shigeru Tokugawa had gathered a few personal things from his bedroom for the trip to Sugamo Prison, renamed, as they all knew, U.S. Army XI Corps Stockade No. 1. Iseda, huddled with his grandmother, had watched the humiliating event unfold, not fully understanding what he was witnessing or why. After all, wasn't his father a patriot, a warrior who'd tried to save his country from destruction by America? And now the American soldiers had arrived to take him away.

He remembered the commotion that had broken out, the officers and MPs shouting and crashing into his father's bedroom. His grandfather had tried to intervene but had been clubbed by the MPs. The boy had bolted from his grandmother's side to help his grandfather and had pushed into the bedroom, where the MPs had been working over his father. He remembered seeing his father's crimson-soaked shirt and, on the floor at his side, in a spreading crimson pool, the gleaming ceremonial dagger he'd used to slice open his belly. He'd seen his father's face horribly distorted by pain and the American officer standing over him, a look of open contempt on his white face.

Tokugawa remembered what happened next. The officer had looked down at the dying man and, knowing that the son had been watching, reared back and kicked the father in the head with the toe of his combat boot.

Tokugawa needed a moment to recompose before he could speak to Marshal Jin. "You said that you have arranged transportation of the fissionable material from North Korea to Russia, through the port of Najin. Can American reconnaissance satellites detect this activity?"

"As you know, we deliberately allowed them to see us break the seals on the weapons storage site in the Kangnam Mountains. We want the Americans to know we are serious about defending our homeland. We trucked the material to our missile launching site at Humhung, but under cover so the Americans wouldn't see it. In due time we will reveal to them where it is. Meanwhile we've prepared a separate shipment for delivery by rail to Najin. It will pass inspection from satellites as nothing more than construction materials bound for Vladivostok. It will be trucked from Najin over the new highway the Russians have built, for pickup on the Russian side of the border by the two scientists posing as construction engineers from Vladivostok. The Americans, distracted by the discovery of warheads at Humhung, will not be looking for warheads in Najin. To complete our task requires that you give approval, through protected channels, for the scientists at your facility in Vladivostok to meet the shipment."

"And your contacts in the Philippines, Marshal? They understand the logistics, the process of conversion, the techniques involved?"

"Yes. The brigade in Mindanao is well trained and well financed. As soon as the shipment arrives, they will commence operations. Every link in the chain has been forged."

"Including the submarine?"

Jin offered to pour more brandy for Tokugawa, but he declined with a hand placed over the snifter. Jin took his own, lit another coarse Russian cigarette off the butt of the one he had just finished, then, eyes squinting and tearing from smoke, said, "The *Red Shark*."

"Which may be the weakest link."

"Dear friend, you have so little faith in North Korean technology?" Jin said good-naturedly.

"It's an unproved technology, you said so yourself. One that may potentially hazard the entire enterprise. To put weapons on board this . . . this new craft of yours and transport them safely from Nam'po to Mindanao is very risky. Transporting them via freighter, one of the new ones you purchased from China, would guarantee their delivery."

Jin frowned. "The Americans have stopped and boarded our ships on the high seas. It's illegal, but they do it because they are a law unto themselves. Who can stop them? We can't and neither can the United Nations, which is an American puppet."

"The Americans don't stop and search all of your ships."

"True, but I'm not willing to gamble on which one they might stop. Even Chinese ships are harassed by the American navy. No, the only way we can ship the weapons to the Philippine attack brigades is by submarine."

Jin's smoke hung in the air for a moment before being whisked away by the breeze. He saw that Tokugawa was still skeptical and said, "The *Red Shark* was constructed using the latest German submarine technologies. She is more than a match for anything that the United States Navy has at sea, including their new Virginia-class submarines. She has an air-independent propulsion—AIP—system and, I am told, is so quiet she cannot be found by even the most sophisticated sonar systems. In addition, she—"

Tokugawa waved this away. "Yes, yes, I'm familiar with these hijacked German technologies. But you fail to understand my point, which is that we risk everything by relying on this *Red Shark* to make delivery."

"Are we not also risking everything on your scientists in Vladivostok; on the brigades in the Philippines; on the goodwill of the Japanese people toward the Koreans; and even on our personal relationship. Everything we have planned so far involves risk. If we are afraid to take risks, our plan will fail."

"Of course we must take risks!" Tokugawa snapped. "I've taken risks all my life. But I never take risks backed by promises or dreams. That road leads to failure."

General Jin bowed low. "My apologies, Tokugawa-*san*. I would not presume to suggest that your judgment in this matter could be influenced by the weakness that derives from sentiment or illusion. I had hoped that the trust I had demonstrated in the *Red Shark* would be sufficient to convince you that there is nothing to fear, that she will perform as promised. I am willing to stake my future and the future of the DPRK on this vessel."

Mollified, Tokugawa sniffed. "If you believe that we must utilize this submarine of yours, then I accept it. You have been a man of your word, so I have no reason to doubt you now. I leave it in your hands."

Downstairs in a locked pantry in the villa's busy kitchen, Wu Chow Fat's secret audio and video recording equipment kept running as Tokugawa and Jin raised a toast to the *Red Shark*.

13

The *Reno,* northwest of Matsu Shan

Scott eased back the slide on a Sig Saur P220 pistol and confirmed a 9mm round was chambered. He dropped the magazine in his palm and saw sixteen gleaming brass cartridge cases through the magazine's witness holes. Satisfied, he slapped the magazine home; the sharp *clack* got Jefferson's attention.

"Going hunting?" Jefferson said, looking up from making an adjustment to the manual add valve of his Draeger LAR V rebreather. It was a compact, chest-worn oxygen breathing device that allowed a diver to breathe his repurified expended air without releasing bubbles that would reveal his presence. But because the SEALs were swimming in from the ASDS on the surface, not underwater, they would use them only for emergency backup.

Under the watchful eye of Senior Chief Brodie, the other members of the team had assembled their gear and run through final checks on weapons and communications equipment. The ASDS had passed its final pre-flight, and both pilot and copilot were aboard. Now the SEALs waited, lost in their own thoughts, their normally cocky attitudes and profane jabber on hold. The *Reno*'s sailors gave them a wide berth, not wanting to jinx the mission by intruding in their ritual preparation.

Jefferson's shaved head gleamed wetly in the glare from strip lights in the overhead; sweat had soaked his cammie T-shirt. "We're about six, seven miles from launch, right?"

"Pretty close," Scott said. "Skipper's working the boat around to the northwestern side of the island. I want to take a good look at that channel and the beach. It's a little too tight for my taste. "

Scott knew that turtlebacking ashore through the channel was potentially the most difficult part of the op. It was narrow, and even though they were going in on slack water, strong, treacherous currents might be present. And there was no way to know what else they might encounter. Neither SRO nor JDIH intelligence knew if the narco-traffickers had planted obstacles offshore—anti-swimmer detection devices or mines.

"Too late to change plans now," Jefferson said. "Besides, that channel's the only way in there."

Jefferson examined the blade of his K-Bar, testing its glittering edge with the ball of a thumb. "Besides, this isn't as tough an approach as some. Dubrovnik, for instance."

Scott thumbed the hammer-drop to safe the Sig and slammed it into a ballistic nylon thigh holster. "Dubrovnik. What about it?"

"Scuttlebutt has it that you cocked up."

"I wouldn't believe everything you hear."

"No? They say you had a chance to kill that bastard, Franjo Karst, but didn't."

Karst, the multimillionaire Croatian general with a private militia and beautiful rock star wife. Karst had bragged that to cleanse Croatia of Serbian influence, he had massacred two thousand Serbian women and children rounded up from a refugee camp in Nova Varos. Karst, the man who had cheated death time and again. Karst, the man with the merciless iron-gray eyes, the fire-scarred face, and a price on his head. Karst, the scourge of the Balkans.

"They say you had him in your sights. That true?"

Karst had stood in the open doorway of his office, eyes flaring like two laser beams, a 9mm Zastava aimed at Scott's chest. Scott could have fired a one-handed burst from the MP5 he'd swung and aimed at Karst, blown him backward into the courtyard outside. And been blown away himself. Instead he'd hesitated. Karst's laser eyes had flicked to the SEALs placing explosive charges, to his dead rebel compatriots sprawled on the floor, to the rifled files and computer drives. He'd spun around and, like the gray wraith he was, fled a split second before Scott had opened fire. Minutes later Karst's headquarters, torture chamber, and armory had blown sky high over Dubrovnik's waterfront.

Scott thought to tell Jefferson that he had had explicit orders to not kill Karst but to try and arrest him. Politics. Trying Karst at the Hague, not summary execution by Navy SEALs, would have lent legitimacy to NATO's Balkans operation. Even so, Scott regretted that he hadn't pulled the trigger: Karst was still at large, which meant, despite the tactical success, that the mission had been a failure. The Navy still blamed Scott for that, and for the near disaster in the Yellow Sea off North Korea. If something went wrong at Matsu Shan, he was damn sure he'd be their scapegoat again.

Jefferson sheathed the K-Bar and said, "Well, it takes a shooter to lead a shooter."

The *Reno*'s 1MC hummed and Kramer announced, "Commander Scott, Colonel Jefferson . . . would you please come to the control room."

Jefferson caught the urgency in Kramer's voice and looked questioningly at Scott.

"Something's up," Scott said.

Deacon ordered, "Rig ship for ultra-quiet." At the same time, the interior lighting throughout the *Reno* cycled from white to red, to inform the crew that conditions had changed.

"Weps, what's your status?" Deacon said.

"Sir, all tubes loaded but not flooded, outer doors closed. Power units for all torpedoes activated and on standby."

Deacon eyed the main console in Fire-control Alley. It displayed a wide-area geographic view of the *Reno*'s position, now east of Taiwan near Matou Shan. A blue pinpoint of light on the display—the *Reno*—moved slowly northwest. Myriad green pinpoints represented "friendlies"—merchantmen. A blinking red light on the display indicated the position of an unidentified sound contact classified by the fire-control party as Sierra One.

Deacon saw Scott enter the red-lit control room, followed by Jefferson. "Sonar's picked up a tonal we haven't yet identified, but it might be a Chinese sub."

"Diesel or nuke?" Scott asked.

"Diesel."

"Is it that Kilo?"

Deacon nodded. "More than likely."

"Jesus Christ," Jefferson said. "What the fuck's he doing around here?"

"What's his bearing?" Scott asked.

"One-one-four," Kramer, in fire control, said. "We're working on the range, have it in a minute."

"Can he hear us?" Jefferson asked, trailing Scott and Deacon into the sonar room forward and starboard of the control room.

The compartment had four positions occupied by watchstanders, including the supervisor, a master chief petty officer. Each man was seated in front of a pair of vertical sonar monitors whose eerie greenish-blue glow illuminated both the darkened sonar room and the men's faces.

On each monitor a row of vertical lines, called a waterfall, provided a visual display of what the *Reno*'s spherical BSY-2 bow sonar array was hearing. Three junior sonarmen sifted through this broadband display of noise, searching for the specific tonal attributes of a Kilo-class diesel-electric submarine.

Scott, Deacon, and Jefferson looked over the chief's shoulder as he pointed to a faint white line almost hidden among all the bright green ones in a waterfall display slowly crawling down a monitor's screen.

"That's him," the chief said. "Faint, barely there."

The white line represented a weak sound picked up by the BSY-2 array. Its lack of brightness was proportional to its intensity. Below it, on another monitor, was a graphic display of the sound's strength and frequency.

"That his tonal you have there, Chief?" asked Scott.

"Yes, sir, it is. And I'm willing to bet it's comin' from the electric generators and shafting of a Kilo 636. The acoustic spectrum analyzer's huntin' for a match. Earlier we had a couple of biologicals and a spit-kit that sounded like a Kilo fadin' in and out. He's been damn hard to pin down."

Scott knew how quiet Kilo 636s were: 242 feet long and displacing 2,350 tons, a 636 with AIP was as quiet submerged as an Improved Los Angeles–class submarine like the *Reno*, maybe even quieter. Equipped with advanced Klub antiship missiles, wake-homing torpedoes, and multiple-targeting electronic fire control systems, a 636 would be a formidable opponent, especially in littoral waters, where large nuclear submarines like the *Reno* were often at a disadvantage. And right now a Kilo belonging to China's PLAN might be lurking close by the *Reno*, perhaps even tracking her.

Scott knew that identifying the sound, whether it was a sub or just phantom noise, boiled down to an arcane mix of art and science and a sonarman's skill at picking out the specific narrowband frequency from all the background clutter. And though the analyzer made the task easier, it was not foolproof. Sometimes even experts could be fooled into thinking a cooling whale was the slowly turning propeller on a submarine.

As the task of Target Motion Analysis—TMA—continued, time counted down to the ASDS's liftoff from the *Reno*.

Jefferson bit his lip. "I'm thinking we're fucked if that's a Chinese sub and he hears us. Our window for insertion won't stay open long."

Scott said, "If he hears us we'll have to deal with him."

Jefferson's grip on Scott's arm was like a steel vise. " '*Deal with him?*' Jesus Christ, you mean sink him?"

"That's up to the skipper."

"What, and start a war with the Chinese? Are you nuts?"

Scott pulled his arm away. "Better tell the pilot and copilot to stand down, the others, too, until we get this situation under control."

Jefferson, shaking his head, headed aft, to the compartment from which the ASDS was accessed via its lock-in/lock-out chamber mated to the *Reno*'s hull and after hatch.

"How are we doing, Chief?" said Deacon.

The tone line on the upper monitor had brightened, while on the lower monitor the sound's intensity and frequency showed an increase.

"Got a turn count, Captain," said the chief, after narrowing the acoustic search and weighing the evidence. "Indicates a speed of three knots. I'd say for sure we got us a PLAN Kilo 636."

Aboard the Kilo, Captain Deng Zemin donned headphones and listened to a faint pulsing hiss, like an asthmatic's labored breathing. As he listened, he studied the two MGK Rubikon sonar monitors on which a weak green blip, looking like one from an EKG hooked to a dying man, crept across the screen. Zemin shelved his lower lip: too weak to identify. He narrowed his eyes as if doing it would sharpen his hearing. Maybe what he heard was an American Los Angeles–class submarine. Then again, maybe not. He switched channels and heard the guttural boom of a pair of twin diesel engines heading due north. Fat's *White Dragon*. Where to now?

The Rubikon's audio spectrum analyzer sifted what it had collected, then recycled. An analyzed tone line appeared on the monitor and under it, in flashing red: UNDETERMINED.

The senior sonarman pointed to it. "Comrade Captain."

Zemin switched back to the other channel and listened. *Undetermined.* If it was a U.S. 688I, Zemin was risking detection by the American. Still, he had to know. He tore off the headphones and commanded, "Main motors stop. Silence in the boat."

The first officer repeated Zemin's orders. A moment later the Kilo's three-knot headway began scrubbing off.

Zemin climbed into the captain's conning chair bolted to the deck in the attack center and folded his arms. "Now we will listen carefully to learn if we are hearing a ghost or a nosy American submarine."

"Conn, Sonar. Sierra One just stopped his prop."

Deacon toggled the mike. "Sonar, Conn. Do you still have him?"

"Barely, sir. Fadin' . . ."

Scott entered the sonar room. "There he is, Commander," said the chief. "What's left of him." He pointed to two weak tonals. "This here blip is his shaft spinning down. This here one—you can barely see it now—is turbulence coming off his prop as it stopped turning. He's just about dead in the water."

"He's got a silent creep motor and may be using it."

"No, sir, I don't think so, he's stopped."

"Maybe he heard something," Scott said.

"Yes, sir. *Us.*"

The chief's report triggered a "Man silent battle stations," from Deacon.

The control room got crowded fast. Phonetalkers manned their sound-powered phones; a full complement of officers took their places in plot and at the attack consoles; a fresh watch took over the helm and planes.

"All stations manned and ready, Captain," Kramer reported.

Deacon queried the senior attack coordinator. "Did we have a final bearing on the Chinaman before he went invisible? Come on, come on, we don't have all day."

"It's one-four-four, sir."

"Christ, that's a thirty-degree shift, he must be damn close. What's his range—and don't finesse it . . . whatever you have."

"Sir, under six thousand yards."

"Less than three miles." Deacon gave Scott a look. "It's your call."

Scott considered while the fire-control party worked a torpedo firing solution on Sierra One. The clock was running, the window closing. Not good, not good at all. "Shut her down. Let's see if we can wait him out."

Zemin scratched his cheek. He glanced at the ship's chronometer: 2135. An hour had passed since their first contact with what he was almost convinced now, had been a phantom tonal, not a 688I. Almost but not quite.

They'd inched along on the Kilo's utterly silent creep motor, the depth gauge needles hung at 195 meters. The Rubikon's narrowband trace line lay dead flat on the monitor. Nothing. Zemin pressed the headphone earmuffs tight to his head and listened. An oil tanker and ro-ro to the west. Small craft—luggers, spit-kits, sampans, and coastal junks—swarming along the Taiwan coast.

The first officer said, "Comrade Captain, we have had no further contact for over twenty minutes. Perhaps we should shift operations to the north and commence tracking and reacquire the *White Dragon*."

Zemin considered. Admiral Chou, commander in chief Northern Fleet, would not be pleased to learn that a 688I snooping around Matsu Shan had gone unchallenged.

"Why would a U.S. Navy 688I show up off Matsu Shan?" Zemin asked.

"Comrade Captain, with respect, we don't know for sure that the contact was a 688I."

"Wu Chow Fat and his *White Dragon,* Matsu Shan, the *Sugun,* the North Korean crisis—a coincidence, no?"

The first officer said nothing.

The Rubikon's narrowband trace line still lay dead flat on the monitor.

"There is nothing more we can do here, Comrade Captain."

Zemin stood. "I agree. These are my orders: Both motors ahead one-half; make our course due north; commence a search for the *White Dragon.*"

"Aye, Comrade Captain."

Zemin hoped he had not been fooled by a clever skipper in a 688I. If he had, it would put Admiral Chou into a towering rage. He saw himself being led from his submarine in leg irons by Admiral Chou's Navy police, to the submarine base brig at Bohai Bay.

"He's on the move!"

"Where to, Chief?" asked Deacon.

"Due north at about ten knots."

Deacon exhaled heavily and said to Scott, "It's still your call."

Scott felt Jefferson's gaze boring into his back. He turned and said, "Ready to move?"

"Hell, been ready to move for the last hour and a half. Damn window's almost closed."

Scott said to Deacon, "All right, let's jock it up."

14

Matsu Shan, inbound

Scott looked through the ASDS's open lower hatch and saw Rus Kramer's upturned face.

"We'll be waiting right here for you, Commander. Good luck."

Scott sketched Kramer a salute, then sealed the hatch. Moments later, the midnight black, bullet-shaped vehicle lifted off its four latching pylons. Aboard the *Reno*, Deacon retrimmed to compensate for the sudden loss of fifty-five tons of shock-hardened titanium and steel and ten men and their gear. The mini-sub, maneuvering on its thrusters and a six-bladed prop powered by a compact lithium-ion battery, cleared the *Reno*'s afterdeck, and, with Deitrich and Allen at the controls, surged toward Matsu Shan.

Inside the red-lit ASDS, Scott, Jefferson, and the six SEALs, faces blackened, wearing dry suits over cammies, their gear ready and staged, sat facing each other across a narrow aisle. They would soon lock out of the mini-sub for a stealthy surface swim onto an island controlled by heavily armed drug-traffickers. They knew that if they were caught there'd be no backup for rescue; they'd either have to fight their way out, E and E—evade and escape—or risk capture and possibly torture. Scott remembered Carter Ellsworth saying it would be a piece of cake. Too bad Ellsworth wasn't sitting across the aisle, thought Scott, H-gear weighing him down, nervous sweat seeping into his eyeballs, knees quaking. Scott just once wanted to have Ellsworth and Radford along on a balls-in-a-vice op so they could see what it was really like to be a gun fighter.

For the rest of the team it was gut-check time. Time to mull what the possibility was of getting in and out without blowing something or someone away, including themselves. Scott hoped Deitrich and Allen were fully occupied flying the vehicle and not, like him, deep-thinking.

Scott looked at Jefferson, and saw that his eyes were closed. Was he thinking about Scott's fuckup in Dubrovnik or how they'd fly the micro air vehicles into the villa without the bugs being discovered and smacked with a fly swatter? If they were, it'd be all over and they'd be in for a fight. Matsu Shan wasn't Dubrovnik, and Wu Chow Fat wasn't Karst.

Scott did box drills in his head, reviewing their direction of travel, how far it was to the beach, and, as best he could, accounting for tides and currents. They'd done a time hack before liftoff, and now he rucked back his dry suit's wrist dam and looked at his watch: soon, very soon.

The ASDS hummed quietly as it cruised toward shore at six knots, ten feet below the surface. Up forward, Deitrich had a hand on the joystick, thumb on its roller-controller, and both eyes on the computer screens used for controlling ballast and trim.

Directly in front of copilot Allen and to Deitrich's

right were two monitors, both enabled but blank, linked to the craft's sonar system and the electro-optical periscope, which they'd use to surveil the AO—area of operation—as the ASDS closed the island.

Before liftoff, Scott had taken a trick at the *Reno*'s scope. From two thousand yards offshore, the channel and beach, seen in eerie green NV mode, looked deserted except for the motor launch tied up at the dock. There was no sign of anyone, nor was there any sign of the *White Dragon*. There was also no sign of the chopper, though it was hard to be sure, since Scott's sea-level view of the landing pad/parking area where the craft would have been parked was partially cut off by the sheer height of the bluff. Still, he should have been able to see something, at least the tops of its drooping rotor blades. Scott had a premonition but kept it to himself.

The villa appeared quiet—too quiet. He spotted a heat bloom in IR, a still-warm truck engine, but no warm bodies moving around inside or outside the villa's walls. He toggled the scope to normal view and saw the effect that moonlight, blunted by cloud cover, had on the sea: The dim canopy of light that made the water shimmer like silver might also make eight swimmers' heads easy targets from shore.

Jefferson had taken a look, too. While he had, the fingers of both hands had beaten a nervous tattoo on the scope's training handles. His eye had come away from the buffer, and he'd turned to Scott. "You're right. I don't see the chopper. Maybe they moved it. Or camouflaged it."

"Maybe."

"Nothing we can do about the moon," Jefferson had said, beating his tattoo. "Your call."

"We go."

Now Scott felt the mini-sub slow and, like the others, leaned into the craft's deceleration. He tightened the straps on his H-gear, checked everything again to make sure his first line gear was all there: two canteens of water, ammo, penlight, compass, pocketknife. And in his rucksack, Carb-Boom energy packets, Handi Wipes, insect repellant; the rest of it—boots, extra ammo, and weapons—in waterproof baggies. He confirmed, too, that the medical gear he carried was stowed in its standard location on the H harness so it could be easily located if needed.

Check, check, check, and recheck: the mini-sub's interior crackled with tension, the SEALs on guard against mistakes that could prove fatal.

Jefferson touched his earphone connected to the pilot's throat mike. "Roger that," Jefferson said into his own throat mike. Then to Scott, "Deitrich says the beach looks clear. He'll have us in position in another five minutes."

The men stirred. Van Kirk, the designated scout swimmer, moved first. He slipped swim fins over his booties, strapped on and tested his Draeger, and fitted the mouthpiece. He adjusted a pair of underwater night-vision goggles and got set to drop through the ASDS's moon pool to begin an underwater recon of currents, obstacles, and anti-swimmer devices. Strapped to one of his legs was a computer "light box" linked to the mini-sub's GPS. The box would indicate, in real time, his position relative to X-Ray, the SEALs' designated landing patch on the beach.

Deitrich deployed the sub's hovering thrusters and dropped the fore and aft anchors to hold the craft in position against a light current they could feel like an invisible hand against the titanium hull.

Van Kirk, looking like a grotesque sea monster, with bulging goggles clamped over his eyes and the Draeger's mouthpiece in place, eased finned feet first over the coaming around the open moon pool. To prevent flooding of the mini-sub, the seawater in the moon pool was held in check by an equivalent pressure head pushing against it from inside the sub's hull. Van Kirk, armed with a K-Bar and Sig Saur, gave Scott a thumbs-up, then dropped into the pool and swam out.

Time stood still.

Scott remembered reconnoitering the obstacle-strewn harbor at Dubrovnik: sunken vessels, debris of all kinds, including a steam locomotive and tender lying on their sides near the base of the pier where the ASDS had anchored.

Scott had finned through the cold, murky water to discover rudimentary antipersonnel mines anchored to the harbor bottom not far from the ASDS. These he had marked with laser flags. He had also marked the barnacle-encrusted anti-swimmer cages wrapped around the wharf's pilings. These had had hundreds of sharp, hooked needles designed to impale a swimmer and trap him underwater.

But here, off Matsu Shan, the water was warmer and less turbid. The sandy bottom sloped gently up onto the beach. With high tide more than ten hours away, they would have plenty of time to conduct the mission and extract without the mini-sub needing to back down into deeper water.

Scott heard a splash: Van Kirk's head and shoulders popped up in the moon pool.

"Clear all the way in, Skipper," Van Kirk reported. His mates helped him out of the pool and out of his dripping gear. "About a two-knot current setting inshore and a bottom so smooth we can walk in the last twenty yards. No tricks, no mines, no traps. I went ashore and planted a laser homing beam as a guidon."

He had marked their position and the position of the laser homing beam on the light box. It was a straight-in swim of about 300 yards. Curved lines on the box indicated the surf zone and the depth of the water out to twenty fathoms in ten-foot increments. The mini-sub's mark hovered between the three- and four-fathom lines. Swimming in on the surface after a shallow-water free ascent from the ASDS would avoid the problems associated with deep-water decompression and allow easy entry and exit from the sub.

After digesting this, Jefferson said, "Ready if you are, Scott."

"Go."

One at a time, Scott and the SEALs made their free ascent from the ASDS. Scott surfaced beside Chief Brodie, who immediately made a head count. With everyone present, they turtlebacked toward shore with life vests partially inflated to help carry their towed combat loads. Scott looked back and saw the rest of the team following, their heads in a straight formation. The mini-sub lay to submerged off the bottom, with a glowing laser homing beacon to mark its position for their return.

With Jefferson and Zipolski out front, the team, with help from the light, setting current, advanced along their designated approach lane through the channel until it opened like a fan. Scott felt the bottom come up fast and saw Jefferson signal "stop" with a raised hand.

Scott checked his compass, then, treading water

alongside Jefferson, looked in toward the beach with its pier and moored motor launch. The swimmers were less than a hundred feet from shore and could almost touch bottom with the blades of their fins: Van Kirk had been right about the walk-in.

Scott scanned the beach through NV goggles for activity but saw none. Greenish night-vision anomalies, white blobs, green reflections and yellow starlight, bobbled across the island and on the surface of the sea, ahead of which a light, curling, pale green surf hissed ashore over coarse shingle.

The SEALs regrouped and, weapons ready, scurried ashore in two four-man files, keeping low and staying clear of sight lines Fat's men might use to scan for seaborne intruders. Quickly, they set up a defensive perimeter above the surf line, where they stripped off their fins and dry suits, transitioning from swim gear to land gear, and cached them at what would be their rally point.

Scott surveyed their surroundings. The heavy smell of jungle foliage, wet from an earlier rain squall, struck his nostrils. And something else: diesel fuel. The pier and motor launch were less than fifty yards away to his left. Straight ahead, behind the beach berm, stood a thick wall of dripping cabbage palm and mangrove. It would provide excellent cover to prepare for their move inshore. Through it, Scott saw lights on in the villa high up on the bluff above them. It was, he judged, another hundred yards from their present hide to the base of the bluff, with its cut-stone stairs leading to the villa.

Scott felt Jefferson come up beside him. Both had flipped up their NV goggles; in the dark, the whites of their eyes seemed unnaturally bright.

"See anybody on the pier?" Jefferson said.

"No. Strange."

"Tell me about it." Jefferson looked around at the others forming up around them and said, "Well, fuck it all. Maybe they're in bed."

Scott said nothing. The diesel reeked, as did the dead seaweed piled against the thick mangrove roots. He slithered forward so he could see better through the wall of foliage. He flipped down the NV goggles and surveyed their line of approach to the bluff. Still nothing. All he heard were humming insects, a night bird calling, and rustling palm fronds, which sounded like a rushing stream. The terrain they'd have to cross to reach the foot of the bluff was strewn with stacked drums of fuel, an assortment of parked vehicles, and what looked like a toolshed. He didn't see any men patrolling the area.

"Okay," he said, crabbing backward on elbows and knees toward Jefferson. "Where's Caserta?"

Caserta had charge of the micro air vehicles and their control gear; he was the expert flier. The "gizmos," as Caserta called them, were packed in a pressure- and water-proof suitcase-like container strapped to his harness along with his other gear. Scott motioned, and Caserta drew abreast of him and knelt.

"We're going to move out," Scott said, "and set up shop at the base of the bluff."

Caserta nodded his understanding. The others, ready, gripped their M4s.

"Yo, Skipper," Chief Brodie whispered. "Comms from *Reno*." Brodie had charge of the miniaturized satellite communications equipment. The size of a cellular flip-phone, it allowed instant communications with the *Reno*, and, theoretically, via satellite, with anyone in the world, including Radford at SRO and Fumiko at JDIH.

Scott plugged his inter-squad ear and throat mike into the sat-com and pressed the device's thumb key. Viewing through NV goggles, he saw the *Reno*'s three-digit call ID light up. His callback triggered a response from Sam Deacon.

"*Reno* One."

"Copy," said Scott.

"Heads up. *White Dragon*'s about to land."

A hesitation. "Say again."

"*White Dragon*'s about—"

"I heard you. Where?"

"Picked her up twenty minutes ago, inbound from Chi-lung. About now she should be rounding the headland and making for the channel anchorage."

"Roger that—out."

"What is it?" said Jefferson.

"That," said Scott.

They heard throbbing diesels. As they looked seaward, the *White Dragon*, darkened but for red and green running lights, hove into view around the headland, part of which formed the channel that led to the beach.

"Where the hell's she been?" Jefferson said.

Scott and the SEALs moved quickly but silently off the beach into the mangrove for cover. Fat's junk hove to and dropped anchor in the shallows. Lights came on around the pier, and several men carrying weapons appeared and boarded the motor launch. They cast off and swung out to meet the *White Dragon*. At the same time, a big black SUV rattled onto the pier and stopped.

"Something doesn't seem right," Jefferson whispered into Scott's ear. "I mean, who the hell's aboard the *White Dragon*?"

Shortly, the launch pulled away from the junk and nosed alongside the pier. Scott and Jefferson, peering with miniature binoculars through the thick tangle of mangrove, saw Fat hoisted from the launch up on to the pier by a freight elevator installed between pilings. He waddled across the pier and stuffed himself into the SUV, which whisked him away up the service road cut into the bluff, to the back of the villa. Moments later all the lights around the pier and aboard the *White Dragon* went out, and the island once again groped into darkness.

"So maybe he's meeting with the two gents he's put up at the villa. To negotiate his fee," Jefferson said.

"Let's find out," Scott said. He motioned to Caserta. "Get ready for takeoff."

15

Beijing, China

At the Central Military PLAN Headquarters of the Chinese Communist Party a few blocks east of Tiananmen Square, Admiral Shi Yunsheng assumed his place at the head of an impossibly long conference table in the ornate Hall of Ministers. A small man, his mere presence compelled his fellow officers' undivided attention and complete silence.

Shi, commander in chief of PLAN, chairman of its general staff, and head of the Ministry of Defense, gazed the length of the table at a dozen faces all turned in his direction, waiting for him to speak. Shi, known as a Purple Hat for the weighty duties he shouldered, wore a naval uniform decorated with blazing gold braid and row upon row of ribbons and medals. He had prominently displayed on his left breast the gold insignia of the PLAN Submarine Corps.

Shi cleared his throat. Each man, he noted with satisfaction, had lying in front of him a document to which he now made reference.

"Esteemed Comrades, I direct your attention to the copy of Commander Zemin's message transmitted three hours ago, to Admiral Chou's North Sea Fleet Headquarters, Qingdao," Shi said in a lecturing voice. "His submarine has been shadowing this pirate, Fat, in his fancy junk, between the North Korean ship *Sugun*, and Matsu Shan. Fat has apparently concluded his business and has returned to the island."

Shi pressed a clicker. Behind him and facing his listeners, a large plasma video monitor came to life with a map of the area around Taiwan and Matsu Shan. Four bright red dots labeled T-One, T-Two, T-Three, and T-Four appeared at different locations on the map.

"Target-One represents the present position of Commander Zemin's submarine, ten nautical miles east of Matsu Shan. Target-Two is the *Sugun*." Her dot was two hand's-lengths north of Matsu Shan. "Target-Three is Fat's junk, the *White Dragon*, in her anchorage. Target-Four"—and here Shi paused for effect—"is what may be a U.S. Navy 688I-class submarine." He turned and pointed to a red dot just south of Matsu Shan and in a direct line with Fat's anchorage.

Shi's audience greeted the light show with respectful silence. The admiral cleared his throat again and said, "I emphasize that it *may* be a U.S. 688I. Commander Zemin tried to make a positive identification but could not. For our purposes, assume it is a 688I."

Another throat-clearer, an elderly PLAN senior general, spoke around a cigarette stuck between dry lips. "And what is the significance of an American submarine operating off Taiwan? After all, they spy on us whenever they feel like it."

"True, Comrade General," said Shi, "but this time we have an unusual set of circumstances—Wu Chow Fat anchoring off Chi-lung harbor twice in two days—

unheard of. A North Korean ship, the *Sugun*, with a helicopter on board, is spotted on the high seas south of Wen-chou. This helicopter takes off from the *Sugun* for a visit to Matsu Shan. The *Sugun* then lies to off Wen-chou for two days."

"Yes? . . ."

"North Korean cargo ships never carry helicopters. Our spies in Nam'po reported the *Sugun*'s sailing and also the extremely tight security surrounding her departure. They reported that no drugs were loaded, only bags of cement and that someone of high rank may have taken passage."

A hand rose. It belonged to General Liu Huaquing of the PLAN air force. "The North Koreans use helicopters to ferry crews between ships engaged in seismographic exploration and their Yangdok oil drilling platform in Korea Bay. Perhaps this is a case of such—"

"I assure you that is not the case, Comrade General," said Shi.

"And what of the *White Dragon*? What is her business in Chi-lung?" another general asked.

"Fat never ventures into Chi-lung to unload cargoes of drugs. Instead, he always transfers to lighters offshore, out of reach of Taiwanese authorities. But when he anchored off Chi-lung he wasn't delivering drugs. Like the *Sugun*, the *White Dragon* embarked a passenger for Matsu Shan."

General Liu grumbled as he pointed to the plasma screen. "So what does this mean?"

"I think the Americans are investigating why Wu Chow Fat would be meeting with someone important from the new government in North Korea. Perhaps with Marshal Jin himself."

A murmur of disbelief arose from the conferees. It

threatened to drown out Shi until he ordered silence and got it.

"As for the passenger Fat picked up in Chi-lung," he continued, "our people there think he is an influential Japanese with ties to the *yakuza* and North Korean drug trade."

Voices rose again as Shi's audience argued among themselves about the possible implications of what Shi had described.

"Comrades, I have ordered Commander Zemin to determine what the American sub is doing off Matsu Shan. It would not surprise me that they would try to put an armed force on the island to discover who is there with Fat. Surely it has something to do with the American–North Korean standoff and is so worrisome to the Americans that they are willing to risk a criminal violation of sovereign Chinese territory to find out what it is. We all know that the United States never hesitates to cross borders or disregard treaties when it comes to ensuring its national security."

The admiral's audience voiced agreement.

"Always it is the Americans that are the cause of our troubles," General Liu said acidly.

"No," said Shi. "This time it is the North Koreans."

16

On the beach, Matsu Shan

Inside their perimeter at the foot of the bluff, Scott and the SEALs set up shop behind the toolshed. Caserta wore special vision goggles designed for viewing the video monitor and controls he'd use to fly the micro air vehicle, which he'd removed from its padded case. Next he erected a small launching pylon, then prepped the bug for flight.

Meanwhile, Jefferson inched around the perimeter, checking to make sure that the team was ready to take down any of Fat's men should they stumble into the SEAL hornet's nest. Scott ran a final comms check, hissing into his throat mike to confirm he was linked to everyone. They all responded in the same fashion. Ready, Scott touched Caserta on the arm and pointed "up."

Scott heard a low hiss that sounded like a release of gas from a bottle of soda. Caserta toggled the stubby stick on his laptop-sized flight control pack, and the little black bug, its wings a blur, lifted straight up off the pylon, dipped, and vanished skyward with remarkable speed.

Like Caserta, Scott wore goggles to view the control

pack's monitor, and he saw exactly what the bug was seeing. There was a blur of yellowish-green color as the little robot zipped to and fro high over head, orienting itself via its miniature inertial guidance system. Then the image stabilized into an aerial view of the villa. Seen through the bug's NV camera, it looked like it was midday in bright sunlight. Shadows were sharp and black, and the details were astonishingly clear.

"Let's see the helo pad," Scott said.

Caserta finessed the stick and the fly rose high above the bluff, until it was looking straight down on an empty expanse of tarmac.

"Shit," Scott said. "Bird's gone. What's IR say?"

Caserta switched the bug's sensors to infrared and took a sample. The heat trace outline of a vanished helicopter appeared on the screen.

"Says liftoff was about four hours ago."

Scott told Jefferson and got a "Shit!"

Caserta brought the fly down from its 100-foot altitude, until it was hovering over the veranda and he and Scott were seeing into the dining room, from the perspective of a six-foot-tall man.

Suddenly the image went black. A heartbeat later it cleared, and Scott realized that a person had walked in front of the camera. An elderly woman servant, Chinese from her looks, stepped away from the camera and bent to clear dishes from the dining room table.

Under Caserta's control, the bug moved slowly through a pair of open double doors into the main living area. A man appeared, dressed in black and armed with an AK-47. Another armed man came into view. The two conferred, then moved out of camera range.

Caserta made a 360, saw that no one else was present in the room, and moved on. The MAV peeked down a deserted hallway with doors on either side and zipped through an open door into a bedroom. Inside was another man clad in black, asleep in a double bed, an AK-47 at his side. Caserta backed the MAV out. More rooms, more armed men, women, too, lounging, watching TV, drinking, eating. Down a flight of stairs to see kitchen help scouring woks, loading a dishwasher.

Scott heard a "psst," from Jefferson. "Anything?"

"Not yet. You?"

"Clear—uh, wait one . . . shit, somebody's coming."

Scott touched Caserta's arm and pointed left. He flipped the M4 carbine's safety lever forward, giving him the option of three-round bursts or full automatic fire.

"Heads up," Jefferson warned. "Got company."

Scott tensed. He had heard feet crunching on seashells before Jefferson's hissed warning arrived in his ear. Through NV goggles he saw two men, clad in black like those on the monitor, carrying slung submachine guns with long curving magazines. They walked slowly toward the shed, jabbering in Chinese, the red coal-ends of cigarettes in their mouths bobbing as their heads moved.

"Got 'em," Scott whispered into his throat mike. "Stand by to bust 'em."

He saw that Jefferson and the others were hugging the ground, trying to make themselves as invisible as possible. A flashlight snapped on. One of the men swept the beam, flaring bright green in Scott's NV goggles, out ahead of them as the pair picked their way around the stacked fuel drums and headed for the tool-shed where Scott and Caserta were hunkered.

Scott, judging distances and angles, waited for them to come closer. The man with the flashlight separated from his companion and played the beam on the wall of the shed, then over an electrical panel equipped with a thick, rotating control handle. A cable from the panel looped to a pole, then to light standards erected the length of the pier. The flashlight's loom passed barely two feet over Scott's and Caserta's heads. Scott, on his haunches, coiled, muscles bound like steel, got ready to strike.

The flashlight beam swept lower, across Scott's face; the man gawked.

Scott drove the M4's collapsed butt into his gut, doubling him over facedown in his own vomit. Scott scooped up the flashlight and doused it. He heard a grunt, then something that sounded like a wet sack of garbage hitting pavement.

"Both assholes down," Jefferson said, pumping a fist.

"See anyone else?" Scott asked.

"No, but someone's gonna come looking for them."

Scott got his breath. He squatted beside Caserta in time to hear him say, "Fuck!"

Scott didn't have to be told. The bug's camera image wasn't moving on the monitor and its lens was looking into a room but seeing it upside down.

"Crash and burn," Caserta said quietly. "We hit something. Onboard gyros say she's down for the count."

"And still no targets."

"None, Skipper. All I've seen so far are bad guys dressed in black."

"How far did you get?"

"Second floor."

"Upload what you have."

Caserta unloaded the control pack's 100-quad hard drive, shifted to Convert, and fired the video captured by the bug to an orbiting satellite for relay to the SRO in Virginia.

Scott pictured someone stepping on the bug and hearing it go crunch. Scott told Jefferson and got another "Fuck!"

"Have Brodie copy the *Reno* and the mini-sub," Scott said.

"And then what, launch the backup bug?" Jefferson said.

"Have to."

Caserta didn't wait for Scott's orders to activate and launch the backup bug. Scott watched it disappear toward the villa, then decided he should check on the condition of the two downed Chinese.

They were small, hard-bodied men. Leclerc had taped their hands and mouths with black duct. Scott knew they were fighting the clock and that their discovery was almost certain now. He estimated that they had another fifteen minutes before things blew wide open. They'd taken out two men, and he'd seen another six or seven in the house, plus two women. Radford had said there weren't more than twenty bad guys, but Scott knew for sure that that assessment was dead wrong.

He duckwalked to Caserta. "Talk to me."

"Christ, don't see nothin', Skipper. Ain't nobody here we're lookin' for. Just baddies."

"How many more have you seen?"

"At least fifteen in the villa, more outside. And if those big shots we're after were here, they sure as hell ain't here now."

Scott saw more armed men wearing black. An alarm bell sounded in his head; the knot in his gut tightened. He hadn't felt any aftereffect from the adrenaline rush that had come from bashing the Chinese gunman—

only sweaty palms and the knotted gut. But there was that alarm bell getting louder by the second. They'd walked into a potential trap.

"Caserta, break off—"

Caserta reached back and grabbed Scott's arm. "Bingo."

A naked Fat lay on his back in a gargantuan bed fitted with red satin sheets. The room had red satin wall coverings to complement the gold hardware on the doors. The bug, hovering at ceiling height, its camera lens set on wide-angle, showed three young naked Asian women toying with Fat's flaccid penis. As Scott watched, one of the girls climbed on top of Fat and squatted, while the other two girls tried to insert his limp penis into her vagina.

Caserta lowered the bug until it was hovering directly over the bed.

"Careful they don't spot it," Scott said in Caserta's ear.

Scott was looking down at the top of the squatting girl's head and at Fat's doughy face, with its slack mouth yawning wide open and pair of glazed eyes hidden behind partially closed lids.

"Pull back," Scott ordered. "You're too damn close."

Suddenly Fat's eyes snapped wide open. One of his massive arms rose from the bed; a finger jabbed air, pointing to the hovering black bug.

The girl riding Fat looked where he was pointing, made a face, and, lips pursed into a perfect O, mouthed something. Now the other girls were pointing, too. Fat tried to get up, but, immobilized as he was by his vast bulk and the three girls piled on top of him, he couldn't budge.

"Get it out of there!" Scott ordered.

Before Caserta could react, one of the naked girls

sprang to her feet on the bed. Her pretty face, distorted by the bug's wide-angle lens, filled the monitor. Her hand shot forward and the room tilted crazily. Scott saw a red satin-covered wall rush toward him, then black.

"Holy shit!" Caserta yelped.

Scott slapped him on the shoulder. "Right now, send what you have," he ordered, then gave an alert over the squad comm line.

Caserta unloaded the video drive, converted, shot the satellite, then started folding up his gear.

"What the hell happened? . . ." Jefferson said over the comm line.

Before Scott could explain, lights popped on all over the island at the same time a klaxon started honking. Men were shouting, and somewhere a truck engine revved up.

"It's time to go," Scott said.

Jefferson and the others were on their feet, bringing it in around Scott and Caserta, their M4s unlocked and pointed.

"Fat saw the goddamned bug," Scott snapped over a shoulder at Jefferson.

"Christ . . . any sign of our two targets?" Jefferson growled, his attention fully on their immediate surroundings.

"No one home, just Fat."

The shouting men came closer. So did a pair of crackling two-way transceivers: Fat's guards searching for the missing men. A searchlight high up on the bluff snapped on and started sweeping the pier.

Ramos, Van Kirk, Zipolski, and Leclerc, anchoring the perimeter, got ready to disperse if the searchlight's loom got too close. Or to open fire if Fat's gunmen spotted them. Brodie, watching over a shoulder, was on sat-comms to the *Reno* and mini-sub, updating their situation. Scott knew that extracting without a fight and, perhaps, casualties would take a miracle and that none would be coming their way anytime soon.

17

Outside Washington, D.C.

Karl Radford stood in the South Wing of the SRO's Operations Center in Bailey's Crossroads, Virginia, transfixed by what he saw up on the mammoth video monitor, which covered a full wall: black-clad men with weapons; the interior of Fat's villa; Fat frolicking with the naked girls; the bug blacking out.

They're blown, Radford thought. *And the goddamn chopper that brought Jin to the island has blown, too.* "Recycle to our bird, please," Radford said.

The image changed to an overhead view of Matsu Shan from an infrared satellite camera 22,000 miles in space, linked to the SRO's Guild System of linked computer nodes for enhancement and display on the giant screen. He saw lights, scores of heat sources—men moving around on the ground, vehicles—and the L-shaped villa. But even in extreme close-up it was impossible to tell which men were which—the SEALs or Fat's private army. Radford didn't fail to notice that there were far more bodies moving around than he'd counted earlier. And on the helo pad, fading traces of heat left by Jin's chopper, which had departed well ahead of the KH-12's lift over the horizon into camera range.

"Karl." The familiar voice of the president's national security advisor boomed into the room from the op-center's comm-net uplink to the Florida Keys.

"I'm here, Paul," he said into a wireless mini-mike on his lapel, the kind used by news readers in TV studios.

"Can we get them out?"

Radford hesitated a beat. He ran the tip of his tongue over dry lips. "No, I'm afraid not. They'll have to fight their way out—if it comes to it."

"Think it will?"

"Well, as you just saw, Fat and his men have been alerted. There is, I'd say, a fifty-fifty chance Scott and his people can extract without a fight." Radford knew that estimate was too optimistic: more likely thirty-seventy. "We may have underestimated Fat's strength."

"What assets do we have in the area that could help out?" the national security advisor asked.

"Paul, if you mean special-ops, or helos, or—"

"I mean whatever we have—ships, planes, anything."

"Nothing. We have no ships or aircraft within five hundred miles of Taiwan or the Formosa Straits. We didn't want to give the Chinese any reason to suspect we were up to something."

"Damn it. And that North Korean chopper has flown the coop as well?"

"Yes."

"And this other guy that the JDIH is so sure is a Japanese, what about him?"

"We just don't know. Scott reported finding only Fat and his men on the island. Jin and his guest must have concluded their business and departed before Scott and the SEALs landed. We're back-hauling our satellite feeds to see if we can pinpoint the chopper's flight path back to the *Sugun*."

"In other words, we sent Scott, Jefferson, and those SEALs into a trap."

"I wouldn't say it was a trap. I'd say our timing was off a bit, but of course we were relying on information provided by the JDIH and—"

"Never mind the ass-covering, Karl. If Scott and the SEALs have to fight their way out, the Chinese will know it, right?"

"I'm not so sure. They may think it's strictly a local issue, drug lords fighting over turf."

After a long silence Friedman said, "Keep me updated, Karl. I want to know everything that happens."

"Of course."

"Fifty-fifty, you say?"

"If we're lucky."

The uplink went silent. *If we're lucky.*

"General Radford?"

"Ah, Ms. Kida, I almost forgot you were there."

"Have you had any direct contact with Commander Scott?"

"We've had nothing from him, just the video uplinks. Have your people seen them?"

"We made copies for distribution. They're undergoing analysis now."

Radford knew that the Japanese had the lead in feature-recognition software. "Perhaps you'll be able to identify someone on them we can't," he said.

"General, I heard you tell Mr. Friedman that the information I provided was faulty, the timing of the meeting—"

"No one is blaming you, Ms. Kida, least of all me. Oh, no, not at all. I take full responsibility for the planning and execution of the mission. You are blameless."

"General—"

"Don't worry, Ms. Kida, you are not in any way responsible."

"General, if you—"

"I'll keep you informed, Ms. Kida."

"Sir, if you make contact with Commander Scott, please let me know."

18

The Villa

Scott heard three-round bursts from M4s, followed by screams, then silence. Someone shouted something in Chinese. Scott next heard the cracking of AK-47s and hot 7.62mm rounds slapping through foliage, spanging off tree trunks, piercing the toolshed's thin sheet-metal sides.

Jefferson's voice was on the line: "Contact! Contact!" At the same time, Scott saw a dark figure rushing toward him with an AK-47 pointed, ready to fire. Scott swung his M4 up and triggered a three-round burst. Frangible rounds tore through the man's chest, knocked him down hard, and sent his weapon flying through the air. All over the island, birds and animals awoke, cawing and shrieking.

Scott grabbed Caserta, who was struggling with the folded-up MAV control pack, and dragged him to cover.

"You two okay?" Jefferson said over his shoulder, eyes glued to the immediate area around them at the base of the bluff.

"Okay," Scott said, chest heaving. "Any of our guys down?"

"Nope. Just bad-asses." He pointed to four black-clad figures sprawled on the sand in poses that left no doubt that they were dead.

"Any more live ones?"

"On both sides of us. But they don't have a bead on us—yet."

Gunfire coming in at them from the bluff was sporadic and uncontrolled. Scott saw muzzle flashes, like fireflies in the woods. A heavy machine gun burped out several rounds, then stopped. The narco-traffickers seemed confused, and their uneven lay-down of fire proved it. The searchlight's loom swept across the beach, hunting for the SEALs. It swept over the pier, then the stacked fuel drums. Everywhere it fell, long, inky shadows slashed like knife blades across the rumpled sand.

"We have to take that thing out," Scott said, ducking as the blinding beam swept overhead.

"Right, if we don't," Jefferson said, "we won't get off the beach." He hailed Ramos. The SEAL slithered over the sand to Jefferson's side. He gripped an M4 equipped with an M203 grenade launcher.

"When I tell you to, put a flash-bang into those weeds over there by the pier," Jefferson said. "It'll get their attention, maybe they'll put that damn light on it long enough for Van Kirk and Zipolski to shoot it out."

Ramos fetched a 40mm grenade from his rucksack and loaded the weapon. Van Kirk and Zipolski would have only seconds to shoot out the searchlight when it paused—if it paused—before the commotion caused by the grenade's concussion and brilliant flash of light wore off and the light moved on again. If they missed, Fat's men would know where the shooting had come from and start pouring in lead.

But before Jefferson gave the order for Ramos to fire

the grenade, a man with a Russian PK machine gun opened fire, spraying live rounds and green tracers helter-skelter in their direction from a hidden position.

"Think that son of a bitch knows where we are?" Brodie said, face pressed into the sand. Sand tossed in the air by bullets grinding up the beach a yard outside their perimeter rained on their backs.

"Shit, no, he's firing blind," Zipolski said.

"Could've fooled me," Brodie replied.

Rounds snapped overhead while others thunked into the stacked fuel drums. Raw fuel—gasoline and diesel—gurgled out onto the beach, its pungent smell on the wind. Scott thought about hot tracers in contact with liquid fuel.

"EPA's not going to be happy about that," Leclerc said, keeping low.

The shooting stopped.

"Either he burned up that PK or he's reloading," said Caserta.

Jefferson lifted his head. "Can anybody see the shooter?"

The firing started up again, tracers zipping by overhead.

"Yeah, he's behind that Toyota Land Cruiser parked at the end of the pier," Leclerc said. "I saw his muzzle flash."

"All right, when Ramos fires that flash-bang, I'll take him out," Jefferson said.

He gave the order; Ramos, lying on his side, lifted the weapon over his head and, judging distance and angle, fired blind. Hunkered down, Scott felt the grenade's concussion against his back and, even through tightly closed eyes, saw night turned to day from its two-million-candlepower flash.

Van Kirk and Zipolski waited until the wild firing

from the Toyota had stopped and the searchlight had swung to where smoke drifted over the weed patch, then opened fire. The light went out in a shower of sparks, glass, and metal. Except for dim illumination provided by the lights strung on the pier, the surrounding area, including the beach, was in total darkness.

"They're all blind from that flash-bang: can't see a damned thing," Scott said.

As if to prove him wrong, a muzzle flash bloomed from behind the Toyota, the PK spitting out rounds until it ran dry.

"Eat this, mother!" Jefferson reared up and fired on full auto, almost emptying the M4's 20-round magazine at the vehicle, blowing out both windshield and backlight, shredding upholstery, sheet metal, and the shooter, too. He spun out from behind the Toyota, dropped his weapon, and collapsed.

Jefferson said, "That asshole's down for good. Okay, we've got a clear lane to the beach. Let's move!"

Scott grabbed Jefferson's arm. "Not yet. This way." He motioned to the villa.

"Are you nuts? That's finished. We're out of here."

"Not until we search the villa."

"Search the villa? . . ."

"We'll split up. I'll take the steps, you and the others take the service road. Their attention'll be focused on the beach and the pier. They won't be expecting us."

"No way. Fat's got plenty more men up there. We'd have to take them out, plus those guard towers."

"Then do it."

Jefferson gave Scott a long, hard look. "You *are* nuts. If we break contact now, we can get out of here in one piece."

"That's your call, but I've got my orders. If you want, pull back to the mini-sub and I'll signal when I'm done and you can pick me up."

"What the fuck is this, a brass balls contest?"

"I've got a job to do. I need your help, but I'll do it without you if I have to." Scott turned away.

Jefferson grabbed a handful of Scott's cammies. "Don't pull that shit on me."

Scott freed his arm from Jefferson's grip. "Save it for Fat's men."

The SEALs looked from Jefferson to Scott. Chief Brodie hissed, "The bad guys are out there, not here." He looked at Jefferson. "What's it gonna be, Colonel?"

Jefferson glanced at the men. "The villa."

"Conn, Sonar. That Kilo's back."

Deacon hustled into the *Reno*'s sonar room. The sonar supervisor said, "Sierra One, Kilo-class submarine bearing two-four-two. Turns for three knots. There's his tone-line, Captain. Have the range for you in a minute."

Deacon said, "Where's the ASDS?"

"Bearing two-three-eight. Range less than four thousand yards. Still anchored."

"Get me the range on the Kilo—pronto." Deacon returned to the control room. "Rus."

The exec stepped away from Fire-control Alley. "Sir?"

"Get me comms on the ASDS, tell them what we have brewing. And I want a setup on that goddamn Kilo. Just in case."

"Aye, sir."

"Scott's probably got his hands full. Think we can raise him?"

"We can try, sir."

"Do it. We may have to fuck with that Chinaman, and Scott had better know."

Bent low, Scott sprinted up the steps cut into the bluff. A few lights still burned in the villa, but it was mostly dark. He stayed low and moved up slowly, step by step, wondering if he was a moving target for an unseen shooter looking down from the veranda. He stopped briefly to scan the bluff face looming above him through NV goggles but saw nothing alive.

He started up again but stopped cold when something alive moved, something he sensed more than saw. He dropped to his haunches and saw a man armed with an AK-47 materialize from the mounds of sharp rock and loose brush bordering the steps. Scott didn't hesitate; he drew his silenced Sig Saur, aimed, and fired twice. Both hits sent the man reeling, crashing against the bluff's jagged rock face, his weapon clattering into the boulders.

Scott, blood pounding in his ears, leg muscles trembling, forced himself to move *now*, so he wouldn't become a target for another hidden shooter. Eyes scanning left and right, he sprinted up the narrow switchback of steps. He stopped to catch his breath each time he came to a landing, expecting any moment to feel a 7.62mm round's white-hot punch.

He moved out again but missed a step, stumbled, crashed a shoulder against stone, got up, and, legs pumping, breath exploding from his lungs, climbed higher. As he approached the summit of the bluff just below the veranda, he heard a woman scream something unintelligible. Her scream was followed by the deafening staccato of automatic weapons fire coming from the veranda.

"Up! Move!" Scott growled. Jefferson and the SEALs were engaging Fat's men from positions on the road behind the villa and had run into a firestorm unleashed from the veranda.

He heard long bursts of gunfire—the drug-traffickers unloading whole magazines at the SEALs, the SEALs firing back with short controlled bursts. In between he heard the thud of a heavy machine gun and distinctive crack of Russian PKs. Tracers whipped across the black sky and through palm tree tops; rounds smacked off the villa's masonry, splintering wood door frames and piercing windows.

Scott crouched behind the wall around the veranda. He made certain his footing was solid, then peeked over the top of the wall at six black-clad figures aiming weapons over the edge of the opposite wall, slamming rounds down onto the SEALs fighting their way up the road. He felt the weapons' heat on his face and hands as they spit bullets.

Scott ducked behind the wall and caught his breath. He felt inside a bag hung on his H-gear and palmed a fragmentation grenade. He took a deep breath, pulled the pin, and, with a roundhouse swing, hooked the grenade into the mob of shooters before he ducked down behind the wall.

An instant later he felt the concussion and felt a searing blast of heat roll over the top of the wall. He heard a muted cry, and after he confirmed that the shooters were all down he vaulted the wall, one-handing the M4.

The grenade had blown the shooters to pieces, scattering shredded gristle and white bone. He moved toward them cautiously, stepping on piles of spent brass cartridge cases and floor tiles slick with blood. The shooters, two of them women, were dead.

"You're clear up top," Scott said shakily over the squad line, after assessing the carnage.

A heavy *whomp* and another blast of heat forced Scott to duck behind the wall as a white fireball erupted behind the villa. A white phosphorus grenade fired by one of the SEALs had destroyed a guard tower from which a steady rain of machine gun fire had stalled their advance. He raised his head to look and saw screaming, burning figures trapped in the tower, silhouetted against the flare of searing phosphorus.

Scott's ear mike hissed. Jefferson's voice came out edgy and with a rush, "Copy that, Scott. Thanks. Still got our hands full!"

Another WP and the vehicle park went up. Burning men staggered around flaming trucks and SUVs. Another grenade topped yet another guard tower. A few short bursts from M4s and PKs, and it was over.

Scott heard Jefferson on the line say, "Anybody down?"

Zipolski: "Nicked in the hand."

Brodie, Ramos, Caserta, Van Kirk, and Leclerc checked in unhurt.

"Scott, you okay?"

His hands had begun to shake uncontrollably. He willed them to stop, but they wouldn't. He looked at the faces of the dead women in the beam of his penlight. Not young, not old, but hard, very hard. One of them had wound her long black hair tight in a bun on the crown of her skull. It had come apart and now was soaked with her blood, oozing from a gaping head wound that looked black in the pen's red light.

The other woman lay on her back, both arms trapped under her buttocks, dead eyes wide open, lower lip trapped under a row of crooked front teeth. Her black shirt had been torn open by grenade fragments that had penetrated her back and, after shredding vital organs, exited out her front. He wanted to tell himself that they had gotten what they deserved but knew that that wouldn't make him feel less guilty for what he'd done. Nothing would.

"Scott?"

"Right. I'm okay."

"We count at least sixteen dead here. You?"

Scott balled his hands into fists to stop their shaking. "Six up here." How many they'd killed on the beach was anybody's guess. Scott felt something go out of him: Radford had gotten it wrong, way wrong.

"Any sign of Fat?" asked Jefferson.

"What? No, he's probably still holed up somewhere in the villa. We'll do a room-by-room. Give me Ramos and Leclerc."

"You got 'em. Anything else?"

"What about the junk? Is anybody aboard?"

"We're gonna find out."

"Chief Brodie, you there?"

"Aye, Skipper?"

"Better sitrep *Reno* and the SRO."

"Copy that."

Sweaty, dirty, Scott sagged against a wall and peered with NV past the shattered glass doors into the villa's main living area. He desperately wanted to rest, but there was no time. Fat and possibly some of his men might be hiding in the labyrinth of the villa's interior. Fat had to be captured alive and interrogated to find out what had gone wrong, why the mission had been a colossal fuckup.

* * *

Deng Zemin, eye to the periscope, said, "There are fires burning on Matsu Shan." His comment was unnecessary: The first officer was watching the video monitor slaved to the periscope. To him it looked as if the whole island was on fire.

"An accident perhaps? . . ." said the first officer.

"Perhaps, but I don't think so," Zemin said. "Infrared indicates very high temperatures but small thermal cores. Weapons, perhaps."

The first officer made notes on his electronic data pad.

Zemin folded the periscope's training handles and nodded. The scope dropped away. After considering, he said, "Come to new heading, one-nine-zero. Engage creep motor. Observe ultra-quiet routine. Initiate passive sonar search for Target One."

The first officer accorded Zemin a look of understanding. They *had* been fooled: A U.S. 688I was in the area after all. Which meant that U.S. Navy SEALs were likely in the area too. Maybe on Matsu Shan. If so, then a mini-sub had put them ashore and was waiting to take them off. Find the mini-sub, find the 688I.

19

Key Largo, Florida

The president stood, hands in pockets, gazing out over Florida Bay, which was chockablock with pleasure craft, at Coast Guard and Secret Service boats chasing down those that had violated the Florida White House's no-sail zone.

The president turned his attention back to the five men seated by the swimming pool around a table cluttered with sweating glassware, empty potato chip bags, and luncheon plates with uneaten pickles. They had arrived wearing clothes more suitable for the colder weather in Washington, D.C. They had shed their jackets and ties but not the pallor they'd acquired from spending too-long days and nights in conference rooms and offices.

The president sat down again at his place between Carter Ellsworth and Secretary of Defense Dale Gordon. National Security Advisor Paul Friedman faced the president and was flanked by the chairman of the Joint Chiefs of Staff, Admiral Jack Webster, and by the deputy chief of the CIA, Holland Paige.

The president said, "All right, gentlemen, let's get to

business. General Radford is monitoring the progress of our spec-ops team on Matsu Shan. If we need to speak with him, or if something develops that we must know, we'll use the SRO's secure communications network." He pointed to a flying-saucer-like device sitting in the middle of the table. Paige moved a potato chip bag away from it.

"As you all know," the president continued, after a slow, deliberate intake of breath, "the SEALs ran into stronger-than-anticipated resistance on Matsu Shan. While the success of the mission and their safe extraction are paramount, I'm more worried about our discovery that the North Koreans have transported nuclear warheads from storage to their missile launch site at Hamhung and to a railhead at Najin."

The president slowly looked around the table at the conferees, his eyes taking them in one at a time. His look conveyed how serious the actions were that the North Koreans had taken. It was clear to all that the president was more than worried; he was frightened by the uncertainty of what they faced.

"Jesus Christ," was Ellsworth's response, the only one from around the table.

The commander in chief motioned to Paige. "Holland."

"We've had a Humint asset in place in Pyongyang for some time. Until the overthrow of Kim Jong-il, this asset fed us information about North Korea on a regular basis. Now, just when we desperately need more information, our asset has either gone to ground or been discovered. We tend to think the former rather than the latter, because if the NKs had uncovered him, they'd have said so, probably paraded him on TV."

Ellsworth and his boss, Jack Webster, exchanged surprised looks. Friedman saw their exchange and interjected, "What you just heard is above Purple. No one outside this group is cleared for it. I want to add that we had no warning whatsoever from this asset of the coup in Pyongyang. Nor of the weapons transfer."

"In any event," Paige went on, "absent Humint from Pyongyang, Defense, and the SRO have worked hard to connect the unsealing of the nuclear storage facility in the Kangnam Mountains to the crisis we face and how those events relate to the meeting on Matsu Shan between Marshal Jin and this so-called mystery man we haven't yet identified. We believe there's a strong connection between the three events but don't know what it is."

Paige picked at his blue Oxford shirt, which was patched with sweat. "I must caution that while everything points to the transport of weapons to Najin, we just don't know enough to be confident that they were moved. Nevertheless, we think it prudent to assume they're up there."

SecDef Dale Gordon, a former civil rights attorney and Wall Street banker friend of the president, said, "Holland, what's the time frame between the unsealing of the storage facility and the discovery that the warheads may have been moved to Najin? And where in the chain of events does the Matsu Shan caper fit in?"

"We and the SRO confirmed that the NKs moved them out of storage a week ago and trucked them to Hamhung. There was a seventy-two-hour period when we lost track of them. As you know, Mr. Secretary, nuclear weapons–sensing technology isn't foolproof. We eventually found the warheads—at least the truck they'd been in—on its way to Najin, where it's only a short hop across the border to Russia. The transporting of the warheads to Najin coincided with the meeting at Matsu Shan."

They all digested this, after which Ellsworth said, "General Holland, how big are these warheads? I mean, how powerful? Anybody know?"

"We think in the twenty- to fifty-kiloton range."

"In other words, as big as the Hiroshima bomb but maybe bigger."

"There's just no way to know," Paige said. "We've tracked these warheads for years but haven't been able to assess their potential yield with any degree of accuracy. Given what we know of the regime's production facilities, it's safe to assume a number somewhere in the middle."

"They're Pakistani knockoffs, right?" said Webster.

"More than knockoffs," Gordon interjected. "They're Pakistani nuclear weapons with NK labels on them. The Pakis went over there and built the goddamn things for them using NK bomb fuel."

The president cleared his throat. "So we come back to the main question: If we assume the weapons are at the border, what's Jin going to do with them? Why move them to the border with Russia at all? Clearly they don't have a dispute with the Russians that would justify their presence in Najin. Any ideas?"

"He's trying to hide them, move them onto Russian soil so we can't touch them," Ellsworth said. "So they won't have to give up their ace in the hole."

Gordon said, "But to do that they'd have to have the approval and cooperation of the Russians. And as far as we know, they haven't moved them over the border, not yet, anyway."

"Yes, sir, true enough," Ellsworth said, "but Moscow doesn't control everything that happens in Russia. Take the Russian Mafiya for instance. They don't just run drugs and whores, they sell weapons, and if they could get hold of some nuclear weapons, they'd sell them too."

The president massaged the bridge of his nose. "That is, I'm afraid, an all-too-plausible scenario."

"I agree, Mr. President," said Chairman Webster. "The Mafiya has been shopping for nukes for years. The NKs might just be selling to the highest bidder."

"Gentlemen," said Paige, "I remind you that we don't know for sure that they've moved the weapons to the railhead. We need more information to make the case and don't have it."

Ellsworth, stirred, steepled his fingers and put them to his lips. "General, Mr. Secretary, what's on the other side of the border? In Vladivostok, I mean. Don't the Russkis have a high-tech sector over there that employs technicians and scientists from around the world?"

"They do," Gordon said, smiling faintly at Ellsworth's dated Cold War reference to Russkis, not Russians. "The old Vladivostok is gone. No more shipbuilding and whaling. Now it's all high-tech, you know, telecommunications and computers. Why?"

Ellsworth shrugged. "I got to thinking about all those Russki civilian nuclear weapons designers and former Soviet Rocket Force officers that found themselves out of work after the Soviet Union collapsed. I wondered what had happened to them, like where did they go and how did they support themselves and their families? Especially if there were no more nuclear weapons to design and service."

"What are you saying, Carter?" Webster asked. "That the NKs are shipping their nukes over the border to keep the Russians employed? How? By having them build more weapons for them? By having them service the ones they already have? If anything, moving their nukes to Russia means there's little chance they'd try to launch them against South Korea, Japan, or, for that matter, us."

"I hear you." Ellsworth looked around the table, perhaps hoping someone would pick up his idea and expand on it. But no one did. He shrugged. "Just a thought."

"I think it's more likely that they want them out of our reach," the president said, "which may turn out to be a blessing in disguise. After all, as Admiral Webster said, if the weapons do end up in Russia, the North Koreans can't possibly launch them from Russian soil against us or our allies. It's a win-win situation."

"With respect, Mr. President," said Gordon, "and you, Admiral, I'm not convinced that they took them out of North Korea to place them out of our reach. Jin is an old fox and a lot smarter than Kim ever was. Whatever it is that he's up to, it required a trip to Matsu Shan only days after he seized power. General Yi is Jin's right-hand man and controls the country's domestic security forces and spy apparatus. That's a lot of power in one man's hands. And with the officer corps still in turmoil over the coup, Yi could have easily seized control of the country himself in Jin's absence. Jin must have known that that was a possibility, yet even so he left the country in Yi's hands for almost a week while he went off to Matsu Shan. It proves that Jin is not only a risk-taker but a ruthless bastard as well."

The president said, "Which is why I've asked the CIA and Air Force to prepare a plan for a possible air assault on Najin."

Paul Friedman added, "We can't permit the North Koreans to transport their weapons out of the country, not even to Russia. An attack would be aimed at destroying the transportation infrastructure around Najin—roads, bridges, and, if necessary, the transport vehicles themselves, not the weapons. Yes, I know we run the risk of scattering highly enriched nuclear bomb fuel over a wide area of North Korea and Russia. Fortunately the area is mostly uninhabited, aside from a few oil terminals and harbor facilities. If we can immobilize the weapons, it will be impossible for Jin to recover them and, more importantly, use them."

"Paul, have you informed the Russians about this?" Gordon asked. "I mean, do they know? Better yet, are they going to permit the NKs to send nuclear weapons across the border into their country? And why would they?"

"We don't think they know what the NKs are up to, and we've not yet brought them into it," Friedman admitted. "And we won't until we have ironclad proof to make our case. When we do, a chat with the Russians would certainly be in order."

"I should think so. They may have something to say about it, you know. After all, it might be their territory that we'd have to attack."

Webster stirred. "Mr. President, rather than an air assault, I'd like to suggest you consider a Tomahawk strike from a submerged submarine. It would be far less risky than, say, punching in there with a flight of stealth bombers."

"Admiral Webster, can we put an SSN into the Sea of Japan?" Paige asked. "Or won't the Japanese allow it?"

"Hell, we put them in there every day right under their noses. But if that's what you're worried about, we can hit the NKs from the Yellow Sea, overfly North Korea itself with Tomahawks and—"

"Gentlemen, please let's stay focused on the main issue," the president said.

"Admiral Webster," said Friedman, "be assured that if it comes to it, we will consider every option, including a Tomahawk strike."

The president looked toward the house, at his aide coming toward him. "Something for us, Karen?"

She pointed to the flying saucer on the table and said, "Yes, Mr. President, General Radford is waiting on SRO comms."

"Put him through."

A moment later the flying saucer croaked, after which the conferees heard Radford say in a clear, booming voice, "Mr. President, Mr. Secretary, gentlemen, I have some good news. Our special-ops team has taken control of Matsu Shan and is in the process of searching the villa for holdouts and for any intelligence they can find."

"That's *great* news, Karl," said the president, lifting his eyes heavenward. "Have they found any sign of Jin and his guest, any evidence that might tell us who this man is?"

"Not yet, sir. But Scott is pretty certain he'll find something."

Ellsworth gave the president a thumbs-up. The president looked better than he had in days, and so did the others.

"As for Jin," Radford said, "we've reviewed our KH-12 pickups and can confirm that he lifted off Matsu Shan a good two hours before the SEALs arrived. Bad timing is what it was. As for the other party, we think he may have returned to Chi-lung aboard Fat's junk. Not sure, mind you, but everything points to it: Fat's departure and re-turn to the island again after the SEALs had landed. This was confirmed by Commander Deacon aboard the *Reno*."

Another thumbs-up from Ellsworth.

"Any casualties?" asked the president.

"Minor."

"What about Fat's people?" Gordon asked.

"I understand that almost all of his men—and several women—were killed. None have been captured so far."

"Karl, it's the president again . . ."

"Sir?"

"How soon can they extract and get themselves and the *Reno* the hell out of there?"

Radford hesitated, and the others sensed that some-thing bad was coming.

"We have a slight problem on that score, sir. I've been in direct contact with Deacon, and he informs me that they've encountered a Chinese Kilo-class sub in their op area. Unless and until it departs, it'll impede their ability to recover the SEALs and haul out."

"Karl, Carter. Has the Kilo made contact with the *Reno*?"

"Deacon doesn't think the Chinese skipper knows she's there."

SecDef Gordon added, "Deacon knows, doesn't he, the rules of engagement he's operating under?"

The president, surprised, said, "Just what are the rules of engagement Deacon is operating under?"

Radford said, "Sir, if he gets in a jam, he's to open fire and sink the Kilo."

Iseda Tokugawa settled back in the leather-and-wood executive cabin aboard the ToriAir 737 and listened to its engines spool up. As the plane trundled away from the Chiang Kai-shek International cargo terminal onto the taxiway, he shut his eyes and saw Marshal Jin's skull-like head nodding assurance after assurance that nothing would go wrong.

But Tokugawa knew better. The plan was so fragile and so dependent on others for success that it could easily fail. Yet the plan, fragile or not, had taken on a life of its own, propelled by the sheer weight of its consequences, and it was now beyond anyone's control, even his own. Only a technical casualty could derail it. Perhaps the warheads would fail to materialize. Or they would be unsuitable for miniaturization. Or the submarine, *Red Shark*, would sink. Or a million other things.

Airborne, Tokugawa cranked back his seat to snooze, confident that despite attempts to settle the dispute between North Korea and the United States, it was too late to stop what had been put in motion.

20

Matsu Shan, outbound

Scott heard bursts of gunfire. Next he heard shouts, then a grenade exploding somewhere outside. Holdouts. Fat might be among them and Scott hoped that he wasn't dead, because he needed Fat alive and talking.

He eased down a hallway and stopped outside Fat's bedroom, which he recognized from its red satin walls and the bed, big enough to serve as the flight deck of a carrier. Only Navy F-18 Hornets were missing.

Scott slowly pushed the bedroom door open with the muzzle of his M4, the Sig in his left hand, ready if needed. He peeked in. The place was a mess. The bed had been torn apart; clothing, purple satin pillows, and scores of video cassettes and magazines were strewn all over the carpeted floor. There was no sign of Fat, nor any of the naked girls Scott had seen on the MAV monitor. And there was no sign of the downed MAV itself, which had to be retrieved. Then he felt something hard in the small of his back and knew it was a weapon, probably a fully automatic one.

"Fuck you, dude."

She had a tiny voice, like a child's.

"Not so big shot now, huh, dude? You drop guns or I shoot."

"No shoot."

Scott bent his knees and slowly lowered both safed weapons to the floor.

"Now you raise hands."

She didn't order him to stop as he slowly turned around to see that he faced one of the girls he'd seen working on Fat's limp cock. She was small breasted, slim, and very pretty, and naked except for bright red bikini panties and the AK-47 in her hands. Scott estimated she was seventeen or eighteen years old, probably mainland Chinese. But lurking behind the delicate young beauty he saw a woman as hard and merciless as the two women shooters he'd killed on the veranda.

She thrust the AK-47 at Scott. "Hey dude, want to fuck me, huh?"

"Not now."

She lowered the AK and shoved its muzzle against Scott's crotch. "Hey dude, got a hard-on?" she taunted, shoving Scott against the wall.

"No, no hard-on," he said.

"No? You no want to fuck me? Then maybe I blow you balls off, yes?"

Scott wondered what action-hero videos she'd watched to perfect her technique. He knew by the look on her face that she'd do it.

"What you say about that, dude?"

"No, no blow off balls."

She drew back and spit in Scott's face. "Fuck you, American." She lifted the assault rifle from his crotch and planted its muzzle under his right eye, her tiny hand wrapped tightly around the wooden grip. "Maybe I kill you now." Her tiny finger wiggled on the trigger.

A burst of gunfire that sounded like a string of fire-crackers going off made her jump. Scott thought to rush her and knock the weapon aside, but she recovered and slammed the AK's muzzle into his chest, driving him against the wall.

Scott heard boots beating up the stairs at the end of the hallway. "Skipper, you up here?" It was Ramos.

The girl swung the rifle around, toward the stairs. Scott made a grab for it, but she saw it coming and swung the weapon back. He threw up a forearm to fend it off, but the AK's barrel cracked into the side of his head.

"Skipper!"

A blinding hot muzzle flash and a deafening, stuttering roar erupted as the girl walked the AK across the ceiling, bringing down plaster and debris on their heads. Before Scott could act, she fired a long burst into Ramos, almost cutting him in half, blowing him backward down the stairs.

Stunned from the blow to his head, Scott lunged at the girl but missed and went down on all fours. He saw his pistol, snatched it off the floor, and came up in a shooter's crouch, ready to fire, but he didn't. The girl, covered with plaster dust, had the AK leveled not at Scott but at McCoy Jefferson.

On his haunches at the top of the stairs, left hand splayed against the wall to keep his balance, Jefferson had his M4 aimed at the girl, its barrel rising and falling in time to his rapid heartbeat.

The girl had her eyes planted on Jefferson. After a long moment she snapped her head around to look at Scott, then back at Jefferson. Scott had never seen eyes so wild as hers.

"Fuck you, dudes!" she shrieked in a voice that left no doubt about what she intended.

Jefferson fired a burst that hit her in the face. Her head twisted out of shape before it exploded into chunks of brain tissue and splinters of white bone.

In was over in an instant. The hallway smelled of cordite, blood, and feces. A haze of eye-stinging smoke parted as Jefferson inched forward to make sure the girl, in a heap against the wall, was down for good. He saw that she was and only then lowered his weapon. He looked up at Scott standing with the unfired Sig held loosely in his right hand. He was covered with plaster dust and spattered with the girl's blood and brain tissue. Red flecks clung to his cheeks and matted hair.

Jefferson eyed him up and down. Scott knew what he was thinking: Scott, hesitating, missing an opportunity to kill the Croatian, Karst, and now this. Scott looked at the girl—what was left of her—and felt sick, but he refused to give in to it.

He heard voices, turned, and saw Caserta and Leclerc dragging Ramos's ruined body up the stairs. *It wasn't supposed to be like this,* Scott thought. Ramos dead; the girl who had killed him dead too, along with the others. The fear and rage he'd felt in his gut began to dissipate, but its effects made him question why any sane man would do what he had done. Scott wiped his bloody face on a sleeve. As if reading his mind, Jefferson threw him a look and said, "It's too late in the game for regrets."

"It's never too late," Scott said and jammed the unfired Sig into a thigh holster.

Jefferson held Scott's gaze for a beat, then went to Caserta and Leclerc, who had laid Ramos out in the hallway on a remains pouch. They stood looking down at him.

Jefferson said, "What's the body count outside?"

"Thirty-three," Leclerc said. He pointed to the dead girl. "Who's that?"

"The cunt who wasted Ramos."

"Christ."

Caserta started taking weapons and equipment off Ramos's body, preparing it for underwater transport to the ASDS.

"They're still missing," Scott said.

Jefferson rounded. "Who?"

"The other two girls—and Fat."

"I don't know about the girls, but for sure that fat shit can't have gotten very far."

Scott put up a hand, then a finger to his ear, and while the others listened in on the squad line, he said, "Go ahead, Chief."

"Comms from *Reno,*" said Brodie. "That Kilo's back. Cap'n Deacon thinks the Chinaman may be on to us and might be huntin' for our ride home."

"Copy. Wait one."

Scott checked his watch. They'd been ashore not more than forty-five minutes, but it seemed like hours. Deitrich and Allen were anchored offshore in the ASDS, waiting for word that the op had been wrapped up. Now they had to sweat out a possible contact with a Chinese sub.

"Decision time," Jefferson said to Scott as he watched Caserta and Leclerc working on Ramos's body. "Sounds like we aren't going to have time to sweep this place clean *and* get out of town before that Kilo finds the parked mini-sub."

Scott touched his throat mike. "Chief, we've got one of Fat's girls up here, dead. Seen any sign of the other two?"

"Negative."

"Any sign of Fat?"

"Nope."

"All right, you and Van Kirk start wrapping up. I'll get back to you."

"So? . . ." Jefferson said.

"So we split up. You, Caserta, and Leclerc take Ramos back to the mini-sub, mate up with the *Reno* before that damned Kilo sniffs out both subs. Brodie, Van Kirk, and I'll stay and search for Fat and scoop up any intel we can find. You pick us up after it's clear."

"Too risky. So is the three of you hunting for Fat and those two girls. Hell, you saw what this one was capable of."

"Look, if we split up now you all stand a good chance of getting back to the sub in one piece and with Ramos's body before that Chinese skipper finds the mini-sub."

"Don't worry, Scott, I'm not planning to die here."

"Good. Now shove off."

"No way. Don't try to be a hero and do it all yourself."

Scott jerked his head at Ramos. "There's only one hero here."

"You got that right." Jefferson broke out a fresh magazine for his M4. "Can Deacon handle that Kilo?"

"He'll do whatever he has to do to make sure we get a ride home."

Jefferson nodded that he understood what that meant and the risks it entailed.

Caserta and Leclerc had finished their work. Now they stood, weapons ready, anticipating Scott's next order.

"All right, let's find Fat," he said.

* * *

"Conn, Sonar, that Kilo's just about dead in the water."

"Conn, aye," Deacon said. *Okay, the Kilo was hunting for the mini-sub. How?* He glanced at Kramer. "Rus, those Kilos, if I remember correctly, have an advanced digital sonar system, right?"

"Yes, sir. An MGK 400 EM."

"I'm thinking out loud here, Rus. He's seen the fires burning on Matsu Shan, knows something's happened, probably reported it to Northern Fleet Headquarters. Maybe they suspect Uncle Sam's involved and that we've got a spec-ops team ashore. Why would we do that? He hasn't a clue but sure as hell wants to find out what we're up to. So . . . might the Kilo's MGK system have a MAD—magnetic anomaly detector?"

Kramer thought it over. "I'm not sure, Captain. I'll call it up in our system, see what the specs are. If it does—"

"If it does, the Chinaman might not have any trouble locating the ASDS."

"Sir, parts of it are titanium, which as you know, is nonmagnetic and—"

"*Parts* of it, but not all of it are made from titanium. The rest of it is made from HY-80 and HY-100 steel. And if that MAD gear is up to snuff, the Chinaman shouldn't have any trouble locating a big hunk of steel sitting on the bottom of the ocean. Hell, she's a sitting duck."

Kramer called the Kilo's combat system up in the *Reno*'s archives and directed Deacon's attention to the computer display. "You're on the money, sir: MGK systems in Kilo 636s have a MAD detector good for ranges of up to two nautical miles—"

"Excuse me, Captain," said the comms chief. "Incoming from Commander Scott, visual crawler only, can't get their voice transmit."

Deacon and Kramer broke off as the incoming message inched across the RDT's display monitor.

"Christ, they want us to run interference on that Kilo for them while they hunt for Fat," said Deacon. "Well, they better hurry, 'cause that goddamn Kilo's breathing down our necks." Deacon needed only a moment to decide what to do next. "Make ready tubes one and two."

Kramer, Fire-control officer, ordered, "Torpedo room, Fire-control. Make ready tubes one and two. Stand by to open outer doors."

Moments later the torpedo room confirmed the order and Kramer relayed it to Deacon. "Captain, tubes one and two ready in all respects."

"Very well, Fire-control. Firing point procedures on Master One."

The BSY-2 team and fire-control coordinator already had a TMA solution on the Kilo.

Kramer reported, "Target bearing zero-four-zero, course one-seven-zero. Speed two knots. Range sixty-five hundred yards."

Deacon pictured the situation topside: A virtual traffic jam, and with no way to duke it out with the Kilo in private. A 21-inch Mk-48 ADCAP torpedo carried a 295-kilogram warhead of PBXN-103. If they sank that Chinese Kilo, the explosion would be felt in Beijing and for sure would rock Washington, D.C.

"Very well," Deacon said. "Stand by—"

"Conn, Sonar."

Deacon opened the mike. "What's up now, Chief?"

"We've picked up a pair of diesel engines. Pretty sure it's that junk what belongs to the drug-lord, Fat."

"She's underway?"

"Trying to confirm it, sir, busy up there."

"Jesus."

Deacon waited. A minute later the sonar chief said, "Sir, we have the *White Dragon*—Sierra Two—underway at five knots, bearing zero-seven-seven. Course three-one-zero. Range six thousand yards. She's standing out of the island channel."

"Shit. Comms."

"Sir?"

"Send to Scott: 'Report your status. We confirm *White Dragon* underway. Is Fat under your control? Advise action re *White Dragon*.' Copy ASDS and SRO."

Deacon glanced at Kramer in Fire-control Alley. The troubled look on the exec's face confirmed what Deacon already suspected: The situation ashore and at sea was on the brink of spinning out of control.

"Watch it! Watch it!" Jefferson warned

Van Kirk had discovered a six-by-six-foot shaft sunk into the living rock under the villa, hidden under a false section of floor inside an enormous clothes closet in Fat's bedroom. As Van Kirk carefully raised the section of floor, gunfire erupted from a shooter armed with an AK-47 and hiding down in the shaft.

Van Kirk dropped the bullet-splintered cover and rolled away from the shaft's opening. "There's a fuckin' rat down there!" He kicked the cover aside, poked a Remington 12-gauge into the opening, and fired, the blasts drumming their ears. Someone down in the hole screamed in pain. They heard a dropped weapon clattering down the shaft, heard it hit bottom, then silence.

Caserta inched toward the opening.

"Careful," Van Kirk said. "He might be playing possum."

Caserta peeked over the edge. "Fuckin' A, it's an elevator shaft."

"See anybody?" Scott said.

"Yeah. But he ain't goin' nowhere."

Van Kirk and Jefferson kept their weapons aimed at a badly wounded Chinese tangled up in the elevator's gear track and safety cables. He had been hiding just below the upper lip of the shaft. Caserta and Van Kirk reached down and dragged him out by his BDU shirt, onto the closet floor. Pellets had crashed through his chest and shattered his right collarbone. His BDUs ran wet with blood.

"I'll be damned," Scott said as he looked down the shaft and saw an elevator cab parked at the bottom. A musty, oily smell mixed with that of the sea and jungle rose from the shaft. "Fat's a sneaky bastard."

"Where's Fat—Wu Chow Fat?" Jefferson demanded as Caserta searched the wounded man for weapons. He found a long hooked knife and threw it aside. He examined the man's wounds and shook his head.

"Give him some water," Scott said.

Leclerc offered the man his canteen, but he refused to drink.

Jefferson prodded the man with his boot toe. "Fat. Where is Fat?"

The man shook his head and looked away.

"Don't give me that shit, where is he?"

"Want me to raise the cab, Skipper?" said Van Kirk, "ride it down, see where it goes?"

"Fat might be waiting for you down there, plus it could be booby-trapped. You and Caserta go around via the service road, find out where this tunnel comes out at the foot of the bluff." He oriented himself. "It should be facing the pier. Be careful. If it's clear, give us a signal and ride it up here."

"Aye, Skipper."

Scott turned back to the wounded Chinese. Jefferson was using his Sig to poke the shattered collarbone. The man hissed in pain; Scott pushed the Sig away.

"Drink this," Scott said. He lifted the man's head and put the open canteen to his lips to dribble water into his mouth. "English. Do you speak English?"

"You're wasting your time," Jefferson said. "He doesn't understand you."

"Marshal Jin; North Korea—do you know him?"

The Chinese said nothing.

"Was Jin a visitor here? Do you understand what I'm saying?"

"Forget it," Jefferson said. He stood. "He's not going to tell you anything. He's just a grunt."

Chief Brodie came on the comm line. "Skipper, you better have a look at this."

"Where are you?"

"Downstairs in the dining room."

"Be right there."

Scott lifted the canteen to the man's lips again but saw that his dead eyes had glazed over.

Jefferson snorted. "Dumb fuck."

21

Matsu Shan, rally point

Scott found Brodie and Zipolski standing in the wrecked dining room. Brodie pointed to a hand-hammered copper vase from an early Chinese dynasty, perhaps one dating from before the birth of Christ.

"Found this. Take a look." Brodie aimed his penlight inside the vase. "A goddamn mini-video cam and mike, size of a pinhead aimed through a hole—it's almost invisible—drilled in the vase. Digital video direct to etched micro discs. And that ain't the only one." He pointed to a piece of porcelain. "Another one's in here. And there's more, all of 'em instant voice-activated and bubble-wrapped and undetectable by sweepers."

Scott understood the significance of Brodie's discovery: Fat had recorded Jin's meeting, possibly for his own protection, or, more likely, to blackmail Jin in the future.

"Have you traced these pickup devices to their storage media?" Scott asked.

Zipolski led the way into the kitchen, to a small pantry off the main part of the room. Inside the pantry Scott saw stacks of recording gear—computers, drives, and filters—all of it inside a wrenched-open case constructed of zirconium-impregnated glass panels, a bubble impervious to electronic detection, and all of it smashed to bits.

"Someone made sure it was destroyed."

Scott inspected the ruined equipment made by V-Tron, a German company that supplied state-of-the-art clandestine video and audio eavesdropping equipment to intelligence agencies in Western Europe and the United States. How Fat had managed to purchase such highly sensitive equipment was anybody's guess.

"I suppose all the hard drives and discs are gone?" Scott asked.

"All except this one," Zipolski said. He held in his palm a shiny, gold-colored mini-disc the size of a half-dollar. "I found it on the kitchen floor. Damn near stepped on it. They must of dropped it when they bugged out. Bet Fat's got the rest of 'em onboard his junk."

"You're sure there's nothing else here? You looked?"

"Yes, sir. Ain't a thing left but this here pile of junk. And this." Zipolski dangled one of the MAVs by its bent wing for Scott to see. "Found it outside the kitchen."

"That's the first one we lost."

"Yes, sir. No sign of the one we lost in Fat's bedroom."

Scott said, "Chief—," but Brodie had a hand up.

"Comms from *Reno*," Brodie said, squinting. "Message is breakin' up bad, hard to hear." Then, "Jesus H. Christ!"

Scott had an uneasy feeling that things were about to get worse, if that was possible.

"Skipper, *Reno* says they've got the *White Dragon* underway. Fat must be aboard. *Reno* wants us to advise."

"Tell them we're hauling ass."

* * *

Scott, Jefferson, Brodie, Leclerc, and Zipolski had assembled at the rally point on the beach by the mangrove thicket, around Ramos's body, which was zipped into a waterproof remains bag. Caserta and Van Kirk trotted from the area of the pier and joined them.

"You were right, Skipper," said Caserta. "The elevator tunnel exits at the foot of the bluff. We found a path leading from it to the pier."

"The motor launch is still tied up," Van Kirk said. "Fat must have used an inflatable boat to get himself aboard the junk."

"Good job," Scott said. "Now let's get the hell out of here."

Chief Brodie twiddled his comms gear. "Skipper, I've got Deitrich. They're gonna up-anchor and move in close to pick us up off the beach. He'll raise an infrared beacon for us to home in on. We should be able to wade out and meet them and—"

"Holy shit!"

Scott looked where Jefferson pointed—at the *White Dragon,* nosing toward the beach, her diesels throbbing softly.

It took a split second to register and for Scott to bellow, "Take cover!"

The SEALs dove into the mangrove as Scott bellowed again, "Chief, raise Deitrich, tell him to stay put—"

A heavy burst of fire erupted from the *White Dragon*'s Vulcan cannon. Bright green golf-ball-sized tracers and 20-millimeter rounds streaked into the pier, smashing the motor launch to kindling and starting a fire.

"Incendiaries!" Jefferson barked. "He's firing goddamn incendiaries!"

Incendiary rounds walked up the beach into the stacked drums of fuel, which exploded in a gigantic ball of orange fire, a deafening roar, and a wall of searing heat.

Pieces of flaming debris pinwheeled into the air, rained down into the sea, onto the beach and into the mangrove, ripping off branches and igniting the foliage. A huge funnel of black, oily smoke rolled skyward. Secondary explosions went off as the flames reached paint cans and lube oil stored in lockers under the pier.

"Where the fuck did he get that toy?" Jefferson shouted above the Vulcan's hammering.

All Scott and the SEALs could do was keep their heads down and hope that the barrage Fat was laying down didn't sweep the beach in their direction and mow down the mangrove. Fire from the Vulcan, at 3,000 rounds a minute, continued to pour into the island and up the bluff into the villa. Raked with incendiaries, the sprawling structure roared into flame.

Scott heard a yelp. He turned and saw Van Kirk writhing in the sand, clutching his side. Scott bellycrawled to him and saw a dark red stain where a piece of hot metal debris had lacerated Van Kirk's rib cage.

"Jesus Christ, that hurts," Van Kirk rasped, his face contorted with pain.

"I've got him," Caserta said. He ripped open a dressing and parked a syrette between his teeth, ready to plunge it into Van Kirk. "Lay still, will ya?"

"How bad is it?" Scott said.

"Can't tell yet."

"Not bad," Van Kirk said through clenched, chattering teeth.

"Just shut up," Caserta told him and jabbed the syrette into Van Kirk's hip.

The ground shook with the might of the Vulcan's destructive power, its heavy rounds pouring in from the *White Dragon,* pounding the villa, setting the garden and cabanas afire, smashing to bits anything in their path.

Like a giant funeral pyre, flames, smoke, and burning debris from the villa lifted high on the wind across Matsu Shan and fanned out to sea, where it would soon draw ships and planes from miles around. When the Mainland Chinese and Taiwanese governments got word that someone had annihilated Fat's army and that Matsu Shan had been burned down to water level, they'd want answers fast and might start looking for them in Washington. Scott hoped that Radford and the president would have some good ones ready.

Then, as suddenly as it had started, the shooting stopped. Over the crackle and pop of burning fuel and timbers, Scott heard the *White Dragon's* diesels raise their voices: Fat, having completed his work, and with his private army decimated, was hauling out to save himself.

Scott cautiously rose to a knee and looked around: The motor launch and what was left of the pier burned bright orange; the villa was a mass of flaming, blackened joists and rafters and shattered masonry.

"Do you believe this?" Jefferson said as he stood beside Scott, surveying the wreckage.

"It's going to draw a lot of rubberneckers," Scott said. "Let's get packing."

The wind had blown smoke off the beach, leaving clear their escape lane.

Jefferson looked up at what was left of the villa and just shook his head.

"You might want to check on Van Kirk," Scott said.

"Right. I'll do that," Jefferson said and moved off.

Scott located Brodie. "Chief, tell Deitrich to stand by to take us aboard. And give the *Reno* a heads-up. Tell them what happened, but make it quick. Oh, and tell them to keep an eye on Fat. I don't want him to get away."

22

The Kilo 636, off Matsu Shan

Zemin had watched in utter amazement as the *White Dragon*, after raking the island with cannon fire, stood out to sea.

"Fat destroyed his own headquarters and now has withdrawn seaward. I don't understand why he would do such a thing." He turned the periscope over to his first officer.

Puzzled, Zemin pored over the track chart on which he'd marked the positions where, he'd thought, both the U.S. 688I and the ASDS might be found. He checked his calculations again: They confirmed that the ASDS had to be somewhere in a triangular-shaped area less than a mile square, just off Matsu Shan's southern coast in shallow water.

Zemin remembered how his grandfather, a hunter all his life, had taught him that a hunter who employed patience and cunning could sometimes flush a bird by threatening its brood. Find the brood, he'd preached, and the mother bird will come to their rescue.

"Comrade Captain."

Zemin glanced up at the slaved video monitor.

"Sir, the *White Dragon* has cleared Matsu Shan at ten knots."

"Commence tracking."

"Aye, sir."

"Helm, steer new course one-six-five." A heading of 165 led to the triangular-shaped search area Zemin had marked on the chart. "I think that with a little luck we will find both the 688I and her ASDS in under"—he glanced at the chronometer—"thirty minutes. You may start the backup clock."

"Aye, sir."

"Helm, secure creep motor; main motors ahead a half together." He scanned the MGK-400 EM's monitors. "Combat systems officer."

"Sir?"

"Full sweep and range on magnetic sensors," Zemin commanded.

The officer acknowledged the order and threw various fixed-function switches on his console to activate the MAD gear housed in a chin blister under the Kilo's domed bow.

Zemin remembered his grandfather's second edict: First, step easy like the cat; next, step hard like the bull. When the ground shakes, the mother bird takes wing. Well, Zemin thought, the ground might not shake, but he was certain that the bird would take wing.

"Conn, Sonar, I've got Sierra One bearing three-two-zero, making turns for eight knots. Range approximately five-eight-zero-zero yards."

Deacon, standing by the lowered scope, looked slightly stunned by the eruption he, too, had witnessed on Matsu Shan.

Sonar broke the silence in the control room. "Sir, Sierra One—"

"Right. That son of a bitch Kilo must have a MAD contact on the ASDS," Deacon said. "Comms."

"Aye, sir."

"Who's pilot? Deitrich or Allen?"

"Deitrich, sir."

"Feed him our data. Tell him to hold course for rendezvous but be prepared to wait for our beacon. Say it may be a little while, that we've got some housekeeping to do."

"Aye, sir."

"Sonar, Conn. Sierra One still closing?"

"Yes, sir. Speed still eight knots."

"Rus."

"Sir?"

"Let's give the Chinaman something to think about. All ahead one-third. Come to course zero-four-zero. We're going to run interference for Scott. Let's hope he and the SEALs are still in one piece." He shook his head. "Hell, even if they're not, that Chinaman had better back off or he's going to take one up the nose."

"Comrade Captain, the American has turned toward and speeded up. Speed twelve knots, range five thousand yards."

Zemin had stepped hard like the bull and flushed his quarry in less time than he had estimated. But he still had another quarry to flush. "Bearing and range to the ASDS?"

"Sir, two-five-zero, range five thousand two hundred yards. Target is lying to, off the beach."

Zemin looked at the MAD display in the Kilo's Fire-control console and saw a bright green cigar-shaped image of the ASDS. Its spinning prop looked like a shimmering disk, while its various titanium structures didn't register at all on the MAD display.

The 688I, meanwhile, showed no inclination to sheer away or back down.

"The American is inserting his ship between us and the mini-sub," Zemin announced to his first officer. "He's warning us to stand clear. A provocation, especially in waters claimed by the People's Republic of China. We'll give him something to think about."

The first officer nodded that he understood what Zemin intended to do, risky though it was.

"Maintain present speed and heading," Zemin ordered. "Active sonar, shift to standby."

"Comms, anything from Scott?"

"Had him, but the wave channel's garbled."

"Well, at least we know he's alive. Probably have their hands full locking in. Keep trying. I want him to know we may have to go to street-fighter mode."

"Aye, sir."

Deacon rounded to Fire-control. "What's that Kilo doing?"

"Captain, range is now forty-nine hundred yards. He's still comin'."

"The Chinaman's broad on our port beam and wants to play T-bone," Deacon said. "What do you think about that, Rus?"

"I think we should show him how to play chicken instead, see how much brass he's got in his balls."

"So do I. Helm."

"Helm, aye."

"Left full rudder, come to course three-two-zero and clear baffles. All ahead flank."

The *Reno* heeled to port as she accelerated and snapped into a sharp left-hand turn that put her on a collision course with the Kilo.

"Fire-control, stand by to launch—"

"Conn, Sonar, single active ping from Sierra One!"

The sound pulse fired from the Kilo's active sonar suite struck the *Reno* like a bullet, her sound-absorbing anechoic tile coating blunting some, but not all, of its energy. What was left over rebounded into the Kilo's fire-control system, which Deacon knew must have lit up like a fireworks display. But by going active, Zemin had also revealed his own position, and now his boat was as vulnerable as the *Reno* was to a torpedo attack.

"Fucker painted us good, wants to make us think he's going to shoot," Deacon said. On that angry note he barked, "Stand by to launch a Thirty CM—on my mark."

Deacon had selected an AN/SLQ-30, one of the Navy's newest countermeasures. The six-inch-diameter fish could be programmed to follow either a preset course or to search for a target using sonar much like an Mk-48 ADCAP homing torpedo. The device had a small Otto engine capable of propelling it through the water at seventy-five knots into an enemy submarine's hull. The collision between enemy sub and Navy countermeasure would send a very strong message: Haul out now or take a real torpedo up the nose.

"Match bearings on a single Thirty CM and shoot."

After a sharp hiss of compressed air from the launcher and a slight lurch by the *Reno,* Kramer reported, "Thirty away."

"That sounds like a fucking torpedo!" Jefferson bellowed. He looked around the mini-sub's red-lit interior and saw frightened looks on every face but Scott's.

"It's not a torpedo," Scott said. "Deacon fired a countermeasure."

Jefferson and the SEALs instinctively ducked their heads as the little fish, the racket from its contra-rotating props reverberating through the ASDS's hull, whizzed by less than a hundred yards away.

"Jesus Christ, could have fooled me," Jefferson said. "What the hell's Deacon trying to do?"

"Get that Chinese sub off our asses."

"Will that thing do it?"

"You bet."

"Both engines ahead emergency speed! Hard left rudder!" Zemin barked orders as soon as he heard the counter-measure's inbound Doppler and recognized what it was. The 688I had swung onto a collision course and gone to flank speed, now this. *Is the American skipper crazy, or did I underestimate him?* Zemin thought to himself.

Zemin's worried fire-control coordinator said, "Comrade Captain, I have a profile and can confirm a U.S. AN/SLQ-30 in the water!"

Zemin, leaning into the turn, noted on the pit log the Kilo's rapid acceleration to twenty-two knots. Not enough to outrun the decoy but enough to ward off a full-speed collision with it. "Range to U.S. countermeasure?"

"Under three thousand yards, sir."

"Stand by to fire a decoy. Stand by engine orders."

The first officer threw switch blocks to energize the Kilo's sail-mounted decoy launch tube assembly with compressed air. "Ready, sir."

"Launch number one."

"Where'd he go?" Deacon said.

"Conn, Sonar. Lost him behind that screen of bubbles from his decoy. He must have gone to creep."

"Let's hope he got our message and cleared the hell out. So much for having brass balls. So where's that Thirty of ours?"

"Don't hear it, sir. It must have been seduced by his decoy."

"Too bad. Where's Sierra Two, *White Dragon*?"

"Bearing two-one-zero, range fifteen thousand yards. She's flat out at ten knots on base course two-nine-zero."

"Tell me you still have the mini-sub."

"Yes, sir, I do. I'm on her beacon and she's on ours."

"Very well. All stop. Engage hover. Standby recovery evolution. Rus."

"Sir?"

"Let's get Scott and his people aboard. And try not to get their feet wet."

23

The *Reno,* off Matsu Shan

Scott floated on a wave of exhaustion, only half-conscious of his surroundings: voices, the familiar smells of machinery and ozone. He felt cold and wet, and a part of him hurt.

Someone said, "Sir, let me take a look at this."

Scott felt the *Reno*'s chief corpsman poking at his hand. "What's wrong?"

"That's what I want to find out."

Scott was in Deacon's stateroom, stripped to his skivvies, aware that he smelled bad and that his left hand was bloody. He remembered tumbling through the ASDS's lock-in/lock-out chamber into the *Reno.* They'd eased Ramos's body out the hatch, then helped a wounded Van Kirk. The rest of the SEALs had followed with their gear.

"Where's Jefferson?" Scott said.

"Right here," he said from the passageway, looking over Deacon's shoulder into the tiny stateroom.

"How's Van Kirk?"

"He's okay," said the doc.

"What about the others?"

"They're looking after Ramos and cleaning up," Jefferson said.

"Ramos's affects, we'll need a report . . ."

Deacon handed Scott a steaming cup of coffee. "There's a lot to cover, but first you should know we're trailing the *White Dragon*. She's on a heading for Mainland China. We've also got a contact—faint, but a contact—on the Kilo trailing us. We can take them both out if we have to. It's your call."

Scott winced. Doc had shot Scott's hand with anesthetic, and he started to dress a wound that Scott couldn't recollect receiving. While the doc stitched, Deacon rattled off the information Fire-control had on both targets.

"Let's get Radford on the horn," Scott said. "I don't mind starting a war with the Chinese, but let's at least get his blessing before we do."

Finished stitching, Doc departed. Deacon headed for the control room, but Jefferson stayed put. He waited a beat, then said, "Jake. . . what I said before, that it takes a shooter to lead a shooter . . ."

Scott, mute, his gaze planted on Jefferson, stepped into a pair of rumpled khakis. Jefferson, eyes cast down, ran a hand over his mouth. "Look, Skipper, what I'm trying to say is that . . ." He looked up. "Back on Matsu Shan, you were a hell of a shooter. The others, too, they saw what you did."

"I just did my job," Scott said, reaching for a shirt, "no more than you all did. Especially Ramos."

"Yeah, Ramos. But what I said about Karst, that other shit—"

"Forget it. We've got more work to do. And it's going to take more shooting."

Jefferson thrust out a hand and they shook, two men

who respected each other. "I owe you, Jake. Don't hesitate to call it in."

Scott nodded. "If I ever need to, I will. Bet on it."

Radford said, "The president agrees that we can't allow
Fat to be given refuge by the Mainland Chinese, Taiwanese, or anyone else for that matter. If the discs and
videos he has fall into Chinese hands, it will complicate
matters beyond belief. Therefore, I'm issuing orders
in the name of the president for you to destroy the
White Dragon and everyone and everything aboard her.
Totally."

Scott glanced at Deacon, then Jefferson. "Understood," he said.

"As to your question, Commander Scott, about a cover
story, we will tell anyone who asks that we know nothing
about the dealings between, shall we say, rival drug-lords.
We all know that sometimes they fight over territory and
that can lead to unforeseen consequences. Now, why a
vessel would blow up and sink in the Taiwan Strait, well,
Mr. Fat is a known dealer in armaments, which are sometimes dangerous to transport by sea. Especially explo-
sives. People are careless. Ships sink."

"Yes, sir, they do. Or will," Jefferson quipped.

"Nevertheless, you will exercise all reasonable caution
when taking action against the *White Dragon*. I don't want
innocent people killed or injured, or a foreign-flagged
vessel damaged. If it can be done so there are no wit-
nesses, all the better."

"That may be difficult," Scott said. "We're operating
in busy waters."

"I understand. As for the Chinese, well, if they lodge
a protest, we'll play ignorant. We can exert some control over the Taiwanese and perhaps their press reports,

if there are any, will reflect this. What's the *White Dragon*'s current position, Captain Deacon?"

"Sir, she's about a hundred klicks southeast of Matsu Lietao. We're trailing and can take her out in under five minutes."

Radford lit a cigarette. He squinted as he talked through a scrim of smoke drifting across the monitored scene from Crystal City. "Very well. The sooner the better."

"General, what about the Kilo?" Jefferson said. "They're watching every move we make."

"Gentlemen, you will handle her with care. I don't want an incident with the Chinese. Bad enough they've been dogging you and this operation. We may be able to paper over whatever it is they think we're doing, but I can't guarantee it. In any event, the president is quite determined to keep the Chinese out of our plans."

"Yes, sir, we'll do our best," Scott said. "I should tell you, though, that we sent the Kilo a message." Scott explained the game of chicken they'd played. "I expect the Chinese skipper will call home when we hit the *White Dragon*."

"And that's why you will high-tail it out of there after it's done. Any questions? No? Then I want to bring on Ms. Kida in Tokyo."

The monitor went to blue, then split in half. Scott saw Fumiko looking fresh and bright, and with a serious look on her face.

"Commander Scott, Colonel Jefferson," she said, "congratulations on a successful mission. But I also want to express my deepest regrets that one of your men, Petty Officer Ramos, was killed."

"Thank you," Scott said, "I'll tell the others. Ramos made it possible for us to return with intelligence material. I just hope that what we found will prove worthwhile."

"The mini-DVD from their surveillance system. Have you viewed it?"

"No, I don't want to touch it. Better our experts in Yokosuka examine it first."

"Indeed," Radford interjected. "Then I'll want Ms. Kida and her people to view it and see what, if anything, they can determine. They have, as you know, first-rate computer software that might wring something of value from it."

"And how do we get the DVD into Ms. Kida's hands?" Scott asked.

"When your op is secure, you will break off and return immediately to Yokosuka."

Radford was referring to the big base on Honshu, south of Tokyo, home of the U.S. Navy Seventh Fleet.

"After our people in Yokosuka have looked at the disc, Scott, you and Ms. Kida will deliver it to the Japan Defense Intelligence Headquarters in Tokyo."

Scott saw Fumiko's look soften. He was quite sure that he saw a hint of a smile on her lips as the video conference ended.

"That's her, that's Fat's junk." Deacon turned the periscope over to Scott, who had been watching an image of the *White Dragon* on the slaved video monitor. Now, for real, he saw in infrared the junk's stubby outline and the glowing heat blooms from her twin diesels.

"I concur," Scott said.

Deacon ordered, "Down scope. Clear baffles to port."

"Clear baffles to port, aye."

The *Reno* turned ninety degrees left to make sure no other ships, especially the Kilo, had crept up from astern.

"Sonar, Conn, report all contacts," Deacon commanded.

"Conn, Sonar, report all contacts, aye," responded the sonar supervisor. After a short delay he said, "I have four contacts, Sierra One through Four. I have Sierra One, the Kilo, bearing one-three-zero."

The Kilo had approached from the southeast. That her skipper had kept his distance from the *Reno* convinced Deacon that the AN/SLQ-30 countermeasure had sent the warning he'd intended.

"Any commercials?" Deacon asked.

"Sir, I have Sierra Three and Four. Both are single-screw commercial vessels." Sonar read their bearings, which Deacon noted as the quartermaster plotted their positions on the navigation chart.

"*White Dragon?*"

"Sir, I report Sierra Two, the *White Dragon*, making turns for ten knots. Bearing zero-four-two."

"Very well, let's take care of business," Deacon said.

Scott knew what was going through Deacon's head, that he had never fired a live warshot at a target other than in a training exercise and that there were people aboard the *White Dragon* who would be killed. Scott had once had similar thoughts about firing on one of Kim Jong-il's destroyers bearing down on the *Chicago*, off the North Korean coast, but that had been another world and another mission. When it had come time to fire torpedoes, Scott hadn't hesitated. Training made all the difference: When your own life, the lives of your crew, and a mission were on the line, a sub skipper never hesitated to pull the trigger.

"Firing point procedures on Sierra Two, stand by tubes one and two."

Scott knew that two wire-guided Mk-48s fired down

the same track, nose to tail, might home in on each other instead of the intended target and detonate prematurely. Scott agreed with Deacon that it was a risky tactic, and that two Mk-48 ADCAPs were overkill against a wooden-hulled junk, but it would ensure that no one aboard would survive to tell what had happened; at the same time, it would destroy whatever spy material Fat had swept out of the villa.

"Flood tubes, open outer doors," Deacon ordered.

Kramer confirmed Deacon's order and added, "Captain, got a good firing solution." He rattled off the target's course, speed, and range.

"Very well," said Deacon. "Up scope."

The Type-18 hummed out of its well. Deacon snapped the handles down, then put the crosshairs on the *White Dragon*. He pressed the red bearing transmitter button on the focusing grip. "Bearing—mark."

"Zero-four-two."

"Final bearing and *shoot*—tubes one and two."

Kramer repeated and confirmed the command from the weapons-control panel, then ordered, "Fire One." A moment later he ordered, "Fire Two."

Forward, a surge of compressed air and a whine like two runaway buzz saws confirmed that the Mk-48s had surged out of their tubes.

"Tubes one and two fired electrically," Kramer confirmed.

"Down scope!"

Like the classic shooting of fish in a barrel, Scott thought as he swallowed to equalize the rise in air pressure from the release of the two torpedoes.

"What's the time to run?" Deacon asked.

"Under three minutes," Kramer said.

Time inched forward. Deacon, who was worried that

the torpedoes running in tandem might premature, glanced at Scott and said, "So far so good."

Two minutes after launch, Kramer reported, "Both torpedoes have acquired Sierra Two."

Deacon ordered, "Cut the wires; shut the outer doors." He gave Scott a thumbs-up, then issued a command that swung the *Reno* away from the doomed junk.

Wu Chow Fat backed into a chair designed to accommodate his girth and sat down behind a rosewood desk bolted to the deck in the *White Dragon*'s main cabin. As big as a corporate boardroom, the cabin was outfitted with handwoven carpets, antique ceramics, porcelains, as well as all the latest electronic gadgets, including HDTV.

Fat drank chilled white wine and tried without success to calm down while he watched his two female consorts primp and preen for their arrival at Pearl Mountain, the private estate of his friend Heung Kim Wong. The assault on his compound by an unidentified force had left him badly shaken. Not pirates, not a rival, certainly not Chinese. *Americans.* His world was in tatters, and he had been lucky to escape alive! Fat glanced at the gleaming brass compass repeater mounted on gimbals by his desk. Its needle, hovering over the lighted compass card, indicated that the *White Dragon* was heading toward a cluster of small islands off Mainland China at Sensha Wan, where Heung Kim Wong would give him refuge. Fat had to warn Marshal Jin and Tokugawa, but not while at sea, where enemy ears had been pricked. Instead he'd use Wong's overland network.

Fat turned his attention to the smashed micro air vehicle laying on his desk, along with two hard drives and a stack of mini-DVDs. He examined the MAV, turning it over in his hands, marveling that something so small could fly like an insect and capture video images while doing it. The perfect spy machine, he thought. And made in the USA. Friends of his in Beijing would pay a fortune to lay hands on it.

Then a curious thing caught his eye: Two brilliant, white-hot balls of fire had mysteriously blossomed in the center of the cabin. He had only a nanosecond to grasp their significance before they expanded and consumed everything in their path.

At the scope, Scott watched thick twin columns of water rise at least 500 feet into the air and then collapse. Two mighty explosions from the Mk-48s shook the *Reno* to her keel. The *White Dragon* had been vaporized, along with Fat, his consorts, his crew, his wine collection, his fine furnishings, electronic gadgets, and the MAV. There was now a steaming vortex where moments ago she had been chugging across the water.

All Scott saw were infrared traces from hot debris cooling in seawater, which, even as he watched, disappeared like the glowing remains of fireworks on the Fourth of July.

Minutes earlier, sonar had reported hearing two buzz saws, which Zemin had refused to believe were torpedoes in the water. He'd reprimanded his sonarmen for issuing a false report, but an instant later he heard the sharp, rising whine of props and knew there was no mistake. Zemin thought the torpedoes were aimed at him and almost panicked. Before he could issue orders to take evasive action, the trip-hammer double boom of exploding torpedo warheads rattled the Kilo. Only then did Zemin understand what had happened.

The sonarman, badly shaken, said, "Comrade Captain, I have a contact—"

"What?"

"Sir, a contact."

"With *White Dragon*? . . ."

"No, Captain, an American 688I, clearing to the southeast at flank speed."

Zemin wiped his face on the sleeve of his royal blue submarine coveralls, embroidered with three gold bands. "Is there any sign of the *White Dragon*?" he asked hopefully.

"None, Captain."

Zemin stood in the utterly silent control room and tried to piece it together: The Americans had torpedoed Fat's vessel and now were flanking it out of the area. First U.S. Navy SEALs on Matsu Shan. Now this. The Americans seemed determined to start a war in Chinese waters. But why? Why, when they were facing the possibility of war with North Korea? It made no sense, but then he was a warrior, not a politician. It would be for the leaders in Beijing to fathom what the Americans were up to.

"First Officer. Bring us to periscope depth. We'll see if there are any survivors. Meanwhile, draft a message for transmission to Northern Fleet Headquarters. Explain what has happened and prepare to send it Urgent/Priority/Commander One."

"Aye, Captain." He gave the orders, then activated his electronic data pad and called up a standard message format to send on the PLAN's highest-priority network.

"The Americans," said, Zemin, "are crazy. And very dangerous."

24

Key Largo, Florida

Paul Friedman watched the first lady in a white mini-bikini, doing laps in the pool. After a long moment he turned away from the sliding glass doors fronting the pool and back to Karl Radford on the SVTC set up in the Florida White House conference room.

"There's no chance of a mistake, is there, Karl?" said Friedman. "You're sure Marshal Jin is back in Pyongyang?"

"I'm sure of it, Paul," Radford said, slightly annoyed that Friedman would question the SRO's satellite pickups. "You saw the pictures; it's definitely him."

"They're so . . . blurred, but I suppose it's the best you can do."

"Trust me, it's him. As for the Taiwanese, they landed a special forces contingent on Matsu Shan to assess what happened. After all, there was no way to hide the fires and smoke."

"Then we'll just have to wait and see what the Taiwanese say," the president interjected. "Paul, you and State handle it if their ambassador, Hun, starts asking questions."

"Sir, he's a prick and thinks we're in cahoots with the Mainland Chinese to screw them."

The president waved this away. "I know that, just do what you have to, to keep him off our backs."

"Yes, sir. What about Beijing? They sure as hell will ask us what's going on."

"Stall them. What else can we do?"

"I have a thought," Radford said.

"Let's hear it, Karl," said the president.

"It's still possible that the Taiwanese may think it was a local issue, a shoot-out between drug-lords."

"That's not going to hold up for very long," said Friedman.

"But it's better than nothing."

"The Chinese," said the president, "are not stupid. And didn't the *Reno* rough up one of their subs?"

"Yes, sir, but we've done it before and they never kicked," said Friedman.

"And what about the *White Dragon*? Scott reported that they annihilated her, vaporized her, I think he said. You can't hide that."

"No, sir, you can't. But Scott confirmed that there was nothing to tie us to her sinking."

"Nothing but that Kilo trailing them."

"So we play dumb," Friedman said. "The Chinese can't prove anything."

The president rose, went to the doors, and looked out at his wife toweling off after her swim. "All right, I'll buy that—for now," he said over a shoulder. "Paul, you'll have to work both sides of the street on this one. If Beijing starts asking questions, tell them what you tell Ambassador Hun."

"Sir, the Chinese ambassador is a bigger prick than Hun."

"Agreed." The president turned. "Karl, what's the next step?"

"As soon as the *Reno* arrives in Japan, we'll have a chance to assess the intel package Scott found on Matsu Shan."

"It's pretty thin stuff, you said."

"Yes, a single DVD but better than nothing. Scott will liase with the JDIH."

"In Tokyo?"

"Yes, sir. Their people are busting their chops to come up with someone we can tie to Marshal Jin."

"Think we can trust the Japanese on this one?" Friedman said.

"Paul, they've worked with us so far," Radford said. "If it wasn't for them we wouldn't even know about Matsu Shan. I don't understand what your problem is."

"They think the guy who met with Jin is a Japanese national, and they get squirrelly when one of their own people is involved," Friedman said. "It won't surprise me if they bail out on us or simply tell us they won't co-operate."

"Nonsense. I know DG Kabe, and he's committed to helping us. They have a huge stake in stopping Jin from threatening war. They're right in the middle if something goes wrong. Hell, the PM is at our feet over the missile agreement."

The president waved a hand. "Forget the agreement. Do what you think best, vis-à-vis the DG, Karl, but keep him on our side. The NKs have upped the vitriol and we may not have much time left to head off disaster. What's on your mind, Paul?"

"A small thing, but maybe a big thing."

"Well?"

"I seem to remember seeing a report—Karl, you

might be able to confirm this—that Scott's ex is currently in Tokyo with a Navy captain Rich Sterling, our military attaché accredited to the Japanese Self-Defense Force."

The president frowned. "Scott's ex. What of it?"

"Sir, I don't think it's a good idea for Scott and his ex-wife to get together at a time like this."

"Christ, Paul, leave it to you to think about Scott's domestic arrangements."

"Sir, someone has to think about it. Scott will have enough to do and doesn't need any distractions over there."

"My God, Paul, what makes you think Scott will hook up with his ex-wife? Besides, that's his prerogative. I mean, who are we . . ." The president hesitated. "Karl, what do you think?"

"Sir, Paul's right, Scott's ex-wife *is* over there, shacked up with Sterling. But I don't see a problem with that. Scott'll be working with Ms. Kida, at JDIH. She's perfectly capable of keeping his attention focused where it belongs."

"What's that supposed to mean?" asked the president.

"It means, sir," said Radford, "that she's smart and quite a looker."

"Ah, I get it."

Radford gave the president a thumbs-up.

25

Pyongyang

"He asks to see you, Dear Leader."

Marshal Jin, tired from his round trip to Matsu Shan, put aside his breakfast of steamed chicken, rice, and *kimch'i* and turned his attention to General Yi. "What does he want to see me about?"

"A private matter. He would not elaborate."

Jin drummed his fingers on his desk, careful not to disturb a *paduk*—Korean chessboard and pieces—while he studied Yi's pitted face. "I have no interest in hearing Kim speak of his private fantasies." He gave Yi a swift appraisal, saw something flicker behind the general's icy mask of restraint. "You may speak freely, Comrade General."

"With deepest respect, Dear Leader, I believe Kim wishes to discuss with you certain understandings he had with the United States."

Jin snorted. "*Certain understandings.* Which ones—the agreement to disarm, to dismantle our forces so the imperialists can walk into our country unopposed to build shopping malls and McDonald's and movie theaters that will enrich the Jewish financiers who run America? And was it not Kim Jong-il who promised that if war broke out he would kill thousands of GIs; shoot down thousands of American war planes; sink America's prized vessels of the Seventh Fleet, their aircraft carriers and submarines; devastate American bases; have all of this broadcast live on international television; and finally, launch long-range missiles at the United States and Japan? I know all about his so-called understandings with the imperialists. But as soon as they took out their checkbooks he turned into a yapping lapdog. That's why he's in detention in Chungwa and not sitting in this chair, here in Pyongyang."

Yi nodded but said nothing as he tired of standing and stepped back to ease himself into a chair. While Jin drummed his fingers, Yi lit a cigarette and inhaled twice before he said, "Perhaps, Dear Leader, there is something we are not aware of despite having total access to Kim's private files."

Jin's gaze bored into Yi. He despised Yi's tendency to circle endlessly around a matter before coming to the point. How he could command troops in the field was beyond comprehension. "Comrade, you test my patience. Please say what is on your mind."

"As you know, Dear Leader, rumors still circulate that Kim played the Americans for fools regarding the nuclear freeze agreement."

"Yes, what of it?"

"That he played them not only for fools but induced them to provide vast sums of money to ensure that the DPRK complied with the agreement."

"Those rumors have proven true. Five billion dollars have been paid by the United States government to the DPRK through secret Swiss accounts. Yes, Kim the lapdog blackmailed the Americans and they paid. The money went for improvements to our conventional forces and for nuclear engineering studies at Yongbyon. But we have known that for years."

"There are rumors that the Americans also paid Kim a billion dollars personally, which he has in a private account in Switzerland. Perhaps it is this money he wishes to discuss with you."

"You mean, Comrade General, that he wants to buy his way out of detention?"

"To buy his way into exile."

Again, Jin snorted. "He is mad if he thinks he could buy exile. There isn't enough money in the world for him to buy his way out of Chungwa. And if there was, where would he go? Who would have him?"

Yi smoked as he talked. "Perhaps his paymasters would see to it that he was welcome somewhere. A country perhaps in need of hard currency."

Jin said tartly, "I doubt it. The Americans' investment in Kim has gone up in smoke and they know it. What is it the Americans say, something about throwing good money after bad?"

"Perhaps, Dear Leader, but one should ask, what did Kim personally agree to provide in return for his billion dollars?"

Jin's eyes narrowed. "That the DPRK would disarm."

"Which brings us back to where we started."

"You talk in riddles. I have no patience—"

"With respect, Dear Leader, I only report what I have heard. He asked to speak with me as a conduit to you. I am reporting what he said, which was little, and what I could glean by listening to what he did not say. I am convinced he wants us to know that the billion dollars he received from the Americans purchased something of great value to them, which he may believe now might be used to purchase his exile."

"What do you think this valuable thing is?"

"I don't know, but perhaps it would be prudent to find out."

Marshal Jin recalled this conversation with General Yi as he entered the special detention center at Chungwa. If Kim Jong-il had information that was valuable, then Jin had to know what it was, had to get it out of Kim any way he could. He reminded himself to tamp down his irritation over the discovery that Kim, once again, held the upper hand even while in prison. Again and again Jin had asked himself how many other things he didn't know. It would be easy to convince himself that Kim was bluffing, that he had nothing worthy to barter, but he didn't believe it. Kim always had something to barter. This time it was information in return for his life. And money.

Jin hid his shock when he saw Kim Jong-il, first in the prison's video monitor, then in person in his cell. He looked skeletal from the loss of over eighty pounds. His jumpsuit, now prison green instead of powder blue, fit him like a sack. His shaggy gray-black beard and hair and patchy gray skin made him look old, like one of those ancient men who still worked the rice fields of North Korea. Kim didn't rise from his bunk when Jin entered, just shaded his eyes from the light streaming into the cell from the open door behind the marshal.

The door rang shut. Kim didn't look up at Jin, who started to speak but was cut off by Kim's croaking voice.

"What I have to say will not take long. There is a spy in place in the People's Hall of Government. He reports to the Americans everything we do and say."

Jin felt a freeze grip his body.

"He has been in place for over two years. The Americans paid me to have him installed."

Jin, his throat constricted, said, "Paid you a billion dollars—"

"To ensure he would not be uncovered."

"Where does he work?"

"I don't know. Perhaps the Second Directorate."

"How can you not know?"

"His identity was known only to the Americans through a defector. He was chosen by them. Part of the deal was that I not know his identity. It would protect him and me."

Jin exhaled a held-in breath. "The Second Directorate is the executive staff of the National Defense Commission." Like that of Kim Jong-il, Jin's chairmanship of the NDC provided the base for his power in North Korea. He felt sweat break on his bald pate. "Such a thing is not possible."

"Of course you would believe it is impossible."

Jin felt unsteady on his feet; the cell seemed to spin as if he were drunk. Everything that he had ever discussed concerning the partnership with Tokugawa, the Philippine operation, the nuclear weapons transfer to Vladivostok, their shipment by *Red Shark* had had its genesis in his office in the NDC, located in the Second Directorate. A question roared in his head: Tell Tokugawa or keep silent? Jin willed himself to regain equilibrium.

"That is all I have to say," Kim concluded.

"No, there is one more thing," Jin said calmly. "Who is the spy?"

For the first time Kim regarded Marshal Jin. "I told you, I don't know. But I can help you find him."

Jin looked down at the pitiable figure of Kim Jong-il. Once the Dear Leader, now nothing more than dog shit scraped from his boot. Yet in control of the situation. Suddenly Jin saw his plan crumbling to pieces. He saw the Americans launching a preemptive attack on North Korea. He wanted then and there to kill Kim Jong-il. He wanted him to die in agony, boiled alive in a lye vat or hung by his neck by wire that would slowly cause decapitation. He was on the brink of ordering the guards to haul Kim into the chamber from which no one ever emerged alive. Instead he said, "What is the price for your help to find the spy?"

"My freedom."

In Beijing, Admiral Shi Yunsheng greeted the latest decrypts from Admiral Chou's North Sea Fleet headquarters with a mixture of puzzlement and annoyance. He considered: Commander Deng Zemin had a close encounter with a U.S. Navy Los Angeles-class submarine; next he located an American special-operations minisubmarine lurking off Matsu Shan but was driven off; he witnessed the deliberate torpedoing of Wu Chow Far's *White Dragon*, not with one torpedo but two, to ensure there were no survivors.

Shi squared the documents and laced his fingers on top of the pile. It was clear that a standoff between the United States and North Korea was about to spin out of control. If it did, the People's Republic of China would be caught between two countries—one an outlaw nation, the other bent on the political and economic domination of the world—and both on a collision course that could set off a conflagration in East Asia and engulf the entire world.

Shi reached for the phone. "Connect me with President Yang."

*   *   *

Kana Asuka bowed deeply as Tokugawa entered the room. Tokugawa returned the favor and said, "Please join me, Kana-*san*."

Tokugawa escorted Kana through the main room of his villa, past priceless works of Japanese art displayed on walls and in glass cabinets. He led her to a cozy dining area warmed by a stone brazier filled with glowing coals, and to a low table, surrounded by cushions, that had been set for two. From behind floor-to-ceiling glass the dining area gave onto formal outdoor gardens illuminated by stone lanterns spotted along white gravel paths. Located in Noda, a small city just north of Tokyo, the villa was a veritable museum filled with Tokugawa's collection of priceless antique bronze sculpture, scrolls, lacquer work, and ceramics.

"The Iranian project was a great success," Tokugawa said.

"I am glad that Mohammad Khatami is pleased with the arrangement."

"And I am pleased that you have dealt with the matters needing immediate attention in such an efficient manner."

Kana turned from admiring the garden and said, "I am always at your disposal, Tokugawa-*san*. It is my great pleasure to provide whatever service you request."

Tokugawa gazed openly at Kana. She wore a man-tailored black silk suit with frog closures and Mandarin collar and had her hair drawn back in a tight bun that emphasized her flawless skin and makeup, her stunning beauty. Her grandfather, until his death, had been a business associate of Tokugawa's. Tokugawa marveled at how much like him she was—intelligent, devoted, discreet, and always cautious.

A shoji screen slid open and an elderly man entered,

carrying a tray of small covered dishes and glazed stoneware pots of warm saki. He arranged the food and drink to a prescribed fashion on the table, then withdrew.

"And the Japan Pacific War Veterans Association campaign, how does it progress?" Kana asked after a sip of rice wine taken from a paper-thin porcelain cup.

"Ah, we will soon undertake a media campaign to bring Japan's—the world's—attention to the forgotten deeds and sacrifices of our war heroes, men like my father and your grandfather. In their honor we will hold a rally at Yasukuni Shrine on the anniversary of the signing of the Pacific War peace treaty with the U.S."

Kana inclined her head and smiled delicately. "Your loyalty to my family is a treasured resource. I value it above all things."

After a short pause Tokugawa cleared his throat and with eyes sparkling said, "Your grandfather compared our heroes to the cherry blossoms of spring. He had a saying: 'Better to fall to earth after a brief moment of glory than to bloom and wither with time.' Our soldiers did not die in vain. They died for an emperor willing to risk his nation and his life for a cause he believed in."

Kana nodded thoughtfully. "You asked me, Tokugawa-*san,* to undertake certain financial transactions. I do not presume to understand why you want me to do these things; I am only the instrument through which the transactions are consummated. However, I feel it is necessary to point out the enormous risks you will have assumed through these proposed actions in the financial and real estate markets."

Tokugawa waved this aside. "I am fully aware of the risks. The portfolios, you have them with you?"

"Yes, for your review and approval. You will see that I

have organized the real estate portfolios into blocks ready for market. Having taken out the equity, when the U.S. market goes to zero, you can go back in with inflated yen, perhaps as high as twenty percent, and re-purchase. Also, your stocks in U.S. companies and U.S. Treasury bonds are set for sale. The conversion of billions of U.S. dollars to Japanese Government Bonds can be completed with the push of a computer key. If you carry out this plan, you will have turned the world's financial markets upside down overnight."

"Then there is no risk involved at all. Am I not betting on what the Americans would say is a sure thing?"

In the bridge cockpit atop the *Reno*'s sail, Jake Scott and McCoy Jefferson watched a Navy tug warp the sub into a berth at Yokosuka. The enlisted phonetalker had communications with the tug's skipper and relayed Deacon's maneuvering orders between the two vessels. Below, on the *Reno*'s rounded hull, linehandlers prepared to heave their mooring lines to waiting hands on the pier. The tug's screw churned the harbor water to a froth; the *Reno* slid sideways; the gap between her and the pier narrowed.

"Hell of a welcoming committee," Deacon cracked as he leaned out from the cockpit to check on his submarine's swing fore and aft, toward the pier's thick, tarry pilings. All hands topside tried not to notice the ambulance, doubling as a hearse, along with its crew of three Navy corpsmen, waiting to receive Ramos's body.

"Shit, we'll have all the welcoming committee we can handle," Jefferson said under his breath to Scott. "The General'll have a ton of questions for us to answer during debriefing. Hell, we'll be lucky to even see an O-club. Course you're heading for Tokyo and some fun."

Some fun, Scott thought. He gazed out over the glittering harbor, and beyond, the tank farms and structures sited around the sprawling naval base and its gray warships.

Scott knew he didn't have the answers Radford wanted. And he didn't see how what he had learned on Matsu Shan would help the JDIH put a name to the mystery man. He pictured Admiral Ellsworth blaming him for their failure to dig up more material, for setting off a firefight, for whatever else Ellsworth wanted to dredge up.

Maybe Jefferson was right, Scott mused—that he should have stuck to what he did best, driving submarines, not playing commando. He saw the two women dressed in black on Fat's terrace, saw them blown away, and with them the young girl with an AK-47 that was too big for her tiny hands. He felt his stomach lurch. He pictured the *White Dragon* being blown away too.

Still, the trip to Tokyo would be an opportunity to see Fumiko and . . . He forced an image of Tracy from his mind: *Stay away from her,* he told himself, *stay away.*

The OOD barking orders to the linehandlers and the motion of the ship warping in snapped him back to the present. He turned to Jefferson and said, "Come on ashore, Colonel, I'll buy you a drink at the O-club."

Part Three

THE TOKYO EXPRESS

26

Nam'po, DPRK

Commander Tongsun Park ordered the *Red Shark* back to port. A day that had included maneuvers with warships of the Korean People's Navy had turned sour. Poor performance by the *Red Shark*'s crew had angered Park: Officers manning the ship's integrated fire control system had had to abort two live torpedo launches at the last moment due to confusion and error. Park, humiliated by the miscues, had received a savage dressing-down from Admiral Jung-en Woo, Commander West Coast Fleet, who had observed the *Red Shark*'s maneuvers while aboard a destroyer.

Park commanded the most modern and deadly submarine in the DPRK's fleet. Based on a secret German design, the *Red Shark* had been built inside a hidden construction hall in Nam'po, using plans stolen by the DPRK's SPF—Special Purpose Forces—from the Germans. Her construction and shakedown over a four-year period had proven how complicated and demanding a vessel she was. Park still didn't fully comprehend the workings of her propulsion and combat systems.

The *Red Shark*'s propulsion system consisted of three components: a closed-cycle Thyssen diesel engine powered by liquid oxygen, argon gas, and diesel fuel; a lead acid battery set; and an air-independent propulsion—AIP—system. The AIP system utilized nine fuel cells filled with liquid oxygen and hydrogen reactants that produced electricity for low-speed cruising. For high underwater speeds, the *Red Shark* used her ultra-high-performance battery or the diesel engine itself.

Though Park had a hard time keeping the three components sorted out in his brain, he knew that new quieting technologies—rafted machinery platforms, elastic mounts for noise and vibration control—coupled to AIP made the *Red Shark* virtually undetectable. Add to that an ability to cruise submerged for over a month, and the *Red Shark* was the perfect instrument to carry out the mission assigned to her by Pyongyang.

Upon arrival in Nam'po, Park received another dressing-down from his squadron commander, a captain, who then handed Park a lengthy set of orders from Pyongyang. Park, in a black mood and sweating furiously from his ordeal, saw the label Most Secret attached to his orders, and also, in the originator box, a name he didn't recognize.

"General Yi is an aide to Marshal Jin, the Dear Leader," the captain explained.

Park read his orders and felt his mouth turn to cotton. "The Philippines?"

"Yes. The cargo you are to transport there will arrive here in four days."

"But—"

"There is a problem?" The captain's stony look cut Park like a knife.

"Comrade Captain, we, I—"

"Yes?"

"Sir, with respect, the crew of the *Red Shark* will need further training—at minimum another two weeks—if we are to undertake a voyage to the Philippines."

"If you cannot make the necessary preparations in the time allotted, I will relieve you of command."

Park knew there were no other skippers qualified to command the *Red Shark*. Still, he chose his words carefully, knowing that if he didn't say what the captain wanted to hear, he could end up in a penal colony.

Park saluted. "Comrade Captain, as ordered, I will prepare the *Red Shark* for the voyage and to receive the cargo."

"Dismissed!"

Jake Scott said, "I used to speak pretty good Japanese. Not anymore."

Fumiko gave him a test. In Japanese, she said something that required a stock response, heard Scott's garbled reply, and said, "You're right, your Japanese stinks. How long has it been?"

"Two years. Not only is my Japanese bad but Tokyo doesn't look the same either."

"Japan has undergone tremendous change. We almost don't recognize ourselves. Are we Eastern or Western? Who knows?"

"Western culture has had an irreversible influence wherever it touches down," Scott said. "I'm not always comfortable with the results I've seen."

Fumiko wheeled a Nissan Cedric sedan belonging to the JDIH onto the Shuto Expressway No. 4. They'd been battling rush hour since she'd met him with the car at Yokosuka. "Yes, especially in Japan." She took her eyes off

Tokyo traffic to glance at him. "Have you been to the city of Ise, in Mie Prefecture, to visit the shrine of the Sun Goddess Ameterasu-Omaikami?"

"The creator of the Japanese Islands."

"No trip to Japan is complete without a visit to the shrine."

"I've been there," Scott said, watching Fumiko thread through traffic. "A tourist trap is what I remember." He recalled the rituals, the crowds of people clapping their hands in worship, and priests in pastel-colored robes intoning prayers in an ancient tongue. And busloads of camera-snapping tourists.

"It's the price we pay for our Western ways," Fumiko said. "No one I know in Japan believes in gods anymore." She shrugged. "Younger Japanese have little respect for our bedrock traditions of duty and obligation to family and country, the very things that make us a unique and cohesive society."

"It's no different in the U.S."

Fumiko exited the expressway at Kasumigaseki, the government quarter south of the Imperial Palace grounds. "But there's been a resurgence of interest in *Bushido*."

"The way of the warrior."

"*Bushido* and its adherents are very controversial today because many Japanese associate it with the Pacific War. Even so, there are those who revere the Spartan devotion to the arts of war, self-defense, loyalty to comrades. It's almost a religion for a group of older, wealthy Japanese who want to make national heroes of General Tojo and General Yamashita. Amazing, isn't it, that behind our veneer of modernity are men who long for the lost glory and power of Imperial Japan."

"Who are these men?"

"Have you ever heard of the Japan Pacific War Veterans Association?"

"No."

She explained the association's basic aims, then said, "Its members consist of a shadowy group that includes wealthy industrialists, financiers, barons of the ruling party, even former war criminals. Their identities are secret. It's said that these men control Japan, that some even serve as personal advisors to the prime minister and the Diet. The polite term the press uses is *genro*, elder statesmen. In America you would call them a shadow government.

"Of course there's nothing new about this. I mean, just look at the old secret societies like the Order of the Rising Sun, the Cherry Blossom Society, or the Black Dragon Society. Most Japanese are indifferent to the Pacific War, but there are others, members of the association, who see Japan as a victim of Western xenophobia, no matter that we are the most xenophobic people on earth. Our schools teach that Japan has nothing to be ashamed of for her role in the war. And since the right wing essentially rules Japan, they've effectively crushed any opposition to their point of view."

"You mean no one questions the propriety of restoring the reputations of war criminals?"

"Jake, after two newspaper publishers asked why the association would honor war criminals assigned to Unit 731—"

"The unit that conducted medical experiments on U.S. and Chinese prisoners in Manchuria."

"Yes . . . the publishers narrowly escaped assassination. After that, the press backed off its criticism. Believe me, the association knows how to intimidate the opposition. Also, someone fired shots at the house of an author who wrote that Hirohito was a clever politician who manipulated MacArthur and Truman to escape indictment as a war criminal."

"Maybe those publishers and that author forgot that assassination is an honorable tradition in Japan."

"So is dying for a cause, at least that's what the association preaches. As I said, its members are very influential. Rumor has it they recently lobbied the prime minister to accept the missile defense system America has offered and that they want Japan to have a nuclear deterrent. It's been said that a wealthy Japanese has even offered to pay to have one built."

"But that's insane—"

"Is it, now that North Korea has nuclear weapons and is ruled by this Marshal Jin? The question is—"

"The question is, has one of these association members made a secret deal with Jin, perhaps to get hold of nuclear weapons?"

She kept her eyes on the road as she weaved expertly around slower-moving traffic entering central Tokyo. "I've asked myself the same question, which is why I've started delving into who the members of the association are. Maybe one of them has a connection to Marshal Jin."

"Okay, I'm listening."

She touched his arm. "Not until I share what I have with the director of my division."

"Have it your way."

"Jake, I know we're working together on this, but remember, this is Japan, not the States. I have to follow certain procedures. As for the association, I know it sounds crazy, but . . ." She shrugged, perhaps mystified by her country's tendency to embrace such seemingly outdated, if not sinister, concepts. "I guess that's why we Japanese are so misunderstood in the West."

Scott glanced at her and saw a beautiful and modern Japanese woman. And a confident one, too. "I don't know, we seem to be getting along just fine," he said.

She smiled at him and said, "We are, aren't we?"

Uniformed, white-gloved officers waved her through a security barrier and down the steep ramp leading to the underground parking garage of the Japan Defense Intelligence Headquarters, where daylight gave way to sodium vapor lamps. She wheeled into a marked parking space. "Ready to meet the director of my division?"

"Ready."

27

JDIH Headquarters

"*Irasshai*—Welcome—Commander Scott." With hands held flat against his thighs, Director of Technical Services Matsu Kubota, a small, wiry man in a black suit, bowed deeply and said, "It is such a pleasure to meet you." Kubota's eyes lingered momentarily on Scott's bandaged hand, but he said nothing.

Behind Kubota's cordiality Scott sensed a coldness, if not outright hostility, to his presence. Fumiko's confident manner had given way to apprehension, which confirmed for Scott his assessment of Kubota.

Scott returned Kubota's bow, aware that Western-style informality had not yet penetrated the inner sanctums of the male-dominated Japanese intelligence and defense services.

Kubota led them into a cramped conference room deep inside the blocky headquarters. For the first time Scott noticed that the building had no windows. The air was uncomfortably dry and dead from being continuously recycled through the structure's antiradiological and antibiological purification system. Even so, cigarette smoke had permeated the room and its cheap furnishings.

Scott was introduced to a roomful of bowing Japanese, whom Kubota described as his technical aides. The men, like Kubota, wore black suits, white shirts, and narrow gray ties. They smiled politely, and each one said something to Scott in Japanese.

Kubota motioned Scott to sit at the head of the table, a place reserved for special guests. The aides took places around the table, which was cluttered with laptop computers and paper files, and immediately lit cigarettes and passed around ashtrays.

Kubota opened a flush panel in the conference table's surface and manipulated a control to activate a flat-screen video monitor covering most of one wall. Fumiko, without being asked, served everyone bitter green tea and sticky rice cakes, after which Kubota got started in flat, but surprisingly unaccented, English.

"Here, Commander Scott, is the sequence of images from the digital video disc you provided."

Murky at first, the images brightened as two men walked left to right from the main room of Fat's villa, onto the veranda. Scott recognized it and saw where he had come up over the wall around the veranda and thrown the grenade at the drug-traffickers who'd been shooting at the SEALs on the road below the villa. He felt a knot in his guts.

He watched the two men speak and gesture to each other—there was no sound—and though the image wasn't sharp or well lighted, he could easily identify Marshal Jin from his bald head and crisp features. Jin stopped, turned toward the lighted room from which they had just exited, and, lit by both incandescent and candlelight, turned again until he was facing the hidden camera that had recorded the images up on the monitor.

"Commander Scott, the man on your left is North Korean Marshal Kim Gwan Jin," said Kubota.

"Right, we identified him when we viewed the DVD in Yokosuka. It's the other guy we can't put a name to."

"Yes, to put a name to him is not so easy."

Kubota froze the image, stopping Jin's guest in midstride. His face was in deep shadow as he conversed with Jin. A faint scrim of incandescent light revealed that he had a head of silver hair.

"Unfortunately," said Kubota, "we cannot identify this man. Not yet anyway. We have run these images through our identity program, which can turn a figure one hundred and eighty degrees and re-create features we can't see. Yet we have no suitable imagery of his face."

One of the aides said something to Kubota.

Kubota said, *"Hai,"* then to Scott he said, "He says that if we had even a fraction more face to work with, had he turned slightly toward the hidden camera, we could likely reconstruct the face. But without it we are lost."

"And there are no other images suitable, Director-*san*?" Fumiko asked.

"No. None. We have tried to open the dark areas in the image, for instance when the two men step onto the veranda, but the shadow densities are so heavily blocked that we can't alter the pixels."

Another aide spoke up. Kubota nodded. "He says there is an image lasting less than a thousandth of a second, where this other man passes from light to dark, when his face is turned more to the camera. But motion-drag caused by color temperatures above 5500 Kelvin has distorted the image beyond retrieval."

"Director Kubota, please run the sequence again," said Scott.

The men moved from the room to the veranda, then

out of camera range. Kubota ran it three more times. Scott, Jefferson, and Radford, via SVTC, had studied the sequence at Yokosuka until they'd been sick of looking at it. Turn them over to the JDIH, Radford had said. They can work miracles. *Apparently not*, thought Scott.

"If you can't identify him from this DVD, Director Kubota, what other choices do we have?"

"Ah, but Commander Scott, I did not say we could not identify him, I said we could not identify him *yet*. We will work on it until we can. We have some experimental software that we can try out. It is not fully developed, but we Japanese rarely are defeated."

Scott looked around at the smiling faces. At Fumiko with fingers to her lips. "How long will that take?" Scott asked. "We don't have time to waste on experiments that might not work."

"That I can't say. We will start immediately. In the meantime, I can give you some idea what we have been doing to make progress on other fronts."

Fumiko spoke up. "Director-*san*, I have begun to develop a list of possible candidates for investigation. Japanese men who might have legitimate dealings with the North Koreans. Or men that have business interests that would put them in a position to have contact with North Korea, specifically, with Marshal Jin."

"What kind of information?" Scott prompted her.

Kubota interjected, "Ms. Kida is mistaken. We are not investigating only Japanese individuals, but Asian as well as Middle Eastern. The North Koreans conduct business with individuals from all over the world. It would be a mistake to assume that only Japanese have access to North Korea."

Scott said, "You'll pardon my American manners, Director Kubota, I'm not inclined to sugar-coat what I say, but we were told that JDIH cell phone intercepts indicated that this individual was a Japanese national."

Kubota gave Scott a head bob. "I apologize for that, Commander Scott. Unfortunately Miss Kida was wrong, and you were unintentionally given false information."

Fumiko inhaled sharply and said, "But Director—"

Kubota glared at Fumiko, daring her to contradict him.

Scott saw thin smiles appear on the aides' faces, and looming on the video screen over their heads at the end of the conference room, the freeze-framed image of Marshal Jin and the mystery man. "If what you say is so, Director Kubota, do you have any solid leads on who this man might be?"

"Ah, Commander Scott, you ascribe to the JDIH the powers of a, what you call, miracle worker. Yes, we are working on it, as I say. What we have done so far is to comb our import-export license requests for anything out of the ordinary. We look for new shipments of industrial and agricultural goods to North Korea. We have also begun an examination of any recent trade talks that may have been brokered by third parties. For instance, we had a Pakistani group arrive in Japan, which then met with the North Korean trade minister about a food exchange program. We have looked at some rudimentary currency transactions to see if there is anything unusual. A Belgian group recently applied for Japanese trade credits which would be transferable to North Korea. Also the Syrians. So you see, Commander Scott, it is not only the Japanese who have dealings with the North."

One of the aides spoke rapid Japanese to the director.

"Ah, yes, he reminds me, Commander Scott, and I am sure Ms. Kida has told you this, we have checked various airline passenger manifests to determine if any name, an important name, might be found on them."

"But Japan has no air service to North Korea."

"True. But as you know there are other ports of entry to North Korea—China, Taiwan, Cambodia, Vietnam, Singapore . . . you see my point."

"What the Director says is correct," Fumiko said, in an attempt to save face. "And we cannot monitor all possible methods of travel by individuals to countries that have diplomatic relations with the DPRK."

"So what do I tell my people?" Scott asked.

Kubota clicked off the DVD. The aides closed their laptops. Kubota steepled his fingers on the table and, like the prow of a ship, pointed them at Scott. "You can tell General Radford, for whom I have only the greatest respect and esteem, that we are pursuing this, as you Americans would say, twenty-four-seven. What I will do, Commander Scott, is order a full report on the information we have up to the present time. I will, if you wish, transmit this to the general, or you may discuss it with him here, at JDIH Headquarters via secure video link. Understand that our offices are yours. The report will include our conclusions regarding the DVD and also our best guess based on the material we have assembled who we think the man with Marshal Jin may be."

"And when will this report be ready?"

Kubota stood. "I will have the report completed in twenty-four hours, Commander Scott. In the meantime I hope you enjoy your stay in Tokyo."

28

The Ginza

"He's lying."

Fumiko lifted her eyes, from her drink to Scott. "Why would Kubota lie?"

The owner of the *ryotei*—a traditional Japanese restaurant—whom Fumiko knew, arrived with steaming dishes of food.

Fumiko, eyes still on Scott, pretended not to notice as he fumbled chopsticks with his bandaged hand.

"You tell *me* why he'd lie," Scott said.

After a long moment Fumiko said, "They're protecting someone."

Scott said nothing.

"The JDIH is protecting the man who met with Jin," she added.

"Okay, but why?"

"I don't know."

"Sure you do. He's someone important; very important."

"Someone close to the government, to the prime minister," Fumiko said thoughtfully.

"Maybe he's involved in something illegal, something the government would rather not have the out-side world know about."

"Terrorism," she said. "You think this man's a terrorist?"

"No, but maybe he's financing terrorism. After all, that's what Jin is, a terrorist. A nuclear terrorist. Maybe this man is an advocate of *Bushido*."

Fumiko drank saki while she mulled that over.

"If he is, it might make your job easier," Scott said.

"What job is that?"

More food arrived. More saki, too. After the owner departed, Fumiko said, "Would you please explain what you just said?"

Scott sat back on his cushions and said, "Did I tell you, Fumiko-*san*, that *taihen utsukushii desu*—you are very beautiful."

She looked down and blushed. "You have suddenly regained your command of Japanese," she said with mock sternness.

"It took me a while to memorize and was meant as a compliment, not a pass."

"In that case, *arigato. Taihen shinsetsu desu.*"

"What? . . ."

"I said, 'Thank you. You are very kind.' But you didn't answer me. Make what job easier to do?"

"If this man is so important he warrants the protec-tion of the JDIH, it should be fairly easy to figure out who he is. How many men in Japan other than the PM would have access to Jin? Only a handful, right? So who are they? You said you'd started looking into the mem-bership of the Japan Pacific War Veterans Association. You also said they were advocates of *Bushido*. Sounds to me like you might be on to something."

"You heard what the director said. He could be any nationality, not just Japanese."

"And you believe that?"

Fumiko pushed her meal aside. "Even if I don't, I don't see what else I can do. Kubota runs the division, and I can't go through him to get more information. He controls everything. And as you saw, he's not happy with me and with you, an American, looking over his shoulder."

"Me, I can understand, but what did you do to make him unhappy?"

"First of all, Kubota lives in the past, when Japanese women were useful mostly for serving tea and for being fucked."

Her words, Scott realized, were not meant to shock but to demonstrate the depth of her smoldering frustration over the treatment that she and other female employees experienced at JDIH. And throughout Japan itself.

"Second, I brought him the original Jin decrypts I had analyzed and which he dismissed until my evaluation of them forced him to admit I was right, that there was a meeting about to be held on Matsu Shan. He didn't want me to liase with the SRO, but Director General Kabe gave the okay over Kubota's objections. But somewhere along the line something changed. I think maybe when Kubota viewed the DVD."

"Then Kubota's lying about not being able to identify that man from the DVD images."

"Possibly. I don't know enough about their capabilities. They're kept under tight wraps."

"If he's lying, it goes all the way to the top, maybe even to the DG himself."

"Jake, that's a serious charge."

"It's a serious thing we're dealing with, nuclear blackmail, terrorism. Maybe a war on the peninsula."

"Look, if the DG believed they had information about something that could potentially affect not only the U.S. but also Japan and all of East Asia, he wouldn't protect the identity of one of the men involved. After all, the DG and Kubota are friends with General Radford. They wouldn't hide something this important from him, not when North Korea could explode at any minute."

"Okay, maybe I'm way off base, maybe the DG doesn't know what Kubota knows, in which case you should tell him what you suspect."

"No way. The JDIH is layered with protocol. You don't see the DG without a year's advance notice and approval from Kubota. Kubota's the gatekeeper."

Scott considered. "We need to find out what Kubota knows about this mystery man."

Fumiko gave Scott an exasperated look. "Jake, this isn't one of those seat-of-the-pants operations you're famous for. This is the JDIH, and this is Japan."

Scott frowned. "Who told you that? McCoy Jefferson?"

"Let's just say I know some things about you, Dubrovnik, the Yellow Sea. I also know that what happened wasn't your fault."

"Thank you. You seem to be one of the few people who believe that."

"Jake, listen to me. You don't go off freelancing here. It isn't done."

"Even if Kubota's hiding something?"

"He's my boss."

"Do you know what's at stake?"

"Where do you think I've been? On Mars? Of course I know. War's brewing between"—she lowered her voice—"the U.S. and North Korea. I'm the one who cracked the messages, brought them to Kubota's attention, I'm the one—"

"All the more reason to find out what Kubota's covering up."

"I'm sorry, but you're jumping to conclusions."

Scott said no more, and they finished their meal, cold though it was. After dinner, which Fumiko insisted on paying for, they returned to her car. It had started to rain, and the streets were shiny and seemingly running with liquid color from the Ginza's riotous electric signage.

"Think about what I said," Scott said, as they rose in a tiny elevator to the upper level of a narrow parking garage crammed between two high-rises.

"I don't want to think about it," Fumiko said.

They stood in their own envelope of space, taking each other's pulse. He heard her breathing, smelled the musky aroma of her tailored wool suit and perfume. She kept her eyes down, as if to ward off any further discussion that would force her to Scott's position.

The juddering elevator stopped; its doors ground open.

Scott waited for her to unlock the car. She hesitated, then looked up at him, so close he could feel her warmth. "You understand my position? . . ."

"Of course," Scott said. "You'll do what's right, I know you will."

She gave him a questioning look, but he cut it off by putting a fingertip to her chin. "Enough for one night," he said.

"Thank you." Her lips brushed his cheek, and he smelled a hint of alcohol on her breath. "I wanted to say that I was very happy you were not . . ." She touched his bandaged hand. "Injured." She compressed her lips and searched for the right words. "More severely, I mean . . . there was Ramos and . . ."

"I know what you mean. Thanks for your concern."

Somewhere, footsteps echoed off cold concrete. A car door slammed shut. An engine started. Tires squealed down a ramp.

Fumiko unlocked the car. "I'll take you back to your hotel."

The man heard a hiss in his earphone, then the voice of a team member from inside the parking garage. "On their way out."

A moment later, the man, seated behind the wheel of a cab, its red sign showing In Use, spoke into a hidden throat mike, "*Hai*. I have them."

Fumiko swung into Ginza traffic, and the cab fell in behind her car.

29

"Mr. Jacob"

Midnight. The *b-r-r-r-ing* phone sounded like a sub-machine gun rattling in his head. Scott got his bearings, picked up the receiver. "Yeah, Scott."

Silence.

"Who's this?"

"Did you think I would call?" She was on a cell phone, her voice perfectly clear.

A trip-hammer went off in his chest. "Tracy?"

"Are you alone?"

Scott swung his legs out of bed. "Yes. Where are you? How did you find me?"

"I heard you were in town."

"No one knew, or was supposed to know. How? . . ."

"People at the embassy know everything."

His arrival in Tokyo had been arranged to avoid any contact with United States Embassy personnel. But someone, someone Scott knew, had found out he was there and told Tracy.

"What you mean is, Rick Sterling knows everything," he said acidly.

"All Rick said was that you were in town and in

Class-C quarters. I called every cheap hotel in Tokyo asking for a Mr. Jacob. Really, you should change your cover name."

"Is that what Rick said?"

"He doesn't know I'm calling you."

"I'll bet. Be careful he doesn't find out and—"

"Can't you let it go?"

"Sure."

Silence.

"What do you want?" he asked. "Are you all right?"

"I don't want anything."

"Just want to talk, huh?"

"Maybe."

"Where are you? I'll pick you up, we'll have a drink."

"I don't want to."

"What you mean is you don't want to see *me*."

"Maybe that's it. Maybe I don't know."

"Rick seems to have you confused."

"I told you, let it go."

"Sure."

Another silence.

"How long will you be in Tokyo?"

"Trace, this isn't a secure phone. And you know I can't—"

"What, tell me anything? Sure, sure, I know how that works."

"Maybe you'd better let that one go, too."

"Sorry."

"My offer stands."

"To what, get me in bed with you, fuck my brains out, is that what you want? What's the matter, no slant-eyed honey to keep you warm tonight?"

"Knock it off. You're the one who called. What's it going to be?"

"I told you, I just wanted to talk."

Scott waited, listening to her soft breathing.

"I suppose you're okay," she said.

"A few new bumps, that's all."

"Your ship, she's? . . ."

"Trace, I'm just a businessman, Mr. Jacob, here on company business, remember?"

At length Tracy said, "I wanted you to know that I'm not coming back to the States, not for a while, anyway."

Scott's mouth went dry and his breath caught in his throat. She always had that effect on him, even now, in Tokyo, over a cell phone. "Sure, those military attaché assignments are at least two-year hitches. It'll give you and Rick plenty of time to see the sights in Japan together. Maybe even learn Japanese."

"You haven't changed, have you? You're still a bastard, you know that, don't you?"

"So I've been told. Do you want to get together tonight or not?"

"No."

"Then where can I reach you?"

"I have a cell phone." He copied down the number as she gave it to him.

"Where are you living?"

"Never mind that. Look, I'm sorry to call so late. I shouldn't have bothered you."

"Trace, wait." The call ended. He thought to call her back but decided not to. Wait her out, he told himself. See what she really wants. Better yet, don't. Don't risk it. Don't die twice.

30

JDIH Headquarters

Director Kubota bowed to Scott. "*Konnichi wa*—Hello." He smiled without warmth. His aides followed suit. Fumiko, who had arrived separately and slightly out of breath, stood silently to one side. She looked tired and haggard, as if she'd not slept at all last night.

"I am so sorry to report, Commander Scott," said Kubota, "that at this time we cannot identify the other man in the video recording. However, I have prepared a full report on the matter for you and the esteemed General Radford. We will continue to work on this until we identify him, but for now we have, ah, certain technical difficulties with the identity software. The director general has authorized that as we develop information, we pass it on to the SRO as soon as possible."

Kubota lifted a thin bound report off the conference table and handed it to Scott. "These are our conclusions. Photos and appendices are included for your convenience."

"That's it?" Scott said. "This is all you can come up with? There has to be some way to identify this man."

"Not at this time," Kubota said, an edge to his voice.

"I remind you, Director, that the United States is facing a hostile North Korean regime armed with nuclear weapons. What strategy we develop to confront the DPRK may depend on our ability to identify this man, who, we were given to understand, is a Japanese national."

"And I told you yesterday, Commander Scott, Ms. Kida's conclusions that he is a Japanese national have not been confirmed." Kubota said this softly but with an undertone of controlled anger. "You are welcome to use our facilities to discuss this matter with General Radford. Sato, here, will arrange the video conference setup if you wish."

"Director . . ."

Kubota turned his gaze on Fumiko, who gave him a slight head bow.

"Director, I worked through the night to compile this list of names of the men who might possibly have reason to meet with Marshal Jin. The list includes, as you have suggested it might, several influential individuals from Pacific Rim countries. Most prominent, however, are three Japanese who—"

"Give me the list," Kubota commanded.

Fumiko complied, handed Kubota a folder, and flashed Scott a look. Kubota skimmed her data, then quickly closed the folder and tucked it under an arm. There was an air of silent tension in the conference room.

Kubota, in a seemingly pleasant but condescending tone, said, "As you know, Commander Scott, Miss Kida is one of our most valued analysts. She is exceptionally bright and eager to help."

Scott caught Fumiko's embarrassment.

"She is due full recognition for her work on this matter," Kubota continued, "for the way she has conducted the briefings in Washington and for her devotion to maintaining the high professional relationship established between General Radford's office and our own."

"Those names she compiled," Scott said pointedly. "May I see them?"

"Ah, I am so sorry, Commander Scott, but the answer is no. I will take them under study and let you know our conclusions. Until then"—he turned his gaze on Fumiko—"the information in this report is classified *Himitsu*—Secret, Director General Only. Miss Kida is not, therefore, permitted to discuss it further."

Fumiko started to say something but cut herself off.

Scott said, "But you *will* share those names with your esteemed friend General Radford, won't you?"

The room went icy silent. Kubota and the aides seemed frozen in place.

"Thank you for your time, Director, Ms. Kida." Scott gave them each a slight head bob. "I will make separate arrangements to brief General Radford. He'll be very interested in your findings."

Fumiko opened the front door to the apartment block but stopped cold when she saw a shadowy figure approach. "What are you doing here?" she said, not at all pleased to see him.

"We have to talk," Scott said.

"No, we don't. I've been taken off the investigation. My security clearance has been lowered and I've been ordered to have no further contact with you. Now please leave."

"I'm sorry, Fumiko, I can't do that. It's too important."

She made a face. "Jake—"

"Make us some tea."

Fumiko's apartment in the Shibuya section of Tokyo was minuscule: a small room doubling as dining area and bedroom. It was furnished with a sofa, table, and rolled-up futon bedding, and it had a cramped galley kitchen, miniature bathroom, and a postage-stamp-sized window that looked out on an alley crisscrossed with CATV and phone lines strung on poles.

"How did you find me?" she asked, brewing tea. She looked worn from lack of sleep; her lovely, almond-shaped eyes lacked their normal glitter.

"I came to Tokyo fully equipped. The SRO had your personal information on file. I just jumped on the Shibuya JR line and walked on over."

"How did you know I'd come home directly after work?"

"I didn't, just hoped you would. Look, I'm sorry about what happened this morning, but maybe now you'll believe that the JDIH is protecting someone."

Fumiko poured tea and put out sweet rice treats but said nothing.

"The list of names you compiled," Scott said. "You must have made a copy. I have to have it."

"I can't give it to you. You heard what Kubota said, it's *Himitsu*—Secret, Director General Only."

"Bullshit! He's afraid you'll expose someone he or the DG is protecting."

Fumiko balled her hands into fists and said, "This is Japan, not the U.S., damn it. You Americans don't run things here. You don't understand how things work here. You're not our bosses. We take security very seriously, and breaching it is a civil offense, jail and all that."

Scott sat down beside her on the sofa and sipped the brewed tea. "Fumiko, I don't have to tell you how important this is. If you have names, I have to have them." It occurred to him that Fumiko's apartment might be bugged, but he pressed on anyway. "I have to have a starting point for the SRO to find out what the hell the North Koreans are up to."

"And what do the people you work for in Washington think the NKs are up to?" she said, a note of defiance in her voice. "Tell me. You have had plenty of time to figure it out. You were on the submarine and on Matsu Shan. What do *you* think?"

He acknowledged her bitter tone and didn't blame her. She had only done her job, and now she was being treated by the JDIH as if she were a security risk.

"All right, I'll tell you what I think."

He got up and used a wand to turn on the TV set. He raised the volume of the game show on the NHK network to create a voice blocker that might neutralize any hidden listening devices.

"I think the North Koreans want to launch a preemptive attack on the United States but don't have the means. The man Jin met on Matsu Shan plays some part in the NKs' plan. But I don't know what part. Maybe he has something they need to launch an attack. Money, technology, whatever. Right now I don't know why this man would help the North Koreans and I don't have any idea who he is. Maybe what you found in the files will provide answers. All I know is that my gut tells me I'm right."

Fumiko had a hand to her mouth. "A preemptive *nuclear* attack—"

"Yes."

"Launched by missiles or—"

"Or delivered by terrorists."

After a long moment of silence Fumiko looked down at her cold tea and said, "You're right. Kubota and the DG *are* protecting someone. Last night after I dropped you off at your hotel I returned to headquarters and accessed the JDIH deep-classified computer files. It took all night, and I finished just before the meeting this morning. I keyed in the names of eighteen men that I had suspected might have a possible connection to Marshal Jin and the DPRK. I winnowed the list to seven names. Each one came up in what are called Bureau Files, daily updates on an individual's activities both in and outside of Japan. Three of those names had been given Denied Access status. The files were sealed and also had reporting tags linked to the DG's personal computer system."

"By reporting tags, you mean the system records your name and access code so they can tell who's been asking for information." He pictured the JDIH computer system, which was capable of processing over a hundred septillion operations a second and working in time chunks of femtoseconds, tripping over Fumiko's intrusion into the agency's deepest and darkest secrets. He could almost hear the drawbridge squeal as it rose over the moat to block access to such privileged information.

"I got past the seals without any trouble, but it must have set off a secondary alarm in the DG's office and in Kubota's, too. That's why he appropriated and classified the file I presented at the meeting this morning and why, by this afternoon, I'd been downgraded from top clearance to mid. Tomorrow I may even be fired or"—she shrugged her shoulders—"arrested."

"What did you find?" Scott asked.

"Things no one is supposed to know. Like reports to the JDIH by the United States Treasury Department and the Securities and Exchange Commission. The reports are only days old, so I doubt Kubota, much less the DG, has had time to review them."

"What kind of reports?"

"Financial information about business liquidations,

sell-offs, that sort of thing. In one case it seems almost as if the person is preparing for the U.S. financial markets to collapse."

"Where's your copy of the list?"

She looked at him like a child who feared being punished for an infraction of house rules. "Jake, it will only make things worse."

"Jesus Christ. Wake up, Fumiko! What could be worse than a nuclear attack on the U.S.?"

31

Shibuya, Tokyo

She came out of the bathroom after flushing the toilet and handed him the list. Where she'd hidden it, he could only guess. He scanned it and saw that she had assembled not just a list of names but also information on the men's business interests and holdings, as well as their approximate net worth. It was a list that dealt in superlatives: billions of dollars; scores of owned companies. These were seven Japanese tycoons favored with enormous wealth and power, men who likely could influence events at home and abroad by simply picking up a phone and speaking to a president, prime minister, or king anywhere in the world.

"The three names that were sealed are at the top of the list," Fumiko said over the TV game announcer's shrill Japanese.

"Iwao Suzuki, Shinjire Atami, Iseda Tokugawa."

"Three of the wealthiest men in the world," Fumiko affirmed.

"I'm listening," Scott said and sat down again.

"Suzuki and Atami head Japan's largest banks. Suzuki got involved in a series of suspicious transactions of Euro futures through a bank affiliate in Zurich. The Japan central bank, with the help of the central bank of Switzerland, traced the activity to a single wealthy private client of Suzuki. This client, a Saudi, has dealt with North Korea as far back as 1985. Ultimately Suzuki got nailed for illegal transfers of oil and gas equipment, and shipments of crude oil from Saudi Arabia. It was this client, with help from Suzuki, who defrauded several European banks. The Japanese government held off prosecuting Suzuki, who in turn agreed to give his unlimited financial support to the prime minister's current bid for reelection."

"No wonder this was buried in the computer files."

"As for Atami, he had brokered a deal with the South Koreans to expatriate billions of won through South American banks, which, when converted to dollars, would allow the North Korean government to buy raw materials and technology from Pakistan for their reactor complex at Yongbyon."

"And what did Atami get in return?"

"A guarantee that Kim Jong-il would finance all his future industrialization programs through Atami's Japan United Bank. When Japan's Ministry of Finance discovered Atami's dealings with Kim, they threatened to close him down. Instead he—"

"Let me guess, Atami's fortune helped the prime minister get reelected."

Fumiko cleared her throat and said defensively, "Financial corruption is not a disease indigenous just to Japan."

"What about this other guy, Tokugawa?"

"He frightens me, Jake, he really does. He's head of Meji Holdings, a conglomerate of trading companies stretching across East Asia. He also has vast holdings in the U.S. and, lately, Russia.

"Meji was founded after World War II by Jinjiro Asuka, a former war criminal. After his release from prison in 1951, he started his company, literally, in a garage, and when Asuka died in 1968, Meji was the largest trading company of its kind in Asia. Asuka's son, Kaza, took over, ran the company until he died in 1980. Kaza's son took control but died under mysterious circumstances in 1987. There is a granddaughter, but nothing is known about her."

"What mysterious circumstances?"

"*Seppuku*. Suicide."

"How did Tokugawa become involved?"

"His father and Jinjiro Asuka were friends and served in the army during the war."

"At Unit 731?"

"Yes. Both were indicted as war criminals, but Tokugawa's father committed suicide before he was brought to trial in 1946. Tokugawa's mother and siblings perished at Nagasaki. Both incidents apparently had a lasting effect on Tokugawa."

"How so?"

"From what I read, he hates the United States with a passion."

"Yet invests heavily in U.S. corporations. Go on."

"Asuka treated the young Tokugawa as his son, brought him into the business when he was eighteen. Now, Tokugawa has outlived them all." She hesitated.

"What else?"

"The scary part. The file I saw revealed that Tokugawa is head of the Japan Pacific War Veterans Association."

"Christ, one of those *Bushido* devotees," Scott said. "Doesn't surprise me. You?"

"I suppose not, given what we know about him."

Scott got up and paced the tiny apartment. "What businesses does he—Meji—own?"

"Just about everything. Electronics, communications, shipbuilding, steel, airlines, even a high-tech facility in Vladivostok."

"So what connection does he have to North Korea, to Marshal Jin? Did you see anything in the file about that?"

"No, there was nothing."

"Then, what possible reason would he have to finance a North Korean nuclear attack on the U.S.? What proof is there that he would?"

"Jake, he's divested Meji of almost all of its holdings in the United States. For instance, according to the SEC reports I saw, there's been an extraordinary level of activity in stocks owned by Meji: Billions of shares have been sold and apparently converted to yen. The Federal Reserve also reported large-scale liquidation of dollars and their conversion to yen, along with holdings in bonds and other corporate financial instruments."

"How many brokers has he worked through? Any idea?"

"Just a few. Big ones, mostly in New York. Tokugawa held positions in only five names, didn't spread it out, and as a result it was easier for the SEC's Stock Watch to track and report it. Of course there's nothing illegal about what he's done. On top of that, Tokugawa has converted over three billion dollars to yen, which he deposited in JGBs—Japanese government bonds. He's stockpiling cash, Jake, any way he can."

"In yen, not dollars."

"That's right. As for Meji's real estate, it appears that he's decided to take out the equity in over twenty properties owned in New York, Chicago, and Washington,

D.C. Overnight he's refinanced them, converting their equity into yen, but leaving his debt in dollars. And get this—if he wants to, he can later go back into the real estate market with inflated yen and buy it all back for far less than what he sold it for."

"So he's suddenly a high liquidator; he's getting out of U.S. markets; he's reducing his exposure. Why?" Scott said.

"Because he thinks—"

"Because he *knows* that the U.S. financial markets are about to collapse. And why does he *know*? Because his North Korean friends must have a plan to attack the United States with nuclear weapons."

"But why would he help the North Koreans?" Fumiko said. "I mean, *how* would he help them? What are his motives?"

"I was told the North Koreans have nuclear warheads sitting on the border south of Vladivostok, where Tokugawa has high-tech facilities. I'm no expert on nukes, but maybe he has people who can weaponize those crude nukes into miniatures for launching from missiles. Right now there's a debate going on in Washington about whether or not to take out those weapons."

Fumiko shook her head in disbelief. "Jake, if they do, it will solve nothing. The NKs have more warheads hidden in sites all over North Korea."

"But not suitable for launching by missile. Didn't you tell me Tokugawa and the association members offered to finance and build a nuclear arsenal for Japan? Maybe he *can* do it, at that."

"Jake, that doesn't make sense, does it?"

"I don't know." He ran a hand through his hair. "I really don't." He felt confused and totally out of his depth, and he knew he was grasping at straws.

"Motive, you said he had to have a motive."

"Revenge. His father, family. But maybe there's something else, something much more powerful driving him—a chance to make Meji Holdings the biggest player in all of East Asia, including a future North Korea and maybe the West, too. The coup in North Korea would be the perfect cutout for Tokugawa to use to take control of the entire financial structure of Asia and maybe the U.S. Think about it, if the U.S. collapsed after a nuclear attack, say on New York, Chicago, or Washington, who would be there to pick up the pieces?"

"Meji Holdings. Iseda Tokugawa."

Scott considered, then said, "What ties has he had to North Korea in the past?"

"Very few. Deliveries of food from his agri-businesses in Malaysia and Vietnam. A prototype synthetic fuel plant in the north near the border with China. Deliveries of heavy earth-moving equipment from plants he owns in Cambodia."

"A drop in the bucket compared to what he may be after now."

Fumiko took a deep breath. "I don't want to believe any of this, Jake, I really don't."

"Who does?"

"How can we prove it, and who do we tell?"

Scott thought for a moment, then brightened. "How would you like to talk to the president of the United States?"

32

Central Tokyo

It was morning in Washington. The president and his advisors—Friedman, Ellsworth, Radford, SecDef Gordon, Chairman of the Joint Chiefs Webster, and Deputy Chief of CIA Paige—listened as Scott wrapped up the briefing he'd given them over a secure voice-sleeved cell phone.

Fumiko, pressed against Scott, who was sitting on the edge of the bed in his cheap Tokyo hotel, listened in. She heard the president, his voice bleeding from the cell phone, say, "I must tell you, Commander, and Ms. Kida if you can hear me, that we appreciate your analysis of the situation but will need time to digest it. There are some differences of opinion to consider."

Scott felt Fumiko take hold of his hand as she listened.

"Frankly, what you've told us seems far too speculative, and I would be reluctant to initiate any military action against North Korea based on such information. What I need is ironclad proof of what Marshal Jin intends to do. As far as we can tell, the weapons are still in trucks sitting on the border. Question is, what's he going to do with them?"

The president sounded fatigued and hoarse; he cleared his throat before continuing.

"Furthermore, we can't ask the Japanese to detain and question one of their leading citizens and a friend of the prime minister's without good reason. We have no proof that he's plotting with Marshal Jin. That's all I have to say for now. General Radford wants to talk to you."

The line rumbled and Radford said, "Scott, there's nothing more you can do in Tokyo, so I want you back in Yokosuka. I'll have a chat with DG Kabe, and of course I'll not mention anything of what Ms. Kida has told us. I may be able to persuade him to take a look at this Tokugawa, tell Kabe we came up with his name ourselves. I was told we don't have much on him in our files, but we'll wring them out again anyway. Incidentally, Admiral Ellsworth tells me that Deacon's wife had a breakdown, that Com-SubPac has a new skipper headed for the *Reno*, but that we can pull your rabbit out of the hat instead."

"General, I can do more good here than I can aboard the *Reno*."

"Scott, you have my orders and—"

"Sir, I don't know all the facts, but we're on the scene here, where Fumiko has access to information and contacts the SRO and CIA don't have. I believe we could run down intel and deliver the ironclad proof the president needs to confront Jin and to persuade the Japanese to arrest Tokugawa."

He heard Carter Ellsworth talking heatedly in the background. Then he heard a sharp exchange between Gordon and Webster.

"General Radford?" said Scott.

"I'm here."

"Sir, time's running out. Give us a chance to run this

down, see what we can find. We'll keep under the radar, no one has to know."

A pause. "Stand by, Scott. I'll get back to you in a couple of minutes."

"They don't believe us," Fumiko said. She realized she'd been squeezing Scott's hand and now released it.

"It's not that they don't believe us, they don't want a pain-in-the-ass like me and a bright Japanese intelligence agent telling them what to do. But if we give them the proof they need, they can get a bust on this Matsu Shan plan, take it down before it starts so we aren't forced to launch a preemptive nuclear strike on North Korea."

Fumiko looked very worried. "Jake, you made it sound like I have special access to information and people that will prove our case. I don't have any information like that."

"We'll come up with something . . ."

The cell phone chirped. Radford said, "Scott, how much time do you and Ms. Kida need to do what you say you can do?"

"Seventy-two hours."

Fumiko covered her mouth with a hand.

"All right, you've got it."

They fell back on the bed together. At first Scott wasn't sure what to do until Fumiko's mouth was on his, her kisses soft, then more urgent as their tongues touched and danced. He felt her shiver as the intimacy they were suddenly sharing gathered momentum, until her breath was coming in ragged gulps. His mouth moved to her throat, to the pit of her neck, to her small breasts, their nipples hard under a red silk blouse. He put his lips to one of her delicate ears, whispered what he wanted, what he needed.

They undressed quickly, and with an easy, practiced move, Fumiko spread herself open and, looking down into his eyes, mounted him. He sucked in his breath, dug his fingers into the tight flesh of her buttocks, and together they found the rhythm until her urgent gyrations made him peak, then explode. It was good, very good, and they kept at it until he had fully satisfied her, until her long, shuddering climax had tapered off. Spent, she dropped her head to his chest. They lay glued together on the bed in the darkened room, not speaking, just listening to their thumping hearts and still-ragged breathing.

"Jake."

"What?" He ran his hands over her smooth back and buttocks, delighting in the little hollows and satiny textures he found there.

"You knew this would happen, didn't you?" she said, her head resting on his chest in the pool of her long, black, silky hair.

"No, I didn't."

"The first time we met, you knew."

"I never think that far ahead."

"But *I* did," she confessed, and kissed him.

He looked into her dark, sparkling eyes and said, "Then I think our professional relationship has come to an abrupt end."

"It can't; it has to last at least another seventy-two hours."

"Then we'll have to put this on hold till later."

"That's a long time to wait," she said. She eased onto her back and reached her arms up. He rose above her and entered her with long, rhythmic strokes. Afterwards they lay exhausted, arms around each other, until Fumiko's breathing slowed and he pulled away to let her sleep.

* * *

An escorted Mercedes-Benz limousine hurtled across the Taedong River bridge. The big car swept east past the Monument to the Fallen Soldiers of the Korean People's Army, then slowed as it approached the entrance to the Student's and Children's Palace.

The limousine came to a halt inside the palace's walled forecourt, where Marshal Jin and General Yi had arrived to witness a Ping-Pong match between students from Pyongyang and Pyongson.

Marshal Jin peered from behind the limousine's tinted bulletproof glass at staff members and children lined up and waving flags, anxious to greet their new Dear Leader.

Jin turned his gaze on General Yi, while outside, security officers cordoned off the limousine.

"You are satisfied that the weapons have been successfully modified?" Jin said.

"Completely satisfied, Dear Leader. Tokugawa's technicians in Vladivostok worked wonders to meet our schedule."

"They should. After all, he pays them handsomely for the work they do. Perhaps we should consider employing some of these technicians to work in our own nuclear laboratories," Jin observed.

"Russians do not like to give up the comforts their new prosperity provides. They like vodka, not our *soju*."

Jin crushed out a cigarette he'd been smoking, brushed ash from his tunic. "They might change their minds when they see what their work has accomplished."

Yi nodded.

"And the weapons are in Nam'po?"

"Yes. Our technicians there will inspect them and receive instructions on their use from the Russian technicians who installed the krypton timers. Sailing orders went out to Nam'po. Admiral Woo confirmed that the *Red Shark* will get underway as soon as the weapons are loaded out."

Jin watched the children wave their miniature red, blue, and white flags.

"What arrangements have you made for moving Kim from detention to Pyongyang?"

"He is most eager to assist in the unmasking of the spy," Yi said. "But I think it is unwise to move him until he has had a chance to review all the documents relating to personnel working in the Second Directorate. He may be able to ferret him out, and only by promising Kim exile will we keep his mind focused on the task. As soon as we move him to Pyongyang, his diligence will wane, and he will think he has found a weakness he can exploit."

"I see your point: He stays put until we find the spy." Jin's gaze returned to Yi. "Have you made progress finding out who the pig of a spy is?"

"Not yet. But I have ordered the arrests of two translators, one of whom is a woman. They may know something because of their former positions close to Kim. If they do know something, anything, I promise you they will reveal what it is before they die."

"Won't their arrests force the spy underground?"

Yi smiled confidently. "*Underground*, Dear Leader? But in the DPRK there is no *underground*."

Jin didn't respond: instead, he got out of the car and greeted the adoring, flag-waving children with open arms.

Fumiko opened her eyes and sat up in bed with a start. "How long? . . ."

"Four hours," Scott said.

She saw the remains of greasy chicken and ramen noodles, empty bottles of Coke and Sapporo beer sitting on the hotel room dresser.

"Want something to eat?" he asked.

She was on her feet, dressing, finger-combing her hair. "What? No, not now, we've got to get going."

"Where to?"

"My place, for starters. I want to bathe and change. Plus you need a fresh bandage on your hand."

He held up his injured hand, turned it over. The dressing was dirty. "Okay, then what?"

She glanced at the mess on the dresser and said, "I get something decent to eat while we come up with a plan."

"That's what I've been working on while you snoozed."

She fiddled with her watch. "Jake, look at the time. Tell me about it on the way."

The fresh air felt good after the tiny, stuffy hotel room. On the Shinjuku JR line, Scott told her he wanted to investigate the unscheduled flight from Tokyo to CKS International in Taipei by the ToriAir 737, with its cargo of switching gear bound for Iran.

Fumiko looked at Scott, puzzled.

"Your instincts are right," Scott said, "it's Tokugawa. While you slept I read your report. One of the documents you downloaded from the JDIH secure file says ToriAir is owned by Meji Holdings."

"Right, I remember."

"What if that ToriAir flight had more than switching gear aboard? What if Tokugawa hopped a ride on it to Taiwan to meet Wu Chow Fat and the *White Dragon*, say in Chi-lung? The *White Dragon* made the round trip to Chi-lung twice during the time the *Reno* was in the area and we were getting ready to make the insertion."

It dawned on her, and she stole a look at Scott, clearly embarrassed by her lapse.

"We can check if the plane's a cargo ship or an executive jet or both. Then we can check with Japanese immigration to see if Tokugawa made a late-night departure to Taiwan aboard that flight. If he did, Radford and the president may be able to force your boss to act."

"Jake, I don't know if I can get that information from the Ministry of Aviation and from immigration."

"The JDIH hasn't lifted your credentials. Flash them at some overworked *sarariman* at one of the ministries and he'll shit his pants trying to help you out."

She leaned into Scott so other passengers couldn't hear. "Jake, I told you, you're not in the States. Besides, I'm not convinced that even if we got the information you want it would prove anything."

"Do you have a better idea?"

She bit a fingernail and looked away.

They hurried from the station to her apartment in a drizzle. When they reached the top of the stairs on her floor, Fumiko froze in her tracks. Scott looked past her and saw the door to her apartment standing partly open and all the lights on inside.

Scott got in front of Fumiko and eased down the hall ahead of her. When he reached the apartment, he peeked around the door but didn't see anyone. He reared back and kicked the door wide open, checked it as it rebounded. Inside, the apartment was a disaster: Fumiko's clothes and personal belongings were strewn everywhere; furniture had been upset amidst smashed kitchen crockery.

She stood in the doorway with both hands to her mouth, looking sick. A door to another apartment opened; a woman peeked out at them, withdrew, shut and locked the door.

"Come on, let's get out of here," Scott said and took her hand.

She stopped short. "No. I'm not going."

"Yes, you are. They may be back."

"Who? The JDIH?"

"Doesn't matter. You can't stay here, it's not safe, and we can't go back to my hotel because they've probably got it covered too. We'll have to find another hotel, then I'll contact Radford—"

Fumiko pulled her hand away. Her look hardened as she flipped open her cell phone to make a call. "No," she said, "I have a better idea."

33

Korea Bay

The *Red Shark* turned south onto a new heading into the Yellow Sea. To avoid contact with PLAN naval vessels or reconnaissance aircraft, Commander Tongsun Park had shaped a course that lay west of the Chinese Shandong Peninsula. Even so, radar emissions from a PLAN Harbin SH-5 flying boat on anti-submarine patrol out of Qingdao appeared on the *Red Shark*'s ECM. The amphibian lingered beyond visual range for almost a half hour before fading to the north.

Satisfied that they had not been detected, Park commanded, "Comrade Navigator, we will hold this course until south of Shidao, then we will submerge."

"Aye, Captain."

Park knew there was absolutely no room in the schedule for slippage; timing was everything, and he'd had drummed into his brain the absolute necessity of delivering the cargo when promised.

His and his crew's curiosity about the three lead casks loaded aboard the *Red Shark* at Nam'po had been tamped down by the presence of DPRK Internal Security Forces. Lashed to the deck in the torpedo room, the casks had been viewed by the crew with deep suspicion, if not out-right fear. Even Park thought he sensed an aura of evil emanating from them, but he dismissed it as superstition. Meanwhile, provisioning, crew training, and the re-pairing of a fuel cell leaking hydrogen had kept Park's mind focused on the potential difficulties involved in such a long submerged voyage in a new submarine, that, while highly advanced, had also proven balky.

Park climbed a ladder to the bridge high atop the *Red Shark*'s sail and assumed the conn from his first officer. As the submarine steamed steadily south, Park thought about the lead casks: small enough to fit through the sub-marine's thirty-inch-diameter hatches, it still took eight men to lug one. Park, after signing the custody docu-ments, had been about to ask one of the officers what was in the casks, but he'd thought better of it. They would re-port it, and upon his return to Nam'po, he'd be arrested. No, his job was to command the *Red Shark* and deliver the cargo, not to ask questions.

"Comrade First Officer," the bridge speaker croaked, "this is the navigator. Please inform the captain that we have crossed the line south of Shidao."

"Comrade Captain—"

"Submerge the boat," Park commanded.

The train slid silently out of the old red brick Tokyo Sta-tion close by the Imperial Palace, rapidly built up speed, and within seconds was rocketing past ugly concrete apartment blocks, traffic-clotted expressways, and sprawling auto factories. A half hour later, Tokyo's drab industrial plain gave way to its less claustrophobic sub-urbs.

Fumiko, tense, still shaken, returned from the toilet at the end of the car. "I spotted a man who looked at me as if he knew me. He's five rows back on the opposite side."

Scott started to turn, but Fumiko tugged at him. "No, don't."

"I'll check him out." Before she could stop him, Scott was up and gone.

He was an ordinary-looking Japanese with a slight build and short haircut typical of *sararimen*. He had a folded black raincoat on his lap and was reading a magazine. The blank expression on his face didn't change when Scott lurched down the aisle past his seat.

When Scott returned a few minutes later, the man had nodded off. Scott decided it was unlikely that he had an interest in Fumiko, but he knew that in Japan things were not always what they appeared to be. He decided he'd try to keep an eye on him.

From the train station in the village west of Tokyo, Fumiko led Scott down a lane bordered on both sides by small, ramshackle houses. Charcoal smoke and the sharp odor of cooking oil filled the air. At the end of the lane she stopped in front of a house, where a black-and-white cat eyed them from its perch atop a bamboo fence. She rang a small brass bell, slid the door open, and ushered her guest inside.

Fumiko's father greeted them with a deep bow. "Zenjiro Kida at your service. I am deeply honored to meet you, Mr. Scott," he added in excellent English.

Dr. Kida, short, slightly disheveled, wore gold-rimmed glasses and a cardigan. Academics, Scott decided, looked the same the world over, but this one looked younger than his sixty years. Mrs. Kida, a tiny woman dressed in gray kimono, white *tabi*, and *zoris*, bowed deeply, then knelt and saw to the formalities of lining up her guest's shoes with the toes facing the lane. Still kneeling, she slid open a shoji screen and showed Fumiko and

Scott into the tatami room, where a charcoal fire glowed in a *kotatsu*. Scott saw an old woman peering into the room from around a screen.

"My grandmother," Fumiko said.

Mrs. Kida set out a meal. Fumiko waited a decent interval for Scott and her father to get acquainted, then said, "Father, please forgive my rude manners, but as I explained when I called, we don't have much time and need your help."

Dr. Kida said, "Mr. Scott, my daughter said you wanted information about someone—Iseda Tokugawa, I believe."

"I know you teach political science at Tokyo University. Fumiko said that in addition you're involved in issues of nuclear nonproliferation and that you'd have information about Tokugawa that might be useful."

"Useful?" Kida said guardedly. "Useful in what way?"

"We're interested in hearing what you know about his involvement in a plan to build nuclear weapons for Japan."

Kida bristled. "You are mistaken, Mr. Scott, Japan is forbidden by law from building nuclear weapons."

"True." Scott's gaze flicked to Fumiko, then back to Kida. "But I've heard that Tokugawa is close to the prime minster and supports his proposal to strengthen Japan's armed forces, which includes building nuclear weapons."

Kida shook his head. "That is preposterous."

"Father, you know it's true," Fumiko snapped.

"No, it is a fabrication, and I will not discuss that which has no basis in fact."

"You're being rude. Don't embarrass me in front of our guest."

Kida, unaccustomed to being scolded by his daughter, to losing face in front of a stranger, recoiled. He gave Scott a sour look. "My daughter doesn't discuss her work with me, has adopted Western ways, shows disrespect, but doesn't hesitate to come to me for help when it is convenient."

Fumiko brushed this aside and said, "I'm not looking for help, Father, we need *information*, information that only you can provide."

"You flatter me, daughter. I don't know anything about Tokugawa and this plan you speak of to build nuclear weapons in Japan. What you have heard are rumors that started because Tokugawa is one of the most reclusive men in Japan. No one knows anything about him, nor has anyone ever breached the barrier of secrecy he has erected around himself."

"*I* was able to breach it, Father," she said with an air of triumph. "Yes, I did."

Kida looked at his daughter, then at Scott, his eyes wide, full of doubt, and also fear. "Impossible."

"But true." To prove it, she told him what they had discovered about Tokugawa in the JDIH top-secret files.

Kida, his face a mask, listened intently but said nothing. Clearly, it was the first time she had ever revealed to her father anything about her work at the agency.

"Dr. Kida," Scott said after Fumiko had finished, "we need to know whether he can build nuclear weapons or if he's bluffing. Can you tell us?"

Kida looked intently at Scott and said, "Why would you, an American in Japan, want such information? Who are you to come here demanding answers to things that don't concern you?"

"On the contrary, Dr. Kida, they concern me because they concern the United States."

"Father, please," Fumiko said, "we don't have time to argue. Just tell us what you know about Tokugawa. It's vital to the investigation we're conducting."

Kida considered for a very long moment. Then, as if weighing his obligation to Fumiko, as well as the fact that his denials had been upended, making his loss of face all the more painful to bear, he nodded as Fumiko prepared to take notes.

"All I can tell you is that a man who heads an association determined to make demigods of our war criminals would likely want Japan to have the power and prestige that accrue to those nations armed with nuclear weapons. Above all, he would see Japan accepted by America as her equal, if not her better."

"Okay, agreed, but how would he build nuclear weapons?" Scott asked. "What manufacturing capabilities does he have access to? Where would he get fissile material?"

"As my daughter has apparently discovered, he owns high-tech plants in Russia. Russia has hundreds of former Soviet-era weapons designers. Perhaps they could turn their talents to weapons development. As for fissile material, Russia is awash in it. Perhaps Japan already has a stockpile he could use."

Perhaps, perhaps. Scott kept his frustration in check and tried another tack. "What type of weapons did he propose to build? Do you know anything about their design and yield?"

"Mr. Scott, I'm a political scientist, not a nuclear physicist. You should talk to an expert. I'm sorry, I just don't know."

"Dr. Kida, forgive me, but you're involved in issues of nuclear proliferation. That means you understand nuclear weapons technology. Am I wrong?"

Kida looked down at a pair of clenched fists resting on his knees.

"Father, what you have told us is very helpful," Fumiko said gently. "But it's mostly anecdotal and theoretical. What we need is *hard* information—no, *proof*—that Tokugawa has provided the technical assistance North Korea needs to bolster their nuclear arsenal."

The room fell silent but for the hiss of the *kotatsu.*

Kida looked up, his face troubled. "What are you involving my daughter in, Mr. Scott? Why do you come to Japan to stir up trouble? In our country Tokugawa is what you Americans would call an 'untouchable.' You don't understand what you are dealing with, especially the right-wing political atmosphere that grips Japan."

Fumiko interrupted him. "Mr. Scott is not here to stir up trouble. And we understand exactly what we're dealing with. I told you on the phone, I can't go into why we need this information, but . . ." She checked herself, then glanced at Scott. He understood where she had to go and gave her a nod yes.

Fumiko took a deep breath and said, "Father, listen to me." She held his gaze as she spoke in a careful and measured tone. "Everything we have uncovered so far indicates that Iseda Tokugawa is helping the North Koreans prepare to launch a nuclear attack on the United States."

Kida reacted as if he'd been struck across the face. "I don't believe you."

Fumiko told her father about Matsu Shan, the meeting at the villa, the SEAL insertion, the battle, the video DVD and stonewalling by Kabe, her demotion, the ransacking of her apartment.

Kida covered his face with both hands and bent double until his knuckles touched his knees. He moaned, "This can't be possible."

"It *is* possible," Scott said. "If Tokugawa has the means, he also has the motive: revenge."

Fumiko reached out and put a comforting hand on her father's back.

"Doctor, you understand better than anyone," Scott said, "the devastating effects nuclear weapons have had on the Japanese people and nation. It's woven into the fabric of your history and your future. You've had to live with the consequences of nuclear war for over sixty years. Fumiko and I have little time left to prevent it from happening in the United States. If it does . . . well, I don't have to explain."

Kida uncovered his face, sat up, and looked beseechingly at his daughter.

"Father, *please* tell us what you know."

Professor Kida kneaded both fists together into a ball. He glanced at the *kotatsu*, then back to Fumiko, whose gaze was unyielding.

At length Kida said, "Soviet designers had solved the problem of how to miniaturize nuclear weapons at least twenty years ago. Once they mastered the problems associated with casting and machining plutonium cores, they built a series of hydrogen bombs that fit on top of a missile designed to be fired from a mobile launcher or a submarine. They called the warhead a BX, and its design was almost identical to the U.S. W-88."

"W-88s are fitted to Trident II D-5s," Scott said, probing Kida's knowledge of nuclear weaponry.

"Yes. U.S. submarine-launched Trident missiles carry eight such warheads. Like the W-88, the BX has a plutonium primary core the size of an egg but shaped like a watermelon. Below it is a spherical hydrogen fuel element. The design allows for a nose cone configuration about sixteen degrees wide and less than four feet high."

"That's smaller than a W-88," said Scott.

"It has been rumored that plans for the BX were stolen from the Russians sometime in the midnineties by the JDIH. The Japan Self-Defense Force realized that it would be relatively easy to develop even more powerful miniature weapons, which could be hidden in silos around Japan. It has been said that this BX concept was to be secretly funded through Meji Industries and that with the treaty giving Japan access to U.S. missile technology, it would only be a matter of time before Japan had W-88-style nuclear weapons mated to U.S.-supplied missiles capable of reaching China and North Korea. But the prime minister balked at the plan because it was too close to elections, and the weapons were never built."

"Meanwhile Tokugawa was sitting on this technology," Scott said. "And at some point before the coup in North Korea, Tokugawa was approached by Jin to reinvent their nuclear arsenal."

"And Tokugawa saw an opportunity to avenge his family and virtually take control of financial markets in Europe and Asia," said Fumiko.

"I caution that these are rumors, Mr. Scott, only rumors."

"The meeting on Matsu Shan that Fumiko told you about wasn't a rumor."

"Japanese and Koreans place a high value on face-to-face meetings, to demonstrate their loyalty to each other and their unwavering belief in causes they support," Kida offered, as if having suddenly discovered a kernel of truth in what he'd heard.

Scott thought about that for a moment, then said, "North Korea has relatively large, crude nuclear weapons. What they want are small, powerful ones that are easy to conceal and small enough to put on one of their new Daepodong ballistic missiles."

"Perhaps even smaller," Kida said, "small enough to deliver by hand, like a suitcase."

"A *suitcase* nuke," Fumiko said, surprised by her father's assessment. "Jake, is that possible?"

"It is if the warheads trucked to Najin ended up in Vladivostok and were miniaturized for use against the U.S. by terrorists."

Scott saw it now: North Korean terrorists, or terrorists working for the North Koreans, would smuggle suitcase-sized nuclear weapons into U.S. cities and detonate them. The North Koreans would claim that they had had nothing to do with the attacks, and the U.S. would be hard-pressed to prove otherwise. Meanwhile, Tokugawa would be gearing up through his multinational companies, to help rebuild America's devastated cities and shattered economy without interference.

"Then we're too late, Jake," Fumiko said. "By now the weapons could be anywhere." Her eyes were red rimmed, dulled by fatigue and, now, fear.

Fumiko's mother entered the tatami room on mincing steps and whispered something, first to her daughter, then to her husband. Fumiko sprang to her feet; Professor Kida rose and hurried from the room.

"What is it?" Scott said, on his feet too.

"Mother said she saw a stranger walk past the house. We have to get out of here."

Mrs. Kida stood off to one side, wringing her hands, while Fumiko and her father investigated. Minutes later they returned, worry written all over their faces.

Fumiko grabbed her things. "Mother's right. He's at the end of the lane."

"A stranger? How do you know he's watching us?" Scott asked.

"Jake, the people who live in this neighborhood don't go around wearing double-breasted suits."

"Right. Let's move it."

"Quick, go out the front before he comes back," Dr. Kida said. "Cut across the lane to my friend Higashi-san's house and take the path to the canal."

"I'm sorry, Doctor," Scott said, "that I've brought trouble to your door."

"No, Tokugawa brings the trouble. Go! *Now!*"

"Father, the three of you can't stay here," Fumiko protested. "You have to come with us."

He pushed Fumiko toward the door. *"Go!"*

34

West of Tokyo

"This way," Scott called. But Fumiko stood rooted in place by the open door of her parents' house.

It took a heartbeat for Scott to register the roar of a black Mercedes-Benz charging down the lane like a rampaging killing machine. He heard Fumiko's scream, a warning to the elderly Higashi-*san* pedaling home on his bicycle. Too late, Scott saw the Benz's snout plow into Higashi, watched his twisted, broken body fly into the air, only to be crushed under the car's rear wheels as the driver aimed at Scott and Fumiko.

At the last possible moment Scott lashed an arm around Fumiko's waist and dove with her, headlong, back into the open doorway. The car slewed to stop in front of the house; a rear door flew open; two men tore Fumiko from Scott's grasp and threw her inside the car. The Benz, with Higashi's smashed and twisted bicycle embedded in its grille, rear tires howling, smoking white, accelerated brutally, a trail of carnage in its wake.

There was a moment of shocked silence before the neighborhood erupted and people poured from their homes, shouting, wailing, pointing at Higashi's body, cut almost in half, at the gray rope of guts lying in the gutter running with blood. Scott caught a glimpse of Dr. Kida in the crowd, bent double with grief.

The crowd surged around Scott like an incoming tide. Already a police car with flashing blue lights was working its way up the lane. In another minute he'd be trapped. Scott fought his way upstream through the gapers, not wanting to believe that Higashi-*san* had been brutally murdered, that Fumiko had been snatched from his arms, and he was half expecting, hoping at any moment, to see the car roar back up the street with her inside.

A man in a black raincoat stood on tiptoe, spotted the tall American clawing past pedestrians, and surged after him.

Tokugawa stood elbow in palm, finger to his lips, gazing into the beautifully tended koi pond in the garden. A school of silver, orange, and black koi had massed at water's edge to feed. He watched them and ruminated on the serenity of his surroundings, where one could discover the universe in a grain of sand and experience a measure of well-being missing in the harsh give-and-take of modern Japanese life.

Footsteps crunching on gravel broke his mood as Kana Asuka approached and bowed. Tokugawa reciprocated.

"What are the Taiwanese saying about Matsu Shan?" Tokugawa asked.

"A local issue between druglords settled the old-fashioned way."

Tokugawa continued his study of the feeding koi. "And our friends on the mainland?"

"Naturally they had questions about the *White Dragon* incident but seemed to accept the explanation offered by the Taiwanese. New China News Agency reported it was an accident that sank the vessel and killed Wu Chow Fat."

"And the financial arrangements?"

"They are complete. Deposits have been made to Meji accounts in Tokyo, Zurich, and Paris."

Tokugawa faced Kana. "The girl?"

"Ojima has her. Unfortunately, a problem arose, which of course we will settle with the local authorities."

"What kind of problem?"

"An elderly man was killed. It was unavoidable."

Tokugawa tossed more food to the koi. "And the American?"

"He is under surveillance. Director Kabe assures me that he will be forced to leave Japan within twenty-four hours or face arrest."

"They say he is an individualist, a loner. Unpredictable. Do you get my meaning?"

"*Hai.*"

Tokugawa bowed his thanks. Alone again, he considered: The *Red Shark* had sailed; Jin was committed; the Americans could do nothing that would affect their plans. It was far too late for that.

Scott arrived at the train station certain that it had been Tokugawa's men who had killed Higashi and snatched Fumiko. If he could find her and free her and not get himself killed in the bargain, it would force the JDIH to have Tokugawa arrested. He felt the vise tighten.

At the station in the village, Scott bought a ticket to Tokyo. Outside on the platform, he recognized the man he'd seen on the train from Tokyo that morning. He had on his black raincoat but carried no luggage.

Scott kept his distance. When the train arrived, he

tried to blend in with the passengers boarding coaches. The man boarded the coach behind the one Scott rode in and didn't appear again until the train pulled into Tokyo. Scott joined the crush rushing from the train for cabs and buses, then tried to lose the man in the crowded station. He thought he had but spotted him again, this time at the end of the taxi queue Scott had joined.

Scott broke out of line and blended into a group of British tourists waiting to board a bus. Screened by the tourists, he watched the man standing in the taxi queue move up as the line shortened. When a tour bus pulled up to the curb to load, Scott broke away and ducked behind the bus. Shielded by its bulk, he dashed across three taxi ranks and jumped into a cab that had just rolled to a stop at the end of one of the ranks. Scott ordered the startled white-capped-and-gloved driver to get moving *hayaku*— fast.

The man in the raincoat waiting on line tore after Scott. Amid cries of *buta!*—pig!—from onlookers embarrassed by a public display of rude manners by a Japanese, the man shouldered his way between a Western couple waiting with bags at the head of the line and bolted for the next taxi.

As Scott's cab sped from the station into traffic, he looked back and saw the man in the raincoat tussling with the Westerner, who received for his trouble a vicious chop that smashed him to the pavement.

Scott turned and faced forward. He knew it wouldn't take long for the man in the black raincoat to track him down.

Scott's taxi pulled up in front of a small, run-down fuck-hotel and bar located over a fortune-teller's shop in the heart of Tokyo's pink district in Kabukicho. The driver said, "Number-one place. You like."

The hotel and shop were wedged between the Art Nouveau, a sex club, and a bar called Bottoms Up. The rest of the block was shoulder to shoulder hostess bars, peep shows, and live porno theaters.

The Japanese who managed the hotel and bar introduced himself as Sammy Shin. He showed Scott a room on the top floor. More rooms like it opened off a balcony wrapped around a dreary courtyard containing a lifeless ailanthus tree.

"Private, very private," Sammy Shin assured him, pointing to the room. "Many beautiful girl to fuck. You bring here." He grinned, showing off brown, jagged teeth.

The room smelled of old urine and sweaty sex, and next door, Scott heard a couple rutting away. Worn tatami covered the floor; a stained quilt lay folded on a dirty futon. A small table and two chairs with woven sisal seats stood in a corner. A ceramic lantern, the room's only source of light, hung from the wall over the table. An undersized *kotatsu* provided heat. Scott decided that the place was perfect.

He stepped out on the balcony to pay Sammy for the room. Across the courtyard two couples emerged from adjacent stalls and split up: two teenaged whores waved good-bye to their customers, middle-aged salarymen.

"Many beautiful girl to fuck," Sammy beamed.

"Yeah, many beautiful girls to fuck," Scott mimicked, and handed over some yen.

Sammy started for the stairs, but Scott grabbed his quilted jacket. "Not so fast, Sammy-*san*. I want you to show me something."

The voice booming at Scott over the sleeved cell phone from Virginia was clipped and tight, a sure sign that Radford was not pleased with what Scott had told him. A grunt was all he allowed when he was told of Higashi's murder and Fumiko's kidnapping. Then he said, "That BX warhead, nothing new there, we've tracked rumors that it exists, never been able to prove it. Same with Toku-gawa churning out mini-nukes for the JSDF, paying for them out of his own pocket. Rumors. This Professor Kida you talked to, Ms. Kida's father, he show you any docu-ments to back up his claims?"

"No, General, there wasn't time, we had to get out of there."

Radford grunted. "Arming the NKs with a bunch of mini-nukes is a hell of a stretch. You'll have to do better than that, Scott."

"Sir, why would they have trucked the warheads to Najin, if not to deliver them to Vladivostok, to that elec-tronics plant owned by Meji Industries?"

"Why? To put them out of our reach across the bor-der in Russia, that's why. But that won't keep us from going in there and taking the bunch of them out."

"I assume, General, that you know exactly where they are."

"I'm briefing the president on it shortly," Radford said, a rasp of controlled anger coloring his voice. "Now, we've looked at that plant every way you can, and it's nothing but a bunch of rickety old buildings where they assemble cell phones for EuroCom. As for a bunch of ex-Soviet nu-clear weapons designers building mini-nukes in that place, that's bullshit. The other thing that's bullshit is the idea that even if the NKs had mini-nukes, they'd be able to smuggle them into the U.S."

"They didn't have any trouble smuggling two truck bombs into Manhattan."

When Radford spoke, the anger coloring his voice

was razor sharp and unmistakable. "Commander, listen to me, and listen to me carefully. The director general of JDIH wants you out of Japan in twenty-four hours. As for the reasons why, he seems to have plenty, starting with all the trouble you and Ms. Kida stirred up. If you're not out in twenty-four hours, he'll have you arrested, and if he does, there's not a hell of a lot I can do about it without going through diplomatic channels, which the president will not permit."

"Sir, perhaps you didn't hear me. I'm convinced that Tokugawa's people killed Mr. Higashi and tried to kill us. They didn't kill us and instead kidnapped Fumiko. I've got to find her if I can—I owe her that. If I wait too long, they may kill her."

"Goddamnit, Scott, you don't seem to understand that we can't end up in a fight with the Japanese. Try getting that through your head."

"Sir, the Japanese are covering up for Tokugawa and the North Koreans. Fumiko's kidnapping is all the proof you need."

"Scott, I want you out of Tokyo and at Yokosuka for debriefing ASAP."

"What about Fumiko?"

"I'll spell it out for you: She's expendable! Just like Higashi. Do you understand that?"

Scott said nothing.

"Did you hear me, Scott?"

"Yes, sir."

"You've got twenty-four hours. What happens to Ms. Kida is none of our business. That's how it is." Radford signed off.

Scott looked at the dead cell phone in his hand. "That's *not* how it is," he said to the room.

* * *

He heard the young whores cavorting with their johns. He tried to ignore them while he reran in his mind the events of the last two days and sorted out as best he could the mess he'd gotten mired in. He knew it wouldn't take long for the man tailing him to find the cab driver who had dropped him in the Pink District at Sammy Shin's: He gave him two hours at the outside. Enough time to make Yokosuka, or . . .

He reviewed notes he'd made from Fumiko's file on Tokugawa, then looked at a map of Tokyo and its suburbs. He found Noda, a city twenty-two miles north of Tokyo. A cab or subway was out of the question; so was a bus. Which meant there was only one way to get there. He activated his cell phone and made a call that was answered by voice mail. He left detailed instructions, then settled down to wait.

35

The White House

Despite his stay in Key Largo, the president looked worse than he had before leaving Washington for a rest at his Florida mansion. Radford and Freidman had discussed his condition via SVTC, while they'd waited on the chief executive's arrival in the Situation Room, where the teleconference had been set up.

"Sir, are you feeling all right?" Freidman asked when the president strode in.

"How I feel is the least of our worries," he snapped and took a seat. He looked at Radford's image on the video screen, piped from Crystal City. "Karl, have you located those nukes?"

"No, sir. The images sent by the Global Hawk are inconclusive. We don't see the trucks in Najin, nor do we see them anywhere near Vladivostok."

"Then for sure the warheads have been moved and we didn't see it happen."

"But how?" Friedman asked. "We've had that area under surveillance for days."

The president turned his head to the national security advisor but kept his eyes on Radford. "If those nukes can be made as small as Commander Scott and this Dr. Kida claim, how hard would it be to walk them out of Russia and back to North Korea? Not too hard, I'd say."

Radford gestured to get the president's attention. "Sir, we're reviewing all of our Global Hawk takes, looking for something we may have missed. I think the warheads are still there, we just haven't found them. As I said earlier, I wouldn't put too much stock in Scott's claim that Tokugawa has the means to miniaturize them."

"Karl, unless you can find the goddamn things *right now*, I'm putting all my stock in his claim. I certainly can't put any stock in the SRO's ability to find them, can I?" The president kneaded his forehead. "If in fact we've missed them, by now they could be anywhere. And if we don't find them, then like Scott said, they could end up in New York City, Chicago, or here in Washington."

Radford and Freidman said nothing while the president consulted a handwritten aide-memoir. "All right," he said, "so far we've heard nothing from our conduit in Pyongyang. Karl, any idea why?"

Radford tugged an earlobe. "I think it's understandable—given the situation, he'd not want to risk it. Perhaps in time—"

"Karl, we don't have time."

"Is there any way we can initiate contact with him?" Freidman asked. "I mean, could we give him a nudge, open a secure channel, say, one of our satellites, that he could upload a signal to?"

Radford frowned. "Paul, for his safety, we didn't supply him with any specialized comms gear. If they were to find it, he'd be dead meat."

"How do we normally communicate with him?" the president asked.

"He passes information to the Danish chargé d'affaires.

But that method is dependent on cultural and scientific exchanges hosted at their embassy in Pyongyang. Since the coup, there haven't been any exchanges, so I have to assume our man has had no way to get information to them."

"Have you considered the possibility that he's been exposed?" the president asked.

"Sir, if he had, I think the NKs would have announced it to the world to bolster their contention that we're about to attack them."

"Then ask the Danes for some help. I don't know what, maybe they can set up a conference, throw a cocktail party for NK bigwigs."

"Yes, sir, I'll ask them," Radford said.

"Now, what is Scott's status? He's done a good job for us, but I want him out of Japan before he gets himself arrested or . . . worse. If they go after him again, he may not be so lucky. I don't want to stir up any more trouble with the Japanese."

"Sir, he has his orders, but he also believes he has an obligation to find Ms. Kida."

"I knew it," Friedman moaned, "I just knew it."

The president said, "You tell him, Karl, that if he doesn't get out of Japan immediately, I'll have him court-martialed."

"Sir, I'll do better than that: I'll dispatch Colonel Jefferson to bring him in."

"You do that," the president snorted.

Commander Deng Zemin eyed the decrypted message:

PLAN ~ NORTHSEA ~ LUSHUN ~ NAVAL AIR ARM ~
SH-5 FLT 007 [STOP]
TO PLAN UNIT 002 ADMIRALTY [STOP]

SURFACE RADAR CONTACT 0643 ~ EAST POSITION GRID
21X ~ 80 NM EAST SHIDAO [STOP] BEARING 190
DEGREES ~ SPEED ESTIMATE 8 KTS ~ POSSIBLE DPRK
SUBMARINE [STOP] CONTACT SH-5 FLT 007 FOR LAST
REPORTED COORDINATES [STOP] CALL SIGN EAGLE
[STOP] LOCATE ~ IDENTIFY ~ REPORT SPEED-POSITION-
HEADING-TASKING IF POSSIBLE [EOM]

Zemin tapped the chart with a stylus. "Comrade First Officer, this unidentified diesel-electric is not too far from our present position. Perhaps thirty nautical miles."

The first officer bent to the chart and did some quick math on his electronic data pad. "I make it thirty-two, Captain. We can reach his area in less than two hours surfaced."

Zemin considered. "If he maintains his current speed, yes." Zemin continued to tap the chart. "Is he Japanese or Korean? What do your bones tell you?"

"Korean. North Korean."

"Do you think Marshal Jin is flexing his muscles?"

"The new leader wants to show that he, like Kim, is not afraid to patrol in our Yellow Sea."

"I wonder . . ."

"My bones tell me so, Captain."

"Very well. Come to periscope depth. Communications Officer."

"Captain? . . ."

"Stand by to contact that SH-5 amphibian and download the contact coordinates. Use her call sign 'Eagle.' "

"Aye, Comrade Captain."

"Comrade First Officer," said Zemin, "you are right, we are looking for a North Korean boat. I, too, feel it in my bones."

*   *   *

Tongsun Park looked up as two of his newest officers, both engineers, entered the *Red Shark*'s wardroom. They hesitated when they saw the captain seated at the long green baize-covered table.

"Greetings, Comrades," said Park.

The officers came to attention and cocked their arms in the prescribed manner to display open palms. "All praise our Dear Leader," said the officers in unison.

"Take your places," Park said.

The officers bowed politely and sat down. One of them, a bald lieutenant named Kang, eyed the bottle of *soju* next to Park's open log book and folder of communiqués. The other officer, a lieutenant named Suk, squinted to read the label.

Park moved the bottle of fiery Korean liquor to the center of the table. "Help yourselves," he said.

"Thank you, Captain."

Park watched them pour small amounts into cups he placed in front of them. "You will find, Comrades, that life in the Korean People's Navy aboard a submarine is different from anything you may have experienced in the surface fleet. You will see that we submariners demand high standards of conduct from ourselves and from each other. And that unlike in the surface force, a submarine's commanding officer"—he pointed to the *soju*—"has certain prerogatives." He quaffed his own drink, which seared his throat and brought tears. "Now, to business."

Park produced documents from a case and said, "We are scheduled to arrive in Davao on Mindanao, in exactly nineteen days, a voyage of approximately two thousand eight hundred nautical miles. Our schedule allows no margin of error." Park lit a cigarette of rough-cut tobacco and waved out a match."We must be on our guard at all times."

Park unfolded a small chart of the Yellow Sea and China-Korea-Japan area. "You are familiar with your duties. Now I will familiarize you with our operation in southern waters.

"The Chinese patrol the northern Yellow Sea area with aircraft. From Dalian south, the Chinese have planted a cordon of sonobuoys and other devices to prevent intrusions into Bohai Bay and Huludao, where they have submarine construction yards. Currently we are steaming south on a course that will keep us as far away from the China coast as possible. The patrolling Chinese antisubmarine aircraft we encountered earlier did not take any action, so it is safe to assume we were not detected. Even so, we must be exceptionally vigilant. If we encounter hostile forces, we must evade them or risk delay of our arrival in Davao by hours or even days."

Park watched the two officers' reactions: They were green but eager to learn and also to be part of an important mission which, they sensed, might represent a turning point in the fortunes of the DPRK.

"Also, if we were to have a problem with our propulsion plant, it, too, could delay our arrival. In reality, the *Red Shark* is a floating bomb." Suk's and Kang's eyebrows shot up. "You know, of course, that the liquid oxygen and hydrogen-matrix we carry on board are extremely explosive when combined. And then there is our diesel fuel and weapons propellant and also our battery, which, when its sulfuric acid and seawater mix, emits chlorine gas."

Park blew cigarette smoke into the overhead, tapped ash into a hand-hammered copper receptacle. "You, Lieutenant Kang, have important responsibilities: maintenance and upkeep of our engineering plant and propulsion system, and you, Lieutenant Suk, maintenance of our weapons. There is much to learn and to master, and it will not be easy . . ."

Park was distracted by the flashing red Captain's Light located over the cradled phone screwed to the wardroom sideboard; beneath it an LED panel screamed ENGINE ROOM.

Park grabbed the phone and listened, blood draining from his face. He said, "Confirmed" and hung up the phone. He stood and jammed his billed cap on his head. He looked at Lieutenant Kang and, while crushing out his cigarette, twisting it until it broke apart, said, "Yes, there is much to learn and to master, and it will not be easy. But you will start *now*. The watch in the engine room has just reported a leak in the fuel cell."

36

Kabukicho, Tokyo

Scott heard high heels clattering up the stairs at the end of the balcony, someone taking long strides, clip-clopping to a halt outside his room. He opened the door and discovered a breathless Tracy. And Sammy Shin berating her in his singsong pidgin English.

"*Amerika-jin giru* no work here, leave now," Sammy said, wagging a finger at her. "You no leave I call boss."

"Jake, he thinks I'm a *yujo*—a whore," Tracy said. "He thinks some Jap wants to fuck my brains out. Tell him who I am, that I'm not a whore."

"It's all right, Sammy, she's a friend."

"No *Amerika-jin yujo* allowed here."

Scott stuffed yen in Sammy's fist. "She's a friend." Scott pulled Tracy inside and shut the door.

She looked around first, and then at Scott. "Nice place. You always pick the best."

Scott lit the lantern. It caught, and they regarded each other for a long moment in the cast orange light. She had on a black silk shirt and tight black leggings. Diamonds of rain sparkled in her hair, which was longer than it had been the last time he'd seen her. Less of a helmet, it swept over both ears and down the nape of her neck. She was heavily made up in the hard-edged way Scott had always liked.

"Thanks for coming," he said.

She moistened her lips with the tip of her tongue and said, "Sorry it took so long, but I was—"

"You don't have to explain."

"You didn't think I'd come, did you?"

"I hoped you would. I told you it was important, that I needed your help."

"You never needed my help for anything," she said in a mocking tone. "So why start now?"

"This is different."

"What happened to your hand; what the hell are you involved in now?"

"I can't tell you."

"Then maybe I can't help you."

Tracy sat down on one of the battered chairs, crossed her long legs, opened a small purse, and gave her makeup a detailed once-over, appraising herself in a mirror sewn into the purse flap.

"I'm trying to avoid some people," Scott said, watching her fuss with her hair. "I need to find someone."

Tracy put the purse away. "Who, a woman? It is, isn't it?"

"Look, Trace, this isn't a game I'm playing. I wouldn't have asked for your help if it weren't damned important, more important than you can imagine."

"Then you might need this." She rummaged in her purse and pulled out a black Glock-26 9mm pistol. "It's Rick's. It was issued to him by the Embassy's Marine guard. He doesn't know I took it."

Scott hefted the palm-sized weapon. "Tracy, you've violated just about every rule on the books governing firearms in Japan, to say nothing of getting Rick in a hell of a lot of trouble."

"Since when did you start giving a shit about Rick?"

"I haven't, but if you'd been stopped—"

"Well, I wasn't. I thought you could use it. So sue me."

Scott dropped the Glock's ten-round magazine, then slammed it home. He examined the chamber to see that it was charged, then pocketed the pistol. "What about a car? Did you get one?"

"You want me to sneak you out of here, right?" Tracy said.

"Yes. Did you follow my instructions? Find the parking lot?"

"Yeah." She threw him the keys: he saw the Lexus logo. "It's Rick's."

"Does it have diplomatic plates?"

"I didn't look."

"Thanks, Trace."

Her eyes sparkled in the lantern light. Scott knew that she knew she had him on the hook she was so good at setting and that she could, if she wanted, play him to death.

Tracy came and stood close to him. Her shirt was thin silk, and he felt her heat radiating through it and the hard tips of her breasts against his chest. She studied his face. "You look as if you could use some sleep." She reached up and touched his hair. "Christ, I almost forgot how good looking you are."

He felt his cock stiffen. Her hand went to it, kneading it, teasing it.

"Trace . . . not now . . . not here . . ."

"Why not *here*, of all places?"

Her mouth was on his, tongue probing deep, hands fumbling with his zipper. She pulled it down and was inside his shorts when she felt Scott's steel grip around her wrist.

"*You're hurting me—* What's the matter, afraid you'll come in your pants—?"

He clamped a hand over her mouth. "Shhh. Listen."

He took his hand away from her mouth, zipped up, then motioned that she should get behind him and stay there. He went to the door and listened.

"It's quiet," he whispered. "Too quiet. This place normally goes twenty-four-seven."

The whores and their johns had vanished. The inn was dead silent save for a creak from its ancient timbers. Even the steady hiss of traffic from the street out front seemed to have died.

Scott doused the lantern, then took Tracy's hand. "Come on, time for us to get out of here."

The sonar technician seated at the Kilo's MGK Rubikon monitors alerted Zemin. Zemin studied the thin green blip working down the screen; UNIDENTIFIED flashed red at the bottom. Zemin scratched his cheek. "Range to the target?"

"Fire-control reports approximately twenty thousand yards, Captain. But as you know, sir, the margin for error is great with such a weak contact."

Zemin factored that into his still sketchy strategy for identifying the target, which was on a southerly heading, and, according to information radioed from the SH-5 amphibian, inside Grid 21X due east of Rongcheng.

Zemin moved cautiously. He knew the Kilo's integrated fire-control/sonar system, good as it was, sometimes faltered when given weak low-frequency tones to process for target identification. Should he bend on more speed, close in and risk being detected by the intruder, or should he trail him at a safe distance and learn nothing? Zemin looked at the monitor: The narrowband trace had not fattened at all.

"Very well. Comrade First Officer, both motors ahead together one-third. We'll close slowly. Maintain our present course."

"Aye, Captain." The first officer moved off to relay orders and to update his electronic data pad.

"Sonar watch," Zemin said.

"Sir."

"Do not take your eyes off that band. Let me know the moment it changes."

"Aye, sir."

Zemin thought about his uncle, the hunter, and recalled the American 688I he'd flushed off Matsu Shan: *We will creep like a cat, then step like a bull to make this bird take wing too.*

Park and Kang emerged from the *Red Shark*'s cramped and steaming engine room. Their inspection of the polymer electrolyte membrane, an essential part of the hydrogen fuel cell, revealed that a valve in the main bleeder line connected to the hydrogen burner had iced up. The ice had created a backup in the line, which in turn had caused a bulge to develop around a welded joint behind the valve. This event had resulted in a measurable buildup of pressure in the fuel cell. Park knew there was no safe way to relieve the pressure buildup from inside the submarine's hull. All such valving was located in the superstructure, out of reach.

Park stood in the engine room, wiping his hands on cotton waste, listening to Kang's assessment of the situation, when the Captain's Light in the overhead began flashing again. This time Park saw CONTROL ROOM on the LCD and dashed forward, where he was directed into the sonar cubicle by the first officer.

"Captain, sonar contact, very faint," reported the sonar watch officer. "Bearing zero-two-three." The excited officer wiped his burnished face with a sleeve.

"Put it on external," Park ordered.

The officer toggled an audio interlock on the DBQS sonar system. A quiet, stuttering hiss emerged from the speaker mounted flush with the workstation's top surface. Park inclined his head, listened, and frowned. "Turn count?"

"Thirty turns—four knots, sir. Range coming on, sir."

Park glanced up at the integrated displays. The Konsberg MSI-90U system kept recycling, hunting for data it needed.

Park swung into the control room and snapped, "Helm! Come left to one-two-zero."

The officer of the watch relayed the order and acknowledged with, "Aye, Captain."

Park watched the needle on the compass repeater at the diving station swing left and steady up on 120. Satisfied, Park ordered, "Activate flank sonar array."

Park gambled that the FAS-3 flank passive sonar array, a long, tubular affair mounted on the *Red Shark*'s port side, working in tandem with the bow's wide aperture array, would allow the integrated tracking system to identify the target with greater precision.

The sonar warrant officer lined up switches, then held up his right hand, palm and fingers open. Abruptly he made a fist and said, "Activate array."

A sailor in the sonar room muscled a hydraulic actuator. After a brief delay, a suite of green lights on a panel above the sonar workstation flashed twice to indicate that each of the ten receptor modules in the array had activated.

Park stuck his head into the sonar room. The sonar-man had his eyes glued to the monitor and both hands clamped to the earmuffs of the headphones he wore. He sensed Park's impatience and squirmed in his seat.

"Contact?"

"Yes, Captain. Very clear contact. Bearing, still zero-two-three."

The first officer bulked behind Park in the sonar room.

"We have him now," Park said.

"A PLAN submarine, Comrade Captain?" asked the first officer.

Park gave the officer a thin smile. "We'll know very soon. If he is, we will go to silent operation, and when we do, it will seem as if we have vanished."

The sonar officer twisted around in his seat. "Comrade Captain . . . I have a computed range to the target: eighteen thousand yards." Nine miles.

Park waited while the integrated tracking system ran comparisons, hunting for a positive identification of the target.

If the target *is* a Chinese sub, Park thought, the *Red Shark* would not only have to run silent but possibly seek cover in the littorals, where bottom irregularities, salinity, turbidity, and temperature gradients would provide cover and impede detection. Risky business running silent in the littorals, and he hoped it wouldn't come to that. Better to quietly sidestep the Chinese boat and simply disappear.

The sonar officer started. Park heard it too: a sudden silence. Where there had been a faint stuttering hiss coming from the speaker, now there was nothing.

Park didn't wait. "Commence silent operation," he commanded.

37

Kabukicho, Tokyo

The banister was worn smooth. So were the steps that led downstairs to the back door of the hotel. Tracy, in stocking feet, heels clutched to her chest, followed Scott down the stairs. When they came to the back door of the fortune-teller's shop, he signaled "stop" by raising a hand.

Scott peered between the strands of a beaded curtain into the empty shop. Normally it was busy, but all he saw now was a low table surrounded by pillows and, on the floor, a stack of *utagaruta* cards, the kind fortune-tellers used in the traditional poem-matching games they played with clients. There wasn't a sign of the fortune-teller, an elderly woman in her eighties. And no sign of the whores and their customers, the salarymen. Scott's heart thudded and his palms sweated. At Matsu Shan, he'd been lucky to see his targets before they'd come at him. That wouldn't be the case here, he realized, even though he sensed someone might be hiding in the darkened hallway or behind a door.

Scott held the Glock at his side, muzzle down. He looked to his right, at Tracy: She was trembling and almost on the brink of panic. He tried to calm her by taking her hand and squeezing it; he got a squeeze back.

He shifted his weight, and together they eased past the fortune-teller's doorway, careful not to disturb the beaded curtain and set it clacking, and started down the hallway. Thirty feet away was an open door leading to an alley behind the hotel. Earlier he'd walked the escape route Sammy Shin had shown him to make sure he had it down.

Wood creaked. Scott froze. A door across the hallway shivered open a crack. Scott dove across the hallway, pushing Tracy ahead of him, and landed on a shoulder hard against the wall next to the opening door. He held the Glock out two-handed, prepared to fire, unless it was Sammy Shin or a young whore and her salaryman inside the room. Instead it was the man from the train in his black raincoat and armed with a silenced pistol.

Scott sprang forward into the man, crashing the Glock's short snout into his skull. The man fell backward against the door frame. The silenced pistol spit twice with a dull *phit-phit*, like a can of soda popping open, bullets splintering the lintel over Scott's head.

The man tried to scrabble to his feet, but Scott, legs driving like pistons, slammed a shoulder into the man's gut, pinning him against the doorjamb. The man's free hand tore at Scott's jacket. He grabbed a fistful of it and slammed his body into Scott, knocking him off balance. Scott staggered backward, glimpsed Tracy with both hands clamped over her mouth to cut off a scream.

Scott rebounded off the jamb, his arm a blur as he drove an elbow into the man's throat, and again as he slashed the Glock's snout down on the bridge of his nose, crushing cartilage. The assassin's silenced pistol skittered away into the darkened room. He lunged, the edge of his rigid hand a blade, which he chopped into Scott's rib cage, dropping Scott to both knees.

Scott, ribs seared, rolled away and got to his feet. The Japanese shook his head to clear it, heedless of the red skeins crisscrossing his white shirt front. A wicked-looking knife with a hooked blade appeared as if by magic in his hand. He uttered a blood-chilling cry, suddenly pivoted like a whirling dervish, the skirt of his raincoat flaring wide like the wings of a predator, gave a high leg kick, and charged.

The explosion from the unsilenced Glock inside the narrow hallway sounded like a bomb going off. The 9mm slug tore apart the kneecap of the man's flexed leg, shredded gristle and bone, knocking him off his feet. For a split second he seemed to hang suspended in midair on his predator's wings before crashing to the floor on his back.

The Japanese assassin looked up at Scott, eyes filled with hatred and searing pain. Scott stomped on the man's wrist to immobilize the knife in his hand. He pointed the Glock between the pair of blazing eyes and, fighting for breath, said, "I know you speak English . . . *who sent you?*"

The man writhed like a smashed bug under Scott's boot.

"Was it Tokugawa?"

Scott saw a reaction, not to pain but to Tokugawa's name.

"Where's the girl? Where's Fumiko Kida?"

The man's front teeth dug into his lower lip. His body started to shake as shock set in; a horrid smell rose from his voided bowels.

"I'm not going to kill you," Scott said. "I know that's what you'd like me to do. Instead I'm going to blow your other kneecap off unless you tell me what I want to know."

"Fuck you, man," he croaked, gargling blood from his broken nose.

"Jake, don't do it!" Tracy screamed before she vomited.

Scott aimed the Glock at the man's uninjured kneecap. *"Where's the girl, where's Fumiko Kida?"* he roared. But the man had slumped unconscious.

Scott moved like lightning. He grabbed Tracy's hand and pulled her down the hallway hopping on one foot as she put on her high heels. She tried to wipe vomit off her mouth and shirt front with a handkerchief, but Scott dragged her through the door and down the alley.

"Let go of me! *I hate you!*"

"Hate me later."

They raced down a narrow stone path that led to the main drag and emerged into light, noise, and crowds. Cold drizzle made Kabukicho's streets glitter like jewels. At the Pink Pussy Club, Scott turned down another alley to a minuscule private parking lot, where Tracy had left Rick's silver Lexus wedged in a space between two BMWs, the space for which he'd paid Sammy Shin ten thousand yen.

"You drive." Scott unlocked the car and got in; it reeked of Rick's cologne.

Tracy didn't budge. "You really are a complete *bastard*," she said. "I don't know you, Jake Scott. I didn't know what you were capable of till now."

"You also don't know what I'm up against."

"What's that supposed to mean? That what you did was right?"

Police sirens started hee-hawing from several directions at once.

"Trace, time's running out."

"Goddamnit, Jake, what are you trying to do, save the world again?"

"No, just one part of it."

38

The Yellow Sea Littorals

UNIDENTIFIED flashed red at the bottom of the Rubikon monitor long after the contact had vanished.

Deng Zemin couldn't tear his eyes away. A submarine contact couldn't just disappear in an instant. Fade, yes, but not vanish as if someone had thrown a switch. But vanish it had.

The sonar technician looked up sheepishly at Zemin, waiting for instructions. Zemin's mind raced through the possibilities: sound masking, interference, temperature gradients, the list was endless. But the Rubikon system's failure to identify the contact nagged at him, too.

The Rubikon's archive had the resources to identify almost all of the warships in service around the world, yet it couldn't identify a contact that he was convinced had been a North Korean submarine. The DPRK had only five submarines in commission, all of which were known by their sound signatures to every navy in the world. Was it possible, Zemin mused, that the DPRK had secretly deployed a new type of submarine with advanced quieting technology? It had been assumed that such technologies were beyond their reach. Were they? Chinese intelligence had, in the past, often underestimated the capabilities of North Korea's military. Had they again?

"Segregate the last contact coordinates from the target-tracking module and run an isolation program to dissect what we have," Zemin ordered. "Perhaps it will provide data we can use to start a new search."

While the sonar watch set to work reconfiguring the Rubikon system to search its memory, Zemin reviewed what little he had to go on.

The target had been on a southerly heading at slow speed. Sonar had reported the target's swing toward the coast. *Had they heard something? Us?* Minutes later, with its range a tick less than 18,000 yards, the target had vanished. A review of the Rubikon's data might indicate where to commence a new search, somewhere close to the coast.

"Your orders, Captain? . . ." It was the first officer.

"Maintain our current position while we try to reacquire the target. If he is on a spy mission, we'll try to trap him in the restricted zone surrounding our submarine base at Dingdao. But it won't be easy to find him, because he's running very quiet. Too quiet. It's a mystery."

"Aye, Captain." The first officer hesitated, then said, "Perhaps, sir, he has fallen into what they call a black hole."

At first Zemin ignored the remark, but then it hit him: Not a black hole in space but perhaps a black hole in the ocean.

The hole-in-the-ocean phenomenon posited that an ultra-quiet submarine could be detected by turning its own quieting technology against it. The theory suggested that an ultra-quiet submarine blocks ambient sound generated by the ocean environment around it, in effect creating a silent hole in the ocean. Find the silent hole, so the thinking went, and you'll find the submarine. Zemin knew his Kilo wasn't equipped with sonar designed to find a hole in the ocean, but a careful examination of information they already had might provide a clue to where the illusive target was.

"Sonar! Belay my last order."

"Aye, Captain."

"I want a full review of our audio drives, starting five minutes *before* and ten minutes *after* we lost contact with the target."

The first officer and sonar officers appeared baffled by Zemin's orders.

"You will commence a search for any dead zones in our sonar reception that might indicate a sound block. Find it and we will plot its position. If we allow for its speed of advance, we may find what we are looking for."

Marshal Jin's meeting with the Chinese and Russian ambassadors had not gone well. The ambassadors had blustered and threatened serious consequences if Jin did not back away from his threat to launch a nuclear war on the Korean peninsula. They'd left the meeting looking sour-faced.

Jin, standing behind his massive desk, undid the collar of his tunic and gave General Yi a look. Evening shadows that had crept across Pyongyang cast a gloomy pall over the darkened capital. Jin snapped on a desk lamp, which brightened the room but not his mood. He lit an English Player and crushed the empty box in a fist.

"What have you found out?"

"Nothing, Dear Leader," said Yi.

"Nothing at all?"

"The translators died under torture but knew nothing. If they had, they would have talked."

Jin dragged cigarette smoke deep into his lungs and said as he exhaled, "A waste of time." He picked tobacco from the tip of his tongue. "What has Kim accomplished?"

"Very little. He is more than halfway through the records of personnel assigned to the Second Directorate. So far he has failed to unearth anything incriminating."

"There must be something in those records." Jin threw down his lighter. "Kim is stalling for time."

"In fact, Dear Leader, he has been most diligent in his search. He has cooperated to an amazing degree. Understand, there are over three thousand records to search. It will take time."

"How much time?"

"It is hard to say. Some of the records are voluminous and in some cases the individuals have family members about whom we need more information."

Jin collapsed in his chair. He gazed over a blacked-out Pyongyang and smoked in silence. At length he said, "Tell Kim he has one week to complete his task to find the spy. If by then he has not found him"—he smashed out the Players—"there will be no exile. Tell him that instead I will fulfill my duty to the People's Council of Justice and carry out his execution."

The big Lexus hissed through drizzle toward Noda. Traffic clotting the roads forced Tracy on and off the brakes, to flash the headlights and cut around slower-moving cars.

"Is this man expecting you?"

"Yes."

Tracy glanced at Scott. His face looked spectral in the red instrument panel lights. "What does he do?"

"Big business."

"Ziabatsu?"

"You might say that."

"Who is Fumiko Kida?"

"She works for the Japanese government. She's in trouble and needs help."

"Have you fucked her?"

Scott turned a steely gaze on Tracy. "Pay attention to driving. Fumiko's been snatched by some people involved with terrorists. I know where she is and I'm going to try to free her."

"All by yourself? You're crazy. I was there in Kabukicho at the hotel, remember? I saw what happened. The people who kidnapped her will kill you."

"When you drop me off, return to the Embassy and say nothing. *Nothing!* Understood?"

"You're committing suicide, Jake. I won't do it."

He took hold of her arm and shook her. "Yes, you will, Trace."

"Why should I?"

"Because you love me."

She turned on him, eyes flaring like lasers. "I don't love you, I hate you!"

"But you'll do it."

McCoy Jefferson crashed into Kabukicho in a tiny Daewoo Magnus SUV.

A handheld GPS data link directed him to the fuck-hotel over the Bottoms Up. An SRO satellite had utilized Scott's recorded cell phone calls to Radford and Tracy to pinpoint the hotel.

Jefferson arrived to find a half-dozen white Tokyo Prefecture police cars and an ambulance parked in front. He searched but couldn't find a place to park, wasted precious time hunting for a space until he found a 6,000-yen-an-hour lot two blocks away. He horsed his gear packed in a black nylon bag out of the SUV and arrived just as the police were wrapping up.

Jefferson polled several bystanders until he found one who spoke English, a youth with spiky purple-and-yellow hair.

"What happened?" Jefferson asked.

"Some guy got shot in the hotel."

Jefferson tensed. "A foreigner?"

"Japanese. *Yakuza,* they said." The youth moved on.

Jefferson entered the Bottoms Up and looked around. Two naked Thai girls on a narrow stage over the bar, one of them flaunting a strap-on silver gel dildo, writhed in time to deafening techno. Porn videos played on a dozen TV monitors hung around the bar. The salarymen sitting at the bar, entranced by the action taking place on the stage, ignored Jefferson.

He ordered a beer and said to the bartender, "I'm looking for a friend. *Amerika-jin.* He was staying here, at the hotel. Maybe you saw him." He pushed a 10,000-yen note across the bar.

Sammy Shin came up to Jefferson, eyed him contemptuously, and said, "No *Amerika-jin* here, man." He pushed the beer out of Jefferson's reach and palmed the yen. "You go."

"He's a big guy," Jefferson said evenly. "He might have been with an American girl, dark hair, good looking."

Sammy looked Jefferson up and down as if seeing him for the first time. "No such man or *giru,*" he said. "I said you go, man. This place, Japanese only. No *gaijin.* No niggers. Fuck off!"

Jefferson produced a wad of yen. "I'll buy talk."

Sammy considered for a moment, then motioned that Jefferson should follow him down a narrow hallway. A man at the bar slid off his chair, but at a nod from Sammy, he stayed put.

Sammy led the way into a reeking men's room. He ordered a man to zip up his pants and get out. Sammy turned to Jefferson and said, "How much you pay—"

Jefferson slammed his left forearm into Sammy's throat, driving him back against a wall, pinning him there. He flashed a silenced H&K pistol and jammed it into Sammy's right ear.

"*Amerika-jin.* Where'd he go, asshole?"

Sammy's hands clawed at the thick arm crushing his throat. Jefferson bore down harder, until the flat face contorted in pain and a slimy gray tongue bulged from between two rows of brown teeth. "Talk to me, you fucking Nip, or this nigger's gonna put your brains in the toilet!"

When Sammy finished telling Jefferson what he wanted to know, Jefferson stepped back and thanked him, then drove a knee into his balls and kicked his feet out from under him. He threw the wad of yen at Sammy and left him doubled over on the filthy restroom floor, retching his guts out.

39

The Yellow Sea Littorals

The *Red Shark* hovered, not quite motionless, above a sea bottom that rose gently from the continental shelf toward the coast of China. The first officer thrust his head into the sonar room to say something, but Park held up a hand.

Park had an ear to the speaker; he was listening to a faint sound, what he thought might be a submarine's creep motor. Filtered and enhanced by computers that had flushed out the extraneous noise generated by small coastal craft and large commercial vessels, even the cry of biologicals, the sound Park heard had been analyzed and compared to known sources stored in the computer archives.

A Romanized label crawled across the upper sonar monitor: KILO 636-CLASS CREEP/MANEUVERING MOTORS.

"Now we know," Park said.

He exited the sonar room and, with the first officer, crossed to the chart table behind the periscope stand.

"We have a Chinese Kilo, almost dead in the water," Park said. He sketched a narrow, wedgelike shape on the navigation chart's acetate overlay and saw that it encompassed the area of littorals along the coast of China in which the *Red Shark* was now hovering. Park made two Xs on the chart and scaled the distance between them: less than 10,000 yards—five miles. *We're virtually within hailing distance of each other,* thought Park—*within the sure kill radius.*

Zemin heard the sonar officer report, "Possible dead zones here, here and here."

Zemin marked their positions the length of a shallow six-mile-long arc that ran roughly southeast to southwest along the coast. The zones he'd seen on the monitor were not clearly defined and, to his disappointment, looked more like amorphous blobs than profiles of a submarine. Still, they were better than nothing, but whether they had been caused by the target's sound-masking effects was another matter altogether.

"Range to the farthest zone?" Zemin said.

"Ten thousand yards, sir."

"Range to the nearest zone?"

"Three thousand yards but fading."

Zemin knew that somewhere on that arc was the submarine he'd been tracking. He also knew that the zones wouldn't last much longer and saw that even as he was viewing them on the monitor they had begun to evaporate.

"Disengage creep motor; main motors ahead together; speed seven knots."

The first officer relayed Zemin's orders: The main propulsion plant's quiet hum changed pitch to a lower register, and the Kilo lurched forward and gained speed.

Zemin saw the officer's questioning look and said, "We will close with the near zone, then stop and secure all motors and coast in the rest of the way to see what we can find."

"He's moving again," Park said as the *Red Shark*'s sonar monitors and data displays lit up like exploding fireworks. "He can't possibly know where we are," he added, aware that he didn't sound convinced.

"Hold position, Captain?" asked the first officer.

"What? Of course. Until we see what game he is up to. We're in his territory, where we shouldn't be. He doesn't know who we are and won't attack unless he feels threatened, and then not without approval from his headquarters. If he can't find us, he might give up and move on to a new search box."

Park settled down to wait him out. He doffed his cap and ran a hand over his sweaty, cropped head. *We've coexisted with the Chinese in the Yellow Sea and East China Sea for centuries,* Park thought, *and have never had an armed conflict. The Chinese are a cautious people and do not like to engage in direct confrontation with their adversaries. Taiwan, for instance.* Park put on his cap and frowned. He hoped that the Chinese skipper wouldn't prove him wrong—

"Captain!" The startled sonarman pointed to the twin video monitors on which data captured from the Kilo was being displayed. As Park watched, both monitors rescrolled their data maps to zero. The sonarman, eyes locked on the monitors, furiously punched the system's function keys, but nothing changed. "Sir, the target stopped his engines . . . we are losing contact . . ."

A chime tone warning sounded as the monitors went black, then to solid flashing red.

Karl Radford watched rush-hour traffic outside his Crystal City office inch past the Pentagon on Shirley Highway. He turned away when a slightly out of breath Navy captain entered the office.

"Sorry I'm late, General. Our translator had problems with the file."

Radford's gaze went to the mini-disc the captain held

in his hand, and he saw that it was labeled Purple—Eyes Only. The officer, whose ID tag hanging around his neck identified him as Roth, Allan J., went directly to Radford's desktop computer terminal and inserted the disc, then tapped the proper keys.

A page scrolled up; Roth stepped back. Radford took his seat and skimmed the monitor while Roth eyed the hard copy he'd brought along. Radford looked up. His disappointment, if not bewilderment, wasn't lost on Roth.

"This is it? This is what the Danes flew in for us from Copenhagen overnight?"

"Yes, sir. Ambassador Schlüter confirmed that it went out in the diplomatic bag immediately after they received it at the embassy in Pyongyang."

Radford went back to the page on the monitor. "Okay, well, our man's alive and functioning, but this . . ." He shrugged. "This makes no sense, does it to you?"

Roth said, "No, sir. I don't get the meaning at all. The translation section thinks its an allusion to some Korean mythological being or cultural artifact. G-Section's running it down now while they're working on the second part of the message."

Radford stared at the words on the computer monitor. They were beyond comprehension, perhaps a flight of fantasy concocted by a frightened man trapped in one of the most dangerous cities in the world: *Red Shark, Red Shark, Red Shark.*

Scott got out of the Lexus parked in front of the Prince Kota Hotel in Noda and leaned into the open window. "I'll call you at the Embassy when this is over. Now get out of here."

"Jake, don't go." Tracy reached for him, but he walked

away quickly. Fearing she wouldn't leave if he looked back, he didn't. He waited to be sure she had departed, then entered the hotel's dingy lobby and roused the sleepy manager.

"I need a *karuma*."

The man glanced at the clock, saw it was past midnight. "Impossible. No one on duty."

Scott stuffed yen in the man's fist. Twenty minutes after showing a passport and international driver's license that identified Scott as Mr. T. Jacobs, he squeezed behind the wheel of a tiny commuter car.

Noda's streets were not well marked, and none were marked in English. Even though he had an address gleaned from Fumiko's classified file, he couldn't find Tokugawa's villa, which was described as having a high stone wall around it, and, at the entrance, an ancient iron gate with pikes. He drove through the streets until he found a narrow lane half hidden by cryptomeria and wild foliage. *There!* At the end of a narrow lane, a high stone wall and a gate with pikes. He parked up against a stand of shrubbery, aware that if the prefecture police entered the lane, they'd see the car and investigate. He had no choice.

Scott switched off the engine and rolled down the window. He heard the Tokyo Express on the Chiba Line overpass and, after it had gone, ticking from the car's hot engine and exhaust system. He sat there, not moving, needing time to sort through what he had to do, and to let the tension in his body ebb after the encounter with Tracy. Even the short time they'd been thrown together had made him willing to risk smashing his psyche.

He forced himself to wait a beat, then he scanned the villa's gates and a section of the ten-foot-high wall for intrusion sensors. He didn't see any. Though the wall had no chinks or cuts suitable for use as handholds or footholds, a stand of spruce, its boughs overgrowing the wall, presented possibilities.

Scott got out of the car and, bent low, trotted across the lane. Back against the wall, he crept through shadows until he reached the trees. He climbed one using its branches for a ladder. After making sure there were no sharp obstacles or hidden sensors on top of the wall, he dropped to the ground on the other side into a garden of moso bamboo.

Crouching, he faced the villa, which had been built as two separate wings, each surrounded by a gallery. The wings, set at a forty-five-degree angle, were connected by an arch through which passed a cobblestone driveway. A courtyard facing a closed four-car garage was illuminated by light spilling from a row of small windows in one of the wings.

Scott gripped Rick's Glock in his right hand. Still crouching, he inched toward the villa. He'd advanced barely ten feet when he saw a dot of blue light suspended above the ground: a laser beam motion detector. He scanned to either side and saw its mate by the driveway. Break the invisible beam and alarms would go off in the house. There had to be more sensors, perhaps ground motion pads and trip wires. It had been too easy so far. He approached the beam path and stopped to scan the garden for a way around the beam, but he didn't see one.

Suddenly a white light exploded in his head. He felt his knees cave, and for an instant he saw Tracy. *Why had she come back? Why wasn't she at the Embassy with Rick, and what the hell was she doing in Japan anyway?*

Part Four

RED SHARK

40

Noda, Japan

Scott, flat on his back on a tatami mat, opened his eyes and saw a face enter his circle of vision.

"Welcome to Noda, Commander Scott," Tokugawa said in excellent English. Resplendent in a royal blue kimono, white *tabi* and *getas*, he looked every bit the shogun. "I was expecting you."

The fog cleared and Scott sat up. He looked around and thought for a moment he was in an art museum filled with lacquer work, scrolls, and ceramics. Then he remembered the hammer blow delivered to the back of his neck by someone unseen, perhaps the man standing motionless, like a statue, in a corner of the room. He was solidly built and looked like a dozing Buddha with both arms folded across his chest and a pair of hooded eyes, but his tense facial muscles and rigid stance said otherwise. Even now he seemed to sense something and lifted his head, as if sniffing the air.

Tokugawa offered Scott a cup of hot saki, which he refused. "I am puzzled, Commander Scott. What did you think you were going to do? Storm my home and free Ms. Kida?"

"Where is she? I want to see her."

"Who sent you?"

Scott slowly got to his feet and felt shaky for it. "No one. I'm acting on my own. I want to see Fumiko." He rotated his head to work out pain and stiffness.

Tokugawa frowned. "You are in no position to make demands. You were ordered out of Japan, but since you saw fit to disobey, I summoned security forces, who are on their way here to arrest you and Ms. Kida. You have violated Japanese security laws, a very serious offense."

"The director general of JDIH keeps you pretty well informed." Scott saw his cell phone, passport, and Rick's Glock lying on a small table across the room. "I know why you tried to kill us—because we discovered your secret plan to attack the United States with nuclear weapons. But the old man—Higashi—you didn't have to kill him."

Tokugawa, unfazed, wiped an eye. "Nuclear weapons? You and Ms. Kida seem to have a penchant for fantasy, Commander. Perhaps it is fueled by your country's habit of bullying weaker countries into submission under the pretext of making America secure. You see terrorist plots and treachery everywhere. Even in Japan, your ally."

"Does the director general know about your collaboration with Marshal Jin?"

Tokugawa's face turned stony. "Unlike you, he does not meddle in my affairs. You are involved in something you don't understand."

"I understand Jin's a madman. But what can you possibly gain?"

Tokugawa felt behind him for a chair and sat down. "In the seventeenth century, Ashikaga Yoshimitsu, the sworn enemy of Ieyasu, the first Tokugawa Shogun, wrote on the subject of a man's duty to his family. He said that a man who does not avenge his father's death in battle is a coward and traitor. Every Japanese soldier who fought in the Pacific War understood Yoshimitsu's words. But they also understood something else: *gyoku-sai*, a word that describes what it means for a Japanese to face an overwhelming enemy force and to die a glorious and courageous death."

"And you want revenge."

"For men like my father who fought against American imperialism, the war was *seisen*—sacred. A man who fought for Japan and in defeat was condemned to death by the victorious Americans had to be avenged."

"By destroying the United States?"

Tokugawa's voice took on an edge. "Not destroying but crippling the United States to halt its relentless pursuit of global hegemony."

Scott looked at the old man with loathing. Powerful, corrupt, willing to collaborate in the murder of millions for an ancient cause no sane man would embrace. But how to stop it? Tokugawa was old and immune to fear and guilt, and even the prospect of death would only harden his warped beliefs.

A *shoji* screen slid open, and an elderly man and woman bearing trays of covered dishes entered the room. The couple kept their eyes on their work while Tokugawa watched them arrange the dishes on a table. Finished, they bowed deeply and withdrew.

Tokugawa said, "Please join me, Commander. It is late, and you must be hungry."

"I want to see Fumiko," Scott said.

Tokugawa considered. At length he clapped his hands, and another *shoji* screen slid open. A wiry man in a powder-blue suit entered the room and bowed. Tokugawa spoke to him in Japanese, then turned to Scott and said, "Ojima will bring her."

McCoy Jefferson left the Daewoo SUV parked in a deep drainage ditch a short distance from the villa. He found Scott's rental car and looked it over and saw that it was empty. In shadow, Jefferson dug out black cammies, black balaclava, and gloves from his bag, put them on, and jammed the silenced pistol into a thigh holster.

Ready to go, he checked his watch, then unclipped a miniature transmitter from his belt and pressed a button to send a burst signal, to activate the transmitter's built-in homing beacon. As he did this, a digital timer on the transmitter started counting down from thirty minutes. All he was missing, Jefferson lamented, was a mini MAV, like the ones they'd used on Matsu Shan, to probe Tokugawa's villa to find Scott.

Moments later he had a small grapnel and line laid over the wall. He tested it with his weight and vaulted over the top in one fluid motion. On the other side he used a magno-discriminator to locate and avoid hidden laser beams and motion pads, then he tucked himself into a shadow cast by the short roof that overhung the gallery surrounding one of the villa's wings. Set, he eased onto the gallery's deck and duckwalked to one of the low windows. Inside he saw a large, modern kitchen and an elderly Japanese couple busy cleaning up.

Jefferson noticed a bamboo and cedar trash storage crib next to the kitchen door. He ran a pencil light over the crib's simple guillotine latch, which held the crib's double doors shut. He lifted the latch, opened the doors, and looked inside at four large, open metal trash cans awaiting the thrice-weekly trash pickup. Neatly packed inside the cans were the requisite transparent plastic bags of sorted paper, glass, aluminum, and organics. He rocked a can back and forth to test its weight.

Perfect.

He tugged and kicked, and a can crashed onto the cobblestones from the crib and rolled across the courtyard, disgorging its contents. Jefferson sprang to the kitchen door and got ready.

A spotlight came on, then the old man, armed with a broom, stuck his head out the door and shouted, "Shoo, shoo, shoo!" He stepped outside and waved the broom to scare away the pesky sika deer he thought had raided the trash.

Jefferson clamped a gloved hand over the man's mouth and dug the silencer into his neck. "Don't make a sound or I'll kill you," he warned in Japanese. "Understand?"

The old man's jaw stuttered, but no words came from his mouth. "*Understand?*"

He nodded, and Jefferson lifted his hand away. "How many inside?"

"Don't kill me."

"*How many?*"

"Five. The *gaijin*—he is an American. And a woman." He hesitated, but the silencer's cold steel made him speak again. "Master Tokugawa and two bodyguards."

"The *gaijin*, where is he?"

"With Master Tokugawa."

"The woman?"

The old man pointed to the second floor.

"The bodyguards?"

"Ito is with Master Tokugawa and the *gaijin*. Ojima— I don't know."

Jefferson pressed the muzzle against the man's cheek.

"Please, I don't know."

Jefferson believed him. "Call your wife. Tell her you need help."

The old woman almost fainted in Jefferson's arms. He herded the couple back inside the kitchen at gunpoint and stood them in a corner facing the wall. The old man tried to calm his wife by patting her back.

Jefferson found a container of rice flour, dumped it on a counter, and spread it out in a thin layer.

"Draw a layout of the house," he ordered the old man.

With a finger the old man drew a crude sketch in the flour. It placed the main room of the villa at the end of a dogleg off a long corridor from the kitchen. The old man also made marks in the flour to show the locations of the villa's half-dozen entrances, and he drew a box in the adjoining wing that represented the upstairs room where he said the girl was being held.

Jefferson scattered the rice flour. "Okay," he said, "face the wall."

He taped their mouths with Plastex and bound their hands and feet with nylon wire ties. The timer said he had twenty minutes left.

41

Villa Tokugawa

Jefferson held the automatic pistol loosely against his leg, silencer pointed down. He took a deep breath and moved out. At the dogleg, he stopped and heard voices: Scott's and that of someone he guessed was Tokugawa.

Jefferson flattened himself against a sliding door facing a wall of floor-to-ceiling glass panels, in which he saw his own reflection mingled with the softly lit garden outside. He inched forward; where the hallway turned into the main room, he rolled on a shoulder and peeked around the corner. Scott and Tokugawa were alone in the room. Jefferson pulled back, unsettled that there was no sign of the two bodyguards. *Not good.* He checked the timer on the transmitter: He had to move, *now.*

A bright reflection in the glass across the corridor caught his eye. He looked left, where a *shoji* screen had silently slid open, leaving a tall black rectangle in the wall. Light from an outdoor fixture had struck a shiny object inside the rectangle, and for a split second Jefferson had seen its flare reflected in the glass.

A fury of splintering wood and shredded paper

exploded into the narrow corridor like a bomb. A muscular man holding a knife in his fist burst through the thin *shoji* screen at Jefferson.

Jefferson saw the flashing blade, rapier-thin, and instinctively whipped his head back as the point whistled past his chin. He reacted on pure instinct, ducked, pivoted on his haunches, and swung the automatic up in a one-handed grip. The man lunged again; Jefferson shot him in the face.

The silenced 9-millimeter round tore the top of the man's head off, pulping his brains into a raspberry-colored mist, knocking him backward to the polished floor.

Jefferson sprang to his feet, spun around, and thrust the pistol, cradled in the cup of his left hand, at Jake Scott.

"Nice to see you again, Scott," said Jefferson, "but you really should have followed the general's orders." He yanked the balaclava off his head, motioned with the pistol that Scott and Tokugawa should back up, and, eyes locked on them, stooped cautiously to pick up the dead bodyguard's knife and the single spent cartridge case.

Scott looked past Jefferson at Ito, lying faceup in the hallway, his head shattered, brains stuck to the woodwork. Scott cycled through possible scenarios, searching for one that fit the current situation. Jefferson's look of cold determination said what Scott had realized perhaps too late: He, like Fumiko, was expendable too.

"You've got a date in Yokosuka," Jefferson said, eyes darting around the big room. "I'm here to see that you keep it."

"Some unfinished business needed attention," Scott said.

"Is that so?"

Tokugawa, seemingly unfazed by what had just happened, said calmly, "Your business, it seems, is to break into my home like common criminals and murder my servant. And now will you kill me too?"

Jefferson thrust the pistol at Tokugawa. "Shut up!" He jerked his head at the dead man. "Where's the other one?"

"He's bringing Fumiko down from upstairs," Scott said.

"The hell for? She's not our problem. You are. We're getting out of here."

"Uh-uh," Scott said. "I came for Fumiko and I'm not leaving without her."

Jefferson leveled the automatic at Scott. "My orders are to bring you in one way or another. She's not part of the deal, get it?"

"She is now," Scott said, looking behind Jefferson.

Jefferson warily shifted partway around, pistol still leveled on Scott and Tokugawa, and saw the blue-suited Ojima standing in the hallway behind Fumiko, an arm lashed around her neck. He had a Sig Saur pressed to her head. Scott saw an ugly purple bruise on her cheek, which, he thought, made her look totally helpless. Repelled yet hypnotized by the sight of Ito, she croaked something unintelligible, which Ojima choked off.

"How quickly the tables turn," Tokugawa said triumphantly. "Put down your weapon."

Jefferson hesitated, the silenced automatic rocksteady in his fist.

"Do as I say!" Tokugawa barked, "or Ojima will kill her." The old man's veneer of civility had suddenly cracked.

Scott saw a twitch of resistance building in Jefferson's stance—strained muscles, clenched jaw, tightened finger on the trigger. Scott chanced a move toward him with both palms up. Jefferson's eyes flicked from Scott to Tokugawa to Ojima and Fumiko. "Put it down, McCoy," Scott ordered. "He'll kill her."

Jefferson's eyes flared like hot coals.

"Remember what you said, that it takes a shooter to lead a shooter?" Scott said. "Well, I'm the shooter. You owe me, and I'm calling it in. Now."

At length Jefferson nodded, slowly stooped, and laid the pistol on the floor.

Tokugawa gave it a nudge with his *geta*, out of reach. "If you were dispatched to take Commander Scott into custody before he was arrested, you arrived too late. Now you are trapped. I could have *all* of you killed if I wanted to, and no one in Tokyo would ask any questions."

Fumiko's fingers clawed at Ojima's arm around her throat. "They'll ask plenty of questions after they trace those nuclear weapons to you and after they find out you murdered Higashi—"

Ojima cut her off with a brutal choke hold that snapped her head back.

"Ms. Kida seems to have made several incorrect assumptions," Tokugawa said, pivoting toward Scott, his eyes narrowed to mere slits.

"Actually, she has most of it right," Scott said, his gaze planted on her bruised face. "As you discovered, she's a brilliant analyst. Also tough."

"And *you*, Commander Scott, they tell me are a commander of submarines, that your record, too, is brilliant yet blemished by your nonconformist attitudes, that your exploits at sea are nothing short of mythical. But here you are, out of your element. Why? Why would your superiors send a submarine commander to do what a thug like Mr. McCoy can do?"

"It's Jefferson, McCoy Jefferson," said Scott. "I told you, I'm acting on my own."

"So you said, but that's not an answer. I was amused by Ms. Kida's wild theories about nuclear weapons being smuggled into the U.S. by terrorists. Do you accept her theories?"

"She didn't tell me everything she knows."

"Ms. Kida thinks the North Koreans are capable of delivering such weapons by ship. What do you think?"

"Probably they can," Scott said. "But North Korean ships are sometimes interdicted by the U.S. Navy. Seems to me they'd be pretty dumb to try it."

"Yes, your Navy patrols Asian waters and tracks certain vessels. The North Koreans are not fools."

"On the other hand, Meji Holdings has a fleet of ships that circle the globe. The weapons could be loaded in a container aboard one of your ships. You've got the motive and the means. The U.S. Navy is hardly going to board and inspect every merchant vessel you own."

"What the fuck are you two talking about?" Jefferson snapped.

"Didn't Radford tell you?" Scott said.

"Tell me what, for Christ's sake? He said you and the woman had broken into JDIH security files, that you were wanted by the Japanese, and that we had to get you out before a shit storm hit D.C. He sure as hell didn't say anything about smuggled nukes."

"I'll spell it out. Tokugawa and Jin are going to launch a terrorist nuclear attack on the U.S. That's right—you're looking at the mystery man from Matsu Shan. Fumiko and I were out to prove his involvement with Jin. His people killed an innocent man—ran him down with a car—then almost killed us but instead snatched Fumiko. Then he sent one of his people to kill me at the hotel."

"I was there, saw them take someone away that you'd shot," Jefferson said. "That was Tokugawa's man?"

"Now you know."

"Everything you have said are lies fabricated by the U.S. to justify a preemptive attack on North Korea," Tokugawa said sharply. "America has a reputation for concocting doomsday tales to justify its imperialist aims."

As he stared at Tokugawa, Jefferson's incredulity slowly turned to anger. His right hand, extended like a weapon, slowly rose. "You're fucking insane, mister!"

"McCoy, don't do it . . ." Scott grabbed Jefferson's wrist.

Tokugawa's hand was a blur. A ceremonial dagger appeared from inside the folds of his kimono. He thrust the dagger's needlelike point against Jefferson's belly, piercing his cammies, pricking flesh. Jefferson froze, his face inches from Tokugawa's, Scott's iron grip locked around his wrist.

They stood pinioned, motionless, until they heard the faint *whock-whock-whocking* of an approaching helicopter.

Tokugawa stepped away from Jefferson, but with the dagger still pointed at his belly. "The security forces have arrived," he said, his breath coming in ragged bursts.

The clatter of the helo's rotors and thunder of its turboshaft engine grew louder, until the villa itself began to vibrate. Ojima looked up, as if expecting any second to hear armed men rappelling down lines, landing on the roof.

Scott forced himself to think clearly, to gauge distances, timing, and, above all, the odds. Time had run out and there was only one avenue left. He ached to move, now, like lightning, but he feared that anything he did would only get Fumiko killed.

Suddenly the mini-talker in Jefferson's cammie shirt pocket chirped. A muffled voice said, *"Tango One, I'm on your beacon—stand by."*

Tokugawa, looking stunned, grasped what was happening: A Navy Seahawk helicopter was swinging in over the villa, its pilot homing in on the signal from the mini-transponder that Jefferson had activated before going over the wall.

"Tango One, I need a final—copy?" crackled over the mini-talker.

Jefferson looked helplessly at Scott: If he didn't reply to the pilot's query, he'd abort.

"Tango One—copy?" said the pilot.

Ojima, his body pressed against Fumiko's, jammed the Sig against her right temple, shoving her head against her left shoulder. She fought Ojima's biting grip and shouted over the helo's racket, "Jake, he knows about the nukes . . . on a ship . . . it's the only way—"

"Kill her!" Tokugawa roared.

Fumiko, a blur of motion, delivered a crippling blow with her right elbow to Ojima's rib cage. At the same instant Scott launched himself at Tokugawa with a lowered shoulder that lifted the old man off his feet onto his back.

Ojima, shocked, paralyzed with pain, backpedaled into a display case, which toppled over and shattered on the floor, shards of glass and ceramic art pinwheeling everywhere. The Sig in his fist exploded twice: one round went wild, the other pierced a glass curtain wall. Before Ojima could fire again, Fumiko took him down with a kick to his groin and a hand-chop delivered between his neck and shoulder, which shattered the collarbone and left him screaming in agony. The Sig skittered away across the floor; she moved like lightning to scoop it up.

"Tango One—aborting—"

Jefferson tore the mini-talker out of his pocket and bellowed, *"Tango Two we copy! We copy! Hang in there, buddy! We're on our way!"*

"Roger that," said the pilot. Then, *"Ah, Tango One, better hurry. We've got company. I count four vehicles approaching your AO. You expecting anybody?"*

Fumiko was on her feet, fighting for breath, a look of triumph on her bruised face.

"You okay?" Scott shouted over the din from the chopper.

She waved him away.

The chopper dropped lower, until it was hovering over the garden, the hurricanelike downdraft from its spinning rotors whipping debris into the air. A powerful beam of light shot from the ship's cabin and played over the garden and villa.

"Move it!" Jefferson shouted.

Fumiko started ransacking cabinets and drawers for papers, jamming whatever she found into a canvas shoulder bag.

"Forget that shit, we don't have time," Jefferson bellowed. He rounded up their gear and weapons, then picked up and threw a heavy chair through one of the glass panels facing the garden. Rotor wash roaring through the shattered panel ripped scrolls and pictures from the walls, tossed furniture around like toys.

Buffeted by the downdraft, Jefferson grabbed the lowered sling and held it open for Fumiko to put over her head and under both arms. A helmeted crewman in the open door 30 feet above got ready to reel her in.

"Where's Jake?" she shouted. "I don't see him!"

"He's coming!" Jefferson urged the sling on Fumiko, but she twisted away and ran back into the villa. Jefferson took off after her as something pinged against the helo's fuselage. Automatic weapons fire began popping and snapping outside the walled garden. More rounds spanged off the helo's rotors and armor plate.

Inside Fumiko found Scott kneeling beside Tokugawa. A deep red stain had soaked through the kimono's blue silk where Ojima's wild shot had pierced his chest above the heart. Frothy blood bubbled from Tokugawa's mouth. Scott tried to help him sit up, but the old man refused and weakly pressed the point of the ceremonial dagger against Scott's throat.

Fumiko dropped to one knee beside Scott. "Jake, is he? . . ."

The noise and wind howling through the villa made it hard to hear what Tokugawa was saying. Something about a warrior's duty to die an honorable death. But the old man didn't have the strength left to cut open his belly in ritual *seppuku*.

"Jesus Christ, are you both crazy?" Jefferson said, standing over them. "Forget him, let's go!"

Scott brushed the dagger aside and leaned close to the dying Tokugawa. He saw that something had changed: Moments ago the man's eyes had shimmered with a cold, pitiless resolve; now they projected a bleak, transparent uncertainty. The man who hated America even as he profited from it, who spoke its language and now plotted to destroy it, looked at Scott with something akin to sorrow.

A thin smile arched Tokugawa's lips. "How unfortunate for America that you won't have the opportunity to test your skills against the shark."

"The 'shark'? What shark? What are you talking about?" Scott felt precious seconds slipping away. The security forces had arrived; the helo couldn't hover forever. He felt control over his anger slipping away. "Where are the weapons? *Tell me, goddamnit!*"

Tokugawa turned a palm up, red from the blood-soaked kimono. Dark red drops trickled down his wrist and wicked into the folded-back cuff. *"Chi."*

"Blood," said Fumiko. "He said, 'Blood.' " She leaned close to hear him say something else. "He says he doesn't want to die disgraced by bleeding to death. It's the *Bushido* Code, he wants to die like a warrior." She looked up. "Jake, he wants you to kill him."

"Then do it so we can get the hell out of here," Jefferson said. He looked over his shoulder into the garden being flailed to ruin by the downdraft from the hovering chopper.

"Tell him," Scott said, "tell him I'll do it if he tells me where the weapons are hidden."

Tokugawa responded in Japanese. "He says surrender is not an option for him," Fumiko translated.

"Then I won't do it."

"Shit, I'll do it," Jefferson said, brandishing his pistol.

"Back off, McCoy!"

Jefferson gave Scott a black look. "We're fucking out of time, Jake."

Scott stood, looked down at Tokugawa, who was still holding the dagger weakly in his fist, and said, "Then it ends here."

Tokugawa, his strength ebbing, cried out in Japanese. *"Blood shark,"* said Fumiko. "He said, 'Blood shark.' " She shrugged, lost.

Scott knelt again. "What is the blood shark?"

Tokugawa, drawing on his last reserves of strength, said, *"Sang-O—Red Shark.* The weapons are aboard the *Red Shark.* A submarine."

Scott, stunned, said, "You're lying."

Tokugawa slowly shook his head.

"Where is it?"

"The Yellow Sea."

"How many weapons are on board?"

"Kill me . . ."

"Only if you tell me." Scott looked up at Jefferson. "Give me your pistol."

"No, give it to me instead," said Fumiko. "I'll do it—for Higashi."

Jefferson hesitated a moment, then handed it over butt-first. Fumiko made sure Tokugawa saw that the weapon was in her fist before she pressed the silencer against his temple.

"Tell me how many weapons," she said.

Tokugawa sucked air between clenched teeth. "Three."

"Where is the Red Shark headed? To what country? What port?"

Tokugawa didn't respond, and for a heartbeat Scott thought he'd died. But he said, "The Philippines. Davao."

Tokugawa's eyes pleaded for Fumiko to pull the trigger. Instead she gave the pistol back to Jefferson. She leaned close to Tokugawa and said, "You don't deserve to die a warrior's death." She stood and looked down at Tokugawa with undisguised loathing, until the knife fell from his hand onto his chest, inches from the oozing bullet wound. He went limp.

Jefferson took Fumiko's arm. "Jake, you coming . . ."

Scott remembered hearing guns crackling and bullets whining off the helo's skin. Then they were up over Noda and sweeping south toward the Kanto Plain.

42

East, over Tokyo

From the darkness of the Seahawk's cabin, Scott, wedged between pilot and copilot, looked out the windshield at the lights of Tokyo. Seated behind Scott, Fumiko and Jefferson leaned forward to hear his conversation with Karl Radford, who had been patched through to the chopper from Crystal City.

"She's going to be damned hard to find and kill," Scott said into the mouth mike of his headset.

Radford's voice came over distorted by the patch-through and muffled under the noise from the chopper's rotors. "A follow-up to our first message from Pyongyang confirmed what Tokugawa told you. 'Red Shark' made no sense to us either, until we received a second message from Pyongyang about a Type 213 submarine. That, plus the intercepted comm from the North Sea Fleet Lushun, that one of their amphibs reported a contact with an unidentified sub."

"That contact was the *Red Shark*," said Scott. "Bet on it."

"We have. We also have satellite imagery we think is the same target but haven't made a positive ID. Still studying its heat blooms. Looks like diesel-electric, not a nuke. If it was a Chinese nuke, we'd know it from its heat signature."

"Any idea, General, how the NKs got hold of a Type 213?"

"No, but we're working on it. Obviously we missed something, missed it by a mile."

"We've got to find and kill this *Red Shark* while she's still in the Yellow Sea, before she can break out into the Pacific. If she does, we might never find her."

"I'll recommend to the president that he not wait to confront the NKs with what we know, that he should force a showdown to get them to recall the *Red Shark*. No guarantee they will. Might deny everything. At the same time we'll coordinate with Philippine president Santos and order a special-ops force to move out from Guam and link up with Filipino units to find that terrorist base in Davao and take it out. Right now I'm not as worried about the terrorist cell as I am about the *Red Shark* and those goddamned warheads she's carrying. We can deploy SSNs to blockade the Yellow Sea, but if we do, the Chinese will probably go nuts."

"General, you won't kill the *Red Shark* by blockading the Yellow Sea. I know the Yellow Sea—it's shallow, and an AIP sub hiding in the littorals will be virtually invisible. If she finds a hole in the blockade, kiss her goodbye. Keep the blockade in place, but someone has to go in there, hunt her down, and kill her."

Silence from Radford, then, "That *someone* being you."

"Sir, you said the *Reno* needs a skipper, that you could pull my rabbit out of a hat . . ."

Another silence. "Wait one."

"Jake, what's he telling you?" Fumiko asked. Jammed

into a jump seat behind Scott, she looked crushed and exhausted.

"It's all worked out," Scott said. "We're not going to the brig. At least you two aren't."

While Scott waited for Radford's return, the chopper skirted Tokyo at low altitude, then turned southeast toward Tokyo Bay and Yokosuka. The Seahawk flew darkened inside and out, radar and infrared jammers activated, and Scott imagined the uproar it had to be causing at both civilian and military air-control facilities monitoring Japanese airspace.

"Scott," said Radford, back on the patch, "I've talked to Ellsworth, and he agrees with your assessment. I've also talked to the *Reno*. Her reactor is critical, and they've stationed the maneuvering watch. She's all yours. How soon can you get underway?"

"Soon as we touch down."

"Very well. You can also tell Ms. Kida and Colonel Jefferson that I want them to help our people coordinate our hunt for the *Red Shark*. They know the details as well as anyone, and Miss Kida's insights may turn the trick for us. Colonel Jefferson can backstop on the Davao operation."

"Yes, sir, I'll tell them. Ah, there's one other thing: We left a hell of a mess behind in Tokyo and Noda."

"We'll clean it up. You just find and destroy the *Red Shark* and those nuclear weapons."

Commander Deng Zemin shook his head. "Impossible!"

NO CONTACT flashed red at the bottom of the monitor.

The sonar tech kept his eyes down and said, "Captain, Target Zone Six was the last dead zone along the arc we examined. If the North Korean submarine had caused it or was anywhere near it, we would have made contact."

"So where is this Korean boat?" Zemin said. "We had contact with it and now it is gone. But where to?"

NO CONTACT, NO CONTACT, NO CONTACT flashed, as if mocking Zemin.

The sonar tech waited a beat, then said, "Sir, if the target has maintained its southerly heading while in an ultra-quiet configuration, it will not travel very far. Perhaps we might pick it up again . . ."

"Yes, perhaps so." Zemin dropped his hands to his side. "First Officer."

"Sir?"

"Give me a course that will first take us due east."

"East, sir?"

"If he hears us haul out east, he may think we've given up looking for him and continue south. Meanwhile we'll end around from east to south and intercept him as he comes down the coast."

"Aye, Captain."

"You will also prepare a message draft to Admiral Chou at North Sea Fleet Headquarters apprising him of the situation. After I have approved it, and as soon as we are on our new course, you will send the message via Fleet Priority. One more thing. Assemble everything we have archived on non-nuclear submarines in service with foreign navies. Especially the air-independent-propulsion types. I want to see it."

The officer understood. "If the North Korean regime bought this type of a boat, perhaps that would explain why we can't locate it."

Zemin laughed. "*Bought?* The North Koreans never pay for something they can steal."

Tongsun Park put his back against the wet periscope barrel and waited. There had been a sudden burst of acceleration from the Chinese Kilo, then only fading screw noise.

"He is sprinting due east, Captain. Turns for fifteen knots. Bearing zero-nine-zero."

Park pushed away from the periscope, entered the sonar room, and donned headphones. The steady beat of a screw and the fading thrum of motors confirmed what had been reported. Park listened for a time, then put down the earphones and ordered, "Motors ahead one-half. Come to new course one-five-zero."

The first officer gave Park a questioning look. "We will take advantage of his sudden departure," Park explained, "and move to deeper water. Here." He crooked a finger and beckoned the officer to the chart table.

"We are in an area of shallows and bottom uplifts. These cause fluctuating thermals and heavy turbidity, which result in very poor sonar propagation. Even so, if the PLAN dispatches surface units to search for us, I don't want to be trapped in this bight." He pointed to a coastal indentation at Ganyu.

The first officer read the datum on the chart. "Captain, Ganyu has less than ten fathoms at mean low tide."

"When we reach deeper water, we will turn south; we must always keep moving south."

Park took up a steel ruler and clear plastic protractor and penciled a rhumb line on the chart. Next he pulled a bottom contour chart out from under the navigation chart and flattened it with a sweep of his hand. Curved lines and color shading represented the shifting and varying depths of water found along the south China coast from Dingdao to Shanghai.

"You see, at Chenjigang the bottom steps out gradually until it reaches thirty-five fathoms at the north-south shipping lanes. There perhaps we can pick up a merchant vessel heading for, say, Okinawa, and use it to mask our passage across the East China Sea and through the Nansei Shoto."

The first officer nodded his agreement. "Captain, as you say, these routes are heavily traveled by commercial ships. A fleet of submarines could follow in their wakes and remain undiscovered for weeks."

Park put down his instruments. "Until then you will double the sonar watch. If that Kilo returns, this time she may be accompanied by aircraft. You will also maintain a taut ESM watch. I want air- and surface-discriminator reports on the half hour. Meanwhile I am going aft to inspect that damaged bleeder line in the fuel cell."

"Can it be repaired, sir?"

"That's what I intend to find out."

Seated in the Kilo's wardroom, Deng Zemin pored over secret reports on AIP subs. Written by The Chinese People's Naval Intelligence, the report stated that only China, Russia, and Germany had operational AIP boats. Other such boats, scattered among a half-dozen Western navies, were either laid up for lack of funds or serious mechanical problems: damaged fuel cells, valves, and piping. No evidence had been found by naval intelligence to indicate that the DPRK had an operational AIP boat or that it was building one, though the report concluded that North Korea had tried, in the early nineties, to obtain secret computer files containing detailed drawings and descriptions of fabrication methods that would have enabled them to replicate a German Type 213. Various components for such a submarine—engines, electronics, and weaponry—were rumored to have been purchased by the North Koreans on the open market.

The report included a set of grainy pictures taken from a Chinese GUK satellite of a World War II German U-boat-style submarine pen that had been blasted out of the granite bluffs surrounding the port of Nam'po. The pen was said to house a building way where a submersible of some unknown type had been under construction for at least five years.

Chinese naval intelligence asserted that the submarine was a conventional diesel-electric, likely a midget. But that assertion had proven wrong when GUK imagery had discovered that the North Koreans had instead launched a full-sized submarine, one that looked exactly like an old Russian Tango-class diesel-electric, a design at least 35 years old. The report stated that while the launching of the Tango demonstrated the DPRK's capacity to build a submarine on its own, it didn't have the capability to build a modern nuclear or AIP submarine.

Zemin studied the picture of the submarine built inside the pen. For a Tango, its shape seemed all wrong: bulges where there shouldn't be any; hull too short and stubby; sail plating askew here and there, as if it had been hastily applied to cover something up. A poor job of camouflage, he thought.

Zemin tossed the report aside and concluded that Admiral Shi's vaunted intelligence service's assessment was dead wrong. The North Koreans had in fact built a German Type 213 right under Shi's nose. That in itself was amazing enough. More amazing was his discovery of this submarine so far from its base in Nam'po at a time when the DPRK and the U.S. were on the brink of war.

Zemin's mind flooded with possibilities: Find and destroy it—no, capture it in Chinese territorial waters.

To attain such a prize would be worth risking his and his crew's lives. Not only would it tamp down North Korea's ambition to be a regional power but it would also show the U.S. Navy once and for all that it was China, not the U.S., that controlled East Asian waters.

A portable phone warbled in Marshal Jin's quarters, where he was soaking in a steaming tub of bathwater. A halting aide brought the phone, and when Jin heard General Yi's voice, he ordered the aide to leave the room. After a brief exchange, Jin ended the call. Ten minutes later, wrapped in a thick kimono and drinking *soju,* he waved General Yi into a private study.

Yi saw a shaken and deeply worried Jin. "With apologies, Dear Leader, for intruding at such a late hour."

"You said there was a news report that Iseda Tokugawa had been killed, shot to death. How?"

"Yes, it was reported on China's CCTV and in Tokyo on NHK, that he was shot dead by an associate named Ojima, a reputed member of the *yakuza* involved in the Tokyo powder trade. Another man was also shot and killed."

"Where did this happen?"

"At Tokugawa's home in Noda."

Jin, ashen, lowered himself into a chair. "What else have they reported?"

"Nothing, Dear Leader, nothing that concerns us."

"Are you mad? Everything about this concerns us; his murder is a disaster. It will change the complexion of Japan's domestic politics and alter its business dealings with the rest of the world. But more than anything else, it will doom our operation in the Philippines."

"With respect, his death has changed nothing. At this juncture Tokugawa was merely a bystander waiting to step in and help the Americans recover from the attack. We control the entire operation, not Tokugawa."

Yi seated himself without waiting to be asked. He lit a cigarette and waited while Jin, lost in thought, sipped his drink, though not with pleasure. "His murder is not a coincidence," Jin said at length. "First there was the attack on Matsu Shan by an unidentified military force, then the killing of Fat, now this. The Americans must have had a hand in all three. I am sure of it."

"Dear Leader, Tokugawa had enemies. It was his bad fortune to be shot and killed by one of them."

"Do you discount coincidences?"

"No, but I always keep them in perspective, especially in regards to the Japanese and their penchant for secrecy and intrigue. Tokugawa was a master of intrigue."

"That's why nothing in Japan is what it appears to be. *Nothing*. Somehow the Americans penetrated our operation. It's clear that they knew of our meeting and sent a force ashore to get information about it." He bowed his head. "Our element of surprise has been lost."

Yi studied Jin through a scrim of cigarette smoke curling from his own cigarette. "If you believe that, Dear Leader, do you then propose to call off the operation?"

"Not yet. News reports are often wrong and given to exaggeration. Obviously there is more to his death than we know. Can you put our agents in Tokyo to work on this?"

Yi, not surprised by Jin's stubborn reluctance to abandon what he had worked so hard to set in motion, stood and crushed out his cigarette in a heavy glass ashtray on Jin's desk. "I will do as you ask." Yi worked the butt down until it was nothing but flattened paper and ash. Then, looking up at Jin, he said, "Kim has information that bears looking into."

Jin quickly shifted gears. "About the spy?"

"Yes. He's no fool, you know. Working with the material we provided, he connected a series of meetings held at the People's Ministry of Science on the subject of radioactive isotopes to several informal discussions conducted at the Danish Embassy's science section with a group of our scientists. He seems to think the discussions held at the embassy may have been for the purpose of passing secret information to the outside by one of our people."

Yi's news electrified Jin even more than had the news of Tokugawa's death, and it brought Jin to his feet. "Which of our scientists were involved?" he asked. "I want to know and I want them arrested immediately."

"In due time. Kim has not identified them yet but soon will. There may be others involved, others outside the science ministry."

"If so, I want them all rounded up, not just the few who had contact with the Danes."

"As you say, Dear Leader."

"When will this be done?"

"Perhaps the end of the week."

"Excellent." Jin, relieved, smiled. "But I am a terrible host. Please forgive me and have a drink. You bring good news and bad. At least let us toast the good."

43

The *Reno*, west of the Ryukyus

Scott was ready to drop from fatigue. The hum of the *Reno*'s machinery and flow of warmed conditioned air through the control room had a lulling effect. Departure had been a blur of frenzied activity by the crew, linehandlers, and tugs nudging the *Reno* gently out of her berth. Soon thereafter, she was submerged, sprinting for the East China Sea.

On the status board Scott had posted that he wanted flank speed maintained all the way to their op-area except during passage through Osumi Strait at the southern tip of Kyushu. He had no search plan in mind yet, but both instinct and the reports he'd received told him they'd likely find the *Red Shark* somewhere east of longitude 124 and north of the Shanghai-to-Taipei trade routes. Now, after standing out from a ship-congested Osumi Strait, the *Reno* had resumed her headlong sprint to her op area.

"Captain, care for some coffee?"

Scott accepted a cup from his exec, Rus Kramer. Scott liked the way Kramer had handled himself during the Matsu Shan insertion and was glad to have such an experienced officer aboard to back him up. "Thanks, Rus. Appreciate you getting us squared away and to sea in record time."

Kramer appraised Scott's haggard looks, the fresh dressing on his hand, the bruises and scrapes on his face. What he saw underscored the seriousness of their mission. "Captain, every man aboard knows what we have to do and how important it is that we find the *Red Shark*. Our families are at home and, well, it's personal now."

It *was* personal, Scott thought, personal for himself, Kramer, the officers and enlisted men aboard the *Reno*; for Radford, Ellsworth, the president, and the thousands of Americans who would die if the attack succeeded; for the millions who would survive and whose lives would be changed forever; for the cities that would be left in smoking ruins after nuclear attacks by terrorists.

He thought about Tracy, hopefully safe in Tokyo, surprised yet not surprised that he cared and felt a sharp pang of guilt. The bond they'd re-formed in the short time they'd been together in Tokyo was tenuous yet real, even though he'd forgotten all about her in the rush to save Fumiko and break open the terrorist plot. He could have called Tracy from Yokosuka, told her to wait for him, but why should she? Now it was too late for him to do or say anything that would change her mind.

"Captain, excuse me." It was the *Reno*'s plot-control coordinator, Lieutenant Rodriguez. "Request a nav fix."

The *Reno* had steamed west of the Ryukyu Trench and was now speeding over a region of deep ocean bottom faults and uplifts. In another hour they would cross over into the wide continental shelf, a relatively featureless and flat abyssal plain under the East China Sea. Ocean bottom contour position plotting, which relied on feature-matching for its accuracy, was at a disadvantage over smooth surfaces. A nav fix from global positioning satellites would update the *Reno*'s inertial navigation system and thereafter provide extremely accurate plotting data that would prove essential if and when the *Reno* made contact with the *Red Shark*.

"Let's take a look," Scott said.

He and the two officers moved to one of the two plotting tables aft of the watch station. The quartermaster of the watch had taped tracing paper over the navigation chart and on it had penciled in the *Reno*'s track. The quartermaster pointed to a dot that represented the *Reno*'s current position on the track.

"Sir, if we can get a fix now, we won't have to take time to update later if things get hot. Plus with our RDT we don't have to slow down or come to PD."

Scott noted their depth on the digital display: 620 feet. He turned to Kramer and said, "Can we piggyback our nav updates with high-data rate capture from SRO and Yokosuka?"

"No, sir, can't do both simultaneously. We have to reconfigure for each capture. Only takes a few minutes to make the switch."

"We're due for an SVTC conference in less than an hour. By then we'll be crossing the continental shelf. From seven hundred fathoms to less than a hundred," Scott snapped his fingers, "just like that." He pointed to the line of demarcation on the chart where the ocean's depth changed from 4,200 feet to less than 600. "And it'll only get shallower the closer we get to the China coast." He pushed away from the plotting table. "Permission granted to update. When you're finished, break out charts of the coast south of Shanghai. Let's see if we can figure out where the *Red Shark* might be hiding."

* * *

Radford looked frightful on the split SVTC transmission from Washington. Exhausted and drawn, he chain-smoked as he spoke. "A few hours ago we intercepted a message to Admiral Chou at North Sea Fleet Headquarters transmitted from what we are pretty sure is a PLAN submarine on patrol in an area south of Dingdao. To summarize, the message indicated that the unit had made and then lost contact with a DPRK submarine. The PLAN message states that they are in the process of making an end around to hunt for this submarine near Rizhao."

"Has to be the *Red Shark*," said Scott, glancing at Kramer, who had joined him for the broadcast conference in the control room. Kramer nodded agreement. "Seems to confirm, General, that the NKs have a 213 on the loose," Scott added.

"Indeed, except that we've been over our archived material and can't find a thing that points to its existence. No satellite material or electronic intercepts. I just don't see how we missed it." Radford was still distressed over SRO's having been surprised by the existence of the advanced North Korean boat.

"Anything new on satellite?" Scott said, pressing on, thinking that Radford could rake his fingers through the dead coals looking for clues later; right now he had a live sub to find.

"Yes, Ms. Kida can fill you in on that. By the way, she's working for us now."

She appeared on the other half of the monitor looking tired but alert. The brightness Scott liked to see had returned to her eyes, and the bruise on her face had been covered up by skillful application of makeup. "Greetings, Captain Scott. And to your crew."

"Thank you. I'm pleased to see you looking fit again."

"The U.S. Navy's taking good care of me."

"Your family, they were unharmed?"

"Yes." She lowered her eyes. "But Higashi-*san* was considered part of our family. His death has hit my parents very hard."

"I'm sorry, Fumiko. Very sorry. Please tell your father."

At length she looked up and said, "I will." She cleared her throat. "We have updated satellite imagery, which, after analysis, we believe shows the North Korean sub. We'll have another update in eight hours. For now the coordinates you see on the monitor are the latest we have, and they jibe with the position of the PLAN sub at the time of its contact transmission to North Sea Fleet Headquarters. As you can see from the heat bloom—and it's very faint—the DPRK sub has indeed moved south to Rizhao."

"Yes, I see it—barely. We'll adjust our search protocol accordingly."

Kramer was busy roughing out courses and search patterns based on the information Fumiko had just provided. He leaned into Rodriguez, who was standing at the portside plotting table, and filled him in.

"General, anything from the Philippines?" asked Scott.

"The president has spoken to Santos. He's offered full cooperation and is assembling a special-ops contingent of Filipino Special Forces for insertion along with our people. Colonel Jefferson is with a recon unit that lifted out of Guam an hour ago. We've narrowed the search for the terrorists to an abandoned port facility in Santa Cruz, south of Davao City."

"What are the Japanese saying about Tokugawa?"

"They're still reporting Tokugawa was murdered and nothing more. The DG, as you might expect, has threatened to go to the prime minister with all of this, but I told him that if he did, things would turn ugly fast, especially over what happened to Ms. Kida and the cover-up by Kubota."

"Have the North Koreans said anything?" asked Scott.

"Not a word. Ambassador Cummings is meeting with their UN representative later today and will tell him to his face that we know about *Red Shark* and the weapons and the base in the Philippines. Ms. Kida, do you have anything to add?"

"General, just a thought, that if Captain Scott can find the *Red Shark,* perhaps he can force her captain to surrender."

"What do you think about that, Scott?" asked Radford.

"If we can find her we'll likely have only one chance to nail her. Sorry, Fumiko, but I'm not planning to negotiate with her skipper."

"Very well," Radford said. "We'll update you if something breaks, say at the UN."

"Well, it was only an idea," said Fumiko. "Good hunting, Captain Scott."

Scott signed off, thinking about the fanatics who would destroy the U.S. One of them was dead, but there were others waiting for the outcome. In the end, it would come down to the *Reno* vs. the *Red Shark*. Only one would survive. Only one *could* survive.

The dream never changed: the charging North Korean destroyer with a bone in her teeth; the shouted orders; the whine of torpedoes; the deafening twin thunderclaps; the NK tincan folding in half like a V; cotton in his mouth and a churning gut—

"Captain."

Scott's eyes snapped open. "Right." He swung out of

his bunk, sweaty, feeling as if a white-hot knife had
been plunged into his chest. Fully awake now, he read
the bulkhead-mounted digital compass repeater and
pit log. The *Reno* was steaming northwest at ten knots.
Four hours ago, around midnight, when she had
crossed the imaginary line of demarcation between the
East China Sea and Yellow Sea, Scott had quit the control room for a few hours of uninterrupted sleep in his
stateroom. Now, he sensed that something had
changed.

The enlisted duty messenger said, "Sir, command
duty officer says we have a tonal contact bearing three-
two-nine. Possible submarine. Range and speed still undetermined."

"Tell him I'm on my way."

The image of the folded-up tincan lingered in Scott's
brain, a haunting presence as he pushed into the control room crowded with watchstanders. It faded as he
looked around at the manned ship control station and
its glow of instruments; at busy Fire-control Alley and
its row of monitors lit up with data; at the navigation
system and its repeaters; at the phone talkers with their
sound-powered phones, ready to relay orders. Following Scott's standing orders, Rodriguez, the command
duty officer, had called away battle stations lite. Men
had shouldered into position at their stations and
stood easy but ready to take action if Scott ordered it.
Exec Kramer was busy monitoring the inflow of data.

"I have the conn," Scott announced to the officer of
the deck, on duty at the watch station. "What do we
have?"

"Aye, sir, you have the conn," said the OOD, Lieutenant Steve Dozier, one of the *Reno*'s fire-control officers. "Sonar's got a possible diesel-electric sub, range

approximately forty-thousand yards. No speed estimate yet. Contact is intermittent."

"Weapons status?" Scott said.

"Sir, all tubes loaded but not flooded; outer doors closed," reported the weapons officer. "Power units for all torpedoes activated and on standby."

"Very well, weps."

Scott stepped aside to examine a console on which was displayed a wide-area geographic view of the *Reno*'s position relative to the coast of China. A blue pinpoint of light representing the *Reno* surrounded by green-lighted friendlies moved slowly northwest. South of Rizhao, in Haizhou Wan, a blinking red pinpoint indicated the position of the unidentified sound contact now classified by the fire-control party as Sierra One.

Scott turned to Kramer. "Rus, let's take a look at Sonar."

They entered the dimly lit sonar room, its positions fully occupied by watchstanders. The sonar supervisor hovered over the chief petty officer who was wearing headphones and a mike, and facing a vertical row of twin sonar monitors. Each monitor's multicolored waterfall graphics currently displayed what the *Reno*'s spherical bow array had picked up earlier. The sonarmen's faces were intent as they sifted the target's tonals, searching for identifiable attributes.

"Chief, is it a diesel or nuke?" Scott asked.

"Diesel, sir."

"Chinese or NK?"

"Working on it, sir," the chief said. "Huntin' for a match."

The chief pointed to the upper monitor, where a thin, white vertical band moved slowly down the screen.

"Target's been fadin' in and out, but there's something familiar about it. I think we've got ourselves another Kilo 636," said the chief.

"Like the one we ran into off Matsu Shan," said Kramer.

"Maybe the *same* one," said the chief. "Something about its tonals—there we go."

As the analysis continued, the tone line brightened noticeably. Below it, the monitored sound's intensity and frequency showed an increase as well.

"Got him, Captain. Single blade turn rate indicates a speed of five knots," the chief said. "It's a match all right, the same goddamn Chinese Kilo we picked up off Matsu Shan."

"What's he doing here?" Kramer said.

"Training exercise," suggested the sonar officer. "He's probably based at Dingdao."

"But I thought all PLAN subs are based at Huludao," said Kramer.

"Just nukes," the officer said.

"How long ago did we pick him up?" Scott asked.

"About an hour," Kramer said.

"And he hasn't moved?"

"Hardly an inch, sir," the sonar officer answered.

Scott pondered a moment, then said, "All right, let's move in—real careful—and see what he's up to."

"Any ideas, Captain?" said Kramer.

"The Chinese get real twitchy when they think someone's messing around in their private lake up here. We saw how this guy got cozy with us until we took out the *White Dragon*. He sure as hell doesn't know we're here now or he'd be on the move. Maybe, just maybe, he's looking for someone else who doesn't belong here."

44

China's littoral waters

Aboard the Kilo, Captain Deng Zemin watched a faint green blip slide across the dual sonar monitors. Though the blip was still too weak to identify through all the background clutter, the Rubikon's audio spectrum analyzer recycled and recycled until a tone line appeared on the monitor and under it, in flashing red, the message IDENTIFIED.

The sonarman said, "Captain, this tone line matches one of our earlier ones."

"Are you sure?"

"Sir, the two sets of intermittent contacts are an exact match."

Zemin looked at the overlay of lines and saw that indeed they matched perfectly. He turned to his first officer. "Do you agree that we have a match?"

"I do, Captain. I'm convinced it's the submarine we tracked earlier."

"Our orders from Admiral Chou are to find, identify, and take appropriate action against this target. And we will. Identify this contact as DPRK One." Zemin stood erect, satisfied that his end-around tactic had worked:

The North Korean sub had reappeared on sonar, east of due south.

The sonarman began inputting more data to the Rubikon's target analysis program, while the first officer backed it up on his electronic data pad. Moments later the system recycled again; this time DPRK ONE flashed in the message slot at the bottom of the monitor.

"Very well," said a satisfied Zemin. "First Officer, prepare firing point analysis on DPRK One. Initiate constant tracking and update to torpedoes. Make preparations to engage target and launch weapons."

"Aye, sir."

"Maintain silence in the boat. Engage creep motor. Come to new course three-three-zero."

The first officer repeated Zemin's orders, and a moment later, the Kilo, her bow pointed toward the target, slowed to less than walking speed. "Orders confirmed, Captain."

Zemin climbed into the captain's conning chair in the Kilo's deathly silent attack center. "Now, if we can slip in on cat's feet, we may have a prize to present to Admiral Chou."

Captain Park ran a gloved hand over the bulge around the welded joint upstream from the frozen main fuel cell bleeder valve and hydrogen burner. The bulge, larger now, had caused the two-inch-diameter stainless steel line to skew in its hangers. A thermal wrap had not thawed the valve, and engineering officer Kang's face mirrored his concern.

"Can this valve be replaced?" Park asked.

"Captain, not in the prescribed way. The liquid hydrogen is under great pressure, and any unchecked opening of the system will cause a blow-down. The hydrogen will gasify and flood the compartment. The mixture will be explosive and—"

"What will happen if the welded joint bursts under pressure of the ice buildup? Will it not cause a blow-down?"

"Yes, definitely."

"Can the valve and line be bypassed?"

"Not with the materials and tools we have onboard. And not in the position we are currently in . . ."

"Hunted by a Chinese boat." Park ran his hand over the weld and around the pipe like a doctor diagnosing a sick patient's chance of surviving major surgery. The bulge felt even fatter than it had moments ago. "Can you apply more heat to the valve to melt the ice so we can purge the seat? If we can close the valve and tap into the feed line, we can possibly rig a diverter to the hydrogen burner."

Kang said, "Captain, I can try . . ."

Park looked up, distracted by the flashing Captain's Light that shouted he was needed in the control room.

Park's attention was back on Kang. "Well?"

"Sir, we have a gas cutting torch, but using it to heat the valve is out of the question, it's . . . it's too dangerous . . ."

"More dangerous than having the line split and cause a blow-down?"

Kang swallowed hard.

"Do it."

Park threw down his work gloves and went forward.

The first officer directed Park's attention to the sonar monitor. "Contact, sir," he said. "Submerged target. Speed appears to be near zero. Turn count almost inaudible. Sonar heard a transient, perhaps water flow over a hull appendage."

The *Red Shark*'s ultra-sensitive spherical bow array, aimed directly at the target, had missed nothing, not even the ruffle of seawater around a hull fitting.

"What is our present speed?"

"Four knots, Captain."

"Sounding?"

"Twelve fathoms."

"Stop and secure main propulsion and trim pumps."

"Aye, Captain."

Park watched the needle on the pit log at the diving station swing left and come to rest, pegged on zero. He knew they could coast for a while on momentum. But with both sound-mounted trim pumps secured to reduce noise levels, they would not be able to hover. In time the boat would require an ever steeper up-angle to prevent her sinking stern-first into the littoral shallows. Yet Park was willing to gamble that by running ultra-quiet, sonar would positively identify the target and its position, which would then allow for evasive action.

Park waited, his stress building to a climax, like a bomb with a sputtering fuse. He watched the combat system cycle through its target identification programs, various program keys flashing brightly on the monitors like heat lightning.

Park gripped a stanchion and held on as the deck under his feet tilted ever steeper upward. He eyed the silent laser Fathometer display and saw it tick down to ten fathoms: only sixty feet of water separated the *Red Shark*'s rudder bottom from the seabed.

Something caught his eye: The words KILO 636-CLASS TONAL appeared on the upper sonar monitor. Below it was a side-by-side comparison of the old and new tonals, which Park saw at once were identical.

"Our friend," Park said, "is back." He gave the Fathometer a look. Nine fathoms.

Like a mountain climber ascending an icy north face, he hand-over-handed it out of the sonar room to the control room. The first officer, also scrabbling for handholds, followed.

"Rudder hard a-port," Park commanded. "Ultra-slow start on Permasyn motor; three beats then secure. Maintain current depth. Perhaps we can pinpoint him."

"Aye, sir," responded the officer of the watch, who, struggling to hang on, repeated the orders.

A subdued hum and the *Red Shark* lurched ahead, gained momentum, and leveled out.

Park counted down three beats of ten seconds' duration and nodded approval when the officer of the watch rang up Full Stop on the propulsor control. Tonals from Park's start-and-stop, sprint-and-drift technique, even if detected by the Kilo's sonar, wouldn't necessarily give away their position. Park counted on littoral irregularities to partially cover their movements. He gambled, too, that even if the Chinese skipper heard them, he would have a hard time pinning them down.

"Sonar report," Park commanded, impatient.

"Steady contact, Comrade Captain," said the sonar officer, leaning into the control room from the sonar room to make his report.

The *Red Shark* coasted, her deck slowly tilting up, up, up as the planesmen compensated for the sub's gradual loss of speed. A loose technical manual slid across the top of an electronics cabinet; the first officer grabbed it before it crashed to the deck.

"Sonar report."

"No change, sir."

Park nodded approval. "He is still looking for us where he thinks we should be, waiting for us to fall into his arms. Instead we will open out to the east and work around him."

The *Red Shark*'s bow continued its steady rise as she lost more way, making footing ever more treacherous, the deck tilting up at an alarming thirty-five-degree angle.

"Officer of the watch, I want six beats, then secure," Park ordered. "Maintain current depth." He looked at the first officer and allowed a small smile to soften his hard features. "I think he has lost us."

45

The *Reno*, southeast of Haizhou Wan, the Yellow Sea

"Conn, Sonar."

"Conn, aye," replied Scott.

"Captain, we have a new contact bearing three-one zero. Range just a tick under forty thousand yards. No tonal matches, and we only have blade-turn information. Could be a submarine, sir."

"*Could be,*' Chief?"

"Can't say for sure, Captain. You might want to take a look at this baby."

Scott turned the conn over to Kramer and entered the sonar room.

"That there's Sierra One, the Kilo," the chief said. "She ain't hardly moved in the last half hour, not since we picked her up. It's this other one, Sierra Two, what's got me. She's sprintin' and driftin' in a regular six-cycle pattern, each interval between cycles is about ten minutes duration. Pretty sure it's a sub, but what kind, I don't know. Want to give a listen, sir?"

Scott took the sonar officer's seat at the console next to the chief, donned headphones, and heard the tonal

pattern the chief had described, even as he watched the
upper monitor's display of what the bow array was
hearing.

"I hear it," Scott said.

"It's nothing we have archived," said the sonar officer over Scott's shoulder, pointing to the weak tone line
crawling down the monitor.

Scott heard the cycle start again: a pulse from the
target's seven-bladed screw.

"Definitely a sub," said Scott.

The chief turned his gaze on Scott. "Maybe a German Type 213?"

"Bet on it. But what's this Chinese Kilo up to?"

"Maybe he's as curious as we are," the sonar officer
said.

"Or maybe he found the *Red Shark* and doesn't know
it," Scott said, vacating his seat at the console. "No sign
from either of them that they hear us, so we'll take advantage of that as long as we can. We'll run on up there
and see what's what."

Scott returned to the control room to monitor the
progress the tracking party in Fire-control had made
after receiving the target data from sonar. The BSY-2
consoles, manned by a full complement of officers who
had anticipated the fresh inflow of data from Sierra
Two, had begun the tracking process on what everyone
now believed was the *Red Shark*. Kramer, orchestrating
the operation, indicated he would shortly have a fire-
control solution on Sierra Two, now designated as Master Two.

Satisfied, Scott stepped to the center of the control
room and announced, "OOD, I have the conn."

"Aye, sir," said Lieutenant Dozier, you have the
conn."

"Captain, I have range and bearing updates on Master One and Master Two."

"I'm all ears, Rus."

"Master One bears three-four-zero, he's moving west, speed steady, range thirty-five thousand yards. Master Two now bears three-two-zero. Range just a tick under forty thousand yards."

"Okay. So the Kilo's almost due east of Master Two," Scott said.

"Range between targets is twenty-three thousand yards," Kramer confirmed.

To attack the *Red Shark*, Scott had to avoid detection by the Kilo, which was not only east but also north of their present position.

"All ahead two-thirds," Scott commanded, aware that their own tonals would increase at least fifty percent.

"All ahead two-thirds, aye," the helmsman confirmed.

Scott felt the deck vibrate under his feet as the *Reno* accelerated along her course of 340. Somewhere forward a hydraulic actuator thumped, too loud, Scott thought, and made a mental note to have it checked. Too late now to worry about loose ends.

"Conn, Sonar . . ." It was the chief.

Scott toggled a mike dangling from the overhead on a coiled cord. "Sonar, conn, aye."

"Conn, we've lost contact with Master Two."

The chief's words hung in the air like smoke. Scott saw the questioning looks exchanged by men at their stations, of those who had halted in midstride. He turned the conn over to Dozier and headed for Sonar.

"Just like that, sir," said the chief. "*Poof!* Gone. Right off her last bearing and range. Like she fell into a hole."

Scott saw for himself that the *Red Shark*'s tonal waterfall on the monitor had flatlined, while the Kilo's was still there, tracking northwest.

"All right, we'll slow down and start over. No sense giving the Kilo a fresh target—us—if he, too, lost contact on the *Red Shark*. I don't want to piss this guy off again or he might try and put one of *his* fish up *our* nose."

"A 688I Los Angeles-class?" Zemin sprang to the monitors.

"I am positive, Captain. The tonals match those we collected off Matsu Shan."

What is he doing here? What does he know? Zemin pondered this and thought, *Has he heard us? Has he heard the Korean sub?* If so, things would be different this time. The American sub was virtually inside Chinese territorial waters where the rules of engagement dictated that Chinese vessels could respond with deadly force not only if provoked by an enemy but also if that enemy violated restricted waters near North Sea Fleet Headquarters.

This time there would be no gamesmanship, no firing of decoys to send a message. This time, the American, steaming in dangerous waters, was fair game. And though his presence complicated matters, Zemin still had to prevent the North Korean submarine's escape from Chinese territorial waters. And if the American got in the way or was spoiling for another fight, he'd give him one.

"Contacts?"

"Only U.S. Navy One. Steady bearing and speed."

"Maintain primary search mode for DPRK One, use secondary mode for U.S. Navy One."

"Aye, sir."

Zemin strode into the control room. "First Officer."

"Sir?"

"Put us on a reciprocal course with the 688I. You may make turns for ten knots on mains."

The first officer hesitated. "Bows on, sir?"

"Exactly. We will close the range in a fraction of the time it would take if we were to cut back from outside his track. He'll either turn and run or face us down. I think he'll run."

Zemin's gaze drifted over the fire-control panel, its firing point analysis of DPRK One no longer valid. "Initiate constant tracking of U.S. Navy One and update to torpedoes. Make preparations to engage new target and to launch weapons."

Park felt his chest tighten. He heard the familiar but faint sound of reactor circulating pumps, saw their tonals on the monitor: a U.S. Navy 688I. In Chinese waters. Possibilities raced through his mind. Was the American hunting for them, the Chinese Kilo, or was he simply on a recon mission? No matter what the answer, now he had to avoid not one but *two* submarines.

"Captain, sir, the Chinese boat has turned toward the 688I." The startled sonarman twisted around in his seat and looked to Park for an answer.

Park, too, saw it displayed on the monitor: The tracker stylus labeled KILO had turned left and was moving jerkily across the screen toward the stylus labeled 688I.

"Sir, perhaps he has confused the American for us," the sonarman said.

"I don't think so. He knows as well as we do that his target is a 688I. No, I think this Chinese captain wants to show the American he will not be intimidated, that he will not tolerate their intrusion into Chinese territorial waters. The question is, how far is he prepared to go to prevent it? And if he shoots, will the American shoot back?"

Park watched the two points of light on the monitor move closer, into torpedo-firing range. All at once he tore himself away from the spectacle and lurched into the control room, commanding, "Both motors ahead half speed. Steady on course one-six-zero." He sought the first officer and said, "We will let those two fight it out, and while they do, we will slip out the side door and clear the area. Regardless of who wins, we will be long gone."

"Man battle stations! Man battle stations!" sounded through the *Reno*'s compartments over the 1MC.

"Conn, Sonar, target Master One is making turns for twenty knots. Range twelve thousand yards and closing fast."

"I guess we pissed him off and now he's playing Chinese chicken with us."

Scott knew that the Kilo was coming at them at high speed. The *Reno* was suddenly within range of the Kilo's Test-71 ME wire-guided torpedoes. He had no way of knowing if the Chinese skipper intended to shoot or was bluffing. Regardless, Scott had little room to maneuver and didn't have much time left to react. The *Red Shark* flashed through his mind: Tangling with the Kilo would open an avenue of escape for the North Korean sub. Scott knew he had to neutralize the Kilo before the *Red Shark* vanished for good.

"Torpedo room, Fire-control, make ready tubes one and two," Scott commanded. "Open outer doors."

"Tubes one and two, open outer doors, aye," Kramer repeated.

"Anything from Master Two?"

"Captain, I have no contact on Master Two."

"Range and bearing to Master One?"

"Sir, range is now ten-thousand six hundred yards; bearing," a hesitation, then, "sir, dead ahead and comin' at us!"

Scott had to make a decision now—

"Conn, Sonar, single active ping from Master One!"

Shrill as a bullet whining off steel and a prelude to firing torpedoes.

"Shit, it's him all right, just like last time," Scott said, chastened by the Kilo's skipper and his penchant for using active sonar. He recalled Deacon's earlier comment about how much brass the Chinaman had in his balls. "A lot," Scott muttered to himself.

"Conn, Sonar—Master One has opened his outer doors!"

Scott rounded from the watch station to the diving control station. "Right full rudder, all ahead flank; come to course zero-seven-zero; close outer doors," Scott said calmly, his anxiety bottled up and out of sight. "We may have to kick some sand in his face. Stand by to launch decoys."

The *Reno* leaped ahead and heeled into a tight right-hand turn, her screw biting hard, throwing up a knuckle of turbulence between herself and the Kilo.

"Conn, Sonar, torpedo in the water! I say again, torpedo in the water! Test-71 ME!"

"Sonar—torpedo speed?"

"Sir, I . . ."

Scott saw the shocked looks on men's faces in the control room and knew that if he didn't act decisively, some of the younger ones might panic, or worse, freeze at controls vital to the *Reno*'s survival. There was no time for hesitation, only action that would save them. Instinct propelled him to issue commands in a calm, steady voice.

"Chief, just give me its speed."

"Thirty-eight knots, sir."

"Thank you, Chief. Helm, come to course one-seven-zero." The *Reno* turned hard right, putting her stern to the Kilo. "Make your depth one hundred eighty feet. Weps, match target bearing on a single Thirty decoy starboard side and *shoot*."

Kramer, pale, dry-lipped, gave Scott a repeat-back, then hammered the launch key with a fist. A hiss of compressed air, a slight lurch, and Kramer, his voice surprisingly steady, reported, "Single Thirty away."

The *Reno* completed her swing into a high-speed sprint that would hopefully outrun the Kilo's inbound fish.

There was nothing more Scott could do now but wait with his crew for the decoy to screw up the torpedo's acoustics and cause it to detonate, or for the *Reno* to outrun it and in the process make the weapon spend its battery and sink.

Time seemed to have expanded to infinity. A smear of impressions—the crowded control room, its smells, its utter silence—were made altogether surreal by the fearful up-Doppler whine of the racing torpedo's contra-rotating props.

"Rus," said Scott, standing in the center of the control room, where the men could see him with his arms folded in a posture of relaxed confidence he hoped would buoy their spirits, "what's the range on one of those Test-71 MEs?"

"Well, sir, I'm not exactly sure—"

"Twenty klicks," said OOD Dozier. His khaki shirt was black under both arms. So was everyone else's. "I just happened to remember it, sir, uh, sorry, Mr. Kramer."

"Somebody do the math for me," Scott said. "If we're running at forty knots, how much distance can we put between us and that fish—"

A shattering explosion caught up to the *Reno* from astern at the speed of sound underwater. Bolts of pure energy crashed into her hull, shot through her decks and rattled equipment, tossed unstowed gear across compartments, and dumped loose china on the deck in the crews' mess.

Scott, ears ringing from the heavy blast of the decoyed warhead, waved the cheering men to silence.

"Damage control report, on the double," Scott commanded as he heaved across the control room. "Helm, left full rudder, let's see if we can get around behind this guy and shake him off."

46

The Yellow Sea east of the China coast

Zemin had recovered from the shock of the deafening torpedo explosion, but not from the shock of a Test-71 ME torpedo decoyed to self-destruction by the 688I.

"Captain, the target has turned northeast at high speed," announced the sonarman.

An angry Zemin pushed into the control room. He had to concoct a new plan, fast. At the chart table he sketched the situation as he understood it: The 688I was churning away from the point of attack and trying to get behind them. If Zemin turned the Kilo on her heel right now and pursued, he might just catch the 688I, even with its ten-knot speed advantage, by cutting inside her wide turning circle.

"Captain," said a still shaken first officer. "Sir, if we press another attack, we may succeed this time."

Zemin's gaze lifted from the chart to the first officer; Zemin sensed he was inwardly seething at their failure to kill the American sub.

"We must act now, Captain," said the first officer, his fist banging the chart. Then perhaps realizing he had been too forward, even disrespectful, he said, with a head bob, "What I mean, sir, is that I will see to it that your orders are carried out promptly and with precision so that an attack you order will succeed."

"See that you do, Comrade First Officer. Now, here are my orders."

Captain Park's face hardened and his eyes narrowed. At first he didn't want to believe what the *Red Shark*'s battle sensors and his own ears had heard: a torpedo explosion. The Chinese skipper had fired on the American submarine. The underwater detonation had rocked the *Red Shark* in her tracks and, in the bargain, had created a giant gas bubble that had helped screen her escape. Now, slowing but still tracking south southeast, Park heard tonals emanating from the 688I and the Kilo.

"Both targets bear zero-four-zero, Captain," said the sonarman. "Range, eight thousand yards, opening out."

Four miles away. Park listened, hoping to hear another torpedo in the water, but he heard only chugging screws.

"Maintain present course and speed," Park ordered the first officer. "We'll seek deeper water south, in the East China Sea."

"Fire-control, are we still pending on tubes one and two?"

"Aye, Captain, still pending."

"Very well." Scott glanced at the compass repeater and ordered, "Left full rudder; come to new course two-five-zero."

The helmsman brought the *Reno* around, then checked her swing, compensating for momentum that would have taken her on past but instead eased her onto the ordered course as neat as could be.

"Helm, All Stop."

"Aye, sir, answering bells on All Stop."

The *Reno*, her prop secured, slowed her headlong rush through the murky Yellow Sea. Scott estimated they could maintain steerage and depth for maybe only twenty minutes to a half hour, but enough time to reacquire both the Kilo and the *Red Shark*.

"On your toes, Sonar," Scott said. "Report all contacts."

Scott glanced at Kramer in Fire-control Alley, then started the wait.

Sonar interference created by water flowing along the *Reno*'s sides, over her planes and around her stilled prop blades, slowly ebbed.

"Conn, Sonar. Report one contact. Master One, the Kilo, bearing zero-eight-zero."

"Conn, aye," Scott said, "nothing on Master Two?"

"No, sir. Nothin'. Just the Kilo comin' back at us."

"Determined bastard," Kramer said as he monitored the BSY-2's dot-stacking fire-control procedure, which had been developed earlier from bearing data as the Kilo approached from the east southeast.

"Captain, he's turned around, trying to cut in behind us," Kramer said. "If he doesn't change course, he'll merge with our track roughly three thousand yards behind us, in . . . make it another five minutes."

"Very well. Ahead one-third. Come to new course three-three-zero. Rus, let's see if he sticks with us or what. If he does, we may have no choice but to put one up *his* nose. We can't screw around here much longer. If we do, we'll lose the *Red Shark*. Every minute we spend playing tag with this Kilo-driver gives the NKs a chance to hightail it into the East China Sea."

"Aye, sir. Weapons are pre-set."

The *Reno* went ahead and swung onto Scott's ordered heading.

* * *

"Coolant pumps."

Zemin didn't have to be told. He saw the line on the monitor and recognized it. Faint, barely there, but definitely a 688I tone line.

Zemin swung into the control room. "Stand by weapons control! Come to course three-three-zero. Motors ahead three-quarters."

The first officer's hands flew over the firing consoles, throwing fixed function keys and switches that sent data to the torpedoes waiting in their tubes and armed the torpedo air ram ejection system.

Satisfied with what he saw, Zemin swung back into the sonar room. "Report target's position."

"Dead ahead, sir."

"Good. We're in his baffles," Zemin said. He swung back into the control room. "Stand by to fire torpedoes."

"Captain, I don't hear him," said the sonar chief. "Had him when we made that turn onto three-three-zero. I think he may be on our tail."

Scott didn't hesitate. "Clear baffles to port! Stand by to take evasive action!"

The *Reno* heeled left, like a plane banking in flight. If the Kilo was lurking in the dead zone aft of the *Reno*'s screw, she'd be naked now, exposed to the *Reno*'s sonar.

The chief almost came up out of his seat. "Goddamn, she's there all right—*two torpedoes in the water!*"

"All ahead flank!" Scott bellowed. "Right full rudder."

The *Reno*'s coolant pumps accelerated; the boat shook as she leaped ahead and turned away from the incoming torpedoes, Scott and everyone aboard grabbing for handholds.

"Fire decoys port and starboard!" Scott commanded.

The lurch caused by the dual ejection went unnoticed in the turmoil of evasion. Twin Thirty decoys aimed right and left, shot out of the tubes, their noise-making gear a shrill whine over the *Reno*'s thundering engines.

Scott bellowed a tangle of engine and rudder orders that made the *Reno* snake dance to evade the Kilo's incoming torpedoes. *No finessing it now,* Scott thought. *Either outrun the fish or hope to God they kiss the decoys.* And no time either for a snap-shot, much less a well-conceived setup and firing solution. All the target data they had was down the drain. The brass-balled Chinaman had managed to get off two shots, and Scott could only scratch his head in wonder.

Two peals of heavy thunder aft from decoyed torpedoes shook the *Reno* to her keel and made the interior lights blink off and on.

Scott exhaled heavily, as did Kramer and others in the control room. Scott looked around at the sweat-burnished faces, at the slumped shoulders of men who, moments earlier, had thought they might not live another ten minutes. Who among them had dry skivvies, he wondered?

Scott slowed the *Reno* and spun her onto a heading that would bring her around, close to where the Kilo had been when she'd fired.

"Sonar, Conn. Anything?"

"Blast surge, Captain. Waiting for it to clear. Shallow here, and we've got sound pulses running all the way to Okinawa. Probably hear 'em in Pearl, too."

"Which means he can't hear us either," Scott said. "Rig ship for ultra-quiet."

Zemin held his anger in check. Two shots; two misses. Now the American had disappeared.

"First Officer, plot back the course the American shaped off his base course. Check the time line and find out when he broke off. Time it out to see how far he could have steamed. He's not moving at high speed, so he must be within the intercept zone we blocked out on the chart, or at least near it. I want all tubes on ready status."

"Aye, sir. The reload is complete and Fire-control is set to accept fresh target data."

"Very well. Now get me that plot-back."

"Break-up noises?" Park asked.

"None, Comrade Captain."

"And no torpedoes have been fired for over thirty minutes," Park offered. "Then they must be hunting for each other." Park went to the chart table to pinpoint the position of the last set of explosions.

"The attack will draw Chinese naval and air units to the area," Park said. "If they drop a net over the region, China will be at war with the U.S. and with us, too. Prepare to change course to due south in approximately thirty minutes. From that point on we will hunt for a merchant ship suitable for use as a decoy."

A light marked Engine Room went on over the ship's interior communications board. A sailor punched a square button on the board and lifted the phone from its cradle. "Captain, the chief engineer—"

Park didn't take the call. Instead he sprinted aft to see what had happened.

"Got something here, Captain."

Scott and the sonar officer peered over the chief's shoulder. "Merchantman," Scott said.

"Yes, sir, a big one," the chief remarked. "Maybe one of

those hundred-and-eighty-thousand-dead-weight-ton cargo ships outa Japan. Probably heard all the noise and detoured to investigate."

"Great. Next we'll have the PLAN breathing down our necks."

"Them too, sir. But see this?" The chief pointed to a thin tonal line working its way down the BSY-2's waterfall, almost hidden among all the broadband noise.

"Residual from that merchie?"

"Not sure. Sir, could you shift the boat right maybe ten degrees, so I can get a better listen on this?"

Scott gave the order; the *Reno* turned right until her big bow sonar dome was pointing at the source of the noise.

"Better. Got a tonal. It's like embedded in the merchie, but I don't think it is."

Scott straightened and worked a kink from his back. "Where do you want her, Chief? Another ten degrees right?"

"That might do it, sir."

Scott made the change and waited patiently for the tonal to strengthen. It didn't. The merchant vessel, her mammoth diesel pounding relentlessly, drew closer, the passage of her sheer bulk through the water masking all other sounds. Minutes later, the embedded trace vanished.

"Stay with it, Chief," said Scott. He returned to the control room, feeling shot through with fatigue.

"Captain, let me spell you," Kramer said.

"Thanks, Rus, I'll do my part. Everyone else is."

The atmosphere in the control room and throughout the ship felt tense, strained, the men still at battle stations, the ship rigged for ultra-quiet. To Scott, it felt as if the fabric was about to rip wide open, a sense of urgency straining the seams, a sense of something slipping away, the fact of it a mocking defeat.

Scott's mind slid back to the hours he'd spent in Tokyo with Tracy. It was always the same: brutal, intense, a gnawing hunger sated, then the downward spiral. Even in Tokyo she'd held him captive. Now, she'd take his failure to call her at the Embassy as a deliberate rejection. He almost laughed out loud. Tracy's ultimate weapon was jealousy. That and her uncanny ability to make him crave her.

"Conn, Sonar . . ."

The tonal waterfall had thickened, no longer embedded in the tonals from the merchie.

"Bearing's steady, sir, and it ain't the merchie."

"Master One?"

"I think so."

"Are we plugged into Fire-control?"

"Yes, sir," said the sonar officer, who looked as drained as Scott.

"Where's that merchie?" Scott asked.

"We're calling him Sierra Three. He's almost over the detonation site, hasn't slowed though."

"Maybe he'll keep on going," Scott muttered, "if he doesn't find anything."

Scott saw movement in the doorway out to the control room. The communications officer said, "Captain, we're getting an incoming RDT. Eyes Only."

"Ignore it. I don't have time now."

"Sir, pardon me, it's a Must Read Priority."

Scott felt like a pricked balloon. "All right. Patch it into my stateroom."

Scott looked into Fumiko's dark, expressive eyes. He wanted to touch her but had to settle for viewing her image, crisply clear and vital, delivered by satellite to the submerged *Reno*.

"Jake, are you all right?"

"We're alive. Trying to stay that way."

After a pause, she said, "I didn't thank you for what you did in Noda. You saved my life, and I don't know how to express what I feel."

"We all got out; that's what matters."

She hesitated, then said, "Colonel Jefferson said that your wife played a major role in my rescue."

"My ex, you mean. She doesn't know anything about the operation, if that's got you worried."

"I'm not worried, it's just that I didn't know she was in Tokyo, that you had seen her."

"Fumiko, we're on the government's nickel. I know you didn't ring me up to discuss my former domestic arrangements. Where's Radford? I don't see his happy face."

"He's briefing the president and asked me to brief you. There have been some important developments. Within the last hour the Chinese lodged a protest at the UN, charging that we've sent a submarine to spy on their naval facilities at Dingdao. They claim the spying is tied to our dispute with the North Koreans, that we're accusing the Chinese of supporting the Jin regime and are trying to provoke their navy."

"We're provoking them? Did they tell you that we've tracked the *Red Shark* into Chinese territorial waters, and that one of their subs fired on us twice?"

That gave her a genuine start. "Oh, my God, Jake. No, we didn't know any of that."

"What did the Chinese say about the underwater explosions around Haizhou Wan? That they're caused by Chinese oil exploration teams running seismic profiles?

Or Chinese torpedoes? Check your sat infrared imagery and you'll see them."

"They haven't said anything about that, not yet anyway."

"Thanks to the Kilo's attack on us, we lost the *Red Shark*. We're trying to shake the Kilo, but I'm not sure we can. Anyway, we're running out of time to find the *Red Shark* before she can break out into the East China Sea. No one asked my advice, but Radford can tell our UN ambassador that he should remind the Chinese that the Yellow Sea is international waters, not their private lake, and that when one of their subs fires on us, we'll fire back."

Fumiko put a hand to her mouth. "Jake, if you do, you'll start a war with the Chinese."

"Just tell them."

"Jake—"

"Tell them!"

"All right," Fumiko agreed. "I'll tell General Radford what you said."

"What's he done about setting up the SSN blockade?"

"ComSubPac has ordered a surge of SSNs into the area, but they won't all be on station for at least another thirty-six hours. JCS has ordered Seventh Fleet to deploy whatever ASW units it has, to back up the SSN blockade. In the meantime General Radford's authorized a Global Hawk surveillance mission of the region, to help you locate the *Red Shark*. If we can get her image on a round-the-clock basis, SRO can vector you in for an attack."

"The Chinese will protest that it's an overflight of their territory, and it'll only make matters worse."

"I agree, but the general, like you, is concerned that she may give you the slip."

"We're trying not to let that happen, which is why we've got to deal with that Kilo. Look, I've got to go."

"Jake, wait. There's something else. Washington received another signal from their contact in Pyongyang. He gave them the names of the cities that are targeted for destruction—New York, Washington, and Chicago."

"So we were right all along, weren't we?" Scott collected himself and said, "What does Jefferson have to say? Has he helped that spec-ops unit find the base in Davao?"

"Actually, he's with them. He sent his regards and said he'd catch up with you in Pearl."

"What the hell's he doing? I thought he was coordinating their ops, not wrangling to be another gun in the fight."

"He got General Radford's okay, said he didn't want to sit at a desk in front of a computer and push buttons. If they take out the base at Santa Cruz, the terrorists' plan will implode because there'll be no one there waiting for the *Red Shark* to deliver her cargo."

Scott wanted to say he'd put an end to it by killing the *Red Shark*, but he knew that was a promise he might not be able to keep, not even to himself. If he failed and the warheads slipped through, and even if Jefferson and the spec-ops team destroyed the terrorist base, where would those weapons end up? And in whose hands? The plan would implode, but the weapons would still exist—somewhere.

Scott held Fumiko's gaze on the monitor. She seemed to sense his need to say something else, something personal. But he was interrupted by the chirping phone, a summons to the control room. A moment later he was gone, and the screen went blank.

47

Pyongyang

Streets in the capital were deserted. Marshal Jin
looked down on central Pyongyang from his office in
the People's Grand Hall, pleased to see that the planted
rumors of an imminent nuclear attack by the United
States had had the desired effect: People were frightened.
Those who had started hoarding supplies had been shot,
but already heating and cooking oil were in short supply.
Protests against the United States had been scheduled to
take place in Kim il Sung Square, where tomorrow over a
million people would march in support of Jin's threat to
attack South Korea and, if necessary, the U.S.

He turned away from the tall, curtained windows
and returned to his desk. He had finished reading General Yi's report on Kim Jong-il's efforts to identify the
spy embedded in the Second Directorate. All that was
required to initiate the interrogation of almost 3,000
individuals was his signature on a document entitled
"The People's Case Against Internal Subversion and
Treachery Calculated to Overthrow the Elected Leadership of the State."

Jin lit a Players and picked up the report. He regarded General Yi and said, "Where in this report is the spy identified by name? I don't see it."

Yi, seated, hands folded neatly on his lap, said, "He is not named, Dear Leader, and with good reason. He is among the two thousand nine hundred and five individuals we have in custody. As the report states, all of these individuals have connections to the scientists we rounded up earlier who, as you know, have had contact with the Danes. We intend to interrogate each of them and work our way to the hard kernel of truth at the center of this ring of subversion. I suspect that none of these individuals is innocent of crimes against the State, and that in the course of our interrogation we will make new discoveries. The point is, however, we have the main body of traitors. There, I suspect, we will find the person who has been serving the imperialists."

Impressed, Jin said, "Kim proved as good as his word."

"Prison life hasn't diminished his arrogant manner, but he is a changed man and eager to assist in the interrogations."

"Where is he now?"

"I had him moved to the lower detention center at the People's Ministry of Internal Security. The food there is better than at Chungwa."

"I see." Jin tapped the report with a finger. "And my signature will initiate the interrogations."

"And authorize Kim's execution."

"You are certain you no longer need his assistance?"

"Yes, Dear Leader, I am. Kim has outlived his usefulness."

Jin grunted. He bent to the task with a gold pen plucked from a well on his desk and, with short, deft strokes, put his name to the report.

Yi placed the report in a leather portfolio, bowed,

and took his leave. When he reached the door, Jin said, "One moment, General. I received a call from Admiral Woo in Nam'po."

Yi, curious, returned to Jin's desk. "And how is Admiral Woo?"

"He says that the Chinese have reported explosions in the Yellow Sea. As you know, the *Red Shark* is at present in the Yellow Sea. Admiral Woo didn't venture what these explosions were."

"The Chinese have oil exploration teams in the Yellow Sea," said Yi. "Did he mention that? Or are you concerned, Dear Leader, that perhaps the explosions are linked to the *Red Shark*?"

"A reasonable assumption. The Chinese operate submarines in the Yellow Sea and East China Sea. We have had run-ins with them in the past. The Americans also operate there. Anything can happen. There is also the death of Iseda Tokugawa to consider."

"Then, Dear Leader, I would say that Admiral Woo must radio the *Red Shark* at once and order her captain to report his status."

"But if he does, the Americans will pick up his signal."

"Oh, yes, they will. But picking it up and breaking our code are two different things. To put your concerns to rest, I would advise Woo to send the message regardless of the Americans."

Yi sensed that Jin, isolated from the outside world, hearing and believing only what fit his preconceptions, was paralyzed almost to inaction by his own plan. Yi waited while Jin debated.

"Have Woo send the message."

"Got him!" said the chief.

They had the Kilo, and it wasn't far away. With time,

patience, and skill, the sonar watch had stripped the Chinese sub's tonals out of the background cacophony of broadband noise.

"Master One bears zero-one-zero, Captain," the sonar chief advised.

"I have the conn," said Scott, entering the control room. "Rus, stand by tubes one and two. Do not—say again—*do not* open outer doors."

Kramer acknowledged and passed Scott's orders to the torpedo room.

"We're going to try and work around this guy, see if we can't give him the slip."

Kramer and the other officers exchanged surprised looks. "Work *around* him?" said Kramer.

"If we can. He's not our main target, the *Red Shark* is."

"Sir, with respect, he tried to pick us off."

"And he won't get another chance. Helm, come to course two-three-zero. Make turns for eight knots. We'll work into the littorals off Lianyungang, use them for cover."

"Those are Chinese territorial waters," Kramer observed.

Scott paid no attention as he watched the repeaters until he was satisfied that the *Reno* was moving stealthily away from the Kilo.

"Sonar, Conn. Any sign that he's heard us?"

"Conn, Sonar. Nothin' yet, sir."

A minute passed, then five. Scott, resting quietly at the watch station, gave Kramer a nod and said, "Welcome to China."

Zemin crashed into the control room. "Both motors full ahead! Energize all tubes!"

At the very instant Zemin had concluded from the

first officer's plot-back that the 688I had to be in the intercept zone marked on the chart, the sonarman had picked up a faint tonal, which was now displayed on the sonar repeater in the control room.

"Prepare to launch weapons one through six!" Zemin barked. "Use staggered timing and internal discriminator blocks!"

"Target lock-on confirmed, Comrade Captain," said the first officer.

Zemin spun around and bellowed, "Stand by to fire on my mark!"

"He heard us! He's turning left and closing fast," Kramer confirmed.

"No sense trying to finesse it anymore," Scott said. "He's about to buy it." He followed this with orders to the helm.

Scott stationed himself in the center of the control room, his gaze commanding the consoles and instruments displaying the information he needed to attack the Kilo. He waited until the *Reno* had come about, then commanded, "Firing point procedures on Master One, tubes one and two. Open outer doors."

Kramer confirmed the target data, then prepared to execute Scott's next order by rotating the torpedo switch triggers to their standby positions.

"Match sonar bearings and *shoot*, tube one," Scott commanded.

Kramer, at the weapons-control panel, repeated Scott's command and, at the same time, twisted the trigger clockwise to its fire position.

The crew heard and felt the surge of the *Reno*'s torpedo-ejection air pump and the unmistakable buzz-saw whine of an Mk-48 leaping from its tube.

"Tube one fired electrically," Kramer confirmed, his voice calm as could be.

"Let's see how we do with this one—Chief? . . ."

"Conn, Sonar—he hears it, Captain. He's turning one-eighty and flankin' it."

"Torpedo running hot, straight, and normal," reported Kramer, timing the run. A minute passed. "Torpedo's acquired its target. Time to impact, two minutes."

Scott gave Kramer a nod.

The chief came on. "Conn, Sonar, he's launched decoys."

"Too late," Scott said. "Too fucking late."

The first officer lost control of his bladder, feared he was on the verge of losing his bowels too. Shamed by the huge stain spreading across his coveralls, and for his display of cowardice in front of the captain and crew, he turned his back to the control room and buried his face in his hands. He tried to blot out the high-pitched *scree* of the incoming Mark 48. He heard Zemin hurling curses at him but didn't care; heard Zemin shout orders to the helm; heard the slam of watertight doors; heard cries of fear from men who knew they were about to die.

And then he heard nothing. The first officer had turned in time to see Captain Deng Zemin, his mouth open wide in a silent scream, consumed by a sheet of white-hot flame that enveloped everyone and everything around him.

Tongsun Park listened intently, an ear cocked to the overhead in the engine room. He didn't need sonar to confirm that what he'd just heard and felt had been an exploding torpedo and now breaking-up noises from a submarine. But which one, the Chinese or the American?

Like Park, the engineering officer Kang and the work gang he'd assembled to make repairs to the hydrogen bleeder line halted their work and listened in horror to the hideous shriek of a collapsing hull and moan of tortured steel twisting and grinding against itself as the torpedoed vessel hurtled to the bottom of the Yellow Sea.

Even before the death rattle had ceased, Park was on the intercom to the control room demanding information: bearing, range, tonals. *Now!*

Park caught his breath, felt the terrified gazes of the men on his back. Park's eyes drifted to the frozen bleeder valve, the bulge in the line now bigger than before. He returned Kang's look with one that he hoped was optimistic even though inside he doubted their ability to make repairs that wouldn't blow up the submarine. He glanced at the parts and tools Kang had assembled. What Kang had proposed might thaw the valve but, not done right, could blow up the ship.

Park imagined the consequences that would await him if he failed to carry out his mission. Admiral Woo and his masters in Pyongyang were slogan-spouting idiots and didn't trust anyone, not even each other. They commanded loyalty through fear. If the mission failed for any reason, even something beyond his control, they'd want a scapegoat. *But not me,* thought Park. *Not yet.* Here, at sea, he still had his independence and professional pride. He'd carry out his orders to the best of his abilities even if it meant taking a huge risk. What choice did he have?

"Forget what just happened out there. Tell me how you plan to make the repair."

Kang composed himself. "Captain, with a non-ferrous sleeve that will fit over the damaged section. We can then introduce hot coolant from the reduction gears through a fitting which will heat the valve and line, reducing pressure on the joint. Then we can open the valve and bleed down the entire line to the diverter and hydrogen burner."

Park nodded. "How long will it take?"

Kang ran a hand over his head of cropped hair. Sweat glistened on his face and scalp. "I think, sir, not more than three hours, but I can't be sure."

"I will return in an hour to check on your progress." Park jammed on his cap and headed for the control room.

"Sonar, Conn. Report all contacts," Scott ordered.

A dozen new contacts proved how busy it had gotten topside. The Kilo's death had drawn ships into the impact area from all points of the compass. The Chinese would be furious once they found out what had happened, but when Scott remembered that the U.S. had sort of mistakenly hit the Chinese Embassy in Belgrade with a cruise missile during the Balkans operation, he felt better. Then, the Chinese had threatened action against the U.S. but had later calmed down. *Fuck it*, Scott thought, *let the politicians in Washington deal with the Chinese.* He was a sub driver on a mission, not a diplomat.

"They're all merchies," the sonar chief reported, "every one of 'em. No sign of that Type 213. But if it's out here, we'll find it."

"He might try to make a dash for it by tucking in behind a merchie heading south."

"Captain, we've got all the bases covered."

48

Washington, D.C.

The president stood in the Oval Office and looked dolefully out over the South Lawn, where dark clouds filled with rain bulked over the Washington Monument. His head throbbed; he pressed a thumb and forefinger deep into the corners of both eyes to relieve the pressure. It didn't help. Nothing did anymore.

"Not only has Scott pissed off the Japanese, now he's pissed off the Chinese," said the president, addressing Radford, Friedman, and Ellsworth. "I just concluded a call with President Yang. He gave me hell, said he has a report that one of their submarines was attacked by one of ours, the one he believes we sent to spy on their base in Dingdao. That would be Scott in the *Reno,* wouldn't it, Karl?"

Radford steepled his fingers. "Scott reported to Ms. Kida that they'd been fired on twice by that Chinese Kilo we've been tracking by satellite. The Chinese claimed that those explosions were not from their sub's torpedoes but from seismographic teams working oil fields in the same area. Bullshit, of course. Scott's hunting for the *Red Shark,* and if the Chinese keep getting in the way, he'll do what he's got to do."

"Do you believe he fired torpedoes at that Chinese sub?"

"Yes, sir, I do."

"Christ. Admiral?"

"Scott had to defend himself, Mr. President," said Ellsworth. "More important, we can't let the Chinese prevent us from heading off that weapons delivery."

Friedman erupted, "How, by sinking one of their subs? After this is over we'll still have to live with the Chinese. We'll need their help to settle scores with that madman Jin, and sinking one of their subs is no way to get their cooperation."

"Paul's right," said the president. "We can't provoke the Chinese."

"Sir, I'd like to point out that Scott is the man on the hot seat," Ellsworth said. "He's got little to go on but instinct—"

"We put a Global Hawk up to get more detailed coverage of the area, to help him find the sub," Radford said.

"Sure, Karl," said Ellsworth, "that's great and all, but Scott's out there on a limb, and he's got to do what he's got to do to find that NK boat. He can't be afraid to step on a few toes."

"Jesus Christ," protested Friedman, "sinking a PLAN submarine is not what I'd call stepping on a few toes, it's a goddamn act of war."

Ellsworth, his face florid, his mood dark, said, "What the hell do you call the Chinese sub's attack on Scott? And the NKs and their warheads headed for the U.S.? What would you call that?"

"Gentlemen," said the president, "let's deal with the situation Scott is facing. Karl, can you contact him, find out what's happening out there so that in the event, we can draft an appropriate response to the Chinese?"

"Yes, sir, I can."

"Now, in your earlier briefing, Karl, you said our special-ops group was in Davao."

"Colonel Jefferson's with the unit."

"And have they located the terrorist base?"

"As of"—he looked at his wristwatch—"an hour ago they'd not made contact."

"As soon as they do, you let me know."

"Yes, sir, of course I will."

The president looked up as an aide silently slipped into the Oval Office with a video reader board, a device used by the White House to display super-encrypted Purple messages.

"Pardon me, Mr. President," she said. "I have a priority from SRO for General Radford."

"Let me see that, Karen." Radford twisted around and took the flat-screen board. He keyed in his personal code and read the message.

The president saw Radford's eyebrows twitch up, then fall and meet in the furrow over his nose.

"Mr. President, satellite imagery confirms that the PLAN Kilo President Yang referred to was sunk, we think, by a torpedo fired from one of our submarines."

The president jammed a thumb and forefinger deep into the corners of both eyes. "The *Reno*."

"Yes, sir."

Park stared at the obsolete Russian-made ZEVS communication equipment installed in the *Red Shark*'s control room. The system had been designed originally for Russian submarines to receive burst transmissions from satellites via extremely high frequencies. The DPRK had purchased surplus units, only to find that the sophisticated, land-based, low-frequency antenna array the ZEVS system required had proved difficult to install and maintain in North Korea's mountainous terrain.

Park debated whether or not to respond to the call from Nam'po. The ZEVS signal was a summons to come up to periscope depth and receive a coded burst transmission from an old Russian Molniya-3 satellite for which the DPRK paid Moscow a usage fee. Unlike the U.S. sub that used the U.S. RDT system, which blasted data from space through deep water at a blinding rate, the *Red Shark* would have to loiter near the surface, vulnerable to detection, to receive the ZEVS burst.

The first officer waited for Park's order to come to periscope depth and poke a mast up. Instead a morose Park, his gaze planted on the deck, said, "I think our ZEVS has just malfunctioned. Can it be repaired?"

The first officer understood what Park intended to do. "Why, yes, Captain, it has malfunctioned."

"Will it take more than a day to repair?"

"I'm afraid so, Captain."

"Too bad. See what you can do."

"At once, sir."

Park looked up to examine the sonar contacts displayed on the monitors, his finger tracing their tone lines. None were labeled hostile.

"Captain," said the sonarman, "we do not have contact with the 688I. Only merchant vessels."

"This one, contact three. How close is it?"

"Sir, eleven thousand yards."

A large ship by the look of her tonals, Park noted, and pounding south at eight knots in the outer shipping lanes, away from Shanghai, possibly bound for Pacific ports. Perhaps even the Philippines.

"First Officer, you will put us on a course to intercept contact three. When you have confirmed that the
contact is in fact a merchantman, you will summon me
from the engine room."

The wardroom phone chirped. Scott shoved aside the
remains of a rare filet and French fries and snatched
the receiver. "Captain."

"Officer of the deck," said Dozier. "Sonar's picked
up Chinese warships. They're pinging."

"On my way. Call away battle stations."

"Battle stations, aye, sir."

Scott shouldered past busy officers and sailors and
eased in behind the sonar watch. In a glance, he saw
that the reported frequency tonals were only a few
miles off the China coast, their active sonar displayed
as a pattern of dancing dots.

"Three of 'em, sir, two DDs and a frigate," reported
the chief. "A squall's degrading sound reception, but
the DDs for sure are ex-Russian *Sovremennyys*. No ID
yet on the frigate."

"Probably deployed from Dingdao to find out what
happened to their Kilo."

"Yes, sir, that'd be my guess, too."

"If the *Red Shark* hears them she'll steer clear, which
might push her in our direction. What else have you
got?"

"Merchie headin' south, big one." He rattled off its
bearing and range.

"Okay, let's poke up the ESM and see what's what."

Scott clapped the weary chief on the shoulder and
went back to control. "Bring her up to PD."

"Periscope depth aye," repeated OOD Dozier.

The *Reno*, after conducting a thorough sonar sweep

that confirmed there were no ships in the immediate area, rose slowly, carefully.

Scott, at the Type 18 periscope, motioned "up" with raised thumbs. As the *Reno* approached PD with the scope's head extended toward the surface, Scott got a glimpse of the furrowed bottoms of waves: On the scope's video monitor they looked like the underside of gray cloud cover. "Here we go," Scott said.

A moment later the periscope broke the surface and kicked up a feather. Scott pushed the scope around once, then stopped on the bearing of the pinging PLAN warships. Focused on infinity, Scott saw a sky and ocean the color of gunmetal and, on the horizon miles away, a row of black matchsticks. The Type-18's electronic signals receiver confirmed that a maze of ship-borne radars was active topside.

"Got 'em. They're hull down. I can just see their mast tops. Control, bring me up another five feet so I can see a little more. But watch your depth."

As the *Reno* rose higher, Scott rotated the scope through 360 degrees, looking for intruders, but he saw none. Back on the targets, this time with more scope out of the water and the *Reno*'s sail barely skimming the bottoms of wave troughs, he got a good look at the warships' busy top hamper, the black watch caps on their funnels, a forest of antennas.

Kramer studied the slaved video monitor. "Skipper, those two on the left are definitely *Sovremennyys;* the other one for sure is a *Jiangwei* frigate. See that stepped mast she has?"

"Let's hear what they're saying. Raise the ESM," Scott ordered.

The mast was barely out of the water when the electronic receiver panel lit up like a Christmas tree. The technician monitoring reception announced, "Sir, we've got J-band 700-MA and 756 search radars, also X-band and Y-band commercial, and two airborne Chinese 0J-bands."

Scott angled the scope's optics skyward. "Right, I see them both. Amphibs. They're looking for someone, probably us. See them, Rus?"

"Got 'em; they're SH-5s."

Eye to the scope, Scott said, "Bearing on those X- and Y-bands?"

"X-band bears three-one-zero. Its source is between the *Sovremennyys* and the coast. The Y-band bears two-eight-zero."

Scott spun the scope onto the bearing but saw only gulls and a fast-moving squall. "Rus, check that Y-band bearing against the merchie's last position."

"Aye, sir."

Scott slapped the scope's handles up. "Down scope, down ESM. We'll give those guys a wide berth." He gave Dozier a new course to steer, away from the PLAN warships, and ordered the *Reno* down to 150 feet.

Kramer said, "Captain, Y-band is definitely the merchie. Range twenty-five thousand yards. He's drifting right on a heading of one-eight-zero. Actually, he's picked up the pace a bit: he's making turns for ten knots."

Scott summoned Kramer, Rodriguez, and the quartermaster of the watch to the plotting table.

"So where is she?" said Scott. "Where's the *Red Shark*?"

Kramer said, "Well, for one thing, the NKs probably don't know who's been left standing—us or the Kilo. For another, they're going to stay away from the Chinese Navy. Their mission is to break out of the Yellow Sea, and the only way to do that is to make tracks into deep water and not get hung up south at Zhongxin Gang and Taowang Gang. Hell, those bights are good places to hide in but are as shallow as a kiddy wading pool."

Scott traced the coast of China with his finger, stopped when he got to Shanghai and its sandy Huangpu' River delta. "I agree, Rus, they've got to stay offshore or risk running aground in the shallows."

"Captain," said Rodriguez, "there's another factor to consider."

"Shoot."

"The north-south shipping lanes into Shanghai are like an expressway at rush hour, always busy. I think the *Red Shark*'s skipper wouldn't want to get trapped inside one of those lanes, because if he did, he might not be able to swing out through traffic to get around the delta at Shanghai. He'd want to make his swing starting somewhere around Dongtai, not any later, and make for deep water."

"Maybe he already has," Scott said.

Kramer, tapping his front teeth with a pencil eraser, said, "What would he do once he's past Shanghai? Turn southwest and make a run down the coast until he felt it was safe to break out?"

"No, sir," Rodriguez said, "if he did that he'd just get himself trapped again inside traffic lanes and, well . . ."

Scott looked at the young officer.

"Sir, this may seem a little crazy, but if I was him and once I'm outside the lanes, I'd try to make a run for it by tucking in behind a merchie, maybe that one heading south."

"Conn, Sonar—"

Scott grabbed the mike hanging over the table. "Conn, aye."

"Captain, we've got more active pingers to the southwest," said the sonar chief. "I make it at least six Luda-class DDs. They're workin' down the coast in a staggered forty-five with a four-thousand-yard interval."

Scott acknowledged the report, then went back to the plotting table. "I think, Mr. Rodriguez, that what we just heard bolsters your theory that the *Red Shark*'s skipper wouldn't want to be nailed in littoral waters by Chinese destroyers. So let's take a look at that merchie, the one heading south, and see what we can find."

49

The East China Sea

Park had eased the *Red Shark* into position, submerged three hundred yards behind the sixty-thousand-dead-weight-ton *Pacific Conveyor*. Seen through the periscope he'd poked up in her boiling wake, Park hadn't been able to tell what kind of cargo she carried—vehicles, he'd assumed, from her huge quarter-stern door ramp. The only thing that mattered to him was that the Panamanian-flagged ro-ro provide suitable cover. It would be a bumpy ride, but Park was determined to stick with her as long as he could.

He lowered the scope and turned the conn over to the first officer. "Wake turbulence will degrade sonar reception but not so much that we will not hear hostiles approach. Relieve the control team every two hours; I want fresh personnel at the control station at all times. Call me at once if you have any sonar contacts or if anything changes," Park said, and departed for the wardroom.

The mess attendant had a bottle of *soju* and a ceramic cup waiting for Park at the head of the table. The attendant filled the cup and backed into his tiny galley, shutting the bifold door so Park could ruminate in private.

Park reckoned that their chances of reaching the Philippines on time were less than fifty percent, given their present situation. He knew he was being pessimistic, but he was a realist. Something must have gone terribly wrong in Pyongyang. Perhaps a war had started. It was the only logical answer to why the American and Chinese submarines had fired on each other and why the *Red Shark* was being hunted.

He drank *soju,* its fire scorching his gullet. And what of his refusal to answer Admiral Woo's ZEVS inquiry? Would Woo understand the danger he was facing from both the American sub and the frozen valve in the hydrogen fuel cell? Not likely. The only thing that mattered to Woo was that the cargo be delivered on time.

Park needed time to sort things out, but when he looked at the chronometer on the bulkhead, he saw that it was time to visit the engine room to gauge how the repair had progressed—

"Captain!" the first officer yapped from the intercom as the Captain's Light began to flash.

Park froze. Instinctively he knew it was bad news.

"Comrade Captain, we have something on the flank sonar array. Possible submarine, but the contact is partially masked by wake turbulence from the merchantman."

Park felt his heart leap. He saw a faint contact on the monitor, abaft the starboard beam. Low-frequency interference from the *Pacific Conveyor*'s machinery and tumbling wake made target discrimination difficult but not impossible.

"Range?"

"Under ten thousand yards, sir, and closing. I'll soon have a turn rate."

Park considered his options. Was it the American or Chinese submarine? Had it detected the *Red Shark*? If so, how much time did he have left to decide what to do? Should he call away combat stations and torpedo stations right now or wait to see what developed? As Park watched, the target slowly turned right onto a course parallel to the *Pacific Conveyor* and *Red Shark*.

"Captain, turn rate shows target's speed is fifteen knots."

Park checked their own speed: eight knots. He also saw that as the target slowly drew closer, the earlier unidentified tone line displayed on the monitor got sharper, more precise. In another minute the signal processor would have a match. He wicked sweat from his face onto a sleeve and said, "How could he have heard us? *How?*"

The worried sonarman looked helplessly at Park. Park's gaze snapped to the secondary set of monitors, and he saw nine well-defined tonals radiating from the PLAN warships to the west. His gaze went back to the monitor tracking the submarine closing in: Its white tone line was thin and very sharp.

"Captain, I have positive identification on a U.S. 688I."

The *Red Shark*'s combat system had proven far more sensitive and accurate than Park had thought possible. U.S. Navy SSNs were virtually undetectable, yet the system had plucked this one out of the water as surely as if the sea had parted around it.

Park had no desire to share the Kilo's fate. "First Officer, call away combat stations and torpedo stations!"

The weapons-control panel lit up as sailors energized the *Red Shark*'s six forward tubes loaded with See-hake DM-24A wire-guided torpedoes and started in-putting data to their guidance systems. It took less than a minute for the fire-control system to cycle from standby to ready.

The first officer declared, "Will commence action on your orders, Captain."

"Talk to me, Sonar!"

"Captain, it's only a maybe, too faint to identify. I mean maybe it's that merchie's prop, like it's nicked or out of balance. What I'm hearing, it's down on the low end of the spectrum, I mean real low."

"Come on, Chief, I need more than *maybes*. Can you strip it out of the propwash?"

"Not from this distance, sir. We're pickin' up the garbage that ro-ro's laying down, and it ain't helpin' any."

Scott weighed the risks of speeding up and moving in closer. He'd already laid on turns to catch up with the merchie, and he hesitated to risk exposure by laying on more. But taking risks was what he was trained to do and what submariners thrived on. And caution had no place in the equation if all it did was allow the *Red Shark* to escape. She had to be killed, even if it meant that the *Reno* would be killed too.

"Sonar, Conn. I'm going to move in and kiss that merchie's ass for you. Look alive in there!"

"Sonar, aye!"

"Ten degrees left rudder, all ahead full," Scott commanded. "Move us in."

"Captain! Target has speeded up!"

Park had to gamble; success depended on surprise,

and he was willing to bet that the Americans would not be expecting him to attack, and that in their haste to avoid the *Red Shark*'s torpedoes, they would be unable to counterattack.

"Hard right rudder! Ahead full speed!"

The *Red Shark* exploded to life sharply to starboard out of the *Pacific Conveyor*'s wake, onto a collision course with the *Reno*.

"Comrade First Officer," Park called, "prepare to fire torpedoes!"

"*Red Shark, Red Shark!*" the sonar chief bellowed. "Conn, Sonar, she's coming at us and closing fast!"

"Snap shot!" Scott commanded. "Tubes one and two!"

Kramer, cool, steady, keyed the *Red Shark*'s bearing and speed into both torpedoes and queued them for immediate launch. "Set!"

But before Kramer could report that both fish were ready, their tubes flooded and outer doors open, Sonar warned, "*Torpedoes in the water! Say again, torpedoes in the water!*"

"Fire two decoys!" Scott commanded. Then, "Left full rudder, all ahead flank!" The *Reno* heeled into the *Pacific Conveyor*'s wake; Scott hoped that crossing it at right angles would mask them from the incoming torpedoes.

"They're close, too damn close," Scott said. "Hang on to your asses, people!"

It was too late to fire down the bearing of the torpedoes; there was only enough time—maybe—to outrun them.

Scott held up two fingers. "Rus—fire decoys."

There was a surge of Ottos port and starboard as a

second pair of decoys fizzed out of their launch tubes.

Scott's gaze locked on the pit log: twenty-three knots and ticking up. Not good enough—the four decoys would have to run interference for them. He heard the *screee* of incoming props, tightened his jaw in anticipation. *Twenty-eight knots.* He saw Kramer gnawing a knuckle.

An explosion and shock wave from a decoyed North Korean torpedo hammered the *Reno*. She staggered like a drunk, yawed as if gut-punched, and, like a drunk, struggled to right herself.

Scott saw piping in the control room vibrate to invisibility, saw shock-mounted lighting fixtures shatter, paint chips and dust plume into the air. He felt the deck drop away as if he were riding a runaway elevator. Something carried away topside with a scrape and roar of steel on steel down the length of the pressure hull. Somewhere aft he heard water blowing in under high pressure. Then a stuttering water hammer.

The ship's emergency lighting recycled twice, then kicked back to service normal. The smell of scorched insulation stung Scott's nostrils, and a moment later he was viewing the control room through a blue haze. The roar he'd heard was a fire extinguisher honking on empty.

"Damage report, all compartments!" Scott bellowed over the 1MC.

"Skipper," said Kramer, his chest heaving, "reactor's at full power, we're making turns for thirty-three knots, depth one-eighty. Course zero-seven-five."

"Very well, but get that damage report in here on the double." Scott toggled a mike. "Sonar, Conn, where's that other NK fish?"

"Lost it, sir, took off after one of our decoys. All I've

got is the *Red Shark,* fading on a bearing of two-six-zero."

"What's the merchie doing?"

"Slowing, probably gonna heave to and change his drawers."

"Yeah, like us. What about those DDs and frigates?"

"Speeding up. I've got nine contacts now moving east, not west."

"All right. Keep on them. They're on their way here for sure."

"Aye, sir."

"I want a plot on the *Red Shark*. My guess is she's heading for that littoral zone south of Chenjigang. If I was him now, I'd want shallow water to hide in, and there's plenty there." Scott found the OOD. "Put us on two-six-zero. All ahead flank."

"Sir . . ."

Scott turned to Kramer. "Damage?"

"Not too bad." He rattled off a short list of cracked lines and spun-open valves that needed attention, food stores strewn in the galley, and a small fire that had broken out in an electrical cabinet in the sonar equipment room. "That torpedo went off close aboard. Engine room said they saw the hull dish in and pop out again. They put this baby together real good, Skipper."

"Let's see if she can hold together long enough to find that North Korean bastard so we put him away for keeps."

Park sat slumped in the captain's chair in the control room. Water trickled down the scope from a packing gland damaged by their own torpedo detonation closer aboard than he had at first realized. The engineering officer warned that the explosion had damaged two shock-mounted rafts that supported a portion of the fuel cell's manifold connected via flexible joints to the frozen valve. His report of a potential sound short to the hull, as well as the possibility that the valve and line had been wrenched out of alignment, had thrown Park into a depression from which the first officer couldn't rouse him.

"Comrade Captain, please, sir, your orders."

Park avoided the officer's pleas. The crew kept their eyes glued to their work and stood like mannequins at their stations, not daring to look away.

"Sir, we are south of the Chinese warships patrolling the coast. There is no trace of the American submarine. Perhaps it was damaged or is fleeing from the Chinese. With deepest respect, sir, if we maintain a southerly course, we can reach Shanghai at sunset and make our transit to deep water. By daybreak we will be south of Shanghai and from there can proceed east for Okinawa. I am sure we can pick up another merchant vessel along the way."

Park looked at him but said nothing.

"Perhaps, sir, you should now respond to Admiral Woo's signal. Tell him we have been under attack, that we have damaged an American submarine. He will understand your reluctance to reply earlier. He must have good reasons for wanting us to risk sending a message. Perhaps even that he is recalling us."

Park roused himself. "Recalling us?" he said. "Is that what you hope for, to return to Nam'po?"

"Why, no, Comrade Captain, I'm only suggesting that—"

"We will carry out our mission as ordered." Park stood and took a deep breath, obviously in control of his emotions again. "When we have cleared the area I will radio Admiral Woo and advise him of our situation. In the meantime you will maintain our present course until we reach Taowang Gang, then turn us southeast. Maintain combat and torpedo stations until further orders. The men can take their meals at their stations."

"Aye, Captain."

Park seemed to have found a reserve of strength. He started for the wardroom, then stopped. "Prepare a message for Admiral Woo. Tell him we have been delayed by the presence of an American submarine but will be back on schedule soon. Tell him nothing about our torpedo attack but say that the American is being hunted by the Chinese. I will fill in the details later."

"Aye, Captain."

Park stomped into the wardroom. He needed a moment to gather his wits. In hindsight he realized that he'd made a terrible mistake. He should have held position, hidden in the *Pacific Conveyor*'s wake. Instead he'd panicked, sure that he'd been discovered, when in fact the American sub might have just taken a sniff and gone on by. Instead he'd broken cover and fired, perhaps damaging the 688I but not sinking it. But now he understood: The Chinese were hunting for the American sub that had sunk their Kilo. He'd inadvertently poked a stick into a hornet's nest, and he had to flee their stings.

The through-ship talker squawked, and Park froze: "Comrade Captain! We have an emergency in the engine room!"

50

North of Taowang Gang

Lieutenant Kang had a look of death. Park examined the sleeve that had been installed around the valve earlier and saw to his horror that it, too, had swelled, a sure sign that the line was about to rupture and release hydrogen into the compartment. Liquefied, it would, if released under high pressure, instantly solidify, then evaporate. Small comfort. No matter how it was released, combined with oxygen, it might explode.

"Evacuate and seal the compartment," he ordered. "Later we will surface and try to reach the main valve in the line from the fuel cell under the superstructure. We'll shut it, then bleed off the hydrogen in the compartment and purge it with fresh air."

Park turned and headed forward, his legs unsteady, his hands balled into fists to hide their shaking.

The *Reno* picked her way along the coast, where marine life, bars and channels, turbidity, and pollution degraded sonar reception. Scott knew the *Reno* was too big and ungainly for close littoral combat, her 7,000-ton bulk too hard to maneuver and too easy to detect, unlike the *Red Shark*. But Scott was sure that's where the North Korean sub had fled after their encounter, and he had little choice but to track her down there.

He tried to put himself in the North Korean skipper's mind. The man either lacked patience or was too easily spooked to action. Why else would he have broken cover and fired at the *Reno*? Could he be spooked again? Scott thought he could, especially with the pressure the Chinese DDs and frigates were applying. He felt the pressure himself and knew he didn't have much time left to find and hit the *Red Shark* before the Chinese were down his throat. The NK skipper had to be feeling the pressure too, which might cause him to make another mistake. *Just don't* you *make a mistake,* Scott reminded himself.

He looked at the ship's clock: 2120. How many junks and steamers had they underrun? How many fishing boats with gill nets over the side waiting to snag a diving plane? Scott had run up the scope at least a dozen times to check bearings against known landmarks on the navigation charts only to see lights coming at them out of the gloom, usually a lantern-festooned junk oblivious to the *Reno*'s presence. They'd been steaming in shallow water for over six hours, the sandy bottom at times coming within yards of the *Reno*'s keel. Another coat of paint, Kramer had joked, and then there was the damage topside caused by the torpedo . . .

"Conn, Sonar, I've got a contact."

Scott slipped into the sonar room. "Let's see it, Chief."

"Here." The chief pointed out a hair-thin line. Low-frequency background tonals cluttered up the display. "Lotsa bottom scatter. Makes it hard to home in on this baby, but it's mechanical, not biological."

"You're sure, Chief?"

"Too regular for a biological. Pretty much dead ahead of us but with a drift toward the west, like it's hugging the coast and trying to high step over obstacles, if you know what I mean, sir."

"Start tracking it."

"Aye, sir, we'll call it Sierra One. Oops, where'd it go?"

The line had vanished off the screen. Scott waited while the chief tried to reacquire it, but several minutes passed without success.

"Call me when you have it—"

"There it is again, sir. *See it?*"

"Yeah. Still faint. Maybe if we pull left, get out from behind it—"

"Might work."

Scott, in the control room, gave orders that put the *Reno*'s wide aperture array where the chief wanted it.

"Chief?"

"Conn, I've got a solid contact but can't put a name to it."

"OOD, sound silent battle stations, rig for ultra-quiet."

"Silent battle stations, ultra-quiet, aye."

After his orders had been passed by mouth throughout the ship, and with all stations manned, Scott stood over the plotting table. The target had to be the *Red Shark*, he reasoned. And unless the NKs had picked up the *Reno* again, there was no way they'd know they were being tracked from astern, in the *Red Shark*'s baffles. If they knew, Scott was certain that her skipper would have reacted by now.

He waited, silently urging the chief to make an ID. They were slowly running out of room to maneuver and fight: Shanghai was less than ninety miles south and they'd soon be entering its busy seaward approaches.

"Conn, Sonar, Skipper, can you please come west a touch, I'm gettin' a turn rate, but I need another angle on it to be sure."

The *Reno* jinked west; Scott waited, the control room dead quiet.

"Conn, Sonar, I can identify Sierra One as *Red Shark*. Tonals match our previous line. *Exactly.*"

Electricity seemed to crackle through the control room. "Chief, you're absolutely sure?"

"Yes, sir. No doubt about it. She's making turns for five knots. Uh . . . wait one."

"Wait, aye." *Come on, come on*, Scott thought. *She won't be deaf forever.*

"Conn, sonar, I've lost contact with Sierra One."

The *Red Shark,* motors secured, rigged for ultra-silent, drifted south, listening. Sonar had heard something, perhaps a S6G reactor aboard a 688I.

"Bearing?" Park asked.

He'd had to force the image of the buckled hydrogen line in the engine room from his mind in order to concentrate on the 688I. So had every man aboard. Word of the worsening situation in the engine room had spread quickly among the crew. *Keep them focused on the enemy,* Park thought, *or they'll panic.*

"Astern, slightly east."

Park checked their speed: four knots in a three-knot current setting to the southwest, toward shore. Did they have enough momentum to turn left and set up for a shot as the 688I crossed their bow, or would he have to kick her ahead into the turn? Would the Americans hear the screw turn over? Park blew through his teeth. He looked at the fire-control panel, saw the first officer's white-knuckled hand wrapped around the firing pistol's grip, finger resting lightly on the trigger. His other hand hovered over the six torpedo tube arming keys, which had to be thrown first to activate the trigger.

Park said to the first officer, "I'm going to bring her around. When you have a full-green fire-control solution, you may shoot torpedoes when the 688I crosses our bow."

Park watched the compass repeater unwind counterclockwise as the *Red Shark* turned ninety degrees left and, barely making steerage, moved into position.

Park wiped his face, felt his chest tighten. Why was it taking so long?

"Comrade Captain. We have a full-green firing solution."

Park heard the arming keys snap to their armed positions. He saw the RANGE TO TARGET display tick down, yard by yard.

"Sounding?" Scott said.

Rodriguez had it from the laser Fathometer. "One thousand eighty feet, Captain. Amazing, but we're over a canyon. It must be part of a fracture zone that's not shown on the chart."

"A lot of things aren't shown on the charts. Not this close to the mainland. Any idea how wide it is?"

"So far, over a mile."

"Very well. Sonar, Conn. Anything at all?"

"No, sir. Deader 'n a doornail."

"Rus, her last position was almost dead ahead, slightly to the right," Scott said. "If he'd hauled out we'd have heard him. Let's work around behind where we think he is and see if we can shake him loose."

"Get between him and the coast?"

"Right. Looks like we've got deep water here, so let's take advantage of it and flush that bird."

"The American . . . he turned off his track, to the right!" snapped the first officer, unable to hide his frustration and anger.

The fire-control solution voided and went to red.

Park felt like he was trapped in quicksand. He tried to move, to make his brain work faster, but he couldn't. He was sure the 688I was getting ready to fire torpedoes. His plan was about to fall apart. The mission was doomed. *He* was doomed. *Everything* was doomed.

Orders, he told himself, *issue orders.* "Ahead full speed! Hard left rudder!"

The *Red Shark* leaped forward and heeled around to bring her tubes to bear on the *Reno,* closing in behind her. At short range, with wire-guidance, Park gambled that his torpedoes wouldn't miss.

"Comrade Captain!"

Park rounded on Kang, framed in the open doorway at the after end of the control room. He lurched into the control room screaming, *"The valve—a hydrogen leak in the engine room!"*

"Got him! He's breaking left, comin' around on us."

"Snap shot!" Scott commanded. "Stand by tubes one through four!"

Kramer rapped in the data—bearing change, range, speed.

Scott kept himself in check, but the urgency had built a head of steam that he thought would burst from his chest.

"Set! Tubes flooded, outer doors open!" Kramer confirmed.

"Match generated bearings and *fire one!*"

Kramer hit the trigger and rolled his eyes to the overhead. "Tube fired electrically. Fish is on its way!"

The Mark-48 slammed out of its tube like a bolt of lightning and accelerated to fifty knots. Two thousand yards out, on commands transmitted down its guidance wire, it jinked right and, like a jet fighter, homed in on the *Red Shark*.

"Fish has acquired its target," Kramer said with forced nonchalance and a genuine look of satisfaction on his face. He held up an old-fashioned stopwatch, finger poised over the stem, timing the runs. It was his grandfather's, everyone knew, from his sub service in World War II, when they timed the runs of cranky Mark-14 torpedoes by hand.

"Conn, Sonar. Fish is pingin' on its target. . . . He hears it, he's turnin' right, makin' a dash for it. Ain't gonna make it."

No, Scott told himself, *he ain't gonna make it, the son of a bitch. Neither will the nuclear warheads.* He leaned against a periscope, exhausted, remembering the hours, the days spent on the run, trying to save himself, his crew, and a good part of the U.S. from oblivion. What happened after this was over wasn't up to him but to the men who controlled that world from centers of power in the East and West. No one would ever know how close the world had come to nuclear war. Better, Scott thought, not to think about things he couldn't control.

"Conn, Sonar. Skipper, I just heard something strange . . . a thud, an explosion, not a warhead."

"In the water?"

"No, sir, aboard the *Red Shark*."

* * *

Park heard and felt it too. And he saw something the chief couldn't see: A solid wall of blue flame from exploding hydrogen bursting into the control room at the same instant an exploding Mark-48 torpedo warhead tore the *Red Shark* into a million white-hot fragments that erupted from the sea, trailing angry plumes of steam until, energy spent, they fell like rain into the thousand-fathom abyss.

EPILOGUE

The Pacific, south of Japan

Scott and Fumiko looked into each others' eyes on the monitor.

"You can put my picture on the piano and mix the drinks," Scott said. "We're heading in."

"Put your picture on the piano? I don't understand."

"It has a special meaning for submariners. I'll tell you about it when I see you."

"General Radford is on his way here from Washington. He's met with the president, and now he's anxious to meet with you."

"I'll bet he is."

"Jake, it's over. Colonel Jefferson and the special-ops team captured the terrorist base and killed over a hundred terrorists. The North Koreans are asking for a meeting with us at the UN. General Radford and the president are very impressed with what you and your crew have accomplished."

"Are they? What about you? We couldn't have done it without your help."

"Jake, it was you who took all the risks."

"What about your former employer? What have they said?"

"Nothing. They're keeping very quiet."

"And the Chinese?"

"The same."

"How about dinner?"

"What?"

"In Tokyo. Something expensive."

"Everything in Tokyo is expensive. We'll see . . ."

"What does that mean?"

"It means we'll see."

"No it doesn't, it means something else. What?"

Fumiko looked away, then back. "Your wife, she called General Radford."

"Ah."

"Jake, she didn't hear from you. General Radford told her you were scheduled for arrival in Yokosuka. I think she plans to meet the *Reno*."

Scott said nothing.

"Of course it is understandable that you would want to see her," Fumiko said frostily.

"If you think that, Fumiko Kida, you don't understand anything."

Fumiko's eyes glittered. She looked around, then quickly kissed her fingers and planted them on the camera lens.

Pyongyang

The door's security bolts slammed open and General Yi and a companion marched into the Dear Leader's office.

Marshal Jin sprang to his feet and gaped from behind his desk. "What are you doing here? What is *he* doing here?"

Yi turned to a fashionably slim Kim Jong-il, who was dressed in a tailored olive-green jumpsuit and gleaming

Italian loafers. "We are here to deliver the final report on the spy investigation you authorized. And to discuss other matters as well."

Jin, his face stony, said, "I have no time to discuss the spy investigation. Certain events have occurred that require my attention in a meeting of the People's Defense Ministry this morning, and I am already late for the meeting."

"By certain events," Yi said, "you mean the destruction of the terrorist base in Davao and the sinking of the *Red Shark*."

Jin looked at Yi with deep suspicion. "What do you know about this?"

"Quite a bit, actually." He motioned that Kim should take a seat in front of Jin's massive desk. Jin frowned as Yi said, "I know that the *Red Shark* was destroyed by the Americans, that the base in Davao was attacked last night, that the Americans will attack Pyongyang and our nuclear facilities if we do not admit our intention to attack U.S. cities with smuggled nuclear weapons."

Jin blanched. "You're mad. None of what you say is true. We will never surrender to U.S. demands. I will admit nothing. In fact, after the U.S. cities are destroyed, I will order an attack on Seoul as well."

"Marshal, please, your scheme is finished. Why do you insist on pretending otherwise? I know, too, that you have requested a meeting with the U.S. representative at the United Nations to find a way out of our dilemma."

Jin was mute as he slowly sank to his chair.

Yi took time to light a cigarette for himself and one for Kim. He blew smoke toward the ceiling and said, "I have certain contacts with foreign governments—the Danes, for instance. It is a way for me, and for them, to discuss matters of importance that would be of interest to other governments. You understand, Marshal," said Yi, "that change can often bring with it benefits. The right kind of change, of course, not the changes you recently initiated."

"You traitor! Now you try to absolve yourself by assuming the role of a statesman."

"I had to try to stop you from executing your mad scheme, which would have worked as long as you had the unwavering loyalty of the heads of the army and navy and of our nuclear forces. They've been arrested."

"You were just as eager as I was, as they were," Jin shouted, "to destroy our enemies and to kill *him!*" He pointed to Kim Jong-il.

"No, I never shared your hatred for the West, for the United States. All that your hatred would have accomplished is to turn the DPRK into an ash pit."

Jin stared at Yi, the hatred Yi spoke of evident in his twisted features and searing gaze.

Yi loudly tap-tapped his cigarette lighter on Jin's desk, then stepped aside as two uniformed security officers entered Jin's office.

"Marshal Jin, in the name of the Democratic People's Republic of Korea, I arrest you for treason against the State."

Jin didn't resist. The security officers frog-marched him out of his office and down the corridor, his boot heels echoing like gunshots on the polished marble. Yi gestured that Kim should take Jin's place behind the desk. Kim rose, and, relishing the moment, swept everything off the desktop and then sat down.

Yi bowed to Kim and said, "Dear Leader, I await your orders."

Acknowledgments

Red Shark could not have been written without the guidance and support of many people. Chief among them is my literary agent, Ethan Ellenberg, one of the best in the business. Also, the professionals at Simon & Schuster/Pocket Books, and especially my editor Kevin Smith and copyeditor Judith Gelman, whose editorial advice and attention to detail proved invaluable. And of course, without my wife Karen, none of this would have been possible in the first place.

As for research, I sought guidance from individuals with expertise in submarines, Navy SEALs, Eastern culture, and international finance. And though these individuals eagerly provided the information I sought and were quick to stress what was possible and what was not, I am solely responsible for how I used the information or, in some cases, ignored it.

As always, I'm indebted to Captain Donald C. Shelton, U.S. Navy (Ret.) for his patience (sorely tested, I'm sure) and dogged assistance. My thanks also to Captain Dick Couch, U.S.N.R. (Ret.), Tom and Tina Bell, Jerry Cummin, Steve Ernst, Armando Rodriguez, Thad Shelly, and Carole Sivin, all of whom provided important material, counsel, and critical advice.

Not sure what to read next?

Visit Pocket Books online at
www.simonsays.com

Reading suggestions for
you and your reading group
New release news
Author appearances
Online chats with your favorite writers
Special offers
Order books online
And much, much more!

POCKET BOOKS
A Division of Simon & Schuster
A VIACOM COMPANY

POCKET
STAR BOOKS
A Division of Simon & Schuster
A VIACOM COMPANY